Prince of Darkness

Also by Rebecca Zanetti

The Dark Protector series
Fated
Claimed
Tempted
Hunted
Consumed
Provoked
Twisted
Shadowed
Tamed
Marked
Talen
Vampire's Faith
Demon's Mercy
Alpha's Promise
Hero's Haven
Guardian's Grace
Rebel's Karma
Immortal's Honor
Garrett's Destiny
Warrior's Hope
Prince of Darkness

The Realm Witch Enforcers series
Wicked Ride
Wicked Edge
Wicked Burn
Wicked Kiss
Wicked Bite

The Scorpius Syndrome series
Scorpius Rising
Mercury Striking

Shadow Falling
Justice Ascending

The Deep Ops series
Hidden
Taken (e-novella)
Fallen
Shaken (e-novella)
Broken
Driven
Unforgiven
Frostbitten

Laurel Snow Thrillers
You Can Run
You Can Hide
You Can Die
You Can Kill

PRINCE OF DARKNESS

Dark Protectors

Rebecca Zanetti

LYRICAL PRESS
Kensington Publishing Corp.
www.kensingtonbooks.com

Kensington Books are published by

Kensington Publishing Corp.
119 West 40th Street
New York, NY 10018

Special book excerpts or customized printings can also be created to fit specific needs. For details, write or phone the office of the Kensington Sales Manager: Kensington Publishing Corp., 119 West 40th Street, New York, NY 10018. Attn. Sales Department. Phone: 1-800-221-2647.

Lyrical Press and the Kensington eBooks logo Reg. U.S. Pat. & TM Off.

First Electronic Edition: June 2025
ISBN: 978-1-4967-5189-8 (ebook)

First Print Edition: June 2025
ISBN: 978-1-4967-5190-4
ISBN: 978-1-516-11183-1

The authorized representative in the EU for product safety and compliance
Is eucomply OU, Parnu mnt 139b-14, Apt 123
Tallinn, Berlin 11317, hello@eucompliancepartner.com

151442730

To the readers who crave danger laced with desire, love forged in fire, and heroes who would burn the world for their fated mates—this one's for you. For those who've been with me from the start, your passion keeps this world alive.

And to the brave souls diving in for the first time to this paranormal world where the vampires are fully alive, drink wine, and make humans immortal but still human, welcome to the shadows, the seduction, and the sparks that will never fade.

Here's to new beginnings…and a heat that never dies.

Acknowledgments

So many books in, and I'm still amazed by the incredible people who make this journey possible. To every reader, supporter, and believer in this world—thank you for your passion, your excitement, and your love for these characters. To the dream team behind the scenes, the family and friends who cheer me on, and everyone who helps bring these stories to life—you have my deepest gratitude. I'd especially like to shout out thank yous to:

Big Tone for being my rock, my fire, and the one who always believes in me—even when the world I'm creating is filled with chaos, danger, and impossible love stories. Thank you for being my hero, my partner, and my biggest supporter. You're the steady heartbeat in all the madness, and I couldn't do this without you. Here's to forever, in this world and every other.

Our brilliant and talented daughter, Karlina—your artistry and creativity inspire me every day. Thank you for being my light, my sounding board, and for bringing beauty into this world in ways only you can. Watching you create is a reminder of the magic that lives in all of us. Never stop dreaming, because the world is better with your art in it.

Our son Gabe—builder of bridges, solver of problems, and quiet storm of strength. Watching you take lessons from the field and carry them into the real world has been nothing short of extraordinary. You've always had a way of making the impossible look easy—whether it's conquering the gridiron or tackling the challenges of engineering. It's a bit supernatural, if you ask me. Keep building, keep leading, and keep showing the world what you're made of.

Caitlin Blasdell, my brilliant agent with the uncanny ability to see the big picture—and the small tweaks that make it all come together. Your insights are like magic, guiding every twist and turn with precision and care. Thank you for believing in this world and for always knowing just what it needs, even if it's a quick tweak…through the whole book. You're a force, and I'm so lucky to have you in my corner. Thank you also to the entire Liza Dawson Agency for your support.

Elizabeth May, my fearless editor at Kensington—here we are on our second book together, and I can only hope you knew what you were getting into when you took on four front-list series with me! Your sharp eye, endless patience, and unwavering support mean the world to me. Thank you for helping me shape these stories and for tackling the chaos with grace and humor. Here's to many more adventures together.

Thank you also to everyone who works so hard at Kensington: Alexandra Nicolajsen, Steven Zacharias, Adam Zacharias, Alicia Condon, Lynn Cully, Jackie Dinas, Jane Nutter, Lauren Jernigan, Vida Engstrand, Barbara Bennett, Sarah Selim, Kait Johnson, Justine Willis, Renee Rocco, Carly Sommerstein, Cassandra Farrin, Sharon Turner Mulvihill, and Kelsy Thompson. We've published more than forty stories together, and I really do feel like I'm part of the family.

A special thank you to the Rebels, my fierce and loyal street team—you're the pulse of this world's magic. Eternal gratitude to my social media sorceresses, Anissa Beatty and Kristin Ashenfelter, and to Rebels Madison Fairbanks, Joan Lai, Kimberly Frost, Heather Frost, Gabi Brockelsby, Leanna Feazel, Karen Clementi, Suzi Zuber, and Asmaa Qayyum.

Thanks to my incredible publicity teams, Book Brush and Writerspace, for wielding the creative magic that brings my vision to life and for helping me forge lasting connections with readers in ways that truly matter.

Thank you to my family, friends, and loved ones who have stood by me through every late-night plot twist, test, and moment of doubt: Gail and Jim English, Kathy and Herbie Zanetti, Debbie and Travis Smith, Stephanie and Don West, Jessica and Jonah Namson, and Chelli and Jason Younker. Your unwavering support, love, and belief in me light the way even in the darkest moments. I'm endlessly grateful for each and every one of you.

Chapter One

In modern vernacular, or rather, the human vernacular, today fucking sucked.

Vero Phoenix sat behind an ancient iron-and-oak desk, his body screaming for action. For anything. He'd even climb an ice-covered tree if that meant moving his legs.

"Mr., ah, Phoenix?" A petite, dark-haired female, who looked around twenty but was actually only seventeen years old, hovered hesitantly in the doorway of his office.

He had a damn office—as well as a surname. He somewhat understood the reasoning of creating family units by employing surnames, but adjusting took time. Just a month before, he'd discovered he had a brother named Paxton Phoenix, so when Pax became their king, Vero figured he should adopt the surname. If nothing else, it showed their enemies where his allegiance lay. "Yes?"

The female paled. "Sir, I mean, um, Mr. Phoenix?"

He bit back a snarl. Smiling was too much for him right now, so he tried to keep his brows from slashing down. Apparently that looked frightening—for some unfathomable reason. "Genevieve, you can call me Vero. Remember?" He couldn't do anything about the hoarseness of his low voice, so he didn't try.

She flushed from her chest to her hairline, her bluish-green gaze darting away. "Yes, sir. I mean, I'm sorry, sir."

Jesus. "It's okay." He had to find somebody else to work as his secretary. Or administrative assistant. How in the hell did he have an administrative assistant? "What?" His voice sounded rusty because he rarely spoke.

She hovered, her shoulders down. "Um, Miss, I mean Ms., ah, Lyrica is here to see you."

Well, double fuck. "Fine. Please send her in." Now he sounded like some human stockbroker. Or worse, an attorney. If he had half a brain, he'd take off for the Himalayas and live by himself in a cabin blanketed with snow. Maybe he could make friends with a bear.

Screw that. He'd never had a real friend. Sure, he'd thought he had, but Hunter had ended up being a two-faced, lying, spying asshole. If Vero made friends with a bear, it would eat him.

That would be preferable to his current situation.

Lyrica Graves swept inside, somehow looking both regal and indignant while wearing jeans and a scarlet sweater that fit her curvy body perfectly, her cheeks red from the cold. She'd apparently ditched her coat in the outer office but still wore thick blue snow boots.

If he asked her to just shoot him, would she?

Her pretty brown eyes sparked. "You are totally screwing all this up."

Yep. She'd definitely shoot him. He considered making the request for all of five seconds, then decided he didn't want to give her that much satisfaction. In the saddle of life, she was a burr biting *his* skin, and she had been for the past weeks as they'd tried to bring the Kurjan nation, his nation, into modern times. "What do you want now?"

She drew to her full and unimpressive height of about five foot six inches and tossed her head in a way only angry females could achieve.

His body reacted instantly, going hard as a rock, head to toe—and worse yet, everywhere in between.

An unholy, feminine, and unreal peach bloomed beneath her smooth skin. "I heard you told Eudokia Guavras she could stay with her mate."

If he had an emotion, he'd blink. Instead, he kept his voice level and forced himself to talk. "I spoke with her—alone—for more than an hour. She wants to remain with her mate. I thought that allowing females to do as they wish was your goal?"

She put both hands on her voluptuous hips, her eyes glittering like a dark disco ball. "Allow? Did you say *allow*?"

Damn it. That was one of the expressions he was supposed to banish. But the word fit the situation. He *had* allowed the female to stay with her mate of more than five hundred years. She'd begged and pleaded to do so. He shoved down irritation. "Yes. She loves her mate. They've been together since the Byzantine Empire, and she has borne him three sons. Good ones." All three were, in fact, excellent soldiers.

Lyrica lifted her face to the ceiling as if he was just too stupid to deal with at the moment. "Eudokia doesn't know what she wants. She has been a Kurjan mate for centuries, man. She has no clue about the life that could be hers out in the world."

Yet her mate and her sons would remain with the Kurjan nation. A headache loomed at the base of Vero's skull, and he allowed his jaw to firm. Now wasn't the time to once again correct her that he wasn't a man. Not human. Not even close. "Perhaps Eudokia doesn't care about the outside world."

Lyrica's chin lowered. With her dark hair curling over her shoulders and her smooth skin begging for a kiss, she looked far more appealing than dangerous. Like a kitten hissing at a cobra, clueless to the dangerous bite about to strike her. "That's because she's had no exposure to freedom."

He stood, unable to sit any longer. "We are not having this argument again."

She took a step toward him. Completely misunderstanding the moment, as usual. How did she not see the killer lurking beneath his black uniform? The animal, barely leashed, that heated his very soul?

"We are not arguing," she said through gritted teeth. "We are discussing the situation."

Discussing? The female had no right to smell like fresh juniper berries while challenging him with every movement. No right at all. "What do you want, Lyrica?" he asked, curling his fingers into fists and resting them on the innocuous desktop.

For the first time, she faltered. "I—I'm not sure. I guess I want to show her the world. The possibilities available to her."

"Why?" He truly didn't understand. Eudokia had mated a high-ranking Kurjan soldier, which gave her status. She'd given birth to three strong and able-bodied sons who adored her. She also routinely won the pie bake-off every autumn during the fall season, when life calmed down. What more could a female want?

Lyrica rolled her eyes this time. "How do you know what you're missing if you have no clue what's out there? These females who've lived with your people for eons? They're like three-dimensional beings who've been forced to live in a two-dimensional world for centuries. They can't remotely comprehend that third dimension...until they actually look up."

If he shot himself, he'd just take too long to heal. The only way to truly end his torment was to cut off his head today...and fuck him. He couldn't do it. His loyalty to a nation that had wronged him—to a brother who didn't understand him—to a friend who'd betrayed him...was absolute. He didn't make a bit of sense, and yet, he wouldn't abandon those who'd abandoned him. For now. Every cell in his immortal body knew with certainty that his end would come bloody, and it would no doubt come soon.

Even immortality had its limits—a good beheading from an enemy lay in his future.

It was a pity he truly didn't care.

Worse yet, this stubborn female, who courted danger she couldn't even see, called to him. Who would protect her if he left? He couldn't worry about that, nor could he think about that wide, three-dimensional world that kept tempting him. So much so that his dreams centered on blue oceans and worlds through portals that might finally be opening for him—if he'd been somebody else. Somebody destined to live after the current year. After Paxton consolidated power next week at the Convexus. If he didn't get the powerful coalition of forty Cyst soldiers to join with them again during the night of the Kurjan Dark Solstice, they wouldn't survive as a nation.

Phenomenal soldiers, the Cyst traditionally served as the spiritual leaders for the nation, and without them, this new world would never work. Most had left when Paxton had become their king. Vero needed to focus all his attention on securing them back with his people.

But this female. She tempted Vero—and failed to hear her own siren call. He cleared his throat but knew it wouldn't make him sound any less Kurjan. While his vocal cords weren't quite as mangled as a demon's, but they were close. "You need to understand that some females want to stay here, with their mates."

Her nostrils flared as she drew in air, obviously biting her tongue before speaking. "No female wants to live subjected to a male. Ever."

His temper licked at the base of his neck. "Nobody is being subjected." Not anymore, anyway. He crossed around the desk, allowing himself to enjoy the scent of berries—just for a moment. "Eudokia loves her mate, and if she feels submissive to him, it seems to work. They have a good union." Her eyes widened, barely, as he approached her.

Her chin lowered. "He's possessive."

"Of course he's possessive. She's *his* mate."

Lyrica instantly shoved him, both hands on his chest. He captured her wrists and pulled her body in closer, his head lowering, his blood thundering through his veins.

* * * *

Fire lanced through Lyrica, head to toe. Anger and something else. A breath-stealing sensation that winged wild flutters through her abdomen. "I really don't like you," she snapped through gritted teeth, ignoring those flutters.

Vero lowered his head even more, and shards of black cut through the unholy blue of his eyes. "I don't like you, either."

Her legs trembled. While Vero wasn't as tall as some Kurjan soldiers, at only about six foot seven, he still stood a foot taller than her. And he was broader across the chest than most Kurjans. The Kurjans, who procreated only males, had black hair tipped with red. Not Vero. The pure black mass of his hair curled below his ears. His skin wasn't as pale as most of his people's, either. In fact, out in the real world, he could nearly pass for human. Almost. If he wore dark sunglasses to veil his eyes.

She had to stop dreaming about those eyes. "Let go of me."

He glanced at his hands, wrapped easily around her small wrists. His head jerked and he released her as if she'd burst into flames. "My apologies."

Yet another difference in him. She hadn't heard any other Kurjan soldier apologize. Ever.

He crossed massive arms across his chest. Why? To keep from grabbing her again? "Genevieve," he called out softly.

The door instantly opened. "Yes, sir?" Genevieve hovered on the threshold.

His sigh held heat. "Set up an appointment for Eudokia to meet with Lyrica again."

Genevieve released the door, turned, and could be heard running down the hallway to the main room of the lodge that temporarily served as their headquarters.

"You terrify her." Lyrica stared at the closed oak door before returning her focus to him.

"I know." He leaned back against the monstrous desk. "She has a brain."

Lyrica's gaze narrowed as she studied him. "Can you blame her? When your people kidnapped us, one of your Cyst generals beat the crap out of her when she protested." The Cyst were the ultimate soldiers and spiritual leaders to the Kurjan nation. They were also a bag of dicks.

"He's dead," Vero said flatly. "So I can't exactly beat him senseless to even the score, can I?"

Her head snapped back and heat flared down her torso. "That's your solution?"

The impossibly hard angles of his face didn't soften. "Yes."

How could she even start to explain why that was wrong? "Solving violence with violence is not the answer."

One of his dark eyebrows rose. "You just shoved me."

Huh. Good point. "I didn't think I could hurt you." The idea seemed ridiculous. He stood twice her size and remained immortal.

"My feelings are devastated."

She blinked. "Did you just make a joke?"

He shrugged one muscled shoulder. "I'm hilarious to most who meet me."

Another joke? No. Absolutely not. He could not be this dangerously sexy and also have a sense of humor. No. She couldn't stand him, and he still overwhelmed her dreams in a way that left her feeling desperate and needy. She absolutely could not like him. If she did, even a little, what then? Her work was way too important for her to be distracted. Plus, his picture could be plastered under "wounded and solitary animal" in the dictionary. As an empath, very rarely she could feel the desperate pain and hollow loneliness he hid so well, since he was an immortal.

She cleared her throat. "I need you to sign up for speed dating tomorrow night."

He straightened. "No." Somehow, his guttural voice lowered even more.

Now she crossed her arms. "Listen. Your people have spent eons kidnapping enhanced females from around the world, and right now, you won't let any of them go free. Some of them, after being guaranteed they control their choices, are interested in getting to know Kurjan males. Immortality is an impressive draw."

Kurjans were male, only. They passed on their K chromosome with every birth, making only males. Much like the vampires only created males as well. Like all immortals, Kurjan males could mate with other species, including enhanced human females. While the females would not become Kurjans, or vampires, or demons, their chromosomal pairs would increase to grant them immortality after a mating—which meant they'd be bonded forever. "As the second-in-command for the entire Kurjan nation, you could set a good example by attending the evening. It'll only take two hours."

"No." His gaze bored into her.

She opened her mouth to argue just as the door opened again and a young Kurjan soldier poked his head into the room, his black hair tipped with red. "Vero? We have a line on a rogue Kurjan group that recently kidnapped several enhanced human females. They've established a rough camp in Alaska. You mentioned you were ready for a fight?"

"Thank fucking God. I'll get my knives." Vero sidestepped her and didn't look back.

Temper jerked her around to watch his retreating back. "I hope you get stabbed in the neck," she yelled.

"One can only wish," he returned before disappearing around a corner.

She clenched her hands into fists. The man was the most irritating person she'd ever met. Yet he wasn't a man. The male. Yeah. That took some talent, to be the biggest pain in the butt of all the males in all the species.

Hurrying out of his office, she bypassed Genevieve and strode down the hallway to her own office, where she took several deep breaths. Why did he affect her like this? She couldn't breathe when the jackass stood in her vicinity.

It took thirty minutes of deep breathing to completely calm herself. Then she sat and primly typed notes into her files regarding the occupants of the camp. All two hundred of them. Finally, not worrying about Vero out on a mission at all, she sat back. That male was not hers to worry about. Her job kept her more than busy. Once again, she'd missed supper.

Genevieve hovered in the doorway again. "Um, Lukas had to go train with the soldiers, so I don't have an escort back to the barracks. It's dark outside."

Lyrica paused as the woman's emotions hit her like a punch. Warmth and giddiness? "Lukas?" She vaguely remembered the young soldier being around lately.

"Um, yeah. Lukas Macrame. His grandmother chose their new last name." Genevieve smiled. "He's sweet."

Sweet? Just because Lukas might look twenty didn't mean he wasn't two hundred years old. "You're not dating him, are you?"

"Of course not." The emotions rolling from the girl said otherwise. Then she looked toward the darkened window. "I don't want to walk alone."

Lyrica needed to shield her empathic abilities better. Fear did wash from the girl to her. Now she needed to figure out more about this Lukas. "It's okay, Genevieve. I'm happy to walk with you." The barracks sat only a couple of minutes away, but darkness felt heavy this high in the Canadian mountains.

"Thank you." The rush of gratitude warmed Lyrica's skin. As did the fact that Genevieve was loosening up enough to trust her. Lyrica, after her time as a mathematician who worked in crisis management for corporations in financial trouble, often felt a little bossy, and she kept trying to temper that instinct. Yet she had to be organized, and bossiness made that happen.

She drew on her coat and scarf, following Genevieve from the office, through the lodge, and outside. The freezing cold instantly blasted into her. She shivered but still took comfort. The best times of her young and often unsteady childhood had involved visiting or living with her grandfather in the mountains of Alaska.

Lyrica walked briskly with Genevieve huddled next to her as a couple of patrol soldiers passed by, nodding at them. The sprawling camp seemed as safe as possible, yet these immortals were still a dangerous unknown. Lyrica's foot slipped on the ice and she regained her balance as they hustled past a maintenance shed.

Genevieve suddenly stopped and grabbed Lyrica's arm. "There's something…over there," she whispered, pointing toward a parked snowplow.

Lyrica followed her gaze and caught the faint outline of something sticking out—bare toes, frozen over with ice and already blue. "Stay here," she said quickly.

"No." Genevieve clutched her coat buttons tighter as they moved cautiously closer.

Rounding the snowplow, Lyrica stopped abruptly. Frozen solid, a nude female body lay sprawled awkwardly, as if she'd fallen and never moved again. Bruises covered her neck, which appeared mottled with frost.

"Oh my God," Genevieve breathed next to Lyrica. "She's dead."

Chapter Two

Vero sat back against the smooth interior of the Phantom Hawk helicopter, his fingers itching for the control panel up front. He'd designed the entire craft front to back and didn't like somebody else piloting it, but he flanked Paxton with Hunter on Pax's other side.

When Vero had stepped up and forced his half-brother to become king of the Kurjan nation, he committed himself to protecting the soldier at any cost. There had already been two attempts on Paxton's life during the last three weeks as they'd negotiated and nearly come to an agreement, a treaty of sorts with the Realm.

For Vero's entire life, the Realm had been their most dangerous enemy. As a coalition of other immortal beings like vampires, demons, witches, fairies, and shifters, they had been a formidable foe. The idea that they were becoming allies still kept Vero up at night.

Had he made a colossal mistake in declaring Paxton their new king? Since Paxton was the oldest heir, it was his birthright.

Probably.

With the Realm treaty almost in place, now Vero only had to worry about the Convexus next week, where Paxton and he needed to draw the Cyst coalition back into the Kurjan nation. The meeting had to take place at headquarters during the Kurjan Dark Solstice, which only occurred every one thousand years, or any chance they had might be lost forever. Surviving as only half a nation seemed nearly impossible.

Paxton glanced at him sideways. "This is a hell of a craft. You really designed this?"

An unwilling pride filtered through Vero and he banished it instantly. "Yes." He took a moment to study the screens across from him that glowed and displayed real-time battlefield data, enemy positions, and mission objectives. Tension-filled quiet blanketed the craft, which ran silently since he'd built it with fusion-powered engines.

He studied his half-brother from the side of his eye. Was there any resemblance between them? If so, he couldn't see it. Paxton was as tall as Vero and as broad, but he had otherworldly silverly-blue eyes. They were a cross between polished steel and an electric wire. Both males had thick black hair, and Vero supposed their bone structure might be slightly similar. Both angled, both sharp, and Vero's eyes were blue, unlike most Kurjans, who had purple or red eyes and black hair tipped with red or red hair tipped with black.

The fact that Hunter sat on the other side of Paxton still with the implants in his face making him look like a Kurjan was an abomination. Hunter was a demon-vampire mix and had undergone surgery to appear Kurjan. He'd been undercover since he was sixteen years old. Deceiver.

If Pax noticed Vero's tension, he didn't let on. "Tell me again about the helicopter's camouflage," he said.

Vero rolled his shoulders to loosen them before the battle to come. "The exterior is enveloped in an adaptive camouflage that renders the helicopter invisible to radar and the naked eye."

Paxton shook his head. "That's awesome, but what I want to know is how."

"Oh," Vero said. "I created a heat-dissipating system that cools exhaust emissions and eliminates any infrared signatures that might expose us. In addition, the external panels project images of the surrounding environment and render the aircraft invisible to the naked eye. Nobody knows we're coming and nobody knows we're here."

Hunter leaned forward to look at Vero across Paxton's broad chest. "I knew you were the smartest guy around. When you said you were working on a top secret project, I had no idea it would be something this cool."

Vero stared at him implacably. "I didn't trust you as much as you thought I did." He turned his gaze back to watch the enemy on the screen, addressing Hunter for the first time in three weeks.

Paxton cut him a look but remained silent.

"All right, boys," Hope's chipper voice came through his ear-comm. "You're about a minute away."

Vero jolted, then regained his composure. It was an odd experience to hear a female voice coming through the comm lines during a mission. According to Paxton, his young mate had the most strategic mind in the entire Realm.

"Vero, you good?" she asked.

Why was she singling him out? "Affirmative," he said.

"Wonderful. I made sure that you had two of the Realm's newest knives in your pack. I want your opinion about them."

Paxton stretched out his legs. "What about me?"

"You got one too," she said, chuckling. "But you're not as accustomed to the Kurjan fighting methods as Vero."

Yeah, that's because Vero was fighting against his own people. His shoulders stiffened.

Paxton cracked his knuckles. "I'm reading twenty-two heat signatures on the screen, but the picture is fuzzing in and out."

"I can't help that," Hope said. "Our satellites are out of range, and the ones we've hacked are moving and rather out of date. Plus, there's quite the heavy cloud cover, but I can confirm the twenty-two heat signatures. It looks to me like there are two main structures and then several smaller tents scattered around. These folks are just setting up a camp."

Paxton nodded. "Tell us about their location."

"They're in Kelly Creek, a small unincorporated area in the middle of the mountains. It's going to be cold," Hope said slowly. "It's pretty much exactly what you suspected."

The monitor in front of them fuzzed again.

"Our screen has gone blind," Pax said. "Tell me what you see."

Rapid typing came over the line. "I can tell you what I saw five minutes ago. It looks like there are twelve heat signatures in the structure closest to the river. They're not moving much, and my guess is that these are the captured women. It's after midnight there, so everyone's asleep."

It had taken them about two hours to reach the destination. "What about the other structure?" Vero asked.

More typing came across the line. "I see six people prone, obviously sleeping."

"So that's eighteen. We're missing four," Hunter said.

"Yes. I'd say those four are patrolling. We saw some movement before we lost the feed," Hope said.

Vero ensured his combat boots were tightly secured.

"All right," Paxton said. "Stay in my ear, baby."

"Always," Hope said cheerfully.

Vero frowned at the still-fuzzy screen. What would it be like to be that close to a female? He wasn't entirely sure he'd allow his mate to be part of the fighting force, but then again, Hope remained safely back at headquarters. He had to admit the plan she put together was excellent.

The pilot motioned toward them. "Thirty seconds."

Vero hefted to his feet, securing his knives in the sheaths strapped to his legs. He had one gun at the back of his waist, which shot green lasers that would turn into metal upon hitting immortal flesh. His knives and one sword provided additional protection for him. The only method to eliminate one of his enemies was beheading.

"I'd rather not kill anybody," he said somberly.

Pax stood and headed toward the back hatch. "Agreed. The mission is to rescue the kidnapped humans and leave the Kurjans alone, hoping they might someday rejoin the Kurjan nation. Since we've destroyed the Kurjan ability to track enhanced females on the planet by decimating that program in all satellites, they won't be able to continue down their current path."

Hunter reached the hatch first and hit the button so it would slowly open. "In position now."

"On one," the pilot called back. "Three. Two. One."

Hunter winked and leaped out of the moving craft into a somersault that he repeated several times. Vero rolled his eyes. Pax followed and Vero counted to two before jumping out. He rolled several times and dropped the hundred or so feet to touch the ground, his feet sinking through ice and snow before he bounded up, flipped in the air, and repeated the action two more times before he could land without jarring his knees.

He looked around quickly to see both Pax and Hunter slogging through waist-high snow to the tree line. He bounded their way, his ankle protesting slightly from the jump. It would've killed a human, but he likely escaped with just a bruise. He reached them and waited for the rest of their soldiers to catch up.

Hunter leaned over and coughed.

"I'm on lead." Vero itched to hit somebody.

Hunter straightened and shrugged.

Vero immediately dodged into the thick forest and angled around trees and bushes with the snow chilling him through his uniform. They emerged into what had been set up as a camp. The clouds covered the moon, but the snow still glowed enough that he could see nearly perfectly.

Paxton reached his side, his breathing even. "Looks like we expected."

"Hunter and I will take the main building. You three get the hostages and you three find the patrolling males," Vero instructed the raiding party.

Paxton's dark eyebrow rose. "What about me?"

"You stick to the tree line and shoot anybody that comes your way," Vero said curtly.

"That's not how I work." Paxton began striding toward the main building.

Vero grabbed his shoulder and jerked him to a halt. "Whether you like it or not, you're the king of the Kurjan nation. You don't go into battle."

Paxton turned on him, heat rolling off him. They stood eye to eye at the same height. They were both bulky and strong, and for a fleeting second, Vero wondered who'd win a fight between them.

Paxton leaned in. "The only way I'm ever going to get the trust of these people is if I prove myself. Besides, I've never known any leader to sit back when there was a fight happening."

Vero shook his head. It was common for a leader to sit back and strategize. "If you die, we're in a shitload of trouble."

"I'm aware of that," Paxton snarled. "I'm not planning on dying."

Vero turned to Hunter. "Is this how the Realm really does it? You're telling me that King Dage Kayrs goes into battle?"

Hunter nodded, his fake purplish-red eyes swirling. "Yeah, that's exactly how it happens with my father. He's usually the first through the door. Your people seem to be more like humans. If the ones in charge were bleeding and dying, you wouldn't be at war so often."

"Perhaps," Vero said.

Paxton turned and advanced even faster toward a rough log structure larger than the others.

Vero jogged to catch up and shoved his way in front of his brother. "Fine, but at least let me go first."

"Fine," Paxton muttered back.

Vero silently strode up the two stairs and pushed open a rough wooden door. His gaze scanned a wide gathering area with natural rocks placed around

---

for people to sit on. The camp's occupants hadn't had time to secure furniture yet. The Kurjan investigators had discovered this place quickly. Good.

"I'll go left. You go right," he told Hunter. He didn't really care where Paxton went, so long as he remained behind one of them.

"Sounds good." Hunter pivoted.

Vero immediately headed down a short hallway that had only two doors. He shoved open the first one and jumped on the sleeping Kurjan before the guy could blink. "Hi, Zelic. Good to see you again. We miss you in the mechanic's shop." Vero had him tied up with impossible-to-break zip ties and out of the bed within seconds. When Vero turned around, Paxton had vanished. "Damn it."

"I can't believe you're doing this, Vero," his prisoner said, fighting against him.

While several inches taller than Vero, Zelic didn't come close in strength.

"Peace is a good thing." Vero propelled the guy out into the hallway. "Don't you miss home?"

"Drop dead," Zelic snapped.

Paxton emerged with another Kurjan.

"Vero," the older soldier snarled.

"Hi there, Ornot," Vero said, forcing cheer. "Don't you miss the big kitchen?"

The guy ranked among the best chefs in the world and had seemed to enjoy his work.

"Not with a traitor or a demon spawn," Ornot sneered.

Paxton pushed the chef roughly ahead of him and tossed a tablet at Vero. "Plans to assassinate me before a rogue Cyst group has a plan for taking over the nation."

Ornot tried to punch back and missed. "We intercepted those. You are going to die, demon. We're not in contact with any of the assassin teams, and even I can tell the plans are good."

Vero glanced down at the cryptic plan. There was no doubt Ornot had intercepted these, considering none of his team were dangerous. A pit dropped in Vero's gut. He had changed the entire trajectory for the nation, probably for good, but had it been the right decision?

He shoved the mechanic down the hallway and into the main room just as Hunter emerged with two other Kurjans. They had been low-level soldiers before they left the Kurjan nation, and Vero had never worked with either of them.

The first had purple eyes that turned bloodred. "You sided with a demon spawn. Hell, only half of a demon spawn," he snarled. "Traitor."

"Yeah, I get that a lot," Vero drawled, shoving Zelic out the door into the cold.

He looked around to see that part of his team had captured the other soldiers while the others had freed the females. The twelve females wore ragged clothing, like they hadn't changed in a week. They seemed to range in age from probably around seventeen to forty years old. One struggled against one of his soldiers.

"Stop," Vero said, his voice commanding.

The female instantly halted.

"You'll be safe. We're taking you somewhere safe."

"You're kidnapping us again?" a petite redhead snapped, rubbing sleep from her eyes.

He smoothed out his tone. "Not permanently. Let's head toward the helicopters." He looked around and saw several shovels leaning against a nearby tree. "I'll shovel a path for the females." He handed his prisoner off to Paxton. "Zip tie the rest of these guys good and tight. We can leave them in the snow." They wouldn't die, but freezing their junk would teach them a lesson. He'd keep the tablet to see what else he could discover about the assassination plans, but these guys weren't helpful. They'd obviously intercepted a transmission through the satellite system that now no longer existed.

"You won't stop us from finding mates," Ornot snarled.

Vero turned and looked back at him. "The methods you've had for hunting down enhanced females are now destroyed." The Kurjans had created tracking software that traced the energetic emissions of enhanced females, first placed within cities, then used via satellite. He and the Realm had corrupted it so thoroughly it could never be used again.

Ornot fought as Paxton forced him to his knees. "I need a zip tie," Pax said calmly.

The hair on the back of Vero's neck rose. He blinked and stiffened, his instincts barreling alive.

Several lasers fired out from the forest toward Paxton.

Vero shouted a warning and leaped into the air, taking the impact of all three. Two slammed into his armor-covered chest, and one burned right through his jugular. He coughed out blood and started to fall.

"Vero!" Paxton yelled.

Vero's eyes closed. He fell into unconsciousness before he hit the ground.

Chapter Three

Lyrica stepped forward—and froze. A surge of panic cut through her, numbing her more thoroughly than the cold ever could. "Oh no," she whispered, dropping to her knees beside the still figure sprawled in the snow. The nude woman had completely frozen over. Lyrica's gloved hand reached out tentatively toward Tekii Bultungin's lifeless form. "Poor Tekii."

Tekii lay on her back, her sightless eyes fixed on the sky. Ice coated her skin, from the top of her head to her blue feet, the frost creeping into her flesh. Lyrica leaned closer, her breath catching as she studied the marks on the woman's neck—deep bruises blooming across her too-pale skin.

"It wouldn't have taken long for her to freeze out here," Genevieve whispered, her voice shaky behind Lyrica.

Lyrica swallowed hard and leaned in to study the woman's face. Red and purple dots speckled the whites of Tekii's open eyes, her corneas clouded and lifeless. Slowly, Lyrica pushed herself to her feet, stumbling slightly as she tried to back away. "I think she's been strangled."

"What?" Genevieve's voice rose an octave, her panic unconfined and broadcasting wildly. "No, she couldn't have been. I figured she ended up out here sleepwalking or something and froze to death."

"She'd never sleep in the nude," Lyrica said, her voice barely audible as she shielded herself from Genevieve's emotions. None of the kidnapped females would even consider that. A violent shiver racked Lyrica's body, the chill cutting through her layers. "It's too cold out here. We need to get help."

Genevieve's teeth chattered. "How? I mean, who should we tell?"

Lyrica paused, the girl's words sinking in. "That's a good point," she said, her voice tight. She glanced around, her thoughts racing. Vero, Paxton, and Hunter remained away on their mission. The Kurjan and Cyst soldiers who had stayed behind had sworn allegiance to Paxton, but Lyrica still didn't trust them—not fully. How could she, considering their people had kidnapped her?

Genevieve chewed on her bottom lip, uncertainty written all over her face. "Should we wait for Paxton to get back? I mean…it's not like we can save her now."

Sorrow welled up in Lyrica, tightening her chest. She had liked Tekii. The thirty-year-old woman had been kidnapped from Palau, somewhere in the Pacific Islands. She often spoke fondly of her homeland, sharing stories about her culture and traditions. Tekii had been counting the days until her release—she would have returned home within the month.

"No," Lyrica said firmly. Her gaze dropped back to Tekii, her friend's lifeless form a haunting reminder of the fragility of their safety. The reality of the woman being naked speared terror through Lyrica. "I need a light."

"I don't have a light," Genevieve replied quickly. "We don't have cell phones that work out here yet."

Lyrica sighed, the weight of their isolation pressing down on her. Months without a working cell phone still felt surreal, but there were bigger issues at hand. She crouched again, leaning closer to examine Tekii's neck. Her breath caught. "Is that a bite wound?"

Genevieve took a step back, her eyes wide with fear. "I—I can't tell. We need to get her into the light. Should we even try to move her, though?"

"I think she's frozen to the ground." Lyrica straightened, her gaze darting around the darkened camp. The cold bit into her skin, the night's stillness unnerving.

Everyone was either on a mission or resting in bed right now. Sure, sentries patrolled at all times, but considering they lived in the middle of nowhere, nobody from the camp would venture into the mountains or the icy river. Especially in this weather. They were effectively trapped. She stood. "We can't just leave her out here like this." Chewing on her lips, she looked back toward the main lodge. "Come on."

Genevieve's nose had turned a bright red and she pulled her scarf up to cover her face. The wind whistled and fought them, but Lyrica led the way back to the lodge. She hurried through the back door. Heat instantly assailed her, pricking painfully against her freezing skin.

Genevieve winced. "I hate that part."

"Me too." Even her feet protested with furious sharp pains as she moved into the main gathering room.

The familiar space usually provided an odd comfort. Several large sofas formed a cozy TV area, and the rest of the room held pool tables, dartboards, and even an air hockey table. Vero and Paxton had worked hard to make this new camp livable—more than just livable, comfortable. For all the harshness of the location and circumstances, they'd succeeded in carving out a safe haven. More supplies arrived every other day or so. Soon they'd have a city built with outlying homesteads.

Comfort felt fleeting right now.

The lodge housed several private bedrooms for the leaders and coordinators. Lyrica's quarters were on the top floor, in the eastern wing, a secluded sanctuary she barely had time to enjoy.

"Come on," Lyrica whispered, heading to the west side and up the stairs.

A wide, heavy body instantly blocked her way when she reached the top. "What is going on?" No familiarity or warmth showed on the young soldier's face.

Her mouth still felt frozen as she tried to speak. "Hi, Liam or Collin." Identical twins, the two vampires protected Hope, Paxton's mate and their cousin. They'd helped everyone move to the new territory and seemed to be good friends with Paxton. Unfortunately, Lyrica's empathic abilities hadn't developed to the point where she could read the emotions of most immortals, so she couldn't tell if he wanted to be helpful or not. "I need to speak with Hope."

"It's after one in the morning, and it's Liam," he said shortly. "I will be pleased when Hope's home is finished being constructed and we're not here in the middle lodge. It's too...exposed." While his emotions remained veiled, the irritation in his tone came through loud and clear. The vampire did not want to stay in Kurjan territory, and the second Hope decided to return to Realm headquarters, he'd be right at her side.

However, Lyrica had seen the way Paxton and Hope loved each other. If she left, so would he. Right now, he seemed intent on ruling the Kurjans, which was a good thing, so Hope wouldn't go anywhere.

"Lyrica?" Liam growled. "I don't like how easy it is for anybody to reach this landing. You're trustworthy, but this has shown a breach in my security that I don't like. We need to move to a single structure. Soon."

Lyrica tried not to take a step back. When Paxton's home was completed, Vero's would follow, as they sat next to each other against the mountain in a more defensible area. She'd miss being close to Vero. No. Hope. She'd miss Hope. "The homes will be very nice," she said lamely.

Liam's gaze narrowed. "What is the emergency? It's late." The handsome soldier was definitely on edge and she couldn't really blame him, considering he was a vampire in Kurjan territory.

"I really need to talk to her. I found a dead woman."

"Dead? Explain."

Lyrica's back went up. And people thought she was bossy. "No. I would like to speak with Hope, and I'm absolutely fine if you want to listen over her shoulder." Sometimes the only way to deal with these overbearing males was to stand right up to them, even if they were a foot or more taller than her. She had the ability to drown a person with statistics and PowerPoint presentations, for goodness' sake. Not all fights were won with swords.

He studied her with alert green eyes, and she really wished that Vero had returned. Why she'd rather deal with him, a stubborn and slightly mean immortal, was something she chose not to investigate. Of all people, the enforcer for the entire Kurjan nation could not be her soft place to land. There wasn't one soft thing about Vero Phoenix. Talk about a ridiculous feeling for her to embrace.

Finally, Liam took a step back. "All right, stay here." With that, he turned and strode back to knock on a door, even his footsteps sounding grumpy.

"What?" Hope yelped from inside. She threw open the door. "I clocked off the mission when they headed home to get some sleep. Is Paxton okay?"

"Yeah. They're still on their way back," Liam said. "Lyrica's here and wants to speak with you."

Hope walked into the hallway, wearing a short and cami set and nothing else. Her blue eyes appeared cloudy and her auburn hair was wild and curly around her face. A spiraling blue tattoo wound up both sides of her neck, which she'd explained as being the marks of a prophet. Apparently Hope was one of three prophets in the immortal world. "Lyrica, what's wrong? Why are your lips blue?"

"I went outside," Lyrica said. "We have a body."

Liam instantly put himself between her and Hope. "Now it's time you tell me all about this dead female. I've allowed you to speak with Hope, and now you cooperate with me."

Allow? Did he actually just use the word "allow" with her? Lyrica's nostrils flared as she tried to draw in more oxygen and not belt him in his gut, which would surely just hurt her entire hand. Even a well-aimed kick probably wouldn't harm him. These immortals had way too many advantages over all humanity.

Hope pushed him to the side, obviously not intimidated by her much larger cousin. "I'm as well trained as you are, buddy, and you're just pissing off my friend here. She doesn't hide her emotions very well. Move."

"You might be trained, but you don't have my strength or speed," he retorted.

Ah. There were the arguing cousins Lyrica had become accustomed to seeing. Enough of this interplay. They had a problem. A big one, and Lyrica needed to deal with the matter so she could go cry and mourn her friend. Away from all these badasses. "It's Tekii. She's dead."

Hope's jaw dropped. "Dead? How?"

"I don't know," Lyrica said quietly, with Genevieve hovering at her side. "I'm not a doctor, but I think she might've been strangled."

Hope's eyes widened. "All right, just a sec. Let me get dressed."

Liam grasped her bare arm. "I'll take care of it, cousin. If there's somebody out there murdering females, you are remaining here under guard with Collin. In other words, you stay in."

"Not a chance." Hope wrenched free. "Did she freeze to death?"

Lyrica shrugged, her entire body aching from both cold and grief. "She's definitely frozen, but her body showed signs of strangulation, and there was a bite mark on her neck. A deep one." The only thing she knew about strangulation came from television crime shows, but she'd seen enough Kurjan bite marks to recognize one.

"Okay. Give me a minute." Hope turned back into her room.

The image of the dead woman's lifeless eyes wouldn't leave Lyrica's mind. Who would've murdered her?

Chapter Four

Safely back at headquarters before sunrise, Vero leaned against the wall by the door in the small but comfortable gathering room attached to the human female barracks. The comfiness derived from fluffy, light green sofas, luxurious throw blankets, and a crackling fire in a stone fireplace. The window shades remained open, revealing the winding Yukon River and looming snowcapped mountains. A tender light unfurled at the horizon, nudging the night aside.

He'd allowed Paxton to slap a bandage over the wound in his neck so he didn't frighten the humans.

Paxton had been both pissed and somewhat bewildered that Vero had taken bullets for him. He'd gone off to see his mate but had issued an order that he wanted to speak with Vero later.

Vero wasn't much for talking. He couldn't believe that somebody had killed one of the enhanced females the night before while he'd been on a mission too far away to stop it. Dr. Fizzlewick, who'd just chosen his surname from a children's book and insisted upon everyone using it, was currently performing an autopsy and had snarled at everybody to get the hell out of his half-built medical facility. So now Vero stood inside the decidedly feminine space, pushing himself into the shadows away from the lights and windows.

The enhanced females he'd helped rescue sat around, many with throw blankets over their legs, all sipping hot chocolate. These twelve, to be added to the twenty-three already in custody, had huddled together in the rear of the second helicopter on the way to this camp. During the flight, he'd tried to appear reassuring, but they'd all looked terrified. He'd been more than happy to turn them over to the reception team, normally led by Lyrica. It had taken about three hours for him to partially heal the wound in his neck, and he could use a nap. But that wasn't to be.

This morning, Lyrica stood at the front of the room, next to a small desk and a large screen. Today she wore dark jeans and a thick white sweater, looking curvy and delicious, although pale. Finding the body the night before had definitely taken a toll, and he wished he could do something to provide comfort. Instead, he leaned back against the hard wooden wall and crossed his arms.

"Okay." Lyrica clicked a button as the screen filled with a picture of the Earth. "First, I am so sorry that you've been kidnapped and I'm glad you all speak English. We've run into a language barrier a couple of times." She sighed. "You've all had a nice warm shower, and I've reassured you that you're safe, but I know you're feeling anything but."

A couple of the women nodded. Several of them eyed him, and he tried to look as harmless as possible. By the widening of their eyes, he failed.

Lyrica cleared her throat, her brown eyes soft and her voice cultured. "You've probably already figured this out, but since you were only kidnapped a few days ago, I'm going to start at the beginning." She clicked a button and another slide came up, showing a sign advertising the services of a psychic.

Vero didn't have time for this.

Lyrica smiled. "Obviously there are humans on this planet, which you already knew. What you didn't know is there are enhanced humans who have abilities outside of the norm, and you all are included in that category."

Lyrica continued, "Many enhanced humans are empaths, some are psychics, some practice telekinesis. Some are very good with animals. Some have the touch when it comes to plants. There are many enhancements. Nobody knows why certain people have these enhancements. We might be a different species altogether or just cousins to the witches or—we really don't know. But the key is, enhanced females can mate with immortals."

A redhead with bright green eyes turned to eye Vero head to toe. He almost felt like blushing.

Lyrica pointed to the screen. "There are immortals among us. First, there are Kurjans." She clicked a button and another slide came up, showing a Kurjan with his fangs extended.

Vero's jaw almost dropped. Seriously?

A murmuring set up among the crowd, and a woman turned to stare pointedly at Vero's mouth. He fought the urge to let his fangs extend.

Lyrica pointed at the screen. "These are the people who kidnapped you. They used to be the bad guys. Now they're aligned with the good guys. Well, some of them. Obviously, the ones who kidnapped you are not good." She squinted, looking around. "Vero?"

He stepped forward and allowed a board to creak beneath his feet.

She jolted. "There you are."

Yeah. He had the ability to blend into backgrounds. Most immortals had otherworldly abilities—even the vampires were known to change the weather or halt their enemies with a wall of ice-cold air.

Lyrica eyed him. "That's Vero. He helped to rescue you and is one of the good guys." The doubt in her voice nearly made him smile. If he remembered how.

A very tall woman with platinum-blond hair looked over her shoulder at Vero, then turned back toward Lyrica. "How do you know they're not all bad?"

"We don't," Lyrica said simply. "But we've signed a treaty and they're more than willing to let you go."

The blonde placed her hot chocolate down on the sofa table. "Right now?"

"No," Lyrica said. "Not quite yet. First, we need to make sure you're all right. Then there's an NDA for you to sign. But I'll get to that." She clicked the button before anybody could interrupt her. "There are also vampires, demons, shifters, and fairies alive today."

"Demons?" a strawberry-blonde from the front asked, her voice trembling. "Like actual demons from hell?"

"No." Lyrica waved a hand in the air. "They're just another species. They're all immortal, unlike humans."

A twenty-something dark-haired girl glanced at Vero and then scooted herself farther away from him on the sofa. "So they can turn us into vampires or Kurjans?"

"No, no, no," Lyrica said, shaking her head. "They can't turn you into anything. Species do not change. If an enhanced female mates with an immortal, she gains immortality by an increase in her chromosomal pairs. But she wouldn't turn into a vampire, demon, or anything other than a human who's now immortal. None of the immortals or mates need to drink any blood, so don't believe vampire stories. Unfortunately, most mates don't get any extra strength or speed."

Another blonde piped up, partially raising her hand. "They just live forever?"

"Yeah, unless they're beheaded," Lyrica said. "Everybody can die by beheading and by a really intense fire."

A couple of females looked back at Vero as if they wished they had a sword in their hands right now. They both paled.

Lyrica looked at him and sighed. "Vero is a Kurjan, but he's actually here to help you."

Something warmed him throughout. He'd wondered what she thought.

"At least, I'm fairly certain," she said dryly. "Now, back to my little PowerPoint presentation here."

Vero shook his head. It was preposterous and frankly a little insulting to think that his people had been reduced to a PowerPoint presentation. He'd never even heard of PowerPoint until Lyrica had insisted on installing it on the few computers currently in the territory. An entire computer bank and upgraded system should be installed soon, and Vero would be damned before he put PowerPoint on his hard drive.

However, Lyrica seemed right at home and well-settled with the organization of the entire presentation. She did like to be organized, didn't she? In fact, her bossiness in that area was cute. Very.

A curvy brunette raised her hand from one of the sofas.

"Yes?" Lyrica asked.

"Did you say shifter? As in humans who shift into animals, like in the movies?"

Lyrica turned from the screen. "I've never seen one, but I'm assured that there are immortals who look human and turn into felines, wolves, bears, and even dragons." She shrugged. "The dragon part might be myth. I can't tell."

The female who'd asked the question shook her head. "This is unreal. So, another question. Why are the Kurjans so pale?" she asked. "I saw one the other day who had a strip of white hair bisecting the scalp and down his back. He was really creepy."

Lyrica nodded. "Those are the Cyst. They're the spiritual leaders, and I think the top soldiers for the Kurjan nation. Not many of them stayed when the Kurjans decided to ally with the other species. They're so pale because until a short time ago, Kurjans and Cysts couldn't go out in the sun without being fried."

"And now they can?" the platinum blonde asked.

"Yes," Lyrica said. "Their scientists came up with a way for them to do so. So now they can go out into the sun anytime they want."

That wasn't exactly true, but Vero chose not to disabuse her of the notion about the Sunshine Cure. For a time, they'd thought they could genetically enhance embryos in utero but had soon learned that protection only lasted a few years. Then those toddlers required inoculations like the rest of them. Right now, they still had to limit their time in the sun. While better than years before, too much exposure would still kill many of his people. He was able to withstand more sunlight than most and actually enjoyed it. Every minute he spent in the sun darkened his skin just a little bit. He had no doubt someday his people would be able to spend as much time outdoors as the other species.

Another hand rose.

"Yes, Lucy?" Lyrica asked.

"What if we…I mean, what if we want to be immortal?" Lucy asked quietly.

Lyrica smiled. "That's definitely an option. And it's completely up to you. We are going to do some speed dating with the Kurjan soldiers here with anybody who's interested. If you're not, no worries."

The idea of speed dating also felt like an insult. Vero frowned and the female closest to him moved down her couch as if afraid he'd bite her.

Lyrica watched the movement. Then she looked at him and faltered. Blinked. Shook her head and returned to her presentation.

So he did affect her.

She cleared her throat. "Also, Kurjan blood usually burns other species, so if you see an injured Kurjan, don't rush to help."

"Usually?" another blonde asked.

Lyrica tapped the control against her jeans. "Yes. It appears that true mates to Kurjans aren't burned by their blood."

"Blood?" a forty-something brunette asked. "You said that nobody drinks blood. So why do they have fangs?"

Lyrica frowned. "Um—"

"We do drink blood," Vero said quietly. "Any immortal can take the blood of humans or other immortal species without a problem. We only do so if we're injured, or during sex. We don't need to drink blood as a food source, and a mate never needs to do so unless she's injured. Also, Lyrica is correct that Kurjan blood does burn the skin of most other immortals and humans, unless we're a fated mate."

Lyrica's head jerked up, and her gaze met his. She quickly looked away.

"This is all fascinating, but what if we want to get the hell out of here?" the platinum blonde snapped.

Lyrica nodded. "I completely understand. As soon as we make sure you're healthy and you sign the NDA, we'll take you anywhere you want and give you a million dollars. If you want to be somebody other than who you were, we'll also give you a brand-new identity."

"And the million bucks?" the blonde asked.

"Absolutely," Lyrica said. "Regardless of whether you want to stay or go, you are free to call anybody from your life to let them know you're all right. But you must come up with a cover story about why you'll be out of town for a few more days." She winced. "As well as where you've been since you were taken."

Vero nodded. "We want your loved ones, if you have them, not to worry. I believe your kidnappers only took unmarried females without children?"

"Gee, that was nice of them," the brunette snapped.

Vero didn't blame her for the sarcasm. "Keep in mind that you'll sign an NDA agreeing to keep silent about immortal species."

The curvy brunette raised her hand again. "What if we sign the NDA and tell the truth anyway?"

Lyrica sobered. "Well, for one thing, nobody will believe you. So I'd be real careful because you'll end up in an asylum somewhere. However, I have been told, and I don't agree with this, that you will be kidnapped again, this time for good."

"And murdered?" the redhead asked, her voice shaking.

"No, no, not murdered." Lyrica vigorously shook her head. "Absolutely not. But you will be kept somewhere—in absolute luxury, I'm sure—but not where you want to be. So if you sign that NDA, I certainly wouldn't break it."

Vero straightened. "She's not wrong." He let authority ride his voice. "You don't want to cross us."

Lyrica's eyes widened and her jaw tightened. "I don't need help here, Vero."

"Apparently you do." A couple of the females didn't look nearly alarmed enough. "We're happy to give you money and freedom, but you will sign

the NDA and you will adhere to your promise," he said curtly. They needed
to grasp the seriousness of his people's commitment to concealing their
existence from humans.

The platinum blonde threw her hands up. "Why? I mean, this is
ridiculous. Why don't you want anybody to know you exist? Why not
coexist with the rest of us?"

Vero stared at her until she paled and then he spoke. "If humans
discovered we have immortality, they'd do anything to get it, wouldn't
they? Wouldn't you?"

Slowly the blonde gulped and nodded.

"Exactly. There's no way to get it without mating us. And if you're just
human and not enhanced, it can't happen. But you'd still try, wouldn't you?"

"Yes," the blonde said, her voice trembling.

Vero chose not to gentle his voice. Not about this. "So then we'd be
at war with the humans. Who do you think would win that?"

She licked her lips nervously. "Probably you."

"Exactly. If we took out the human race, we wouldn't have enhanced
humans to mate through the coming eons. Since Kurjans are male only,
same with vampires, us wiping out so many potential female mates is an
untenable idea."

Lyrica's eyes spit fury at him.

He shrugged. "They need to know the truth."

She snapped her teeth together. "All right, now they understand the
truth. Just so you also know, ladies, this very handsome, hunky, sweet soldier
who's telling you like it is will be one of the eligible immortal bachelors
attending the speed dating event tonight. Won't that be fun?"

Chapter Five

Vero stood over the dead girl's body as fire, then ice roared through his veins. "Say that again," he said, his brother at his side in the makeshift medical facility.

Dr. Fizzlewick shook his head. "She was strangled, raped, bitten, and left to freeze. I haven't found any DNA evidence, not that I really expect to." The ancient Kurjan scientist crossed his arms and leaned against the far wall. He had to be at least three thousand years old, and the red tips in his hair had faded to more of a maroon, but his purple eyes remained sharp and his body well-honed. He'd returned to the Kurjan nation under the new leadership, having been exiled centuries ago for pissing off somebody in charge. Vero still hadn't gotten the story from him.

"Can you tell me anything?" Paxton asked, anger vibrating low in his voice.

Fizzlewick shook his head, his bloodred lips turned down. "No, just that she was assaulted and killed last night."

Fury swirled in Paxton's green eyes. "You said she was raped. There has to be DNA evidence. Condoms rarely work with immortals."

Fizzlewick glanced at Vero, his eyebrows drawing down. "Uh, yeah. No doubt the killer controlled his seminal emission."

"What are you talking about?" Paxton snapped.

Fizzlewick's jaw went slack. "Um. Er."

Vero shrugged, heat tinging his ears. "Are you saying males from other species can't control, well, orgasmic discharge?" He tried to sound as scientific as possible.

Paxton turned his head to face his brother. "No. Are you saying that the Kurjans can come without ejaculating?"

Leave it to Paxton to forgo scientific platitudes. "Yes," Vero said simply.

"No shit?" Hunter asked from Pax's other side, looking more Kurjan than Vero did. He shook his head. "I don't want to ask this, considering you've mated my cousin, Pax, but can you do that?"

A muscle ticked in Paxton's jaw. "I don't know. Never tried."

"It's not easy," Vero admitted. "Nearly impossible with your own mate, so I've heard." He could do it and had, considering he'd never wanted to mate anybody he'd dated. Or rather, anybody he'd had sex with—which had always been consensual. "Guess you didn't uncover all our secrets while you were spying on us, Harold." He stressed the fake name Hunter had used for years. It wasn't like they'd talked about sex.

Hunter met his gaze evenly. "Guess not."

"What else?" Pax asked shortly.

Fizzlewick rubbed his clean-shaven jaw. "From the bruising, I'd say she was strangled with one hand. The bite marks, and there are several on her body, are from fangs. I've found no evidence, visible or in energy, that her attacker mated her."

So someone had bitten and raped her but not mated her. Most immortals could sense the energy of a mated female, and nothing in the air hinted at that.

Paxton stared at Vero. "Do Kurjans get mating marks on their palms?"

"No," Vero said. A mating brand usually showed up on the palm of anybody with demon lineage when they met their mate, and it transferred during sex and with a bite to create the mating bond. Other immortals mated with a good bite during sex, and Kurjans permanently marked the bone of the female.

Pax glanced down at the faded mark of a *P* on his right hand. "I like that I transferred a mark to Hope."

Vero couldn't care less that Paxton was half-demon.

Dr. Fizzlewick gave a half bow to Paxton. "King? Thank you for giving me the time to do an autopsy."

"Of course." Paxton leveled his gaze at the scientist. "I'm not sure about the king label, but we're on the same side now, right?"

Fizzlewick cut a glance at Vero and looked back at Paxton. "Of course, my king. You gave us all a choice and I decided to return home. I can't say that I'm comfortable with this new arrangement, but I'm not averse to giving it a try." Ancient wisdom echoed in his tone. He shook his head, his eyes softening as he looked down at the dark-haired female. "One more thing." He lifted her head carefully and turned it to the side. "There's a wound at the back of her neck. Fresh."

Vero ducked down to study the raw wound. "What is that?"

"Some symbol? I took several photographs." Fizzlewick gently released the victim's head and reached for a file folder on the counter. "It's a circle with three slashes through it. Her attacker dug a blue ballpoint pen deep into her flesh to scratch in the pattern."

Vero accepted the printouts and scrutinized the design. "Some vigilante group taking credit? A warning?" He looked at Paxton. "Is this familiar to you?"

"No," Paxton said, his eyes spitting fire as he looked at the paper. "I'll reach out to the Realm and see if they have any info."

Fizzlewick sighed. "Such a pity. She was so young."

Paxton looked at Vero. "What do you know about her?"

"Not much," Vero admitted. "She was kidnapped three months ago."

Paxton turned, anger flushing across his high cheekbones. "Did she have an intended mate before I took over as king?"

Vero shook his head. "I don't think so."

The Kurjans had been kidnapping enhanced females for eons. Some became mates to soldiers and others were used as experiments that involved injecting Cyst blood into their brains. Survivors from these experiments were being rounded up and treated by the Realm. All remaining females in Kurjan territory had been tested and were perfectly healthy, even if they had been experimented upon earlier.

Vero rolled his shoulders. "I don't think anybody had tried to claim her, but I'll look into the matter."

"We both will," Paxton said. "Doc, if you discover anything else, let me know." He turned and strode out the door, Hunter on his heels, Pax's boots leaving a trail of melted snow.

Vero looked at the scientist. "You have no idea who killed her?"

"None," Fizzlewick said. "I'm telling the truth. There was no forensic evidence. Most of our soldiers have lived hundreds of years. Anybody who wanted to kill her would've made sure they weren't discovered."

Vero's throat ached. "True."

"Do you need me to do anything with that?" Fizzlewick jerked his head toward the still-healing wound in Vero's neck.

"No," Vero muttered. Paxton had already offered him blood, but he had refused it. "I'm healing fine." He had already sent all his healing cells to the area and could speak again, so it shouldn't be too long until the injury stitched over and disappeared.

Fizzlewick glanced at the empty doorway. "You're due for your injection."

"I know." Vero shrugged out of his jacket and shoved up the long sleeve of his black T-shirt. Fizzlewick removed a syringe from a drawer and plunged the blue liquid into Vero's arm.

The doctor pulled out the needle. "The Realm scientists are still requesting samples of this concoction, and I've denied them so far. Paxton hasn't pushed it."

Heat flushed down Vero's torso as the injection warmed his blood. "Stop worrying about it. Hunter surely sent them a sample while he spied on us." Guilt that Vero had failed to read the duplicity in his one friend tried to take him and he shoved it away.

"I doubt anybody thought the Sunshine Cure needed to be hidden." The doctor tossed the empty syringe into a garbage can.

No kidding. "Is everyone up to date with the injections?" They needed the shot once a month to be able to venture into the sunlight. For now, anyway. Vero hoped that their bodies would take over for the injections and make the process a natural one that they'd pass down to their children through the years. He needed more time in the lab to make that happen.

"Almost," Fizzlewick said. "We're keeping to a regular schedule of so many per day. I've finally seen positive results in the blood I've been studying. Yours is the most changed, and I believe you're close to not needing the injection every month. Right now, no one else is near your level. I have enough of your blood in stock to study but haven't figured out why it's different. Do you think your brother will put enough resources toward this endeavor?"

Vero kept his expression blank. "I don't know. I just met the guy in person a month ago." Paxton played both sides right now to try to keep the peace, but he *had* shown loyalty, at least, to the Kurjan nation. A peace treaty didn't require them giving up details that could get them killed should they go to war again.

Fizzlewick rubbed his neck. "Does he understand the importance of the Convexus next week during the Dark Solstice?"

"Yes." If Pax didn't reach an agreement with the Cyst on that night of all holy nights, it'd never happen. "It's all or nothing. He gets it." Vero strode out of the makeshift examination room/morgue and outside down the steps. He had to find the killer before the Cyst descended on the territory for the Convexus. A cool rush of air hit him, and he breathed in deep. Canada had always been one of his favorite places, and not just because they could live in the mountains surrounded by snow with very little sunlight. The mountains stood solid, the weather predictable, and the people jovial. He paused at seeing his brother pacing on an icy trail, speaking on the phone.

Paxton clicked off and looked up. "You get your injection?"

Vero smoothed out his expression. "I did."

"How bad do you need it?" Pax asked.

Vero shrugged. "Not sure. What do you know about the concoction?"

"Not a damn thing," Paxton said. "It's not something I'm worried about right now."

Vero tucked his thumbs into the black pants of his uniform. Accustomed to wearing the black outfit at all times, he considered obtaining jeans and more casual clothing now that vampires and demons mingled in the territory. It'd be nice to dress down once in a while. Even as the king, today Paxton wore ripped jeans, snow boots, and a black puffer jacket.

"We need a larger medical and scientific building." Vero had agreed to move to their current location, but the infrastructure needed to be built faster.

Paxton looked up at the bulbous clouds above them. "I've let the construction crew know the order of priority, and additional materials are being ordered as we speak. After they finish the construction for the meeting area, which is outside, they'll move to the other projects. It's going to snow again."

"We're in the middle of Canada by the Yukon River," Vero said slowly. "It's always going to snow again."

Paxton grinned. "That's a good point. I wanted to ask you a couple of questions."

"Go ahead."

Paxton looked toward the main lodge. The chill in the air kept most people inside except for the patrolling soldiers and the mechanics working on different snowplows and snowmobiles near the river. "Does the Kurjan nation have any sort of police force?"

Vero stared at him. "No. Not really." The last three weeks had been spent moving from Eastern Canada to Western Canada and rescuing any kidnapped females they could find. They really hadn't sat down and discussed how Paxton planned to govern the nation.

"Yeah, same with the Realm."

Vero shook his head. "Usually, the enforcers take care of any problems, but we've never had anything like this." He still couldn't fathom why anybody would've killed that poor female. He took a deep breath, filling his lungs with frigid air. "We've never had a crime like this, and you should look at the demons and vampires you're slowly filtering into the community here."

Paxton blinked once, his silvery-blue eyes blazing. "You think it's one of mine?" He paused, then shook his head. "Wait a minute, they're *all* mine." He tapped his chin thoughtfully. "I need to get my head around that. Sorry. I only discovered I was a Kurjan three weeks ago, and then you pretty much made me king."

"Yeah, I feel for you," Vero said dryly. "You need to look at the newcomers because this isn't something that happens in Kurjan territory. If somebody wanted a mate, they took that person as a mate."

"I get the feeling that things haven't been all that consensual around here," Paxton drawled.

Vero nodded. "There's some truth to that. However, there are plenty of enhanced females who wanted immortality and gladly mated. At least, through the years."

Paxton kicked at a chunk of ice, shadows dancing across the hard planes of his face. "How is your progress going with interviewing the mated couples?"

Vero had no clue what he was doing. "I'm about halfway through."

"Has anybody wanted to leave?"

"No," Vero said.

Paxton shook his head. "Statistically, that's impossible. You're missing something."

"Maybe," Vero noted. "I'm having Lyrica meet with each of the females on their own, and we'll see." So far, he hadn't seen any indication that anyone wanted to leave or take a fairly new virus that could negate the mating bond—something no Kurjan mate with a still-living partner had ever done. It was a risk, that was for sure.

"Also, I want you to make up with Hunter."

Vero blinked once and then again. "Excuse me?"

"You and Hunter. You were best friends. You need to hash it out."

Temper ticked through Vero and he forced his body to remain relaxed. "Hunter lied to me for years." Hunter had infiltrated the camp as a Kurjan when they'd been only sixteen. "And you need to get his face changed back to whatever it looked like before. Everybody knows that he isn't actually a Kurjan, and it's an insult to look at his face arranged as one."

"I couldn't agree more," Hunter said, stepping around the weapons depot, irritation rolling off his muscled form. "Why don't you go ahead and try to rearrange it right now?"

Vero's fists clenched. He'd like nothing better.

"Absolutely not," Paxton said. "You both need to grow the hell up and handle with your problems away from everybody else. I have enough dissent in this community without having to deal with the two of you morons. Fix it." He glanced at his watch. "Oh, and both of you report to the main lodge tonight. You're joining the speed dating event."

Fucking great.

Chapter Six

"I like your hips. They're wide and will no doubt help produce many sons," the Kurjan across the narrow table from her said.

Lyrica sat back and shook her head. How in the world did she end up caught in her own trap? While she had thought it hilarious that both Hunter and Vero had to attend the speed dating event, she hadn't once considered that they'd have one entrant too many and that she would have to fill in. "Gee, that's really nice of you, Jonathan."

Jonathan smiled widely. Like most of the Kurjans, his pale skin had darkened slightly, and his face looked brutally carved. His eyes were a mellow purple and his dark hair was gathered at his nape. The red tips seemed to have faded, and she wondered if the Sunshine Cure caused that.

"I think females would prefer to hear a different sort of compliment," she murmured slowly.

Jonathan's lighter brows drew down. "Really? Isn't that the greatest compliment?"

Oh, man. It was going to take her forever to bring these guys into the current century. "No."

"I see." Jonathan looked her up and down. "Well, that's a pretty yellow dress you're wearing."

"Thank you," she said, smiling. He was kind of getting it. The luxurious silk with a few sequins dotted throughout seemed a little old-fashioned, but truth be told, she felt pretty in it. She liked the way the waist nipped in and then flared. "How old are you?"

"I'm about one hundred and fifty years old, so pretty young," he said, nodding. "I like this idea of speed dating. We've never done anything like it."

She leaned forward and tried to ignore the fact that Vero sat only a few tables down. This close to him, she could feel his heat. Somehow. The guy burned like an inferno. "You're being a good sport, Jonathan."

Jonathan cleared his throat and looked around as if searching for something to say. "Um, you decorated this place, no?"

"Yes." She had decorated the main room in the lodge with streamers and balloons they'd ordered in, hoping to add a festive vibe to the winter evening. A full bar sat in the corner with every type of alcohol and soda available. She had found that Kurjans enjoyed Guinness beer, so she made sure to have plenty of it on hand. Then she'd had her assistants slice tables into small two-tops scattered around the room.

"It's pretty. You did a good job making the place, uh, lighthearted." He glanced toward a pretty blonde at the next table, his chin lifting. "I hope the females feel comfortable."

It had surprised her how many of the kidnapped females wanted to participate, and she knew full well that Paxton had had to order many of the immortals to join in. Besides the several Kurjans, she recognized a few vampires and demons. Vero was currently chatting with a young woman named Louise from Buffalo. Well, it'd be more accurate to say that Louise chattered on and Vero sat there with his arms crossed. Lyrica cut him a glare. He could at least try. He stared back, his blue eyes so dark they appeared nearly black. Dead and unfeeling. Even so, he unfolded his arms.

Jonathan looked down at his green long-sleeved shirt and jeans. "I have to tell you, I like dressing casually. It's enjoyable wearing clothing that is not a uniform."

The Kurjan nation seemed rather regimented.

"I'm glad you're liking it," she said, "and speed dating as well."

He shrugged. "Back in my day, we'd just go ask a father's permission to take a mate, and we still gave dowries. This is a whole new world. I guess." He looked around. "We still have kidnapped females everywhere, but that was never my thing."

"I'm glad to hear that," she said.

He leaned forward. "It'd be fun if you could get a few feline shifters to join in someday. I know I'm meant for a human, but still, I wouldn't mind trying to court a lioness."

Lyrica frowned. "How do you know you were meant for a human?"

"I'm one of our best soldiers, the strongest—it's true." A deep red flush started at his collarbone and washed up over his face. "I was injured badly as a child. Fell off a horse and the rotten animal kicked me in the head."

What in the world? "What does that mean? You sustained brain damage?" His amethyst eyes appeared intelligent.

"Yes." His voice lowered to a hush. "My IQ is probably only around two hundred. Not nearly high enough for a shifter. So it's a human I'll mate."

"Hey," she protested.

He ticked his head to the side. "What?"

"Are you saying that humans are dumb?"

He sat back as if realizing the impact of his words. "No. Just not as smart as shifters or most Kurjans."

How insulting. "You don't know that." She glanced toward Vero to see him focusing intently on Louise. Her stomach clenched. Hard. She drew in air. That was good. She wanted Louise to find somebody, if that's what she wished. Although why anybody would want the grumpy, ice-cold enforcer was beyond her. Sure, he was sex personified and had the old wounded-badass-dangerous thing going on, but that could only last for so long. She jolted back to see Jonathan watching her carefully. "What?"

He smiled, showing sparkling white teeth. Apparently, the Kurjans had had more yellowish teeth and fangs in the past, but the injections had brought this interesting side effect. "Vero's one of the most intelligent Kurjans ever born."

She stiffened and couldn't help her eyebrows rising. "Seriously?"

Jonathan nodded. "Yes. He had much to do with advancing our cure against the sun. He has the mind of a scientist. A great one. Not his soul, though."

Lyrica's heartbeat picked up. For absolutely no reason. "What about his soul?"

"That one? He has the soul of a warrior. A killer, really." Sympathy, soft and real, tinged Jonathan's tone. "I've watched him fight his dual nature for years, until finally the killer won."

She held her breath, wanting more information. Oh, she shouldn't. But she'd been fascinated with Vero from the second she'd arrived in the other camp, just after having been kidnapped. That first day, their eyes had met, and she'd felt that ice-cold blue touch her soul. Even more so, any time she saw him interacting with any of the females, he'd been distant but kind. Then he'd helped Paxton defeat the evil leader of the Kurjans before declaring Pax to be the rightful king.

Poor Paxton had grown up not knowing he had Kurjan blood in him. The guy had had no clue.

Lyrica swallowed. "Why did the killer in Vero win?"

"There was no choice. His father died when he was young, so he was raised by his two uncles. Both enjoyed cruelty, and I think he took one beating too many to enjoy science." Jonathan sighed. "A female, a Kurjan widow, had taken him under her wing. Then a soldier from the Realm kidnapped her, and that's when Vero stopped working in the laboratories and started living in the fighting rings. Before long, nobody wanted to challenge him."

It sounded like he'd been alone. Lyrica could relate to that feeling of being orphaned. Her heart stuttered. No. Bad heart. There was no doubt in her mind that Vero was a killer—one who didn't like her. She cleared her throat. "Then Hunter came along and they became friends?"

"Yeah. Of course, we knew him as Harold. Yet one more betrayal for Vero. I can't remember the last time I saw him smile. Doubt he remembers how."

Lyrica had never seen him smile, now that she thought about it. "At least he has his brother now."

Jonathan snorted. "Right. They don't know each other in the slightest, and most of us believe that Paxton's loyalty is to the Realm and not the Kurjan nation. Vero's loyalty is to us. Someday that will be tested, and only one of them will walk out alive."

Chills skittered down her spine. "That's not true."

Jonathan shrugged. "You'll see. For now—are you involved in the investigation concerning the dead human? We've never had an investigation before. Usually, if somebody killed somebody, we knew who it was and dealt with them appropriately."

"I'm not," she said.

"You might want to think about it," Jonathan noted. "The females trust you. If they know anything, they'll tell you."

She guessed that was true.

Tingles slid up her side, and she knew Vero was looking at her. She didn't know how she knew, but she did. She swallowed and forced a bright smile on her face. "So the next female you meet, what are you going to say?"

Jonathan rubbed his smooth, shaven jaw. "I'm going to say that…I don't know. What am I going to say?"

Lyrica sighed. "Give her a compliment that has nothing to do with hips and bearing sons."

"Oh, yeah, yeah, yeah. What about eyes? Can I remark upon her eyes?"

"Yes, that'd be perfect."

"Excellent. You have stunningly beautiful chocolate-brown eyes. There's a sweetness to them I can't describe," he said.

She sat back and heat filtered into her face. "That's about perfect."

"I can do this," he said. A buzzer rang and he stood. "I enjoyed our chat," he said formally.

"As did I." She had purposely set up the evening so the males had to move and not the females. It created a different dynamic than they had grown accustomed to, and she remained determined that they begin to see females as equals. Even human ones with their lower-than-two-hundred IQs.

Hunter sat across from her. "Hi, Lyrica," he said dryly. "Great night."

"I'm so glad you decided to attend." She tried not to smile. Even with the implants in his face, he appeared disgruntled. What did he actually look like? She caught the glares of a couple of other Kurjans in the room focused right on him. He didn't seem to notice. She sighed. "They won't forgive you, will they?"

He lifted powerful shoulders. "Why would they? I lied to them for years. Ever since I was a kid."

She leaned forward. "It's surprising to me that the king of the entire Realm sent his own son into the enemy camp as a spy."

Hunter nodded. "Yeah, exactly. No one suspected it. I just showed up, saying that my small group of Kurjans had been in a battle. They took me right in." He glanced at Vero and then looked back at her. "I understand why some people are pissed. I would be too." He rubbed his jaw and winced as if in pain.

"Do the implants hurt?" she asked.

"They are not comfortable," he noted, "especially as I've grown through the years." There was no doubt Hunter Kayrs had an impressive physique. Incredibly tall and broad, he likely resembled his father, the king of the Realm. She'd heard rumors from Kurjan mates about the king's striking handsomeness.

She couldn't imagine living with foreign objects in her face. "When are you undergoing the surgery to get all that removed?"

"Soon," Hunter said. "Apparently, my face just ticks people off, so I wouldn't mind going back to myself. Although," he grinned, widening his eyes that swirled an odd purple, "I kind of don't remember what I looked like before. You know?"

"No." She couldn't even imagine.

He leaned in. "You know most Kurjan soldiers aren't really looking for mates, right?"

"I do," she said, "but these females were given a choice whether they wanted to just go free or if they wanted to talk about immortality, so we had to fill the chairs." To her right, Jonathan laughed across from an accountant from Russia. The woman was named Sasha and she had long blond hair and startling green eyes. She laughed and patted his hand. Lyrica smiled. This may work out after all. Even if she got just one couple to start dating, she'd take it as a success.

"If you say so." Hunter shook his head. "I am not going to mate for a long time. Last thing I want to worry about is taking care of somebody else."

She leaned forward, curious. "What are you looking for in a mate?"

He blinked. "I don't know, probably somebody like my mom or my aunts. Brilliant."

She had heard many things about the Queen of the Realm. The woman was known to be a genius and an obsessed scientist. She wanted to cure every disease out there. It made sense that Hunter would be interested in somebody similar. "You know that what we want in our heads and what we actually get in our hearts is usually different, right?"

He chuckled. "I have no doubt. I'm sure my dad as the king had a much different idea in mind than a female who is constantly wearing a lab coat, forcing everyone to give blood samples, and driving herself to exhaustion. But you love who you love."

"True," Lyrica said. She wished she could keep Hunter here talking to her. He felt like he could be a good friend. Next, she'd have to deal with Vero.

Her body flushed at the thought. The buzzer went off much too soon. Hunter patted her hand and stood, looking to follow Jonathan.

Vero kicked back the chair and sat, heat rolling off him. "Having a good time?" His voice was more of a growl.

"Yes. I hadn't planned on participating," she admitted, which probably wasn't fair.

His gaze swept her light-yellow dress and pinned-back hair. "You look lovely."

She jolted. "Thank you. I like to see you dressed casually." He wore a long-sleeved black T-shirt and faded jeans with combat boots. His black hair had been swept back from his face and his eyes glittered a dangerous and chilling blue. His face was all planes and angles, and unlike most Kurjans, he looked like he nearly had a tan. Truth be told, he was probably the most handsome male she'd ever seen, which made his chilly attitude all the more unbearable. "Have you found your mate?"

He stared at her, not moving an inch. Appearing relaxed and lazy—when she knew he was neither. "No. Have you?"

"No. I'm not here to find a mate."

"Neither am I," he rumbled. "Yet, you seemed to force us all into this."

Genevieve bustled toward them, delivering two bottles of sparkling water from a tray laden with them. "We opened the new shipment of supplies. Enjoy." She moved to the next table.

Vero kept Lyrica's gaze as he twisted open the bottle and took a deep drink. His eyes widened. He held out the bottle and looked at it, then lifted it to his mouth again, drinking half of it down. "This is incredible."

Lyrica cocked her head. "You've never had sparkling water?"

"No." He finished the drink. "It's magic."

Amusement filtered through her. She glanced over to where Jonathan was waving at Sasha even from a different table. "We might have a love match happening right now."

Vero sighed, looking big and broad across from her, a restless energy vibrating from him. "This is a waste of time. If somebody's interested in dating, they can go about it themselves. We aren't humans."

"I know you're not humans, but you might want to take a lesson from how we do things. You can't just kidnap your future mate," she spit out.

"Yet we did." He looked around at all the tables. "All these females are here trying to touch immortality." The male had a point. Plus, even though the Kurjans were pale and a little too tall, they had a dangerous predatory vibe that many found sexy.

She could see the draw. Lyrica crossed her arms, feeling vulnerable in the pale dress. She liked to deal with Vero while wearing more clothing.

Worse yet, her body hummed with an energy she couldn't pin down. Her breasts felt heavy beneath the corset, and her heartbeat thrummed between her legs. For him. "Exactly how do you think you're going to meet your mate?" she muttered.

He carelessly lifted one powerful shoulder. "I don't know if I'll live long enough to mate. But if by some miracle I do, when I see her, I'll take her."

She blinked and ignored the fact that her traitorous body wanted him. Perhaps humans *were* stupid. "That behavior is what we're trying to unlearn here."

"Maybe, but my mate will know her place and it'll be easy."

She might actually have to hit him.

Chapter Seven

The smell of juniper berries was slowly driving Vero insane. His clothes felt too tight. He had already met with three of the females, and he had spoken more words in the last half hour than he had the entire past two years. He had to get out of this room. This was ridiculous.

"What?" Lyrica asked, her eyes spitting mad.

He had heard Jonathan refer to her eyes as warm chocolate, and he disagreed with that assessment. Her eyes were more of a dark, burnt honey with a depth that tempted him too much. Somehow they reflected hints of gold, chestnut, and earth tones, turning her into a female of mystery. Those eyes held secrets…and sadness. Both drew him, and that irritated him more than anything else.

He heard the back door open, and then one of his soldiers peered around the corner from the kitchen. The relief that filtered through him would embarrass him later. "Come." He stood and grasped Lyrica's arm, pulling her up.

"What are you doing?" she asked.

"I'm not leaving you sitting at the table alone." He might not be a gentleman or anything close to it, but even he knew that much. Plus, he had tired of her speaking with other males.

She looked around, then gathered her skirts, falling into step beside him. Apparently he wasn't the only one wanting to flee the stupid speed dating.

Jonathan waved to her and she waved back.

Vero looked down at her pert nose. "He's our burliest and strongest soldier, it's true. However, he was kicked in the head by a horse, you know."

"I heard," she murmured.

"His IQ is only around two hundred at the very most," Vero muttered, pulling her along. "The injury occurred when he was young enough to affect him for the rest of his life." They reached the kitchen. "Silas," Vero said quietly.

At around three hundred years old, Silas had red eyes several shades lighter than his lips. His torso tapered from a muscled chest to a narrow waist. He craned his neck to see beyond Vero. "That looks miserable."

"Yes." Vero saw no need to go into detail. "Why are you still in camp?"

"I wanted to review the surveillance and computer equipment orders again." He pulled a piece of paper out of his back pocket and unfolded it.

Vero read it over quickly. "The list is complete."

"Cameras and computers?" Lyrica asked, leaning closer, her breast brushing Vero's arm.

Electricity arced through him, landing forcefully in his groin. His growl had her stiffening.

"The cameras for the interior of the encampment, and the computers to connect us to the outside world," Silas said, clueless to the undercurrents. "We worked on ammunition supply, military infrastructure, and safety from outside attack first, although we don't have satellite or internet reach yet. Also, we didn't think we'd need interior surveillance. Apparently we do since someone attacked and killed that poor human female. Yet one more thing to worry about."

Vero edged toward the door. "Silas, there's a break in the snowfall now."

Silas puffed out his chest and smiled at Lyrica. "You look real pretty in that dress, Lyrica."

Pink filtered across her cheekbones. "Thank you, Silas. That's nice of you to say."

Irritation climbed down Vero's back. "You want to join the speed dating?"

"No. Hell no." Silas straightened his uniform with the silver medallions on his left breast.

"Change clothes," Vero reminded him.

Silas glanced down at his pressed uniform. "I know. The mechanics are getting the helicopter warmed up. I have time to become more humanlike."

He cleared his throat. "I saw Doc for my injection and he wanted me to remind you that the facility in Dakota with the mind-wiping protocol needs funds."

Damn it. Vero glared at him. "On it."

Lyrica jerked. "What? Mind wiping?"

Silas nodded, obviously missing the tone of her voice. "Sure. For the females we release back to the human world." He winked at Lyrica and hustled out into the cold, shutting the door loudly.

Vero just might have to kill the guy.

She whirled on him. "Wait a minute. You and Paxton said you liked my idea of giving them a million dollars and having NDAs. You can't mess with their minds."

He didn't want to deal with this. "We do like your idea."

She stared at him. "So you are not going to wipe their memories."

"We haven't decided." That was the truth, and he needed to speak with Paxton about it.

She drew up. "Okay. Then I want to discuss the matter with you both."

"Fine."

Lyrica looked over her shoulder as the buzzer rang for everybody to move tables. "I don't suppose we have to go back in," she said softly, hope in her voice.

Amusement ticked through him. "No."

She looked toward the window in the top of the door. "It's a beautiful night. The moon is bright." She bit her bottom lip as if undecided.

"I'm finished," he said curtly. It seemed a waste of time to meet the females since he had no plans to mate one of them.

Her face lit up. "Then I can't go back in. Perhaps I'll run to the warehouse for more of the sparkling water. Apparently, it's a huge hit."

"Good," Vero grunted. "I'll escort you."

"I can make it," she said, reaching for the door.

He grasped her arm and pulled her back. "Jacket." He looked at the multitude of coats and jackets on every hook in the mudroom just off the kitchen. He had no idea where they all had come from. "Where is yours?"

She shook her head. "Upstairs in my room. I hadn't planned to leave the main lodge."

The female needed a keeper. He removed a long wool coat off a rack. "Wear this." The deep blue cashmere felt soft against his skin.

"That's not mine," she said.

"It's not anybody's." He took her arm and pulled it through, before doing the same with the other one. While she protested, he buttoned up the coat and grabbed a heavy black scarf out of a cubby to wrap around her neck. He looked down at her little shoes. "Huh." Ducking, he rummaged in the nearest basket and removed a pair of snow boots. "Step in."

"They're not mine," she protested.

He leveled up, meeting her gaze. "Now."

"You might try a complete sentence once in a while." She stepped into the boots, keeping her flats on. "They're too big."

He tied them both. "They'll keep your feet warm." There. That was a complete fucking sentence. She was human and had no clue how frozen she could get. The image of the dead and frozen female from the night before flashed through his head. "Gloves."

"No. I'll use my pockets. I'm not taking someone else's gloves." She slapped his abs, branding him without knowing it. That touch. It tore through him with the force of a gale, filling every pore. She had no clue the danger she courted.

He opened the door. "Fine."

She faltered. "Don't you need a coat?"

"No." He hadn't felt the cold in a decade. Maybe longer.

Giving him a look, one of pure sass, she stomped outside in the large boots and down the two steps to the frozen ground. He shut the door, relieved as the frigid night air washed over him. Years ago he'd been taken by a rival Cyst group and tortured before his uncles had rescued him. Speed dating had been worse.

He gripped her upper arm, careful to keep from flexing his fingers. As a human female, her fragility couldn't be overestimated. "It's icy."

"I know." She clopped awkwardly in the boots. With the moonlight shining down, her eyes shone like rare brown diamonds with all their alluring facets. "Can I ask you something?"

He grunted his assent, his senses tuning into the environment around them, searching for threats.

"Are you a virgin?" she blurted out.

He halted them both and turned, staring down at her rapidly reddening face. What the fuck?

* * * *

Lyrica barely kept herself from slapping a hand over her mouth. The question about Kurjans had been on her mind since she had come up with the speed dating idea, but she hadn't known how to ask. Not once had she meant to be personal just with Vero. Except, she couldn't stop thinking about him. Big and dangerous, his too-blue eyes held a sadness that no amount of his anger could veil. That drew her. More than his hard-assed and muscular body. "I'm sorry," she breathed. "That's not how I meant to broach the subject."

"The subject?" He barely cocked his head while brushing a piece of her too-wild hair away from her face.

Desire dropped into her abdomen while her skin heated. Just from one tiny touch. She stared up, way up, to his sharply carved face. "Yes. It's part of my job to know what I'm working with when it comes to matching prospective mates." Did that make sense? Her mouth had taken over and was just spewing out words.

He blinked. Just once. Then he tapped the bridge of his nose as if trying to concentrate, his eyelids briefly closing.

She winced. "I really didn't mean to be rude."

His eyelids opened and the world filled with blue. For a second. "No."

"You're not a virgin?" A surprising disappointment flickered through her. Why? Seriously. Had she thought she could introduce him to pleasure? What was wrong with her head? Her body. Yeah, that was it. Her body was trying to take over. Bad body. Bad. "Vero?"

"No. Why?"

She took a deep breath and winced as frozen air burned her lungs. "It's just, well, that the Kurjans have been so isolated from everyone else. Look where you live. In the middle of mountain ranges away from all civilization." Her hands were freezing in the pockets so she scrunched her fingers into a fist. "I didn't mean to embarrass you."

One of his dark eyebrows rose. They were so much darker than most Kurjans'. "Do I look embarrassed?"

She studied his face. His bone structure appeared sharp enough to hurt anybody who tried to punch him in his immortal face. His eyes glowed a Prussian blue, and mere curiosity hinted in his expression. No doubt because he let it. Heat and an undefinable tension rolled off him to surround them both with a hint of warmth. Power. Yeah, that was it. Power streamed from the guy. "No, you don't look embarrassed."

"Why do you?"

Apparently, some of the heat in her face resulted from a furious blush. "I don't usually talk about sex with, um, friends."

"Is that what we are? Friends?"

Was he mocking her? His expression hadn't changed, but his lips had pursed with just a bit of arrogance. "Yes. We're friends."

"Hm." He slid his fingers into her hair and brushed his callused thumb gently across her cheekbone.

She blinked rapidly, her breath quickening, her knees locking. Her clit aching. "What are you doing?"

"Not feeling friendly." He leaned down, his mouth an inch from hers. "Talking about sex doesn't bother me. Why does it turn you red?" His hot breath warmed her lips and somehow seeped into her mouth, heating down her throat, past her breasts, right to her aching sex.

"Vero." It was the only word that came to mind. She tried to shake her head to get her bearings, but his casual touch kept her firmly facing him. Desire fired even stronger inside her, and she bit back a moan. This wasn't healthy. Or normal. For the love of Pete, she had to get herself under control. Under her own control. Not his. "So you've had girlfriends?"

His lips twitched but didn't curve into a smile. "No. I've had extensive training in sexual practices, like all Kurjans."

What? She jolted. "Excuse me?"

"When we turn sixteen, we're sent to one of several houses to learn about sex. How to perfect it. Those places are not on this continent."

Should she be disgusted or curious? Was it possible to be both? "The partners? They were willing?"

"Very. Apparently, Kurjans are unique even in the world of sex and money. Don't forget that we can read people. I promise, with my utmost assurance, that I've never been with an unwilling partner. We're not the monsters you think."

It was the most he'd ever said to her at once. "But you've forced females to mate through the centuries."

"So have the vampires and demons, until recently. Same with humans—who still do so. There are plenty of human countries where fathers give daughters away, even today."

She couldn't argue with his facts. "It's wrong."

"Yes. Which is why we're changing. You saw Paxton sign the new directives into law."

She had, which is why she felt comfortable with the speed dating. "Besides these sex houses, have you ever been with a female? Or a male?" Curiosity. It had its grasp on her.

"Yes. Female, not male. No judgment, but I like females." Still too close to her, his gaze swept her body, leaving tingles everywhere those twilight blue eyes lingered. "The sun harms us. Not the moon. My cousin and I often ventured into human cities and bars to meet females." His thumb caressed her cheekbone again. "That's a familiar practice for all Kurjans. By masking the red if there's any in our hair, wearing contacts, and darkening our skin, we look almost human."

Oh. Well, all righty then. "Good. I'm happy for you."

His lips parted. Not in a smile but perhaps the promise of one. "Disappointed?"

"No," she lied.

"Hmm." Now his gaze dropped to her lips. "Falsehoods from you don't seem right," he mused. His fingers tangled in her hair and he tugged back her head, his mouth on hers before she could take a breath.

Rough, wet, and hard, he kissed her, forcing every thought out of her brain. Liquid magma poured down her throat, turning her body into an inferno surrounded by frigid air.

Hot and cold.

Fire and ice.

Passion and need.

His tongue swept hers, and her body burned hotter. Blood pounded into her clit. He pulled her closer, against unmovable hard muscle.

She kissed him back, overtaken. All of her softening into pure female, a hundred percent, in a way she'd never imagined.

He lifted away, and she murmured in protest, slowly opening her eyelids. Needing him. He slowly turned his head, his gaze sharpening as it landed on the main lodge.

"Wha—" she started.

Then the windows on the top floor blew out in a shattering explosion, glass flying and fire shooting outside only to be sucked back in as if swallowed by a massive vacuum.

"Paxton!" Vero yelled, releasing her and running toward the flames.

Chapter Eight

Vero barreled toward the burning building and cleared the stairs before kicking open the front door and running inside. Jonathan and the other males herded the females outside to safety. "Go with them," Vero ordered Lyrica.

She grasped a visibly shaking Genevieve to escort out.

Smoke had already filtered down the stairs to choke the air in the main gathering room. He ran to the right and took the stairs five at a time, skidding on the landing just as Paxton careened out of his room with Hope in his arms.

Vero reached him almost immediately. "Is she okay? How bad is she hurt?"

Hope looked at him, her blue eyes blinking. "I'm fine. I might've gotten crushed by this guy when he jumped to cover me, but I'm good."

Paxton stood in black boxers and nothing else. Smoke lifted from behind him, surrounding his face.

Vero squinted through the murky air as the smell of burned flesh filled his senses. "Shit. You're on fire." He immediately pivoted around his brother and started slapping out flames with his bare hands.

Paxton didn't so much as grunt.

Hope struggled in his arms, looking over his shoulder at Vero. "The explosion happened between our room and the twins'."

Flames licked across the floor. Vero slapped a flame out on Pax's lower back. "I've got it. You take her outside." He couldn't see through the smoke and his lungs rapidly began to protest. Embers and ash floated down to burn his head, but he pushed his way through the crackling air and kicked open the bedroom next to his brother's.

"Collin, Liam!" he yelled, his eyes watering, his body shuddering.

He coughed several times, squinting through the thick, dark smoke. Fire licked up the entire wall by the windows. He knelt down, hoping to see better beneath the smoke, and spotted a foot. Grunting, he grabbed an ankle and pulled an unconscious body toward him. Fire burned over the male's torso, so Vero wildly slapped out the flames with his hands before ducking his head and jerking the body over his shoulder. He didn't know which twin he carried, but he turned, coughing, stumbling and limping into the hallway.

Paxton immediately stood in front of him, burns down the side of his face. His black hair smoked, and his eyes blazed through the darkness.

"I got one," Vero coughed. "Wait for me."

"Take him outside," Paxton ordered, his breath emerging raspy and rough. He coughed and then hurried beyond Vero toward the burning room.

Damn it. Vero jogged toward the stairwell and descended, taking the stairs quickly and bursting outside where Hope and Lyrica waited. He looked wildly around.

"Liam!" Hope cried out, running behind Vero to check her cousin. How she managed to tell the twins apart, Vero would never know.

The scientific medical building. That's all they had. Cold air smashed into him, a balming relief to his burning skin.

Vero careened across the icy ground as soldiers and civilians began to pour out of the different barracks. He kicked open the door to the medical lab and ran inside, ducking his head to flip Liam over onto his back on one of the three medical tables. A sheet covered the dead human female on the first table.

The twin didn't move. Vero reached for the pulse in the male's neck. It pounded strong and steady. He looked to see Hope and Lyrica behind him. Good. He much preferred they stay inside. "Take care of him."

Hope immediately reached for her cousin's wrist.

Lyrica grabbed Vero's arm. Her pretty brown eyes glowed, full of concern. "Be careful. You can die by fire," she implored.

He was well aware that he could die by fire. He nodded gruffly. Nobody had ever told him to be careful before or even remotely expressed concern for his well-being. He shook off the sense of unease and ran back outside, where a powerfully rough snow had started to fall in heavy and painful sheets of near ice. Good.

He saw two of his soldiers, ones he trusted. "Guard the medical building. Don't let anybody in unless it's Paxton or me. Got it?"

"Yes, sir," the first male said, immediately taking point.

"Find somebody to guard the back also," he ordered the other guy. While there was only one door to the place, the wide window looking toward the river could easily be breached.

"I'm on it," the soldier replied.

Then Vero ran back toward the lodge, which now had flames billowing out of the roof above Paxton's room along with soot. He hurried back inside, ducking his head against the painful smoke just as Paxton reached him, his leg on fire, the other twin over his shoulder.

"I've got him," Vero said, fitting his shoulder to Paxton's and pulling the vampire onto it. The guy weighed a ton. "Extinguish the fire on your leg."

"I am."

Vero looked over his other shoulder. "Do we have everyone?"

Paxton coughed as he stumbled outside into the cool night air. "Yes, only two bedrooms and two bathrooms make up the west wing's second level. We'd just gone to bed about an hour ago."

Vero carried the unconscious vampire, who weighed a good three hundred pounds of solid muscle, over the ice and into the medical building. Once there, he gently flipped Collin over next to his twin on an examination bed. An angry-looking purple-and-red lump had formed on Collin's forehead. The blast must have thrown him across his room.

Vero immediately sought Lyrica to calm himself. She stood next to Liam, looking fragile and defenseless in the wool coat. Something settled in his chest upon seeing her still safe. "You good?"

"Yeah." She pulled a heavy blanket up over Liam's convulsing body.

"They both took wounds to the head and have inhaled a lot of smoke," Hope said briskly, making sure Collin was covered as well. "My guess is they'll be out for an hour or so as their bodies repair themselves." She gazed down Vero's torso. "How badly are you burned?"

He shook his head. "I'm fine."

Lyrica frowned and grabbed his hand, flipping it over to show the skin burned away to the bone. "That is not fine," she said in a hushed voice.

Hope winced, somehow looking regal in a white nightgown with the bottom burned away and spots of soot everywhere, including on her nose and above her right eye. Her hair stood up in a tangle of curls, and the prophesy markings up her neck seemed to darken. "I agree. Let me at least put a salve on that."

"It's fine." Vero sent healing cells to the damaged tissues. That would take a while.

Lyrica stamped her foot. "At least put on a glove."

He didn't have a glove. "I will. I'll grab one. On my way back in," he lied. "You two stay here. I have guards at each possible entry point."

With that, he hustled back outside and looked at the flames reaching into the sky. The ice and fire collided right above the roofline with an ear-shaking hiss as steam blew in every direction.

Paxton stood between a group of soldiers, still in burned boxers and his feet bare as they all grabbed chunks of snow and pieces of ice off the ground to hurtle at the flames. Working rapidly, faster than any human eye could detect, they launched more ice and snow even as the skies mercifully granted assistance with sleet. Soon the fire gave up the fight and sputtered out with an angry crackle. More steam rolled into the night.

Paxton looked down at his burned feet, then over at Vero. "You okay?"

"I'm fine," Vero said. "How badly are you injured?"

Paxton leaned slightly to look at Vero's back. "About the same as you, I suppose."

The frigid night air helped, and the angry sleet stung as it hit his flesh, but then it provided a balming relief. Vero sent more healing cells to the deeper burns on his body. He stared at the damaged log facade. "I heard just one detonation."

"Affirmative," Paxton said. "I think the explosives were set in the small bathroom between our room and the twins' bedroom."

"You all four got out," Vero said slowly. "So either those weren't meant to kill you, or…" He looked uneasily toward the silent building.

Paxton stiffened. "Or there are more explosives in there that did not detonate. We also need to check your bedroom in the east wing."

"I'll go." Vero's right foot felt numb, but no doubt the healing cells would do their job. Their enemies needed to kill Paxton before the Convexus—in exactly seven days.

"No. I'll go," Paxton said.

Vero shoved him not too gently to the side. "In case you forgot, you're the king. We need you to stay alive." Without waiting for an answer, he pivoted away, fury hotter than the explosion erupting through him.

Fury that Paxton didn't know to keep himself safe, and fury that somebody had dared try to blow up his brother. He had felt little loyalty during his life, but he'd at least tried to be loyal to his family members and to his nation as a whole. This was different. This *felt* different. There was a depth to Vero's fury that caused him to go stone-cold. He hadn't known his brother for long, but they shared blood. That meant something, and he would find whoever had tried to kill not only the king of their nation, but his brother.

A wisp of sound behind him caught his attention as he walked inside the smoking lodge. He looked over his shoulder, unsurprised to see Paxton. "What the fuck are you doing?"

Paxton shook his head. "I'm not letting you go up there alone. Now come on, let's get this done."

Irritation climbing through him, Vero stomped up the damaged steps, unsurprised as one gave way beneath his uninjured foot. He hopped up and kept moving without missing a stride. His brother truly did not understand his duties as the leader. At the moment he should be protected, guarded, and safe. Instead, the idiot was following him, burned head to toe, wearing only tattered boxers.

His brother had big feet.

Vero had no clue where that thought came from, but he moved farther down the hallway, acidic black smoke attacking him from every angle. He reached the room formerly occupied by the twins and shoved inside, noting some of the smoke had dissipated out the burned-away wall. Dirty chunks of ice littered still-smoldering bedclothes as well as weapons leaning against the far wall.

He stalked past the nearest bed into what had been the twins' bathroom. The room now stood as a burned-out shell of black charcoal and torn wood. He pointed toward where the sink had been. "They hid the explosives under there."

Paxton stood behind him, tall and sure, seemingly not noticing that his feet were burned to a crisp. It had to hurt to stand on them. He looked around. "There was nowhere in here for a secondary device."

"Agreed." Vero turned back to the bedroom and they quickly searched it, spending extra time in the closet and tossing the beds out of the way. He cocked his head. "That leaves one room on this wing."

"I'm aware," Paxton said grimly, pivoting toward the door and heading into the hallway before Vero could jump in front of him.

Enough of this shit. "We really have to get you accustomed to acting like a king," Vero snapped, shoving his brother behind him.

"I am acting like a king," Paxton said, knocking him on the arm.

Vero grit his teeth and kicked open the door of what had been Paxton's large room. The bed had fallen and was a smoldering heap of mattress and blankets. He hurried toward the closet and rifled through it, looking for another device, while Paxton went into the adjoining bath and did the same.

Paxton emerged, shaking his head, soot covering the right side of his body. "There's nothing in there. Maybe they thought the one bomb would take us all out."

"I don't think so," Vero said, his gaze caught on the one dresser to the side of the closet. He stumbled over crispy black wood and shattered belongings as well as ice from the windows and immediately began pulling out and dumping out drawers. No explosives.

Paxton shrugged. "Let's search your bedroom and then go check on the twins. I guess this was it."

"This wasn't it." Vero knew to his very soul there was some danger here. He could feel it. He could smell it. Grunting, he grabbed the heavy oak dresser, lifted it, and heaved it across the room. Looking down, he could see a bomb of sorts embedded in the floor. The left side of it glowed yellow and began to flash to red.

Panic gripped him. Fuck. He turned, grabbed his brother around the shoulders, and threw them both out of the gaping hole in the wall. The explosion rocked the room the second he hit the air and propelled them both, along with a flash of fire, several yards up to the heavens.

Vero gripped his brother tight, holding on, wanting to make sure they landed on him and not Paxton. As they rolled around, fire licking at them, smoke surrounding them, momentum smashed them both into the depot building. Darkness crashed through his head, and he didn't feel the hard, icy ground when he finally landed, fully unconscious.

Again.

Chapter Nine

The explosion from the main lodge rocked the entire camp, and Lyrica grabbed the counter in the medical building for balance but still went down to her knees.

"Damn it." Hope fell and quickly rolled up to her feet. She looked wildly around. "Do we have weapons in here?"

"I don't know." Lyrica started pulling open drawers to see gauze, tape, medication, and scalpels. Was Vero all right? How many explosions could his body take? "We have scalpels."

Hope looked over her shoulder at Lyrica, shivering in her ruined nightie. "I don't think scalpels are going to do us any good."

"Agreed," Lyrica said, rubbing her eye. Spikes of ice, rapidly melting into mushy soot, covered her yellow dress. "You need a blanket." She hurried toward a basket in the corner where she grabbed a fleece blanket and immediately returned to wrap it around Hope's shoulders. "You must be freezing."

"That's okay," Hope said quietly. "I'm immortal. I can't die." She rubbed soot beneath her eye and smeared gray mush across her pretty face.

Lyrica studied her, having wondered about her new friend since Hope had arrived in camp only a month before. "You're the only female vampire ever born, right?"

"Yeah," Hope said, wincing, her blue eyes bloodshot. "Until my birth, vampires only created males, just like Kurjans, I guess. I'm a mixture of pretty much every species out there, but my dad is a demon-vampire and my mom is an enhanced human. All immortals take on one aspect of their heritage. So, for example, if your dad's a demon and your mom is a shifter, you're likely to be only one of those. Your true nature."

"Oh." Since Lyrica had known only Kurjans as immortals since her kidnapping months ago, she was just learning about the other species.

Hope sighed heavily, looking at her cousins, both still unconscious on the beds. "I've never shown any extra strength or abilities." She pursed her lips. "There was a prevailing thought that perhaps I'm more human than immortal, and we never really found out, although the prophet markings on my neck show that I'm definitely immortal somehow."

"Fascinating." Lyrica nodded. "But now that you've mated Paxton, you'd be immortal regardless. Correct?"

Hope brightened. "That's correct. However, it's been less than a month, and no one quite knows when immortality kicks in. In all the tests, it's a different time frame for each person. Genetics and all that."

"Oh," Lyrica said, quickly checking over Liam again.

The vampire hadn't moved, but the air popped wildly around him. She'd sensed the healing cells that immortals could employ, and somehow they altered the air, or rather atmosphere, around whoever was using them.

"So that's why Paxton is so overprotective of you." Lyrica had wondered.

Hope grinned, a dimple appearing in her cheek. "Yeah, I don't think that's going to change. I may hit five thousand years old someday, and I doubt he's going to be any less protective, but that's okay."

Lyrica wondered for a moment what it would be like to have somebody in her life who cared that much. She never had. "Must be a safe feeling."

Hope glanced at her, awareness darkening her cerulean eyes. "Among other feelings. What about you? Do you have a boyfriend out there searching high and low for you?"

Lyrica snorted. "No." Sadness wandered through her. "Right after the Kurjans kidnapped us, they gave us the option of either just disappearing or emailing our loved ones to let them know we had gone on walkabout and needed space so they wouldn't worry." In fact, she'd heard that Vero had insisted upon the opportunity. "I didn't have anybody to email."

"Not at all?"

"No. I'm an only child, and I never met my mom. My dad and I were poor and lived out of cars and sometimes shelters. In the best times, we stayed with his father in the mountains, and I never wanted to leave, but Dad had wanderlust. He died several years ago. When I was taken by the Kurjans, I'd just moved across the country for a new start and hadn't even found a job yet. I'm a mathematician and an expert in crisis management for financial companies when things go wrong. I love solving problems." How freaking depressing. Nobody knew she'd been kidnapped. Nobody missed her.

The door burst open and Vero hauled an unconscious and bleeding Paxton inside, dragging him over to heft onto the doctor's desk chair.

"Paxton," Hope cried out, rushing around her cousins to reach him.

Vero staggered back, blood flowing from a wound in his forehead. "Another bomb detonated, and we jumped out the window. I landed on him." Vero winced and a cut in his lip bled freely. Burns, bruises, and broken bones showed down his right side.

"Are you sure you landed on him?" Lyrica pushed him into one of the two guest chairs. They only had one more chair left if anybody else came in wounded. "You look like a truck landed on you both. We need to get you a bed."

"I don't need a bed," he growled. "How bad is he?"

Hope touched Paxton's face and brushed back his thick, black hair. She ran her fingers down his neck, torso, and legs as he slumped in the chair, his head against the wall.

"Here." Lyrica rushed to fetch another blanket from the basket.

"Thanks." Hope covered him, careful of his left side. "I feel a few broken ribs, obvious contusion from a lump above his ear, and probably some internal damage."

The air heated and swept around the room.

Hope's eyes widened as she looked around. "Apparently, his healing cells have gone into action."

"Good," Vero grunted, sitting in the chair. The fire and explosion had burned away much of his jeans and sweater, leaving raw skin and wounded flesh visible.

Lyrica grabbed the final blanket and brought it over. "Here. You need to stay warm." She leaned in to look at the bleeding wound on his head and the room began to swim.

"Whoa. Take a deep breath." He grabbed her arm.

"Sorry, not great with blood," she said. "I think we need to stitch that up."

He leaned in, his blue eyes intense. Lighter than normal. Icy. "No, I'm fine, and my blood will burn you. Toss me a cotton ball."

Lyrica's stomach dropped, but she turned away to rummage in one of the drawers for gauze. "Here you go."

"Thanks." He took the bunch and slapped the mass onto his head. The flimsy material immediately turned red with blood.

She reached for the hand he wasn't hiding from her. "What injuries do you have?"

"Minor concussion. The explosion knocked me out for a brief moment before I came to and hauled him in here." Vero pulled free and reached behind his back to pull out a weapon. "Who's guarding this place? I didn't see anybody out front. I gave orders."

Lyrica's eyes widened. "Nobody is guarding the front?"

"No," Vero bit out. "However, it's entirely possible that after the explosion, they went to see who was harmed. I saw a couple of people down but getting back up. We were the only ones in the actual explosion." He turned the chair, winced as pain no doubt engulfed his damaged body, and aimed his gun at the only door. "Hope, do you have any weapons on you?"

"No." She stared at her cousins, who'd arrived wearing only boxers. "Nobody here has any weapons other than yours."

"Fantastic," Vero growled, looking furious and deadly even though blood poured from several injuries in his chest. The blanket fell down to his waist. He shifted, pain in his eyes.

Lyrica felt a desperate urge to assist him. "What do you need?"

"Help me remove this shirt, would you?"

She blinked. "Okay."

No doubt the material continued burning him in several areas, and he probably needed his skin free. The cool air would hopefully soothe some of the burns.

She reached for the bottom of his shirt and gently lifted up. He gave her one arm and then the other, and she pulled it over his head. Truth be told, she'd imagined taking his shirt off before, but not like this. Whoa. Muscle, dangerously cut, shifted beneath his skin. Yet the wounds kept pouring out blood.

Her gaze caught on a piece of wood that had embedded itself in his heart, with only a small bit still visible. "Oh my God." Panic grabbed her. She took a step back, stumbling and slipping on a chunk of ice and falling to her knees.

"Whoa." He reached down and grasped her arm, lifting her up even though it appeared as if one of his wrist bones poked through his skin. It was like he didn't even notice.

She stood. "How are you breathing? Did the stake not go through your heart?"

In answer, he slowly looked down to see the wedge of wood poking out of his skin. "Huh?"

Hope snorted behind Lyrica.

"What?" Lyrica snarled. "It's not funny. There might as well be a stake in his heart."

"A stake?" Hope looked at her unconscious mate overwhelming the chair. "I know it's not funny." She chuckled. "I'm sorry." Her eyes filled with merriment that glowed in her pale face.

Vero snorted, but pain rode the sound.

Lyrica put her hands on her hips. "I don't think you understand. If we pull that stake out, you could die, Vero Phoenix. You took it to the heart."

Vero looked up, his face, at least the part that was working, in a frown. "What are you talking about?"

She pointed to the wood. "You've been staked through the heart."

"Jesus." He grabbed the edge of the stick with two fingers and started to pull.

"No," she yelled, trying to grab his hand.

Before she could reach him, he yanked out the fragment. Blood spurted from his chest. Wincing, he tossed the offending wood onto the ground. "A stake to the heart doesn't kill us, sweetheart. You need to stop believing movies made by humans."

Embarrassment warred with panic inside her. She shook her head, walked slowly to the drawer, and brought out more gauze. "At least let me cover the wound." Gently, she laid the white mesh over his heart, removing her hand before his blood could burn her. If they mated, his blood wouldn't harm her. The thought came out of nowhere, and she shoved it away. "You can't tell me that a stake to the heart doesn't cause damage."

"I'm not telling you that." Vero closed his eyes and leaned his head back on the wall. "It takes a while to repair a heart, but the wood only nicked the edge of it. I'm okay."

He didn't sound like he was okay. Even so, with his eyes closed and his head back, his gun remained leveled evenly and unwaveringly at the doorway. The air shimmered around him. Not quite with glitter or anything too shiny, but somehow, the very oxygen appeared filled with a hint of magic. Healing cells at work.

With a gasp, Paxton sat straight up, sucking in air. His eyes had morphed to a shockingly electric green as he looked around and took in the entire area. "Hope?" Urgency rode the first word he said.

"I'm safe." Hope leaned toward him and cupped the side of his face with her hand. "Are you all right? My gut feeling says you're experiencing internal bleeding."

As an empath, Lyrica could feel Hope's concern. Had Hope allowed that since they were friends, or was Lyrica gaining more skills?

"I'm fine," Paxton said shortly, turning to look at his brother, blood still sliding from a cut above his ear. "What were you doing trying to put your body between me and the bomb?"

Vero opened his eyelids almost lazily to focus on his brother. "I was doing my job. It's to keep you safe at all costs."

"Meaning even your own life?" Paxton spat, fury rolling off him in waves.

Lyrica took a step closer to Vero and away from the king of the Kurjans.

"Yes, dumbass," Vero said.

Lyrica's eyes widened and she let herself fall onto the chair next to him. She just couldn't handle this right now.

"Did you just call me a dumbass?" Paxton growled, blood dripping from the side of his mouth.

"Only because you're acting like one," Vero muttered, shutting his eyes again and leaning his head back.

Even in the current bizarre circumstances, Lyrica had to hide a grin. They actually sounded like brothers. She looked over at Hope, who had a soft smile on her face, even as she fussed with the blanket over Paxton.

"What the fuck?" Liam sat bolt upright and bunched his fists as if ready to fight.

Vero sighed and opened his eyes. "You're fine. There was an explosion. Everybody's good. We're fairly safe in this room, although I'm the only one with a gun."

Liam frowned and looked over at his unconscious twin. "How long have we been out?"

"I don't know. An hour maybe," Paxton said.

"More like thirty minutes," Vero corrected.

Liam leaned over and punched his brother in the shoulder. "Collin, wake up. We're in trouble."

His brother didn't move. Lyrica expected panic or concern, but instead, Liam punched his brother harder. "Wake the hell up."

Collin's eyelids opened and he turned only his head to stare at his brother. "You hit me again and I'm ripping out your throat."

An inappropriate giggle emerged from Lyrica.

Hope shook her head. "Now is not the time, you two." It sounded like she'd repeated that mantra to her cousins more than once.

Groaning, Collin pushed himself to a seated position. "Did somebody try to blow us up?"

"Affirmative," Vero said.

"We only have one weapon?" Paxton repeated, looking down at his damaged chest, then over at his brother.

Vero kicked out his legs and something loudly popped back into place. "This is the one gun."

"What about guards?" Paxton asked.

"I assigned two, but they disappeared after the second explosion. My guess is they went to help."

"Huh," Paxton murmured.

The outside door opened again and Dr. Fizzlewick walked inside, followed by Jonathan. "Dear Lord," the doctor said. "You all look terrible."

Paxton cleared his throat. "We're fine. Have you checked for injured outside?"

The doctor waved a hand in the air. "Of course. We have some burns, a couple of concussions. Nothing major." He leaned his head to the side to look at Vero's chest. "You get hit in the heart?"

"I did," Vero said, the sound more of a grunt.

"You better heal that first," Fizzlewick said helpfully.

Vero stared, his eyes flat. "No shit, Doc." He sounded grumpier than a trapped bear.

"Don't be so darn cranky." Fizzlewick walked over to Paxton and looked him over. "I feel internal injuries riding the air along with healing cells."

"I know, Doc," Paxton said easily. "I'm sending healing cells to my spleen right now."

"Spleens are more important than you think, kid." Fizzlewick turned to check the twins. "Boy, that's an impressive lump you have on your head," he said, prodding the back of Liam's cranium.

Liam slapped his hand away. "Yeah, my skull felt better before you poked it."

Fizzlewick smiled. "You're all being babies." He looked at Hope and Lyrica. "Are you ladies all right?"

"We're fine," Lyrica answered for both of them, unable to move from her seat. Her sopping dress was heavy now that the ice had melted, and her ears still rang from the explosion.

"Well," Fizzlewick said. "I can feel the healing cells, so everything's going smoothly."

Vero looked at Jonathan. "You armed?"

"Of course," Jonathan said. "I've got two guns. I had no clue if speed dating was going to be dangerous or not, so I loaded for bear, as they say. Of course, we only had enhanced females and no bear shifters there. It'd be fun to meet a bear shifter."

Vero's chin lowered in a purely intimidating move. "Good. I want you to cover the front of this place until we're all healthy enough to move."

Jonathan nodded solemnly. "That's all right, but Thaddeus and Ranton are already out there."

Paxton cut a look at Vero. "Are they trustworthy?"

"Affirmative," Vero said. "They're the two I ordered to cover the building in the first place. They must have gone to help people when they heard the explosion."

The tone of his voice hinted that he'd speak with those two about that later. Hopefully not with a punch to the face, but Lyrica wouldn't bet against that.

Vero focused back on Jonathan. "Then take a soldier or two and search the entire east wing of the lodge for more explosives. My gut feeling is that they would've already blown, but sweep the bedrooms anyway."

"Yes, sir." Jonathan ran back outside.

"All right. We need to regroup," Paxton said. "We have to rebuild so there's no sign of an attack—the coming Cyst can't know we're vulnerable. Also, first thing in the morning, Hope, Collin, and Liam will move to Realm territory."

Hope's head jerked and her eyes burned a wild blue. "Not in a million years."

Paxton looked at her and his smile was slow. Not slow and sweet. Slow and deadly.

A shiver wandered down Lyrica's spine, and she edged her chair closer to Vero.

Paxton reached out and tugged on a piece of Hope's hair. "That's nonnegotiable, my sweet mate. You can check on my dog when you're home and then bring him back with you. I miss him. Until I figure out who all is trying to kill me, or kill you, you're going to visit your family."

Hope's chin lifted. "You are my family."

Paxton's gaze softened in a way Lyrica never would've imagined from the leader. "I know, baby. Which is exactly why you're going. It's nonnegotiable."

Vero sat up, losing the lazy look. "Family. Speaking of whom...where the hell is Hunter?"

Chapter Ten

The first light of dawn emerged through jagged peaks, revealing the aftermath of last night's vicious storm. The mountains stood sharp and dark, their edges brutal against the bruised sky, where heavy clouds still hung. White tipped the peaks and spread down the mountains to the flowing Yukon River. Even with a storm having cleansed the area, the stench of burned wood and destroyed flesh filled the morning.

Vero had searched through the night, but with the smell of the fire clogging the air, he couldn't catch his friend's scent. Now he stood in front of the lodge noting the damage. They'd built it in less than a week, so they'd probably be able to rebuild that side in a few days. Well, if they had supplies.

The whir of a helicopter filled the air and he paused, stiffening as he saw Silas land in the helicopter area closer to the edge of camp.

Liam and Collin jogged up, both bruised and moving slowly, their green eyes determined. "All of the buildings have been searched, and we just ran the length of the forest to the south. Found nothing," Liam said. At least Vero thought he was Liam.

The other one nodded. "Liam climbed several trees. My left leg is still healing."

So, Vero had guessed correctly. Good. Liam had a gash above his right eye, distinguishing them. For now, anyway. Vero pinched the bridge of his nose. "Okay." He glanced uneasily at the icy river that flowed too smoothly. "We may have to dive."

"I'm up for it," Paxton said, walking out of the building.

"You're not going anywhere," Vero protested. "I don't know why I have to remind you all the time that you're the fucking king."

One of Paxton's dark eyebrows rose. "Hunter Kayrs is my family just like you," he retorted. "I'm going to find him."

The helicopter's blade silenced and Silas jumped out before reaching in the back for several large bags.

"At least the surveillance cameras have arrived," Vero muttered.

The lodge door opened again and Lyrica walked out, wearing jeans, a heavy coat, and tall snow boots. She brought him a cup of coffee. His heart warmed, even though the chill of losing Hunter wouldn't quite leave him. The guy had to be somewhere.

"I can help you search," she said, her hands encased in thick mittens.

"No, I need you to interview everybody again," Vero ordered. "Everybody who attended speed dating first. I know they all ran outside when they heard the explosion, but I want to know who saw Hunter last. Where did he go?"

There wasn't a doubt in Vero's mind that Hunter would have headed right for the explosion, especially since his cousins lived on that side of the house, and yet he remained nowhere to be seen. Vero hadn't even thought about him until he could take a breath.

Paxton's face darkened. "He would never have left Hope inside like that. Something happened to him."

Silas jogged up, his eyes a mellow red as he grunted when he dropped the camera materials gently on the porch. "What happened? It looks more like an explosion than just a fire."

"It was," Paxton said curtly. "Did you get everything we needed?"

"I did." Silas looked around. "Is everybody all right? Was anybody hurt?"

Lyrica leaned closer to Vero, probably without knowing it. He liked that she sought shelter from him.

He shook his head. "We don't think so, but we can't find Hunter. When you flew over the camp, did you see anything suspicious?"

Silas scratched his chin. "No. All I saw was white snow and the aftermath of a storm. It looked like the wind whipped a few trees bare. That's why I couldn't come back till this morning."

Paxton glanced at the now silent helicopter, which was far beyond anything the humans had yet to invent. "Maybe we should look for him from the air. We've searched everywhere in camp, every building, every vehicle, every possible hiding place."

Vero's gut hurt. Hunter fought brutally well, and yet he'd disappeared without so much as a whisper. Who could have managed that? How many people would it have taken to get him away?

The door opened yet again, and Hope walked outside, encased in a thick, long, black puffer jacket, a hat on her head. "Who needs coffee? I have more brewing. We'll bring out a pot in just a minute." Worry pinched her face, which had gone pale. "Nobody's found Hunter?"

"Negative," Vero said.

Paxton slipped his arm over her shoulders. "We'll find him, Hope. I promise." He glanced at the twins. "However, you two need to get her out of here. Go to Realm headquarters."

Instantly all three protested. "We're not going anywhere," Liam snarled, "until we find my cousin."

"Agreed," Collin said, his voice low.

Hope nodded vigorously. "We can't go home without him. We don't know where he is, Paxton. You have to understand that." Her lips pressed into a firm line.

Vero looked at them, wondering what that kind of loyalty felt like. He thought he and his cousin had had loyalty, but he'd been wrong. His cousin, who was now dead, had known about Vero's lineage for years and had never said a word. Had never told Vero that he even had a brother. It had been as much of a shock to him as it had been to Paxton.

Paxton looked over at him. "What do you say? We take the helicopter up and look?"

Vero nodded. "Yeah." Guilt filtered through him. He hadn't really talked to Hunter since discovering his spying on the Kurjan nation the day Paxton became their king. Should he feel guilty? He didn't even know anymore.

"We'll go too," Liam said, standing shoulder to shoulder with his brother.

"No." Paxton looked at them, his face unyielding, no give in his voice. "I need you to keep an eye on Hope. Protect her and Lyrica. I promise if we see anything, we'll call it in."

Collin's face hardened in front of their eyes, but he nodded. "Agreed."

Vero fought the very real urge to place a kiss on Lyrica's nose and instead shoved his hands in his pockets and started walking toward the helicopter. His heart hadn't mended all the way from the wooden shard, and one of his knees still felt out of joint, but he'd healed the internal damage he had sustained from the explosion.

Next to him, his brother limped just enough for Vero to notice. "You want to fly or want me to fly?" Vero asked.

"How's your head?" Paxton murmured.

Vero rubbed a lump behind his right ear. "It's good. Vision's still a little blurry, though."

Paxton looked sideways at him. "I'll pilot the craft."

"Fair enough." At this point, Vero didn't really give a shit.

The fact that they hadn't been able to find Hunter or even a hint of him didn't look good. The guy could fight. And disappearing without a word, well, that just didn't make any sense.

Vero cleared his throat. He had a question and he didn't like it, but he had to ask it. "I'm not saying that it has happened, but if somebody killed the King of the Realm's son, I take it this newfound peace we have is over?"

Paxton's jaw stiffened. "Nobody killed Hunter."

All right, so they'd go with denial. Vero could be as nonlogical as the rest of them. "All righty then. Let's hop in the helicopter. I'm sure we'll spot him right away."

"We'd better," Paxton growled, opening the pilot side of the souped-up craft.

Vero limped around the front and jumped up into the passenger seat, fastening his belt and shutting the door tight. The thing would be soundproof the minute Paxton started up the rotors and they'd have no need for headphones. Vero made sure his knives remained securely sheathed down his legs, with his gun at the back of his waist.

The helicopter started up silently and Paxton easily lifted them into the air. "What do you think?"

"Let's follow the river." From their position, it ran northwest before taking a sharp west turn in Alaska and emptying into the Bering Sea.

Paxton banked left. "You think he fell into the river?"

"I think if he was being attacked and he was outnumbered, he dove into the river." It's what Vero would have done. He wouldn't allow himself to consider alternatives.

"Agreed," Paxton said, his jaw hard. The male no doubt worried about Hope and how she would take Hunter's death.

Vero would mourn his friend later if they found him without his head. For now, he worried about his nation. Peace was tenuous, and if somebody in his camp had killed the future leader of the Realm, then peace had been very short-lived.

They remained silent as they followed the river north and Vero kept his gaze peeled to the white ground beneath them, looking for any hint of the soldier. Only brush trees and wildlife filled his gaze. Nobody large enough to be Hunter. They continued for another twenty minutes.

"Do you think he would have floated this far?" Paxton asked.

Vero nodded. He'd lived in various parts of Canada his entire life, and he knew how far one of these rivers could take a body. "Yes. Plus, it was a hell of a storm last night. The water would have been rushing fast, even beneath the ice."

His gaze caught on something up ahead. He pointed.

"What is that?" Paxton banked the helicopter left and lowered.

"I don't know. You see what I'm seeing?" Vero asked.

"Yes, but I can't tell what it is. It might be a deer."

Whatever it was had stopped halfway between the river and a bend, snarled in a low-hanging tree.

Vero squinted to see better, his heart rate kicking up. "I think that's a boot."

Paxton leaned down. "Maybe." He looked around. "There's a flat area right there." He flew even lower.

Vero could barely make out the shape of a hand. His gut clenched. "We have a body," he said. "I see a large hand." He didn't recognize the boots, but when was the last time he had noticed anybody's boots?

Paxton circled before slowly lowering the craft.

"You stay here," Vero said.

"Not a chance." Paxton cut the engines and jumped out.

Vero shook his head. Keeping the leader of the Kurjan nation safe was becoming a pain in his ass. He opened his door and dropped out, sinking to the top of his rib cage in snow. His body heated the mass and he kicked his way through with Paxton at his side. It made a lot more sense for Paxton to get behind him since he was already creating a trail, but Pax doggedly moved forward with him. Vero was much too stubborn to step behind his brother. As they neared the river, they both increased their speed.

A scent hit Vero. Hunter, the smell of forest and snow. He launched into a run, barreling through the snowdrifts, as Paxton did the same. Getting closer, Vero skidded on his knees toward Hunter's legs.

Hunter lay face down with his boots submerged, one caught on a rock. Dread filled Vero's chest and he gently started to rip branches and even a small log out of the way.

"Is his head attached?" Paxton asked, his voice low as he tugged the boot free of the rock.

"I can't tell yet," Vero said, his gut cramping. He lifted the last of the branches to see Hunter's thick black hair caught on even more branches. "I see his head," he said, leaning up, feeling around Hunter's neck. Blood instantly coated his hand. That was good, though. He was still producing blood.

Relief blew through Vero as he looked closer. "He's got a neck and head wound." In fact, it looked like a knife had gone through the side of his neck almost to his spine. Vero felt for a pulse.

Paxton jumped over Hunter and crashed on the other side, helping to remove the rest of the brambles. He peered in. "His neck is still half attached. It's not a death strike."

"No, but it was close." Vero shrugged out of his jacket and tore off his shirt. The jacket was too heavy, but he could bind Hunter's neck with a shirt and at least keep his head on his body. Blood instantly filled the material as the wind whipped against Vero's bare torso. He didn't feel a thing.

Paxton leaned in. "That's too close."

"Agreed. It looks like they got about half of his neck. My guess is that he dove into the river and let the current bring him out of danger. He'll be out for a while healing, but he's not going to die."

"We'll see," Paxton said. "We don't know the rest of his injuries."

As long as Hunter's head remained halfway attached to his body, he would live. "Roll him over and we can carry him back to the helicopter." Vero took a deep breath. "Hunter, I have no idea if you're even remotely awake, but buddy, this is going to hurt."

Chapter Eleven

Lyrica couldn't get rid of the vision of Hunter's head hanging by a tendon. Right now, Dr. Fizzlewick was working on the soldier, and he'd kicked everybody else out of the medical building. The smell of the burned lodge filled the air along with thick wisps of smoke. A crew already worked on removing debris, and she could hear them coming up with a construction plan. Did they need help with that? She could create a PowerPoint presentation for them.

She stood outside with Vero, unsure of what to do next. She always had a plan.

Paxton stared at his brother. "My side of the lodge is burned out, but I can bunk with the soldiers."

Vero's head jerked up so quickly he must've given himself a headache. "You are not bunking anywhere but in the lodge with me and the soldiers I've put in place. There are two empty bedrooms in the wing Lyrica and I have been using. You are now assigned to the room between mine and Lazart, who has been a soldier for five hundred years. We can trust him, I promise you."

Paxton's eyes flashed fire.

Lyrica retreated a step. She couldn't see Vero's expression, but if it remotely matched his brother's, she wanted to get out of the snowy night and now.

Paxton exhaled. "I think you've forgotten that you named me the fucking king, brother."

"Yes, I did, which means you stay fucking safe." Vero sounded every bit as angry as Paxton. "Letting them kill you isn't in my plans. So, get used to being covered at all times."

Paxton stretched his neck like a stallion fighting a bit. "You have misunderstood me. I've put up with the extra detail and lack of privacy because Hope's safety is paramount. But she's going to return to Realm headquarters as soon as Hunter can be moved—to the safest place in the world for her. I'm not standing down. Whoever put her in danger and tried to kill us is going to pay, Vero. All I have to do is find them."

"It's my job to find them, and using you as bait is not going to happen," Vero returned evenly, his back one long line of pissed-off muscle.

"Who's going to stop me?" Paxton asked softly, his expression a cold mask.

Vero stilled. Completely. "I am."

Paxton's smile lacked humor. "How's that, little brother? You wouldn't dare hit your king, now would you?"

For an answer, Vero struck Paxton so quickly in the jaw that Paxton didn't have time to block.

Lyrica gasped, slapping both hands over her mouth.

Paxton studied Vero.

Vero instantly dropped to one knee, loudly smacking a closed fist against his chest. "Your Highness. There's no excuse for my behavior."

Paxton cocked his head to the side and held out a hand.

Vero hesitated, then took it, standing back up.

Paxton instantly clocked him with a hard right, sending Vero to the side. "I don't think this is between members of the royal family. This is between brothers." He punctuated the last with a hard drive into Vero's gut.

Vero let out an angry oof, paused, and as if a demon unleashed, burst forward and partially lifted Paxton before laying him out in a tackle, both of them in the snow. Paxton roared and clapped his hands against Vero's head, shoving him over. Vero growled and punched Paxton in both sides of his rib cage, held on, and flipped them over with him on top.

Paxton let out a battle cry and did the same, and the two threw up handfuls of snow as they rolled over and over.

"Wait!" Lyrica shouted, kicking into the deeper snow to get to them. "Just wait." She tried to reach them, but immortal rolling-over speed was faster than a boulder tumbling down a hill. Finally, she caught up and shrieked. "Stop it. Both of you, right now."

At this point, Vero was on top of Paxton, his fist cocked. He slowly looked to the side, his eyes an unbearable blue. "Time out."

"Time out?" Lyrica yelled. Seriously? The guy knew what "time out" meant?

Paxton paused with a punch an inch away from Vero's neck. Slowly, he turned to look at her, snow covering his head. "Okay."

Vero let out a shrill whistle, and two Kurjan soldiers rushed toward them from behind the weapons depot. The first looked at them and hesitated. "King? Do you require assistance?"

"No," Paxton said, sounding almost cheerful even though he lay on the frozen ground buried in snow. "This is family business."

Vero flicked his gaze from the soldiers to Lyrica. "Take her into the main lodge. Nicely. If she's bruised, I'll kill you."

She stomped a foot in the snow. "I will not be—"

As if she hadn't spoken, the two ultra-tall soldiers each tucked an arm beneath hers, lifted, and easily started carrying her away. "You are so going to pay for this, Vero Phoenix," she bellowed, kicking her legs uselessly three feet off the ground.

The only sound that came back was fists on flesh and an occasional pained grunt.

Finally, the two carrying her deposited her inside the door of the half-demolished lodge. Apparently one fact crossed species, immortal and human. As they shut the door behind her, she turned and stared at the slightly damaged oak. "Boys are stupid," she yelled.

* * * *

An hour after throwing the first punch, Vero panted wildly, spitting out blood. He sat with his back against the weapons depot, his arm broken, his legs stretched out in front of him. Blood, ice, and snow covered his new jeans.

His brother sat next to him, his body and face in similar shape. "Feel better?" Paxton grunted, blood dribbling from his mouth.

Vero sent healing cells to his damaged cornea and thoughtfully considered the question. "I believe I do." Suspicion tickled the base of his mangled neck. "You mentioned this was a brother thing. Do brothers often break each other's bones?"

Paxton snorted. "You're the first brother I've had, but I've seen how other vampire and demon families relate to each other. I know you're torn up about Hunter, and since you can't hit him right now, I figured I'd be a good substitute. Plus, I'm not entirely sure I appreciate you declaring me the king of the Kurjan nation."

Vero licked at a split in his bottom lip. "Yeah, I understand. I should've realized you'd have a huge bullseye on your back." Yet he probably would've made the same decision. It was time to bring the Kurjan nation into the modern times and create coalitions with other immortal species, and having Paxton as their king made the most sense. Plus, as the eldest son of the ruling family, the title belonged to him. "I didn't consider the danger to you."

Paxton's shoulder loudly popped back into place. "I don't care about the danger, except when it comes to Hope. It's the responsibility. I grew up with a vampire dad who wasn't my dad who hated my guts. Then I traveled with my uncle, who was in a secret society that still wants to hurt everything we believe in. I had two friends my whole life, and they're both females. I mated one of them. I know fuck all about how to run a nation. How to protect people and create lasting bonds."

Vero hadn't considered self-doubt when it came to Paxton. His father and uncles had never shown an iota of self-doubt. They'd viewed doubt as an unforgivable weakness. "I figure the fact that you care makes you a good leader. Plus, you have me." Not that he'd been of much good his entire life. "At the very least, I can cover your back."

"Because we're brothers or because I'm the king?"

It was a good question. A fair one. "Either way, I'd kill or die for you." It was the truth.

Paxton slapped him on his newly healed thigh. "I guess it's a good start."

Vero lifted his head to allow snow to fall on his flesh and calm his wounded skin. "I felt a kinship to my now deceased cousin while growing up, but he didn't really care about me. He certainly never told me I had a brother."

"Well, you do, and I would never keep a secret like that from you. No secrets, period." Paxton turned and looked at him, blood on his face, and mellow flames in his powerful eyes.

"We're a pair," Vero muttered. They'd both grown up with more punches than compliments thrown at them. "I hadn't considered that we might be too damaged to actually fix the Kurjan nation and build a good future for everyone." His spine needed attention, so he sent more healing cells to the base. "When Hope faced certain death if she didn't pick Drake as her mate, and she chose you, I thought you were the luckiest male in the world." Vero's cousin had dragged her in front of cameras so the young Realm heir could choose him publicly. She hadn't—regardless of the cost.

Paxton nodded, then groaned. "So did I. Believe me, I didn't expect her declaration. I figured she'd agree to mate him to save everyone. But in the end, she said only one answer existed."

That kind of loyalty proved rare. "So I thought that she knew something about you that I didn't. She's the Realm princess—the heir to everything. She chose you, Pax. So I figured I should, too."

Paxton coughed, turned to the side, and spit out a couple of blood clots. "You have a great uppercut."

"Ditto."

Pax lifted an ankle and his boot jerked to the right as it healed with a loud crack. "When Hunter heals—"

"No. I don't want to talk about Hunter."

Paxton sighed heavily. "He was just doing his job. The one the King of the Realm, his father, ordered him to do."

"I know," Vero said softly. "I understand. I really do." Vero had always followed the orders of his superiors as well. But Hunter had pretended to be his friend for years. They'd trained and had gone on missions together, always having each other's backs. More than that. They'd geeked out together in the science labs in a way other soldiers would never appreciate.

"You're related to him now. I mated his cousin and you're my brother."

The words weighed heavily but Vero kept his focus pure. "You can deal with them all you like, but I'm not. I'm your enforcer here and out in the world. And I hope to hell, if you somehow come to an agreement at the Convexus and save the Kurjan nation, that you're not planning to settle the Kurjan nation in Idaho near demon and vampire headquarters." Vero would never live that close to them, even if they became allies. The idea of losing this brother he'd just found felt like another fist to the gut, but he'd never admit it.

Paxton chuckled. "No. Canada is the place for us." He cleared his throat. "If things go south and the Kurjan nation crumbles, there's a place for you in the Realm. Just so you know."

"You can't have a plan B, Paxton. It's the Kurjan nation or nothing." Sad but true.

"All right. Well then, I will succeed in bringing the Cyst soldiers back into the nation. There's no alternative."

Vero's gut actually ached. "I'm glad you understand that."

Paxton sighed. "For the record, I'd love to reach a point where we are true allies with the Realm. Maybe even friends."

That would take centuries. Maybe. "The easiest way to do that is to arrange for matings, if the Cyst return home. While vampires and Kurjans are male only, a lot of demons, shifters, and fairies align with the Realm. Maybe we start speed dating with other species in a few years."

"Speaking of speed dating, what's up with you and Lyrica?"

The mention of the stubborn female's name heated his blood. "Nothing. The female is impossible." But that kiss. That was something.

"You like her," Paxton said, his voice light.

"Do not." Vero could finally see out of his left eye.

Paxton punched him in the thigh. "Do too."

Vero swiveled and grabbed Paxton around the waist, throwing them both into a snowbank. "Do not." He punched first without hesitation this time.

Chapter Twelve

Lyrica sat straight up in bed, blinking her eyes. She gingerly removed the laptop from her chest. She must've fallen asleep while planning the next few activities for the community. So far, she'd had a difficult time drawing out the long-standing Kurjan mates. The females seemed to keep to themselves. But finally, a few had started confiding in her. They had dreams. She wanted to help them succeed in life so badly.

What had awakened her? A loud thump and a groan came from the next bedroom. She pushed off the warm covers and yanked on yoga pants before tiptoeing to the door. A bump and a muffled curse came through the night. That was Vero. She'd recognize his low tenor anywhere, but he didn't usually use expletives. Around her, anyway.

Her heart pounded and she took several deep breaths to calm herself. Then she slowly opened her door and looked out into the darkened hallway. Nothing.

Swallowing, she padded in her bare feet to Vero's doorway and knocked softly.

Nothing. What if he was hurt? Steeling her shoulders, she opened his door to see him sprawled across his ultra large bed, face down, his powerful frame dominating the space. His broad shoulders were motionless, the thick, defined muscles hidden beneath layers of bloody and snow-covered fabric. His back, normally taut and imposing, seemed oddly slack, but even in stillness, his sheer physical presence was undeniable. The fabric of his jacket clung to him, soaked through in places, revealing hints of the hard planes beneath. Ice had formed in jagged patterns down the backs of his legs, encasing the ridges of muscle there in a crystalline sheen. Water dripped steadily from his combat boots, pooling onto the floor, the sound unnervingly loud in the silence.

"Vero?" she whispered. Had he been attacked? Glancing at his hands, she could see bloody knuckles. He'd definitely fought and hard. Shaking her head, she moved into the room. A scent immediately assailed her, filling her senses with full-blooded male. Fresh, wild, and foresty.

At the very least, she could help the guy take off his boots.

Grabbing his ankle, she tried to push him onto his back. "Vero," she whispered. "Turn over." When he didn't comply, she moved up his body and nudged his shoulder. "Roll over so I can at least get your boots off."

He turned his head to the side, his gaze cloudy. "Lyrica? Pax and I had it out but we're good now. Are you in my bedroom?"

"Yes." She prodded him again, wishing she'd tossed on a sweatshirt over her thin cami top.

He moved then, rolling over with a sudden, unrestrained strength that caught her completely off guard, somehow taking her with him in the fluid motion. For a heartbeat, she was on top of him, her hands pressed against the solid expanse of his chest, the unyielding muscle beneath his shirt like steel under her palms. Then, just as quickly, she was beneath him, pinned under the full weight of him—broad shoulders framing her view, the powerful lines of his body surrounding her. His chest was impossibly hard, his muscles tense and coiled like a predator poised to strike, and every inch of him radiated a heat that was both overwhelming and inescapable.

"Hey," she protested as his wet clothes permeated her cami and yoga pants.

"Hey," he breathed back, his hands tunneling through her thick hair.

Her mouth dried up. Even though he weighed a ton, somehow he kept from crushing her by positioning his elbows near her shoulders. As he breathed, she could actually feel his ripped abs move against her thin shirt. "This is a bad idea."

"I know." His voice deepened.

Her body shuddered in pure, feminine response. "I-I can't do this. Can't live this life." It was too late to pretend that physical attraction didn't pound between them. Heck. Even the emotional attraction turned her all girly. Even though his people were slowly moving into the modern world, they'd never get there all the way. As independent a woman as she was, she didn't know how to change and had no intention of learning. Not even for somebody as intriguing as the Kurjan enforcer. Or was he a prince? Did it matter?

"True." He turned on his side, taking her with him, and spooning his impossibly warm form around her. "But you need cover, and I'm gonna provide it." His voice remained sleepy and slightly slurred. "I have an idea how but I'm not ready to convince you. Not tonight."

Convince her? What in the world was he talking about? Her thoughts tumbled into a jumbled mess, and she tried to form coherent words. "Um. You're kind of enveloping me," she managed, though the protest lacked conviction.

And it wasn't entirely true. He wasn't just enveloping her—he was everywhere. The solid wall of his chest pressed against her back, the heat of his body sinking into her own, and his arms caged her with a strength that felt both unyielding and oddly comforting. The rough edges of him, the hard lines of muscle and strength, should have been intimidating, but instead, they left her feeling…safe. Too safe. He felt way too good surrounding her, and she hated herself a little for not wanting to move.

He didn't move. "You remind me of somebody. She was perfect."

She blinked, fighting the irrational urge to lean into the solid warmth of his protection, his strength a magnetic pull. Her mind raced, torn between curiosity and a hint of dread. Did he want to tell her about an ex-girlfriend? The thought was as bizarre as it was unsettling. Did the Kurjans even have ex-girlfriends? The idea seemed foreign, almost laughable. Yet here she was, asking anyway. "Who?" she whispered, not really wanting the answer.

Vero snuggled his nose into her neck. "Her name was Karma."

What a beautiful name. A poker-hot and very unwelcome jealousy flowed through Lyrica's veins. "That's nice."

"Yeah." His lips brushed her nape. How had he moved her head to the side? Fire lashed through her, lighting her skin into need. "She was the closest female I ever had to a mother. I mean, she wasn't my mother, but she acted maternal. She cared, you know?"

Lyrica's head jerked. "Wait a minute. You find me matronly?"

His chuckle warmed her already electrified skin. "Not even close. Believe me. All I meant was that Karma seemed tough and was very soft. Perhaps too kind. At least, she was to me."

Lyrica's heart hurt for him. More than a little. "Yeah. There's nothing like a mother's love, or so I've heard. Wouldn't know."

He jerked against her and then flattened his humongous hand against her abdomen, drawing her closer against him, spooning her like they belonged together. Heat instantly engulfed her from both sides, and desire slammed hard into her core. "You never even met your mother? Not once?" He sounded almost sleepy against her skin.

She trembled, head to toe. The male had no clue what he could do to her with just his breath. "No. Also, before I forget, I've never thanked you for the kindness that you allowed the kidnapped females to contact their loved ones with stupid excuses of where they'd gone." She hadn't had family, but she did check her email just in case her recent ex-boyfriend had reached out. He hadn't. Then Lyrica had heard rumors that Vero had done so without his uncle knowing and had taken a beating from several guards afterward. "They hurt you for that. Right?"

His shrug was so casual, so unbothered, it would've rolled her clean off the bed if his heated palm hadn't been spread firmly across her abdomen, holding her in place. The weight of his hand was solid, grounding, and impossible to ignore. "Pain is temporary," he said, his tone calm, as if discussing the weather. "I'm pleased to have provided the females some relief from worry."

The way his hand spanned her middle, large and impossibly warm, sent a flicker of something through her—a mix of exasperation and something she refused to name. His words, noble as they might have been, felt at odds with the sheer strength of him anchoring her there, like the storm of his presence was only barely contained.

He needed to continue with the kindness, so she nudged him. "It's time to allow the kidnapped females freedom."

"Not yet. The Kurjans aren't the only species that would kill to keep immortality a secret. We need the females to understand the danger that will follow them if they talk, and we need a plan so they don't all return to human society at the same time." When she started to argue, he nipped her nape.

She gasped, her entire body freezing in place as if time itself had stopped. But inside, everything was chaos. Desire rolled through her in an unstoppable wave, leaving a searing trail in its wake. It ignited every nerve, every sensation, zinging them wide awake and painfully alive. Desperately so. Her breaths came quick and shallow, her body betraying her with the intensity of the pull, a hunger she hadn't expected and couldn't seem to control.

He continued as if he wasn't slowly killing her. "In addition, our scientists are tracking what makes a human female enhanced. We're trying to determine if you have a different genetic code than other humans, or if not, if there's a mutation on a gene that gives you gifts. The trials aren't finished, but they will be soon."

Should the Kurjans have such intimate knowledge of available mates? They'd only been the good guys—if they actually were—for a short time. She shook her head, then paused as teeth gently scraped across her vulnerable nape. A needy moan started in her chest and she sucked it down quickly.

He didn't move. Did the guy know what his touch did to her? "I overheard you once speaking with the redhead about your ex-boyfriend. Did he hurt you, to become an ex?" The low rumble against her vibrated down her entire body.

It had always been her and her father against the world. "No. Well, not really. He did call me cold."

"I could kill him for you if you like." The offer sounded kind.

She blinked. "No. Vero...just no. If the Kurjans are going to enter the modern world, you can't go around killing people you don't like."

"I wouldn't. I was offering to kill someone who'd obviously hurt you."

That sincere offer should scare the hell out of her. Truth be told, it did. "Why?" she whispered.

This time he didn't answer, but he did toe off his boots to land on the floor.

She should go. Really go. But his warmth surrounded her, and for the first time in months, she felt safe. Well, from the outside world. Her eyelids closed on their own.

Several dreamless hours later, a loud roar awakened her right before she was thrown from the bed, careening headfirst toward the nearest wall.

Chapter Thirteen

Lyrica shrieked, and right before impact, two strong hands grabbed her around the waist, whirled her around, and planted her back on the bed. She blinked, the blood rushing through her ears. What had just happened?

"Sorry," Vero said, backing away, hands up, his blue eyes wide. "I was having a nightmare."

"You woke up in the nick of time." She sat, still foggy, her heart galloping. She might have broken her neck if she had smashed into the wall. Thank goodness he'd awakened to grab her. "We must've fallen asleep." She blinked sleep from her eyes, the bed solid beneath her thighs.

He stood near the door as if wanting distance between them. "My apologies. I was concussed."

Amusement tickled her. "One might consider that statement insulting."

He cocked his head as if considering her words. "No insult meant."

Sometimes he was adorable. Her eyes focused and her mouth went dry. At some point in the night, he'd shucked his jeans and shirt, leaving him in faded gray boxers. He was all muscle. One hundred percent. She swallowed.

"Are you all right?"

No. Nope. Not even an iota all right. A body like that didn't exist in her world. Males like him didn't, either. When he moved, she could actually see the play of muscle beneath his skin. A part of her wanted to jump him, but it'd be like purposefully smashing herself against a boulder. His form was more solid than the building. Tendrils of heat climbed into her face, and she forced her brain to work. "What was your nightmare about?"

His face went carefully blank. "Nothing."

"That's not good enough." She sprang to her feet. "If you're going to toss me across a room, I'd like to know why."

"It won't happen again," he said. She took a step toward him and tripped over one of his monstrous boots, crashing toward the ground. He caught her again, lifting her up against his hard chest. The door slammed open.

"What's the screaming about?" Paxton Phoenix stood in the doorway wearing only boxers, bruises still visible down his chest. "I have the twins on Hope. What's happening?"

"Nothing," Vero said grimly, dropping her in Paxton's arms and forcing him to catch her. "Here. Take her back to her room."

Pain slashed along Lyrica's arms. Paxton growled, and Lyrica gasped as her skin met his. Paxton immediately reacted and tossed her back on the bed, shaking out his arms. An ugly red rash sprang up.

"Oh, shit." Vero turned toward Lyrica, where her shoulder showed a similar rash. "I'm sorry. I completely forgot about the mating allergy."

"No kidding," Paxton muttered, rubbing his arm. "Are you okay?" he asked Lyrica.

The skin on her arms felt like red ants had enjoyed her for breakfast, but the pain slowly began to ebb. "Yeah. You know, I'd heard about the rash mated immortals get when they touch a member of the opposite sex, but that's real."

"Of course it's real," Vero said. "Why would we lie about that?"

She glared at him. "You all have enough secrets. Who knows?"

To her surprise, he nodded. "Good point."

Paxton's gaze narrowed as he looked at Lyrica, then at Vero, then at the bed.

"Nothing happened," Lyrica said in a rush. But wait a minute, why did she care what he thought? Heat flared into her face. She shouldn't have said anything. She was a grown-ass woman who could sleep with whomever she wanted.

"Right," Paxton said, taking a step back. "I misunderstood the shriek?"

Vero's eyes flared as his gaze dropped to her bare arms. "No. This was my fault. I'm responsible."

Lyrica's chin dropped. "You're not responsible for me."

"I am. My brain was concussed, and you have a soothing scent. And voice. And touch," he said thoughtfully. "I remember rolling over and not allowing you to leave."

Paxton's jaw tightened.

"No," Lyrica said. "I could've easily left if I wanted." She hadn't protested, and every cell in her body promised that if she had, he would've let her go. "I stayed on purpose."

"Why?" Vero asked softly.

She blinked. "I felt safe." Vulnerable and shaky, she shrugged her chilled shoulders. "I'm not used to feeling…protected."

Paxton leaned against the doorjamb and pinched the top of his nose. "Because the Kurjans kidnapped you."

She shook her head. "Even before that. My dad and I were often alone, and he traveled a lot for work, often leaving me with my great-aunt. We were robbed twice." As they both straightened, she held up a hand. "We weren't home either time, but it was still scary."

"I'm sure," Vero murmured.

She inhaled slowly, counted to four, then breathed out to calm herself. "I can take care of myself, gentlemen." Yet being bracketed by a guy strong enough to bench-press a school bus certainly led to a feeling of safety. Maybe she could understand some of the mates wanting to stay. But not her. She had a job to do, then she'd return to her normal life.

Why that didn't fill her with relief, she'd figure out later.

"Again, this is my fault, and I apologize sincerely." Vero looked alert, as if expecting an attack from every direction. "We fell asleep, and I had a nightmare. Nearly broke her neck."

"What?" Paxton asked, stepping back inside again.

Vero shook his head. "I had a nightmare. I struck out and tossed her across the room."

"But he caught me," Lyrica said defensively. Why in the world was she defending him? What was wrong with her? Oh yeah, she just woke up careening through the room. Anybody could be a little off after that. Taking a deep breath, she settled herself. Her gaze instantly caught on the two brothers and their spectacular bodies. They had the same frame. Badass, muscled, and dangerous.

"What was the nightmare about?" Paxton asked.

Vero glowered at his brother. "Nothing. It's just an old nightmare. Let it go."

"No," Paxton said.

Vero sighed. "Listen, we just got done beating the shit out of each other. We can go outside again if you want, but I'm not talking about the nightmare."

Lyrica scooted back and pulled the covers over her legs against the chill in the room. She needed thicker yoga pants. "It helps to talk about it. I used to have nightmares. The more you talk about it, the more you rewrite them in your brain." Plus, she wanted to understand. What would make a warrior like Vero throw her across the room?

"Was it that bad?" Paxton asked. "I still have nightmares from my childhood."

Vero's eyebrows rose.

Lyrica looked at the Kurjan leader, surprised that he'd shared that much.

"It was stupid," Vero said. "I told you about Karma, right?"

Lyrica nodded, her mind spinning and her stomach suddenly cramping. "You said she acted as a mother figure to you."

"Yes. Her mate had died a century or more earlier, and she did her best to look after many of the children." Vero shook his head. "But when I was younger, maybe around, I don't know, ten years old, my uncle wanted her. He often tortured her by yanking on her skirts or threatening to hurt me if she didn't follow his orders."

The anger in his eyes sprang awareness through Lyrica's body. Like any prey would feel when a predator stood nearby. For the first time, she could actually see the warrior Jonathan had warned her about. "What happened?" she whispered.

Vero's blue eyes went flat. Dead. Empty. "My uncle couldn't touch her because she'd been mated, but I think he planned for her to take the virus that might negate the mating bond. Well, before a soldier from the Realm kidnapped her."

Paxton's dark brows drew down. "That soldier saved Karma. Since her mate had died centuries ago, she took the virus and negated the bond. It worked for her. She's now happily mated to a vampire-demon hybrid, Vero. I think they have their third or fourth kid on the way."

"So you say. But you never really know, do you? I remember when Benjamin Reese kidnapped her, after my uncles had tortured him for days. If you ask me, he let them capture him just so he could get ahold of her," Vero muttered. "At least he came back for the twin human girls she'd adopted. I hope they're safe. The Kurjans get a bad rap, but the vampires and demons have kidnapped just as many females through the years as we have."

"So, the nightmare?" Paxton asked softly, obviously not rising to the bait.

Vero shrugged. "My uncle was harassing Karma as she served us dinner one night, and I got between them and told him to knock it off. He was twice my size, so he purposely shoved me into her, and we went down. Her arms were bare and so were mine, and the mating rash immediately sprang up. I pushed her away, but he had stuck his boot at the small of her back, keeping her in place. We touched for long enough that the rash burned us both and remained for several weeks."

"What a dick," Lyrica said.

Vero chuckled, and his shoulders relaxed. "Yeah, he was. Still, I wouldn't mind seeing for myself that Karma's all right."

"I'll see what I can do," Paxton said. "No promises. She mated Benjamin Reese, and he lives by his own rules."

"What does that mean?" Vero asked curtly.

Paxton watched his brother carefully. "Benny's a good guy, but some people think he's insane."

"What?" Vero burst out.

Paxton held up a large hand. "No, he isn't. He's actually quite brilliant, and he adores Karma. He doesn't live within the Realm confines, though." He relaxed again and leaned against the doorjamb. "I'm sure I could track him down. Well, maybe, if Benny wants to be tracked down."

Lyrica gulped as her feet started to warm up.

"So," Paxton said awkwardly, straightening and once again backing out of the room. "I'm sorry to have interrupted."

"You didn't," Lyrica said. Darn it. Why did she keep protesting? She didn't care what the Kurjan leader thought.

Vero's shoulders went back. "I apologize and won't let it happen again." He gave her a shallow nod of his head. "There's no excuse for my behavior, and I hope I didn't frighten you too badly."

Why did he always sound so formal? Well, most of the Kurjans did, actually. Lyrica cleared her throat. "You caught me before I could get hurt, and it's all right. We all understand nightmares, and that sounds like a bad one." How fast were his reflexes, anyway?

Paxton looked from Lyrica to Vero, an unidentifiable light in his sharp eyes. "I was hoping the speed dating had been a success."

"Good night, brother," Vero said firmly.

"Okey doke." Paxton shut the door, and his heavy footsteps sounded down the hallway.

Vero crossed his arms, the sinewed strength beneath his skin tightening like coiled steel, a quiet display of power just below the surface. "I assure you this lodge is as safe as can be. I have all entrances and exits covered with an additional set of guards rotating at irregular intervals. You should be able to sleep well."

Was he kicking her out? It sure sounded like it. Although she should be heading back to her room. Yet something in her wanted to reassure him. "You didn't do anything wrong, Vero. I chose to stay, and we both got some much-needed sleep."

Vero's lids half lowered, casting a shadow over his eyes that gave him the sharp, focused intensity of a hunter locking onto its target. "That short window has given me pause. If anybody tried to take you from me last night, I would've obliterated them." He looked up at the ceiling and back down. "I had no involvement with kidnapping the females, so I don't know if anybody had commitments to other males. We'll need to shore up defenses as the men come for them."

Obliterated? Wow. Her mouth gaped open and she quickly shut it. She absently tugged at a stray thread on the bedspread, her fingers twisting it in a quiet, restless motion. "I've spoken with all the kidnapped females, and nobody is married or committed. That can't be a coincidence. My guess is that the Kurjans only kidnapped single females." It made some sense.

"We'll see. And I need more information about your ex. There's no way he isn't hunting you down, even if you think he's just an ex."

She tried not to laugh. "No. I don't think Mike is the type to hunt down a woman who broke up with him on the phone."

"I don't believe you."

She sat back, studying Vero's hard face. "Why not?"

His searing blue gaze raked her, dark with raw, dangerous intensity. "Because if anyone took you from me, I'd burn the world to ash to find you— and I'd tear through the wreckage with bloody hands until nothing remained."

She couldn't breathe. Her lungs just stuttered, forgetting their job. "You mean, if we were dating?" Her voice trembled.

He blinked once. Slowly. "I think you should return to your room for the remainder of the night."

Chapter Fourteen

In the morning, his body aching from sleeping close to Lyrica but not claiming her the night before, Vero sat on the thick leather chair and looked around the cozy conference room in the main lodge. Claiming? Seriously. He had to get that thought out of his head. Now.

The smell of burned wood and furniture still permeated the space, while the sounds of hammers and saws filled the day as his people reconstructed the fire-damaged part of the building.

The doctor said Hunter wasn't ready to be moved yet, and the ancient Kurjan wouldn't let anybody see him. But hopefully by afternoon Hunter could be flown to the Realm doctors.

Lyrica had insisted upon bringing in the multiple chairs now placed around a coffee table across from a wide window that looked out toward the snowcapped mountains. A coffee station had been set up in the main room of the lodge that included hot chocolate and apple cider. She'd brought carafes of each into the conference room along with several clean mugs. He had discovered an affinity for apple cider, having never enjoyed it before.

Even so, sparkling water with its delicious bubbles must've been created by gods.

He didn't like being away from Paxton with the threats hanging over the guy's head, but he'd put his four strongest soldiers on protection detail, a fact that had seemed to piss off Pax. For some reason that must have something to do with being brothers, that fact had greatly amused Vero.

Lyrica sat across from him, sipping delicately on coffee with no creamer or sugar. She liked it straight and black, which surprised him. Even he didn't like it that strong.

After she'd returned to her room the night before, he'd gone for a run outside in the freezing cold. It had barely cooled his body down. He wasn't sure what he was going to do about her, but right now wasn't the time to figure it out. Also, he felt a little guilty about returning to the lodge and drinking an entire carton of sparkling water earlier that morning.

Today, she was dressed in faded jeans and a taupe-colored sweater that made her eyes glow like molten amber catching the last rays of a sunset, warm and smoldering with an irresistible magnetic pull. And yet, those stunning eyes had yet to focus on him.

Should he say something? Words remained beyond him. He'd wanted her to stay with him more than he'd like to admit. And not to sleep.

When a timid knock came at the door, the relief that swamped him would embarrass him later. He instantly stood.

"I've got it." Lyrica placed her coffee cup on the table and stood, hurrying to the door to open it. "Eudokia. Hello," she said warmly, pulling the female inside.

"Hello to you," Eudokia Guavras said formally, partially turning to face Vero and giving a short curtsy. "Prince."

He had to get rid of that moniker, but he didn't know how. "Please call me Vero," he rumbled, trying to look harmless and no doubt failing horribly. "I've asked you several times, and I don't think formality is necessary. Do you?"

"Probably." Eudokia shrugged out of her wool coat to place over a chair.

Lyrica led her over to the seat she had just vacated. "We have coffee, hot chocolate, and apple cider. Can I get you something?"

"Oh no." Eudokia shook both hands. "Of course not." The female wore a pretty green gown that tucked in at the waist, with her dark hair carefully braided down her back. At several centuries old, she was stunning, with thick black hair, lighter blue eyes, and flawless skin. Vero had never been told where she'd come from, but she had always been kind to him.

He cleared his throat. "Are you sure? We're out of sparkling water here in the main lodge, but I can run to the warehouse and fetch some for you."

Lyrica frowned. "How could we be out? The pantry was full."

He shrugged, trying to look innocent. "If you'd rather have something warm, I'm drinking the apple cider, and it's wonderful." He meant the words. It was truly a pity he'd never tasted it before Lyrica ordered boxes to be delivered to their storage unit in Anchorage. He wanted more sparkling water, however.

"Of course I will," Eudokia said, instantly beginning to stand.

"Oh no, I'll get it." Lyrica patted her shoulder.

Sighing, Vero sat. "You don't have to drink cider. I just thought you might like it."

"I appreciate that, Prince," she said, her eyes sparkling.

He shook his head. "What would it take for you to call me Vero?" He held her in the utmost respect, not only from her age, but because she had always been kind to everybody she knew.

She pursed her lips thoughtfully. "I'm not really certain. You are the prince."

"Yes, but what if we agreed in informal settings such as this that you just call me by my name?" He truly disliked any mention that he had royal blood. As far as he was concerned, the only decent person in his lineage, or at least the only decent male, was Paxton, and he was barely getting to know the guy. "Although, it's perfectly fine to call Paxton king."

Eudokia let out a short burst of laughter and then covered her mouth, her eyes dancing.

Amusement surprised Vero as it bubbled through him. "I know. He hates the designation as much as I do."

"I wonder why?" Eudokia asked softly. Lyrica brought over a steaming cup of cider to place in front of Eudokia.

Vero gave her the truth. "Many of the leaders of the Kurjan nation have not been kind people, and perhaps we'd both like to distance ourselves from that history."

Eudokia tilted her head and studied him. "Should that be the case, then I would think you and your brother would want to use the titles as much as possible and give them a different meaning for the nation."

Lyrica took the chair between the two of them. "Eudokia, I wanted to speak with you. I know you already talked to Vero, and he's more than happy to leave right now if you would like to speak with just me."

He was? He hadn't agreed to that fact, but he chose not to argue.

Eudokia lifted her mug to her mouth and inhaled. "This does smell lovely." She looked at Lyrica, then Vero. "I hold no objection to the prince remaining, though it is not truly my decision to make."

"It is your choice," Lyrica burst out, her eyes widening. "Everything's your choice."

A small smile tugged at Eudokia's lips. "You live in a different world than I do."

"But it doesn't have to be that way." Lyrica leaned forward. "Honest. You can do anything you want in this world. You could travel. Anybody who leaves takes with them a million dollars. You can see the entire world if you want."

"I've already seen much of it." Eudokia sipped delicately.

"But you haven't seen it in modern times," Lyrica returned. "You could wear jeans and let your hair flow loose. I know the rules in the Kurjan nation have been very restrictive."

Eudokia blew softly on the liquid. "Indeed, though we may dress as we please now, I am still fond of my gowns. In truth, with so much hair, binding it in braids proves far easier to manage." She shifted her gaze to Lyrica. "Why is it so difficult for you to believe that some of us desire to remain with our families? In truth, it appears most of us are of that mind."

Lyrica took a big drink of her coffee. "I don't know that you would still want to stay if you had all the information."

"Maybe you don't have all the information," Eudokia returned, not unkindly.

Lyrica nodded. "That's fair."

Vero sat back and studied the females. "How did you and your mate meet?"

Eudokia looked up as if surprised to hear him ask a question. "Centuries past, Georgios first laid eyes upon me at the agora, our common marketplace. He sought me out after and made an offer of substantial property to my father." At Lyrica's small sound of protest, Eudokia reached over and patted her knee. "It was the way things were done centuries ago, and my family paid a dowry of textiles."

Lyrica shook her head. "It's not the way things are done today."

"Maybe not in this country," Vero said, "but you can't say that for all human countries." Lyrica cut him a glare. He tried not to smile. She was irresistibly cute, like a sparrow darting about, and there wasn't much in this world that ever made him back down.

"I do understand how the world works," Eudokia countered. "Georgios and I often traveled. One of his jobs the past couple of centuries has been to acquire goods for the Kurjan nation, and I've shopped all over the world. I've had a good time, too, and I haven't seen any life I'd rather have than the one I do." She looked at Lyrica again. "How about you? Were you happy before you were taken from your current life?"

Lyrica frowned. "I was happy enough. At least I had my freedom."

"Hmm," Eudokia said softly. "Happy enough. That doesn't sound like happy to me."

Lyrica placed her cup back on the table.

"I agree," Vero said, surprising himself. He took a big gulp of his drink. Where had he been that he didn't know apple cider even existed? Maybe it was time he ventured out on his own for a little while. He looked at Eudokia. "Are you content in your mating?"

She smiled. "I'm very content. I love Georgios, and I want to stay with him."

Lyrica finally sat back and looked like her body relaxed. "But from what I've seen of the interaction between you two, he's rather demanding."

"All males are demanding," Eudokia said, her gaze flicking to Vero and back. "Even if they don't know it at first."

Vero fully recognized himself as a demanding male. He'd had no choice when he had to rise up within the soldier ranks. And yet, he remained their finest scientist, though by force of habit he kept that well concealed.

"But a male shouldn't be telling you what to do," Lyrica said softly.

Eudokia chuckled, and a slight accent emerged, but Vero couldn't place it. "We might do things differently here in the Kurjan nation," she said kindly, "but like I said, I'm happy. Yes, Georgios is a little bossy sometimes, especially when it comes to safety, but if you think I don't rule that roost with my mate and my three grown soldiers who have ventured out on their own, then you're not watching closely enough."

Vero had seen Eudokia in full temper at one of her sons once, and he would've backed down as fast as her son did that day.

Eudokia looked Lyrica over. "In fact, all three of them are currently unattached. I would be more than pleased to provide an introduction for you."

Irritation clacked down Vero's spine, but he didn't move. He didn't so much as twitch.

Even so, Eudokia glanced at him beneath her lashes. "Or perhaps not." She smiled again. "May I provide any additional information to you this fine day?"

Lyrica nodded. "Would your mate let you leave?"

Vero stiffened. Talk about a loaded question.

Eudokia's smile brightened her already pretty face. "Not in a thousand lifetimes."

"Exactly." Lyrica slapped her jeans-clad thigh. "You can't really leave."

"No, probably not." Eudokia sipped again. "If I did leave, and that male failed to follow me, I'd sever his head from his fit body. He'd better love me more than that." She sniffed. "Even the thought of it makes me want to burn the gingerbread I planned to bake for him tonight."

Vero's ears perked up. "Please don't do that. Georgios hasn't done anything wrong."

Eudokia lifted one eyebrow. "I'll save you a slice. Prince."

"Thank you," he said sincerely. The woman was a genius with all breads.

Lyrica clasped her hands in her lap. "I don't understand."

A fine line formed between Eudokia's eyes. "I'm sorry. Are you saying you've never met a male who would die for you? Kill for you? Who couldn't live this existence without you?"

"No," Lyrica breathed. "In my world, that's pretty much called stalking and a behavioral abnormality."

Eudokia pursed her lips. "I suppose it's a matter of degree." This time, she leaned toward Lyrica. "Make sure you know yourself before you attend speed dating again. There's no halfway with the thought of a divorce if you mate an immortal."

"I know." Lyrica seemed to be avoiding looking at Vero. "Some of us like freedom."

"Some of us like safety, protection, and undying passionate love," Eudokia said softly. "But again, there's a fine line. Make sure you choose a male who'd give his life to keep you safe, and not one whose ego is dependent upon you or who would even consider harming you. Any male who'd hurt a female should be put down."

Vero finished his drink. "I couldn't agree more." His uncles had been assholes to everyone, even females. How could he explain this to Lyrica? "While I've observed mates like my brother be overbearing and overprotective, he'd do anything in his power to make Hope happy. If she's not happy, he's miserable." Which put the power in Hope's hands, really.

"All right, I'll stop asking about your life." Lyrica paused. "One more question first. I meant to ask you last time how you chose your surname, now that the Kurjans are claiming last names."

Eudokia smoothed out her skirts with one hand. "Guavras was my surname before I mated Georgios. He thinks Georgios Guavras sounds a little too cutesy, but that's what I wanted, so he agreed to the family surname."

Lyrica's eyebrows lifted. So that was a surprise, huh? She cleared her throat. "All right. Is there anybody that you know of who might be in a bad situation?"

"Situation?"

"Yes. Anybody who might not want to stay mated to their current mates."

Eudokia's lips briefly pressed together. "I'm sure I would never speak out of turn like that."

Vero stiffened and forced himself to remain impassive. "Do you mind letting us know, Eudokia? We're attempting to make sure that everybody wants to be in the lives they're inhabiting."

Eudokia looked away and then back. "All right, but I can't think of anybody right now." She stood, and Vero immediately did as well. "We've kept our heads down for so long, mostly from the Kurjan leadership and not from our mates. In fact, many of our mates have tried to shield us from leadership. Now that's changed. I think you're good for us all... Vero."

Lyrica pushed herself to her feet. "What do you think about a field trip? Say we take a few of the mated ladies and, I don't know, go to Vegas and have a weekend?"

Eudokia predictably looked toward Vero as she pulled on her coat and quickly buttoned it to the top.

He thought about it. "I can perhaps see some sort of vacation like that, but there would be security around you at all times."

"Oh no." Lyrica shook her head. "No, no. It would just be several of the women going."

"That's not going to happen," Vero said, keeping his tone level but firm. "The world's a dangerous place, and some of these females haven't been to cities in eons. I would insist upon protection being in place. That's nonnegotiable."

Eudokia chuckled. "He's not the only soldier who will set that rule, Lyrica. Honestly, I wouldn't fight this one." She reached over and gently touched Lyrica's shoulder. "Also, maybe take a look at your thought processing. Just how happy have you been with the males in your life? I sense that something has been missing for you."

Vero didn't want to consider other males in Lyrica's life, although it wasn't any of his business.

Eudokia reached down and retrieved her mug. "May I borrow this? I'd like to finish this delicious drink, and I'll return the mug washed."

"Of course." Vero lifted a pen and pulled one of Lyrica's notebooks in front of him. "You've been with the Kurjan nation for a long time, Eudokia. Have you ever seen this symbol?" He quickly scratched out the circle with the three slashes through it.

Eudokia leaned over and stared at the drawing. "No. I've never seen that before. What is it?"

He figured she hadn't. "This was carved into the back of the neck of a recent human victim here in camp."

Eudokia sobered. "I heard about that. How sad…and odd. Why would anybody kill a human female?"

Vero had no idea.

Lyrica stared at the drawing. "As soon as we have Internet via satellite, I can conduct a search for that." Visibly shaking herself, she looked away. "It was nice chatting with you today, Eudokia."

"Same with you, Lyrica." Eudokia gave another quick curtsy. "My prince." Humor sounded in her voice this time, but her tone remained kind. She turned and headed toward the doorway.

"Eudokia?" Vero asked suddenly.

She paused and looked over her shoulder. "Yes, Prince?"

"Have you heard anything from Karma?" He doubted that any messages from Karma could have made it to Kurjan territory, but still, he had to ask. Ever since the nightmare the previous night, he couldn't stop thinking about the sweet female.

Eudokia's face fell. "No, and I miss her terribly. If you manage to get word to her, would you tell her hello for me?"

"Of course," Vero said.

Eudokia swept outside and shut the door behind her.

He looked at Lyrica. "Why do you think you haven't been happy in past relationships?"

She stood straighter. "I have no idea."

Interesting. "Maybe you've been choosing the wrong males." If anybody needed some cover and a safe place, it was Lyrica Graves.

"Is that an invite?" she snapped back.

His life was filled with danger right now, and he didn't see that reality changing. He had to protect Paxton, and that most likely meant fighting to the death sooner rather than later. However, it was becoming clear to him how he could protect her. From very close to her. "It depends how much you want to take a risk."

Yeah. He meant every word of that.

"I'm not sure what you're talking about."

"I know." He stretched his neck. "I need to scout the territory and then will meet you back here this afternoon along with Paxton. I promised you time to discuss the release of the kidnapped females."

She perked up. "Great. I'll create a presentation."

Amusement took him. "Good. Paxton doesn't realize it yet, but he's leaving with Hunter." Even if Vero had to knock him out first. "Then you and I will discuss…risks."

Chapter Fifteen

After scouting the territory and not finding lurking threats, and still waiting for an update on Hunter, Vero sat back in his chair in the small conference room in the main lodge, watching Lyrica click through a meticulously crafted and very colorful PowerPoint presentation. How in the world had the female created that in less than three hours? Impressive. Very.

Both he and Paxton drank hot chocolate, which wasn't nearly as good as the sparkling water.

"Point three," she said, her tone even but firm, "bribing the females is not only more cost-effective, but it also ensures their cooperation. We maintain goodwill without the messy side effects of mind wiping." She paused, her fingers tapping the sleek remote in her hand. "Screwing with somebody's mind leads to all sorts of problems."

Well, for humans. The Kurjan technology remained infallible. But he couldn't share that fact with her. He watched her, suppressing a smile. The female was in her element. Slightly bossy, a bit impatient. Polished. Structured. Organized to the point of near-perfection. The slides were clean and logical, with bullet points laid out like stepping stones in a crystal-clear stream. Based on what she'd told him of her uncertain childhood, of wandering with her father and living out of cars or shelters, this made sense. How she thrived in the chaos surrounding them. Order in a world of uncertainty.

Still, he wanted to ruffle her. Just a little bit.

"Hypothetically," Vero drawled, tilting his head, "what if one of the females takes the bribe, signs the NDA, then runs to the press anyway? Humans love drama, and this sounds like a social media post that could go absolutely viral. Especially if one or more of them worked together."

Lyrica's fingers gripped the remote tighter. "If you'd let me finish the presentation, you'd see I've accounted for that possibility." She clicked to the next slide, a sharp movement betraying her irritation. "That's why we have follow-up monitoring. Discreet, thorough, and noninvasive. It's pretty simple, even for you."

How adorable. He leaned toward her, invading her space. "Simple? Sounds like a lot of work, to be honest."

She blinked, caught off guard, and for just a second, her voice wavered. "I—what?"

Ah, there it was—a small crack in her armor. He affected her as much as she did him. "Workload, baby."

Her jaw went slack. The word "baby" did it, huh? He liked that.

She regained her footing. "It'd be worth it, and I'm more than happy to head up that committee."

Paxton glanced at Vero, no expression on his face. "Do we have committees?"

"No, but if anybody could start one, it'd be Lyrica," Vero drawled.

"Thank you," she said crisply, clicking through more slides about cost analyses and the fragility of the human brain. "I'm sure you have advanced medical procedures, but nobody, not even you, can fully anticipate how any given brain will react."

There was some truth to that statement. He nodded. "Go on." The more he watched her, the more he felt a prick of unease. Lyrica had immediately emerged as a leader of the kidnapped females and now held a high position in the Kurjan nation as an advisor to both the king and his enforcer. That made her a target, especially right now.

He glanced at Paxton, whose gaze was fixed on Lyrica with the unreadable intensity Vero had come to expect. Paxton knew it too.

"Your analysis is solid," Paxton said finally, his deep voice breaking the silence. "You've done your homework, Lyrica. No one's arguing that. But don't forget—this isn't just about numbers. It's about people. Humans aren't predictable, no matter how many pie charts you throw at them."

"I'm aware," she said, her voice clipped. "But this is the right path."

Vero needed to put more protection on her. In fact, he needed to keep her close to him. Very. "This is good work, and you've made your point. Nice job."

Relief relaxed her expression. "Paxton?"

"Agreed," Paxton said. "Thank you for this."

"Good." She powered off the presentation, pleasure lifting her pretty mouth. "I'm sure we're out of coffee with the construction going on, so I'll go make some. Thank you for changing your minds." She bustled out, her butt adorable in dark jeans.

Paxton looked at him. "Thoughts?"

Vero thought through his options. "We bribe them, wipe their minds, then send them back to their lives. Our methods are safe." As safe as possible, anyway. "I'll destroy all records of them, so nobody will be able to surveil them."

Paxton winced. "All right, but let's keep this between us."

Most definitely. Vero hadn't lied to her because he hadn't promised. Even so, he'd rather she didn't know. Ever. He hoped for another presentation from her soon, although the weight on him grew even heavier. Structure could only take her so far. In their world, turmoil always found its way in. And Lyrica, whether she realized it or not, was now at the crux of the chaos.

* * * *

Late afternoon, Lyrica ran out into the snowy day toward the softly humming helicopter, her boots slipping on ice beneath freshly falling snow. Her arms windmilling in her ultrathick coat, she skidded to a stop near the open doorway. "Hope?"

Hope emerged from the rear of the copter and into the doorway. "Hey. I was just getting Hunter situated. We need to keep him stationary for his neck to heal." The female's blue eyes deepened with worry, but she held her shoulders back, and she moved with her customary grace. She sat in the opening, her boots kicking back and forth. "Thanks for coming to see me off."

Lyrica angled her neck to see Liam in the pilot's seat with Collin next to him. She could finally tell them apart. Their primary duty involved protecting Hope, so it came as no surprise to see them accompanying her and Hunter home. "I wish you didn't have to go, Hope," Lyrica whispered. Their friendship had formed in necessity and from a joint need to take down the former Kurjan leader, and Lyrica didn't want to continue this work without Hope. They made a great team. "When will you be back?"

"When it's safe," rumbled a low voice from behind Lyrica.

She jumped, turning with her hand clapped to her upper chest. "Paxton." How had he moved so silently?

The young king moved toward his mate, brushing snowflakes out of her hair with a gentleness that had Lyrica feeling slightly bereft. Happy for her friend, but still. Paxton was six and a half feet of dangerous muscle with silvery-blue eyes and thick black hair. She could see the resemblance to Vero.

Hope placed a hand on his muscled chest. "We don't have to go."

Paxton leaned over and kissed the top of her head, lifting her out of the craft at the same time. Smoothly. Easily. "You need to go with your cousin, and I don't mind having you safely back at Realm headquarters until we find who's trying to kill me." Then he kissed her, walking toward the back of the helicopter, apparently having no problem with rather heated public displays of affection.

Lyrica glanced up to see Collin rolling his eyes, and she grinned.

"You need to get going to miss the next big storm," a deep male voice said from behind her.

She yelped and whirled around to see Vero standing tall and solid in the winter day. "For the love of all that's holy, you both need to stop doing that."

One of Vero's dark eyebrows rose. "Doing what?"

Her mouth watered. He wore a black leather jacket over jeans, his jet-black hair dotted with snow and his blue eyes the hue of a mysterious ocean. "Sneaking up on people. You should make a little bit of noise as you move—just to be polite if nothing else."

"Noise gets you dead," Vero said, gracefully moving past her to jump into the helicopter. Crouching to keep from hitting the roof, he strode down toward where Hunter lay on his back, unconscious on a stretcher with a blanket covering his body to his wide chest.

Lyrica leaned in to watch.

Vero sat on a bench fastened to the side of the craft, leaning over to look at his friend. In profile, Vero's jaw clenched as he stared at the bandages around Hunter's neck. Other than angling his head to the side for a better look, his muscled body didn't move. But tension rolled from him, hotter than a damaged steam pipe. Up front, both Liam and Collin turned to watch Vero, no expressions on their immortal faces. But their green eyes showed an understanding of sorts. As one, they both turned back to the front of the craft and began a preflight check of all the blinking buttons and readouts.

Feeling like she was spying on Vero, she stepped away from the craft just as Paxton returned with a rosy-faced Hope, who looked like she'd been thoroughly kissed. Still in Paxton's arms, Hope leaned over to hug Lyrica. "I'll miss you. Is there any chance you want to come with me to Realm headquarters?"

What a temptation. But Lyrica's gaze caught on a still-silent Vero, her heart aching for him. "I'd love to visit another time. For now, I still have a job to do." She'd happily taken the offer to serve as liaison with the kidnapped females and the Kurjan leaders as well as Kurjan female mates. Until each of those women found their chosen safe haven, her mission remained active. "Besides, I'm sure it'll be safe here soon." By the fierce look in Paxton's eyes, he planned to root out those would-be assassins— and probably without a hint of mercy. They could've killed Hope, and that seemed to be his line in the sand. Or snow.

Vero cleared his throat. "Pax? I know you want to stay here, but you need to go."

The king looked at his brother. "What are you talking about, and why have you waited until right now, in front of my mate, to bring this up?"

Vero's shoulders widened. "Because I'm not a moron. The Convexus is five days away, and our enemies are going to ramp up their efforts to kill you, or at least destroy more buildings to make us look weak. We have to look strong."

"I don't care about being safe," Paxton growled.

Lyrica shivered.

"I know," Vero said calmly. "While I agree with that sentiment, you're not the only one in danger. This time they took out half the lodge. They could've taken out the entire thing, and we'd have more dead. Go for a very short visit to shore up our treaty with the Realm. Make it public. Let the Cyst know that we have the entire Realm behind us, and they'll be even more willing to negotiate. It's a good plan, and a reasonable reason for you to leave for just a few nights. Come back on Tuesday night for the Convexus."

Lyrica thought through the situation. "Also, if there are spies here, they'll let the Cyst know that you're meeting personally with the Realm and firming things up. That makes sense. They'll feel like they're in a weaker position."

Vero nodded. "Exactly. Go see your family, Pax."

Paxton's chin lifted. "You are my family."

Vero didn't move, but something shifted in his eyes. Something heated and loyal. "Agreed. So please listen to me. For the good of the entire nation."

Paxton faltered.

Hope nodded. "I agree. You know it's better to meet the Realm leaders in person. My family is just like that."

"Trust me. This is the best move, and it looks like a strong one," Vero said. An obvious toll showed on his angled face, but as usual, his duty apparently ruled.

"He's right. Let's go, Pax," Hope said softly.

Paxton looked around. "I don't want to endanger anybody else." He stared at his brother, at his mate, then at his territory for several long moments before speaking. "All right, but you stay alive. Deal?"

"Deal. You're in more danger than I am. I'll draw up plans for you to arrive back home just in time for the Convexus, hopefully with a signed treaty in hand. If you can get one from the demon, shifter, and witch nations, it'd be even better. While they align with the Realm, we should have our own agreements with them." Vero moved toward the doorway of the craft, leaning down to stare at his brother. "Trust me."

"I do," Paxton said softly, jumping into the craft with his mate in his arms and placing her on the bench, carefully securing her with chest and lap straps before sitting next to her.

Vero partially stood and slapped his brother on the arm before moving toward the door.

Hope snagged his arm and dragged him toward her, throwing both arms around his neck, even while encumbered by the straps.

He visibly stiffened, then relaxed, returning her hug but careful not to touch her skin. That mating allergy immortals gained after mating sure kept touching somebody else's mate to a minimum.

Hope released him. "You're my brother now, Vero. Hugs are part of the job."

He nodded solemnly. "Understood." Then he stepped down onto solid ice before looking over his shoulder. "Just don't drag me into any dreamworlds at night, all right?"

Hope chuckled. "I haven't been able to create a dreamworld since Pax and I mated, but I'm still going to try. And this time, when you arrive, I'm going to have you wearing floral board shorts."

Vero almost smiled, then looked back at Hunter, losing the amusement. "Take care of Hunter, would you?"

"I will," Hope said softly.

Vero reached for the door and smoothly slid it shut. "Everyone get clear. Liam likes to make a statement when he lifts off." He gestured Lyrica ahead of him and she turned, following the shoveled but icy path toward the burned-out side of the main lodge.

Liam did, indeed, make a statement as he flew the craft straight up, spinning a couple of times and spraying snow in every direction.

Vero stepped in front of Lyrica and shielded her from the barrage with his broad back.

She felt small and feminine as he protected her, awareness winging through her abdomen. Through the rest of her too. The sadness she'd seen in his deep eyes as he'd looked at his only friend, one who'd lied to him for years, dug down deep inside her heart. Had Vero forgiven Hunter? She wasn't comfortable asking him, regardless of the incredible kiss they'd shared.

The helicopter rose higher into the clouds and disappeared.

Lyrica turned to face Vero. "Who wants Paxton dead so badly?"

Vero still watched the clouds. "If I knew, they'd already be decapitated." His voice remained low. Contained. Absolute.

Lyrica shivered. The male who'd looked with sorrow upon his fallen friend was gone. This soldier, his voice gritty with determination, he remained.

Vero must've caught her movement. "It's snowing out here. Lyrica, I want you back at the main lodge. I have guards I trust in place. Then later, you and I are going to have a chat about your safety."

Why did that sound like a threat?

Chapter Sixteen

A chat about her safety? Seriously? She was always careful. About everything. What had Vero been hinting at? Or about? After a supper of fried chicken, Lyrica slammed her file folders on her desk and kicked off her snow boots. Her ears heated. What had he meant by that? His eyes had warmed as he'd said the words, and there had been definite challenge in his tone.

What in the world did that even mean?

She flopped onto her desk chair and laid her head back on the smooth leather, shutting her eyes and breathing with extreme control. She'd never shied away from her temper. But first, she had to figure out what was ticking her off to this degree.

A soft knock came at her door.

"Come in," she snapped.

After a hesitation, the door slowly opened. "I'm sorry to bother you," Genevieve said quietly, "but you left me a note on my desk, asking me to drop by." The girl looked at her, her eyes wide.

"Oh yes. Sorry." Lyrica forced her tone to calm. "I didn't mean to snap."

"That's okay." Genevieve wrung her hands together. "The prince isn't in his office, so I could help you for a moment if you like."

Actually, Genevieve was supposed to be assisting both of them, but she spent most of her time hovering near Vero's door as if afraid to be caught not working.

"It's after dinner, and you don't need to be working at all," Lyrica said softly. "But since you're here, come in and sit down."

Genevieve gulped and nodded, walking inside and shutting the door. Today, she wore black jeans and a pretty blue sweater that matched the sky on a fully sunny day. "Do you think the prince will be working late?"

"I have absolutely no idea," Lyrica gestured toward one of the two white leather chairs on the other side of her desk. When she'd set up the camp, the Kurjans had given her carte blanche with a credit card, and she'd made good use of it. It must be absolutely fabulous not to have financial worries.

Genevieve sat and crossed her legs, plastering on a placid expression. One of Lyrica's eyebrows rose. "I thought we should have a little talk."

"Oh?" Genevieve asked quietly.

Lyrica took a drink of her third coffee of the day. She liked it strong and could handle about three cups before her stomach became upset. It was rather amusing how much Vero enjoyed both the sparkling water and the apple cider she purchased. He must not be the only one enamored with the bubbly water—the kitchen kept running out of the cold delight. "Yes. I know that you have considered staying here with the Kurjan nation, and I'm happy that you're making choices, considering your difficult time in the beginning."

"I'm fine. I don't really have anywhere to go. And, I don't know, it's kind of cool being on the inside of a huge secret, you know?" Genevieve asked, her eyes sparkling.

"I do know," Lyrica said, enjoying the excitement and positive feelings coming from the girl. "I think it's fascinating that all these immortal beings have been able to keep their secret through the millennia."

Genevieve pushed up the sleeves of her sweater. "Are you going to stay?"

"I don't think so," Lyrica said. "I want to finish the job and maybe move on." But did she? Was there anything inside her that wanted to move on? She did have a life, and she enjoyed her job, and she missed her friends from her previous job, but she had rapidly made new friends out of both necessity and danger. She would miss Genevieve horribly.

The girl shifted on her seat. "I thought maybe you and Vero, you know, had started up something."

Lyrica's head jolted. "Seriously? What gave you that idea?"

"Tension," Genevieve said easily. "Definitely tension. The air kind of pops when the two of you are around each other."

"No, it doesn't," Lyrica protested.

Genevieve grinned and chewed the inside of her lip. "If you say so."

"I do," Lyrica said, cupping her hands around the hot mug. "I wanted to ask you again about this Lukas you mentioned."

Genevieve sobered immediately. "He's nice. Super nice. We hang out sometimes. That's all."

If that wasn't complete baloney, Lyrica couldn't imagine anything more absurd. She could feel the girl's emotions. "Tell me more."

Genevieve paled and looked down at her hands. "There isn't more."

"Uh-huh," Lyrica said. A sharp rap on the door had them both jumping in their seats. Lyrica's lungs compressed. She recognized that heavy hand. "Come in, Vero," she muttered.

He opened the door and poked his head in. "Hi."

Genevieve jumped to her feet. "I'm so sorry I wasn't outside your door. I didn't know you'd gone back to work." She hovered near the chair but didn't move toward him.

"No, I didn't," Vero said slowly. "I won't need anything for the rest of the evening. Please retake your seat."

The girl instantly dropped into the chair.

Lyrica frowned and studied her.

"What?" Genevieve asked.

Lyrica looked up at Vero, then back down. "These guys still scare you, and I don't blame you, but it makes me truly wonder about you possibly dating one."

This time, Genevieve flushed a light pink. "I am not dating one."

Vero's head lifted just slightly. Lyrica zoomed in on him. "What?"

He studied the female, who now faced only Lyrica. "She's not a good liar."

The new color bled out of the girl's face instantly. She looked up at Lyrica, her eyes pleading.

Lyrica ignored the urge to help her out. "I'm sorry, but we really do need to know. Somebody brutally attacked and murdered one of us."

Panic had the girl wringing her hands. "I don't know anything about the murder."

Vero stepped into the room, and a swell of heat, pure and natural, came with him.

Genevieve huddled down in her seat.

"I'm not going to hurt you," Vero said, "and you know that. But you're lying about something, and it looks like Lyrica has a bit in her teeth. I suggest you tell her the truth about whatever you both are discussing right now."

Genevieve looked quickly toward the window, then back at her hands.
"Now," Vero said, his tone firm, but no anger or heat in his low voice.
Genevieve's shoulders slumped. "I haven't done anything wrong."
"I didn't say you did," Lyrica said. "But are you dating Lukas?"
Genevieve remained quiet for a moment, then she let out a heavy sigh.
"Fine. I've been kind of, you know. Just a little bit, but sort of seeing Lukas
Macrame, sort of."
Lyrica stilled. "All right. So that's true." Her eyes slashed up to Vero.
"Yes," Genevieve whispered. "He's very sweet, and we meet up when
he's finished with training for the day. Since I work all day, sometimes we
just hang out at night and go for a walk. We don't go far because it's so cold."
Irritation heated Lyrica's blood. "How old is Lukas?" she demanded.
"Is he another two-hundred-year-old Kurjan?" The girl had just turned
seventeen, for Pete's sake. They had put rules in place for a reason. The
guy could be three centuries old.
Vero chuckled. "No, he's seventeen, as in a legitimate
seventeen-year-old male."
Lyrica's shoulders slowly relaxed as her temper dissipated. Thank
goodness she didn't have to go after the Kurjan. "You're sure he's
actually underage?"
"I'm absolutely positive," Vero said.
Relief tickled through her. "Okay. Well, then." They had set rules in
place that anybody joining the dating pool had to be at least twenty-one
years old, but she hadn't thought of Genevieve, who was the only underage
female who'd been kidnapped. "I guess we need to put some rules in place."
"Why?" Genevieve asked, her chin lifting. "Nobody else has
rules in place."
"Because you're underage," Lyrica said, keeping her voice gentle.
The girl crossed her arms. "Maybe so, but you're not my mother."
Vero obviously masked a grin. "No, but there will be rules." He looked
at Lyrica as if he had no idea what those rules would be.
Lyrica nodded. "I think it's fine if you want to date, but we need to know
when you're out and about. And," she looked up at Vero, "is it possible
for teenagers to mate?"
"Absolutely," he said. "It's rare, but it's not impossible."
"Oh," Lyrica said. "Well, there will be none of that."
Genevieve's eyes narrowed. "Says who?"

"Says me," Lyrica retorted.

"And me," Vero said in his deep voice from the doorway.

The sigh that Genevieve let out sounded long-suffering. She pushed from the chair and stood. "Lyrica, I suppose you're going to talk to Lukas?"

"No. I am," Vero said, moving to the side.

Genevieve tossed her head back and strode out of the office, apparently losing her fear of the Kurjan leader as she disappeared from sight.

Vero watched her go and turned to focus on Lyrica. "Was that a huff?"

"I believe so." Lyrica chuckled. "She's cute, but you do need to speak with Lukas. She's definitely not ready for a lifetime commitment."

"Neither is he." Vero lounged against the door frame, looking deceptively casual, when the tension rolling from him felt heated and intense.

Her heart rate sped up and she had to concentrate to banish the memory of his ripped body in those boxers the night before. "Why are you here, Vero?"

His eyes deepened, taking on the inky hue of an endless, mysterious sea. "A couple of reasons. The first is to update you on the dead female. We're interviewing all the soldiers, and so far, nobody saw anything."

Lyrica gulped. "You noted earlier that this is unprecedented in Kurjan territory. So, they never kill females?"

"Not often, but whoever did this purposefully left her in the snow for us to find. They were making a statement."

She reached for a pen to twirl. "A statement? How so?"

He lifted a shoulder. "That such a crime can take place under Paxton's leadership. That nobody is safe."

"Or there's just a bad guy out there who hates humans," Lyrica said thoughtfully. "It might not be about Paxton."

Vero nodded. "We'll see once we find the killer."

Movement sounded, and Jonathan emerged next to Vero. Flanking him were four Kurjan soldiers. Jonathan's eyes glowed a wild hue. "We were patrolling and found another dead female body."

Chapter Seventeen

Illuminated by powerful flashlights, the naked victim lay face up on the icy terrain, her head close to the Yukon with its thick chunks of ice floating by. Fingers splayed out on the brutal terrain, her hands appeared both bruised and frozen, while spikes of ice covered her bare feet. Her long, black hair spread over the frozen ground, and her face was turned to the side. Dark bruises covered her throat, and a circle with slashes through the center had been dug into her neck with what appeared to be blue ink.

Anger speared through Vero, and he pushed all emotion away, forcing himself to concentrate. He looked up and measured the distance across the river and studied the nearby snow-filled trees and starkly looming mountains. He didn't sense a threat near, but considering Lyrica stood next to him, he remained vigilant.

He crouched down and angled his head. Bruising marred the victim's face, and her nose had been broken. Blood pooled onto the ice around her.

"I don't recognize her." He looked up at the doctor, whom he'd called in immediately.

Fizzlewick dropped to his haunches, fury rolling off him. "I haven't seen her before, but I don't know everybody in the camp yet."

The human victim appeared to be in her mid to late twenties.

Vero angled his head. "We have new Kurjans who have moved to this camp from outlying satellites, so I don't know everybody yet, but I've never seen her."

The doctor looked up at Lyrica, where she hovered closer to the victim's feet. "Do you recognize her?"

Slowly, Lyrica shook her head. "No, I've never spoken to her. She's not one of the kidnapped females, for sure." She paled, and her lips had turned blue from the cold, even though she huddled in a thick, black puffer jacket.

"Why don't you return to the lodge?" Vero tried to make the statement sound like a request.

She stuck her hands in her pockets. "No, I'm good. Was she strangled?"

"It looks like it," Dr. Fizzlewick said. "I'll know more when I get her into the lab."

Vero leaned over again and took another look. "She didn't belong to the Kurjan encampment that I moved from Eastern Canada, and I've met with most of our recent newcomers."

Although it was entirely possible he had met with the female's mate and not with her.

Jonathan stood, anger etching lines into his strong face. "Lyrica, are you sure she's not one of the kidnapped females?"

Lyrica nodded, her nose red from the cold. "Yes. In addition, I've spoken with most of the mated females in the territory, and I don't recognize her. I'll provide you with a list of everyone I've met with so far, which will greatly narrow down your search."

Vero leaned in and smelled only female. The victim's scent still lingered in tones of rich roses, but terror also filled the freezing air with the smell of burned lemons. "I don't sense that she's mated."

"Neither do I," Dr. Fizzlewick said. "However, she's frozen, and she could be newly mated."

That could make sense, but even still, who was she?

Lyrica shifted her snow boots as her body shook with cold. The wind blasted into her, throwing her hair back, but she didn't complain. Not a bit. "Is it possible somebody brought her here from a nearby town?"

Vero wanted to cover the female but knew the doc had to perform an autopsy first. "No. The nearest town is four hundred and thirty miles away, which takes nearly three hours in our most advanced helicopter." Although, he would ask Silas since he'd recently headed to a town. "Even Kurjans on foot, snowmobile, or in a UTV would be gone long enough they'd be missed. Nobody could've left here and brought her back...absent a helicopter."

"We need to speak with every pilot," Jonathan said grimly, standing.

Vero stood and brushed icy snow off his jeans. "Agreed, but other than our raiding party the other day, where you and I were present, only Silas has flown out of here. I'll seek him out immediately."

Ice began to gather in Lyrica's thick hair. "Is there any way a helicopter could be taken without you knowing?"

"Negative," Vero said. "Our hearing is too acute."

Jonathan shoved his hands in his jeans pockets, his angry gaze still on the prone victim. "We also feel the vibrations as they bounce back from the ground. Nobody has taken a helicopter secretly."

Dr. Fizzlewick motioned with his gnarled hands. "Let's get her back to the lab and take a picture of her face once we clean her up, and go door to door. We have to identify her."

Vero looked directly at Lyrica. "Return to your office. Cover both of ours in case somebody comes looking for a missing female. Once we send you a picture, you can meet with the rescued females and ask if anybody knows her."

She hesitated.

"You're needed at our offices now, just in case," he prodded.

Gulping, her brown eyes wide, she turned.

He absolutely did not want her out in the cold for any longer staring at a fragile and broken human. One he hadn't been able to protect.

Dr. Fizzlewick reached for the victim's shoulder. "All right, let's do this."

* * * *

After a night without decent sleep, the sound of hammers and saws slowly drove Vero insane, even though he knew they had to get the lodge back up to standards. He began to turn away from his computer just as Paxton filled the screen from a country away.

"Morning," Pax said. "Good to know that the computers have been updated and we can meet this way, even though I'll be back in a couple of days. For now, I received your message about another dead body with the weird symbol. We need to find this killer."

Vero paused. "Hi. I'm working on it. I saw Fizzlewick this morning, and his prelim didn't provide any additional information. She was raped and strangled like the first victim before freezing. We don't know who she is. How's Realm headquarters?"

"Good. I'm reaching out to the Cyst leader today from the Realm, thinking that might make a statement. Tell me about General Waxton."

Vero needed a sparkling water. Had the stash been replenished? "The general is smart and strong, and actually a decent guy. Has a level head on his shoulders, and while an excellent fighter, I believe he prefers the spiritual side of his job. Use reason and respect with him." Vero had always liked that general. He didn't pick on kids or females. "He has to be at least two thousand years old."

Paxton whistled. "Impressive. Hopefully the news of our problems in the camp hasn't reached him." Paxton leaned closer to the screen. "Before I forget, are you all right after our fight the other night?"

"What fight?" Vero drawled. It had taken him a while to heal his spleen, but he supposed that was a good thing. He wouldn't want his brother to be a wimp when it came to a good scuffle.

"Just checking." Paxton scrubbed both hands down his face. "Back to the victims in our territory. I've been on the phone with various leaders around the world, as have the Realm leaders. Nobody has any clue what the circle with slashes through it means."

Vero sat back and his chair creaked. "On one hand, that's good news. It means there isn't some coalition out there trying to take us down. On the other hand…"

Paxton stretched his neck. "We have no clue who would murder helpless human females. Is this a common thing in the Kurjan nation?"

"Absolutely not," Vero said. "This is an anomaly." He tried to sound casual. "How is Hunter doing?"

"Hunter's doing well. Their doctors are the best in the world, especially his mom. The king said Hunter should be all healed up in probably a week, and he's already talking a little bit. Didn't see who jumped him and managed to dive through the ice and into the river, letting the current take him to where we found him. Guy was smart."

Healing the damage in his neck that quickly was impressive. Reattaching cords and even vertebrae should have taken longer than that. Vero had always known Hunter to be tough, but this feat stood out as remarkable.

"Have you decided if you want our current location to be the permanent headquarters?" Vero asked.

"I think so. It's a good strategic position and we're close to the Realm, but not too close. What do you think?"

Vero picked up a pen to twirl between his fingers. "I like the position of it. If this is it, I will send orders for the complete computer hub to be sent here. I'm having trouble accessing the satellites. It should take about two days to get us up and running if we fully move here."

"We'll need to get going with digging an underground headquarters and some escape routes," Paxton said.

Vero nodded. "I will start sketching up ideas. Back to the current problem. Lyrica checked in and none of the kidnapped females recognized the second victim."

Paxton's brows drew down. "Really? Not one of them?"

Vero shook his head. "No, and she wasn't betrothed to any of the soldiers."

Paxton threw a hand in the air. "She didn't just arrive out of nowhere."

"I know," Vero said, grimly.

Paxton lifted his head, his chin firming. "The only person to leave camp and come back within the last week was Silas."

"Yes, and I have him in a cell. I'm going to leave him there for some time before interrogating him, to keep him off balance," Vero said. "I've known him longer than you have, and I'll be able to tell if he's lying." Maybe. At several centuries old, the male probably had perfected a few talents through the years. "I have to tell you I don't see it being him. I just don't."

"Then maybe I should interview him when I return in a couple of days," Paxton said.

Vero liked that Paxton apparently thought he'd find success. "If he hasn't broken by then, he won't. I'll try and maybe come in sympathetic. We need to figure this out." Nothing in him could see Silas mutilating a human female like that, but Vero had been hit with enough surprises in his life. He should be ready for anything.

"Keep me informed."

"I will." Vero ground one fist into his right eye, trying to push back a looming headache. "I don't want this investigation to interfere with my plans for the females this afternoon."

The human females who wanted to leave had all signed the NDA and accepted the seven-figure bank accounts. He didn't expect any of them to talk—or remember their time in the wild. A fact he had chosen not to share with Lyrica. "I want to stay on schedule with releasing the rescued females today."

"I agree," Paxton said. "They want to go home and they have every right to return to their lives. How many females decided to stay?"

"Twelve," Vero said, surprised. "I guess immortality is a draw."

Paxton nodded. "If they continue to stay, we can invite them to my wedding in the spring." He paled slightly.

Vero exhaled slowly. "Spring's going to be here before we know it. Are you certain the Realm is prepared for Kurjan soldiers to attend an event?"

"I'm certain," Paxton said. "If we're going to ally with the Realm, we need to do it sooner rather than later. I've been looking through Kurjan records, and it appears there are probably five hundred Kurjans alive across the globe and one hundred Cyst soldiers. Is that true?"

"I think there are a few more that we've lost track of," Vero admitted. "More than half decided to stay with the nation when you took over as the king, and we need those forty Cyst leaders. You have to convince them to join us."

Paxton remained quiet for a moment. "I will. You have my word. How many soldiers at that main camp do you think want to take me down?"

"I don't know," Vero said. "Obviously a couple of people or they wouldn't have bombed your room the other night. I haven't had any luck figuring out who that is. It's going to take me a while to interview two hundred soldiers and their mates about the bombing and dead human females. The somewhat good news is that I can combine those interviews with Lyrica's since she's speaking to all of the mates."

"Fair enough," Paxton said. "Hunter should be up and talking within a few days. Do you want him to give you a call?"

"No."

Paxton studied him. "All right. I'm not going to push that, but you have to remember he was doing his job when he infiltrated the Kurjan nation."

"I remember," Vero said.

Paxton chuckled. "Well, if nothing else, I get to miss your little get-together with newcomers tonight. I hate cocktail parties."

"As do I," Vero groused. "But it's Kurjan tradition, and Lyrica is excited to meet the twenty new couples, so she's organized it." The group was a small band that hadn't liked the former leadership but had agreed to join the current nation—so long as Paxton succeeded in bringing home the forty Cyst soldiers. "They should arrive any minute via our helicopters." He hadn't wanted to put off the meeting. More soldiers could only help at this point.

Movement sounded outside his office and Lukas Macrame stood in the doorway. "You wanted to see me?" the kid asked.

"I have to go, Pax. Talk later." Vero ended the video call.

Lukas took a deep breath and strode inside.

Vero released the pen he had been holding. "Have a seat."

The kid stood tall at about six foot seven and remained gangly. His skin carried a tone slightly deeper than pale, complemented by striking amethyst eyes and pure black hair lacking any red. As one of the babies injected with the Sunshine Cure in utero, he hadn't required additional supplements until he turned three years old.

At that time, the Kurjan scientists realized the in-utero cure only lasted a few years, sometimes less. So now the kid received injections just like the rest of them. Lukas had good looks and faced Vero without flinching.

Vero didn't know how to do this. "I wanted to talk to you about Genevieve."

Lukas tugged on his training uniform. "I figured."

Vero had seen him on the field. The strong kid would make a good soldier someday. "She's a human female and she's fragile."

"I understand that," Lukas said. "She's also smart and incredibly kind."

Oh. Vero sat back. He was dealing with puppy love or hell, maybe the real thing. What did he know? "She doesn't have family to protect her, so that leaves me. You understand what I'm saying?"

Lukas gulped. "Yes, I understand what you're saying. I do want to court her."

"You're seventeen years old. You're a little young for courting. You're going to live thousands of years."

"I know." The kid flushed. "But she's it for me."

Vero didn't have time to deal with young love. "That is off the table. There will be no mating until you're well of age. Tell me you get me."

Now an angry flash swirled across Lukas's hard-cut face. "I didn't say I wasn't going to court her for a good twenty years. That's fine with me and that's fine with her. She's the one. When you find the one, you don't sit. You don't wait. I mean, life might be long, but sometimes it's cut off way too early, you know? I wouldn't want to miss a moment."

"You make a good point," Vero said. His mind flashed to Lyrica and their kiss the other night. How many good moments could they have?

Chapter Eighteen

Lyrica watched as the last of the three helicopters lifted into the air and headed south. She'd miss the women, now headed back to their lives much wealthier than when they'd left them, but everyone had promised to stay in touch somehow. She didn't have cell service, but according to Genevieve, a massive haul of computer systems had already arrived. It would be nice to reach out to the rest of the world without having to use a satellite phone.

She nodded at Jonathan and Lukas, who had been assigned to escort her when she left the main lodge. She couldn't believe another body had been found. According to a Kurjan mate she'd spoken with earlier, they'd never had a serial killer in their midst.

So who was doing this? Dr. Fizzlewick had reported that the second victim had also been raped and strangled, with no DNA left behind. Another circle with slashes had been carved into her neck.

What did that mean?

Lyrica shivered in the cold and her boots crunched ice as she made her way back to the nearly repaired lodge. It was impressive how quickly a motivated group of people could work.

Ducking her head, she strode through the main living room back to her office, wanting to make a note of which released women she'd contact first after giving them a short time to get acclimated. For now, she looked at the files on her desk about the remaining Kurjan mates she had yet to meet.

So far, they had all wanted to stay. She had yet to find a truly unhappy mate, and that didn't make sense to her. Twenty additional couples had

arrived early that morning on the helicopters, and she had scheduled time
to speak with a few of the females before the cocktail party that night,
meeting some resistance.

That didn't surprise her.

She glanced at the cold cup of coffee near her tape dispenser. It marked
her fourth of the day, so she should probably pass on her afternoon treat.

A sharp knock had her jumping in her chair.

"Come on in," she said, smoothing her hair. She hadn't seen Vero all
day. Not that it mattered, she reassured herself.

The door opened and a tall Kurjan soldier walked in dressed in a black
uniform with silver medals across his breast. They were all tall, but this
one stood at least six foot eight or nine.

"Hello." She also stood.

He looked her over. His black hair had red tips, and his eyes were a
deep amethyst with a hint of red. "I've been instructed that my mate needs
to see you." He stepped to the side, and a petite redhead walked inside.
Her hair was braided and she wore a pretty green dress that matched her
eyes. She looked calmly at Lyrica.

"Hi. I'm Lyrica." She gestured to the guest chairs. "Would you like to
have a seat?" The woman looked up at the soldier and he nodded, so she
walked over and took the farthest seat.

The soldier looked at Lyrica. "I am Ralstad and this is my mate, Maeve."

"Hi. It's nice to meet you," Lyrica said.

"I prefer to stand," Ralstad said.

Lyrica shook her head. "I would like to speak with Maeve alone, if
you don't mind."

"I do mind," he said.

Maeve remained quiet.

"I'm sorry to hear that," Lyrica said, "but we can check with the king
or his enforcer if you wish."

The male's eyes narrowed. "Very well. I'll be right outside. Don't take
too long." He shut the door sharply behind himself, and heavy footsteps
echoed as he no doubt headed toward the coffee bar in the living room.

"So," Lyrica said as she sat. "It's nice to meet you."

"You as well," Maeve said, a slight accent emerging with her words.

Lyrica pulled out the intake form she had created. "Do you
have a last name?"

"No. Far as I know, we're to pick a family name, but Ralstad hasn't settled on one yet," Maeve said softly.

"I see. Do you have a name you prefer?" The woman looked at her blankly. "Okay, let's start there. If you don't mind telling me, what year were you born?"

"Oh, that's simple enough," the woman said. "I was born in the year 1860."

Wow. To have lived through so many changes in the world. "You sound Irish?"

"Yes."

Lyrica took notes. How could she relax the woman? "Okay. When were you mated?"

"1880," Maeve said.

"I see." Lyrica sat back and gave her most calming smile. "I don't know if you've been informed, but things have changed in the Kurjan nation. Did you mate Ralstad willingly?"

Maeve looked at her and shook her head. "I don't understand."

"Did you want to get mated?"

"Oh, sure. We had a fine arrangement, and Ralstad knew me Da, so it was a match that suited us well."

Geez, that sounded romantic. Lyrica placed the pen next to the paper. "Part of my job here is to make sure that you want to remain mated."

Maeve tilted her head. "Sure, I've not a clue what you're on about."

"I mean that it's your choice. If you don't want to remain with Ralstad, you don't have to stay mated. There's a new virus that we believe ends the mating bond. I don't know that much about it, but I am happy to look into it if you would like to negate the bond."

"Ah, and what would I be doin' in such a way?" Maeve asked, looking nervously at the door.

Lyrica's instincts slowly awakened. Something was off with the woman. "Whatever you want. The Kurjan nation has money and can set you up anywhere, doing anything you want. You're free."

Maeve clasped her hands in her lap. "There's no such thing as freedom."

"But there is." Lyrica looked down at the form. "Where have you been the past year?"

"At a Kurjan outpost in Russia," Maeve said. "We watched the live feed when the current king took over from the last, and everyone was called back home if they wanted to stay part of the Kurjan nation. Ralstad wants to stay, for now, at least."

Lyrica reached out with her senses. While she'd always thought of herself as empathetic, it turned out she truly had gifts, and she'd been trying to strengthen those while with the immortals. All she felt from Maeve was an odd nervousness. "What about you?"

Maeve shook her head. "I've no notion what you're askin'."

"What do you want to do?"

Maeve unclasped her hands. "Choose a surname?"

The woman had no idea about the world outside. "Don't you want freedom? You could explore the world. You could go anywhere you want. Are you happy in your mating?"

"My matchin' suits well enough," Maeve said softly. "Have ye any other questions for me? Ralstad said not to be takin' too long."

Ralstad seemed like kind of a bully.

Lyrica looked down at the form. "Do you have any children?"

"No, not yet. We've not been able to have young so far, but sure it can take hundreds of years for the Kurjans," Maeve added quickly. "It's not on me, so it's not."

"I didn't think it was," Lyrica said, enjoying the woman's brogue. "How would you like to take a weekend away, just girls, go somewhere fun and see an interesting part of the world?"

Maeve's pretty green eyes widened. "Ah, no. I don't reckon Ralstad'd be pleased with that." Her nervousness turned into a low, buzzing panic.

"What does Ralstad do when he's not pleased?"

The door opened. "That's enough time," Ralstad said.

Maeve jumped to her feet. "Grand talkin' with you, Lyrica."

"You too," Lyrica said.

Maeve hustled out of the office and Ralstad gave Lyrica a hard look before shutting the door.

Lyrica took several deep breaths before scratching some notes. This absolutely would not be the only time she spoke with Maeve. She'd just finished up when another knock came on her door. She knew that one. "Come in, Vero," she said.

He opened the door. "How'd you know it was me?"

"Your knock is unique."

His brows drew down. "That's weird." He moved inside and handed her a bouquet. Her heart lurched. She stood and accepted a stunning rustic winter arrangement made of evergreen sprigs, pine cones, and frosted birch twigs. There was a bit of moss gathered throughout, and a few feathers had been tucked delicately into the mixture.

"What is this?" she asked, noting the entire bouquet was tied together with a simple strip of burlap.

He shrugged. "There aren't any flowers anywhere near, so I made my own. The brown and grayish feathers are from the boreal chickadee. There are a bunch around here."

She had the oddest urge to lean in and sniff the bouquet like she would if there were flowers. She did so, and the scent of the trees filled her. It smelled like Christmas.

"This was kind of you," she said awkwardly. "Thank you."

"I've decided to court you." He turned and shut the door before taking the leather guest chair Maeve had vacated. "The closer I keep to you, the safer you are. I don't think we can spend a lot of time together without combusting, and I know you like a structured and methodical approach. I don't know how to use PowerPoint, so I thought I'd just be honest."

Lyrica dropped to her seat, barely keeping shock off her face. "I, ah, I don't have a vase." Courting? What in the world was he talking about? The kiss from the other night as well as the feeling of his hard body bracketing hers in that bed flashed into her brain, and her face slowly heated.

"I don't think we have any vases in the territory. I can put some on the next supply list." He leaned over and took the bouquet, leaning it against the wall.

The smell of pine filled the room.

"We don't like each other," Lyrica finally burst out.

A hint of a smile hovered on his lips. What would he look like truly smiling? Probably devastating. "I know."

"You're confusing me." Also somehow turning her on. Thank goodness she'd worn a bra today.

"Not my intention." His muscled body overwhelmed the pretty leather chair. "The kiss we shared was...explosive. I understand that you plan to leave Kurjan territory with the million-dollar fee after bringing us into this century. I don't ever plan on mating. Since we're being all modern, and I plan on guarding you while you're here in the territory, and since you're most certainly in danger, I thought we could date like the humans do."

Date? Did he mean date or just sleep together? She liked logic, but this was throwing her off. "Why don't you plan on mating?"

His head tilted ever so slightly, as if surprised she latched onto that part of the conversation. "Let's just say that an heir apparent and current enforcer to a king, who many in his nation want dead, does not have a long life expectancy."

A chill swept through her. She tried to reach out with her newly developing senses and just felt hard resolve. No fear. No anticipation. No emotion she could read. "I don't understand."

He gave one short nod as if that made sense. "Anybody wanting to kill Paxton has to go through me first. That means I'm dead before anybody gets to him. Or, in the alternative, if somebody somehow manages to kill him, and they're strong enough to do so, then I'm next. They won't want me ascending as the new king."

How could he sound so matter-of-fact about dying?

"So you, um, want to have a relationship until I leave?" Her breath quickened and she tried to slow her exhales.

"Yes. Consent is imperative in this world, as you've explained, so I'm bringing you a winter bouquet and requesting consent." He sounded ready to negotiate.

She stared blindly for a few seconds at his stunningly dark blue eyes. Unsure, turned on, she fell back on reason. If he could be so honest, so could she. "I'll consider it, but I want, um, a contract in place." Was she actually doing this? Contracting to date somebody? To sleep with the hard-bodied badass? Was she losing her mind? Or was this a reasonable and good idea?

He sat back in the chair and it creaked in protest. "That's a fine idea."

Her mouth went dry as she remembered something from a sitcom she used to watch. "You are actually willing to draw up a relationship agreement?"

"Then consent would be clear, would it not?"

Yeah, but the kiss the other night had been wildly passionate. "I want to draft the contract."

"Of course you do. Or, maybe we should just go on a date and see where it leads us."

Her chin lifted. "I'd rather we were both clear before we kiss again." She could handle this. Control and organize the situation. Her mouth watered. She did want to kiss him again. "I am attracted to you."

"I know." No arrogance there. Just fact.

"Okay. I'll draft something up and we can then decide if we really want to go this route." This was too freaking bizarre. Yet her body flashed to awareness as if knowing an amazing treat was coming her way. The guy had said he'd been trained by the best in the art of, well, sex. "Do you have any stipulations?"

His eyes darkened. "We move into my room so that guards can take the rooms on either side to better protect you. We're exclusive, and I'm not one for public physical affection. However, holding hands is permissible unless Pax has returned and I'm on guard, in which case my hands must be free."

She smartly tapped her pen on a blank piece of paper and began making notes, staring down at her shaking hand. "Is there a sexual requirement?" Yeah. More sarcasm. A boatload of it.

"No. Just a promise that if we do have sex, you'll get off a minimum of four times."

She gulped, her gaze slashing up to his. "Get off? That's slang."

"I know. I learned it from watching movies with my now dead cousin."

She barely shook her head, trying to concentrate. "You can't guarantee that."

"Want to bet?" he asked softly.

That tone zipped right to her clit. She shifted her weight on the chair and cleared her throat. "The Kurjans, even the modern ones, seem to be old-fashioned. There's no way I'll obey you."

"I only expect you to obey me when there's danger involved. You'll give me that whether or not we date."

She stilled. There was something so wrong with that statement. "Vero—"

"No. I'm the enforcer for the king of the Kurjan nation. Everyone in this camp, in this nation, obeys me when it comes to safety and protection. That is nonnegotiable. Period."

Had she been blindly obeying him? Had everyone? The guy always seemed in charge and like he knew what he was doing, so she'd followed along when he'd assigned living quarters, offices, and even jobs. "Huh."

"We'll make the three-month status common knowledge. If people understand we're temporary, they won't try to go through you to get to me."

She didn't like that. Not really. "Of course."

"I want three months from the signing of the agreement, if Paxton brings the Cyst into the nation, and also if I live. Then I'll take you anywhere in the world you want."

Her mind spun. Was this really happening? "If you don't live?" She could barely get the words out.

"If I'm taken out, I've made provisions for you—regardless of our dating status. I promise you'll be safe and that you'll end up back in your former life a very rich person." He studied her and she tried not to squirm. "What are your conditions?"

Conditions? The multiple-orgasm promise sounded good. "Um, you try to ask and not order all the time."

"Done."

What else? Her brain kept blanking. "All physical contact doesn't automatically lead to sex."

"That's fair. What else?"

"You leave me be to conduct my job in the way I see fit." So far, he'd done exactly that, but she hadn't taken many chances. She might be in a bit of danger with Maeve, but she wouldn't abandon the woman.

He seemed to contemplate her words. "So long as you're safe."

They'd just have to agree to disagree there. Was she really going to agree to this? "All right. We can attend the greeting party tonight as a couple." She frowned. "Should we be having get-togethers with murders occurring here?"

He shrugged. "We need to meet the twenty new couples who've joined us today, and it's Kurjan tradition to have a cocktail party in such instances. Plus, you only have three months to modernize us."

So, he'd put a definite deadline on their relationship. Fine. "I'll draw something up."

"Thank you." He stood and crossed to the door.

"Vero?" She waited until he looked over his broad shoulder. "Why?" There was no need to go into more detail.

His eyes remained hard. Flat. "There's no doubt I'm dying soon, and I want something warm and good before I go. In fact, I want to be surrounded by your heat." He opened the door and walked into the hallway, shutting it quietly behind himself.

Chapter Nineteen

The cocktail party felt like a success. Lyrica looked down at her sparkling blue dress. Apparently the Kurjans enjoyed ceremony and often had such parties. She delicately sipped champagne next to Eudokia, whose mate kept a close eye on them from across the room. "Are you sure you're happy?" Lyrica asked.

"Yes," Eudokia murmured, wearing a lovely red ball gown. "We didn't have a choice in remaining out of sight and mind with the old leadership, but Vero and the king are changing things. In fact, I'm not sure you've noticed the lovely sweaters many of us wear?"

Lyrica nodded. "I have. You knit them?"

"Yes. I've been asking some of the newcomers about the world out there. What do you think about us selling them to humans? Or even immortals. It could be a good moneymaker, I think."

Lyrica coughed and swallowed champagne. "You should definitely do that."

Eudokia straightened. "Would you mind speaking with Vero for us? Since you signed that contract that you've made public."

Lyrica glanced at the woman. "You disapprove?"

"That doesn't seem very romantic to me, and you appear to be a romantic. Or perhaps it'll work out." Eudokia shrugged. "Either way, we wouldn't feel comfortable approaching our mates about the idea unless we had the permission of the king and his enforcer. Our mates have spent lifetimes protecting us, of course."

None of this made sense. "I'd be happy to talk to the king and Vero." She could study the market and create a good presentation. Maybe they could open an Etsy store. Or one of their own using one of the many online shopping portals. Her gaze caught on Maeve, who looked lovely in a green gown with her hair piled on her head in an intricate braid. "I'm sure your mate has protected you, but I don't know that's the case for everyone. Excuse me." She moved through the crowd to reach the couple. "Good evening."

"Evening," Ralstad said for them both.

Then Vero stood next to her, grasping her arm. A warmth started in her chest and flowed through her entire body. She had to keep her heart out of this. "Oh, hi. Vero, you've met Ralstad and Maeve, have you not?"

"I have," Vero said, nodding at Ralstad before half bowing to Maeve. "Thank you for joining us here at the main headquarters."

"It seemed like the safest thing to do," Ralstad said.

Lyrica forced a smile. "I wanted to speak with Maeve about having a girls' weekend, maybe somewhere in Seattle where we could all go shopping."

"No," Ralstad said.

Maeve placed her hand gently on her mate's sleeve.

"I didn't ask you," Lyrica said. "I asked Maeve."

Maeve's cheeks turned a pretty shade of pink. "Ah, well, I'm grateful for the kind offer, but I'll have to pass."

"Excuse us." Vero guided her toward the dance floor.

Tingles exploded up her arm, and her abdomen performed a slow roll that heated and flashed warmth through her body. Just from the strength in his hand around hers. Even so, she'd been in the middle of a discussion, and she didn't appreciate the high-handedness. "What in the world do you think you're doing?"

"We're going to dance. Kurjans love dancing, which is a closely guarded secret." He signaled the male managing the music and instantly a slow song came across the many speakers. His arm banded around her waist and he tugged her close, his hand still around hers.

She temporarily lost her voice when pulled against his heated, rock-hard body. Think. She had to concentrate. "You see what's going on there?"

"I saw you interfering."

Irritation heated her to her ears. "That's what I'm talking about. Maeve has every right to do what she wants. She doesn't have to ask her mate's permission."

"Perhaps they have a contract that says otherwise," Vero said, his tone reasonable.

Lyrica tried to remain stiff against his overwhelming heat, but her body fought her. He towered over her, forcing her to tilt her head to meet his gaze. She'd never been small and had always been a curvy girl, but he made her feel petite and oddly safe.

Amusement danced in his blue eyes, but still, no smile.

She gathered her thoughts. "If they did enter into a contract, it was in the eighteen hundreds when women didn't have rights. I think there's something wrong with their relationship."

"Define what you mean by using the word 'wrong.'" Vero swayed her easily to the music.

She hadn't figured he'd be so graceful on the dance floor. In fact, all the Kurjans had surprised her. They were shockingly good at many different styles. Lyrica looked over to see Genevieve and Lukas kissing next to them.

Vero caught her gaze, reached out, and smacked Lukas on top of the head.

"Hey," the kid protested, stepping back.

"Knock it off," Vero muttered.

Flushing, Lukas turned back to hold Genevieve not quite so close.

Lyrica bit back a smile. Now, that was funny. "This seems like a good party," she murmured. "I would like to speak with Maeve alone again. Could you arrange that for me?"

"You've already spoken to her twice, counting tonight."

"I know, but I read feelings of nervousness from her." Lyrica tried to gauge the crowd one person at a time, opening herself up. Several rushes of emotion hit her instantly, and she gasped.

"Stop it," Vero said, looking down at her.

She blinked. His eyes were so blue. "Stop what?"

"You know what you're doing. Knock it off. There are too many people here for you to try to read."

She blinked several times. "How did you know?"

"I can feel it," he said, lifting one shoulder. "You send out an energy signal. And if I could feel it, I assume other people can too."

Yet another facet to her gift she hadn't realized. Why hadn't she trusted her own instincts that she had abilities and learned to develop them long before now? "How do I stop transmitting?"

"You just need to work on it. You're fairly new to using this power, right?"

"Yes," she said. Her skin felt sensitized and her breasts felt heavy. Needy. Even her nipples sharpened against her plain white bra. To ignore her aching body, she focused her empathic attention directly on Maeve. Could she read the woman's emotions from across the entire room?

"I said to stop it," Vero said. "You're going to overwhelm yourself."

Her stomach began to cramp, and a headache formed at the base of her neck. He was right. Slowly, she calmed herself and brought all her senses back inside her body and head, where they belonged. "I need to know what's going on there."

"Not tonight," he said, turning her again, his hand warm across her lower back. "Tonight, we live by the contract."

* * * *

Vero's room smelled like him. Foresty and male. Lyrica sat awkwardly on the bed, plucking at a loose string on the bedspread. She didn't have anything sexy to wear. That shopping trip to Seattle really did sound like an excellent idea. Was she crazy? Most likely. But something about Vero called for her.

She didn't know why, except he was probably the sexiest male she'd ever seen in her entire life. Plus, they had a contract. She wanted to be amused about that, but when they both signed, he had seemed very serious. Even that was sexy.

During the dance, she'd almost combusted from being close to him. What was it about Vero? For the past several months, as she'd lived in the Kurjan world, she hadn't felt a thing for any of the immortals. Nothing. Like not even a casual interest, much less a strong desire.

Tonight for bed, she wore a white T-shirt with her yoga pants like she normally did, wishing for a sexy camisole or negligee.

Quiet drummed around her. Vero had escorted her to his room, rather *their* room, before heading out to check the positions of the soldiers guarding the various areas of camp that needed surveillance, especially the female barracks, and of course, the main lodge.

She thought about how dangerous his life would always be, and for some reason that didn't scare her. She wished she could talk to Hope, and once she received the updated computers, she would definitely reach out.

Hope didn't know much more about the Kurjans than Lyrica did, considering Hope had been raised by the Realm.

Lyrica missed her. They'd become fast friends while fighting against an enemy the day Paxton became the king, and Hope had quickly become a close confidante.

Her stomach turning over, Lyrica rested against the headboard and tucked a pillow more securely behind her back.

Should she just get naked and under the covers? She didn't know what to do. This felt so awkward. What had she been thinking? She had almost talked herself into getting up and leaving when the door opened and Vero walked inside.

His gaze swept her, and heat flared along her every nerve ending. "I take it we're all safe for the night?" Lyrica asked dryly.

He nodded and kicked off his monstrous boots.

"What size are your feet, anyway?"

"Size seventeen. Sometimes sixteen and often eighteen." If he found her desperate attempt to start a conversation amusing, he didn't show it.

She'd have to be careful not to trip over his footwear. She'd probably break her neck. A nervous laugh escaped her.

"Are you all right?" Vero unzipped the perfectly hidden zipper of his uniform top.

"I always wondered if the medals came off or stayed on." During her time as a captive in the Kurjan nation, she'd seen many different silver medals arranged in all sorts of different orders. Not one inch of her cared to learn what any of them meant.

"They pretty much stay on." He shrugged out of the top and strode to the closet.

Smooth, hard muscle showed in every line of his chest and down his arms. She gulped, heat pooling low in her abdomen. She had never seen a chest like that. Maybe computer enhanced on social media with the use of AI, but not in real life.

Then he opened the closet and turned his back to her, hanging up the top.

She failed at masking her gasp. Whip scars marred his entire muscled back, top to bottom, some quite deep and all ridged.

He looked over his shoulder, his eyes a mesmerizing, storm-tossed blue. "What?"

"Your back," she breathed. "I thought immortals didn't scar."

"Depends on the age of the immortal and how brutal the wound." He unbuckled his belt.

The sound sent erotic shock waves through her system. Even so, tears pricked the back of her eyes. "You must've been young and the beating brutal." Her heart hurt for him.

"Beatings, plural. Injury upon injury can also create lasting wounds for us. We have to heal ourselves at least somewhat before being harmed again." His tone remained flat with no emotion.

She felt enough for both of them. "Your uncles?"

"Affirmative."

She didn't feel any loss at their deaths. How horrible for him. While she didn't have the skills yet to reliably read an immortal, she felt enough from him to know that he didn't want sympathy.

He unzipped his pants and took them off to hang in the closet, leaving himself in black boxer briefs.

Wow. A lot of skin and muscle and power all shifted in front of her. "The party went well," she said, searching for anything to say.

"I thought so." He turned to face her.

She couldn't help but count the ridges in his abs. There wasn't a bit of fat on the guy. Could immortals even get fat? "So you're not shy," she said, wishing she'd already ducked beneath the bedcovers.

His blue gaze zeroed in on her rapidly heating face. She must be blushing like a crazy woman, and the raw male appreciation in that gaze weakened her knees even as she sat. "Why would I be shy?" he asked.

Very good question. She didn't imagine anybody who looked like that would be shy. "No reason," she croaked.

His eyes softened just a hint. Not enough to seem mellow or even calm, but she hoped she saw a softening. "We can just sleep tonight if you want," he rumbled.

She latched onto the offer, a raft in an unforgiving sea. "That might be a good idea." Her body tingled in absolute protest. "This is just weird," she added.

"Weird? How so?" He walked around the bed and sat on the other side before lifting her up and settling her on his lap.

She'd never been cradled by a man like this before, or rather, a male. Like this. She had to stop thinking of him as human. He wasn't anywhere close.

Her body naturally stiffened while her muscles wanted to relax right into his strength. "I guess it's all the talking and agreeing and the contractual obligations. I mean, the other night when you kissed me, it was passionate and wild." Why couldn't he just sweep her away again?

"This is more honest."

She swallowed, fully aware of how hard he was beneath her. All of him. Every inch.

Desire flamed through her and she tried to concentrate.

He brushed the hair back from her face, his touch oddly gentle for a giant of his size. "I thought consent and talking and agreement was what you wanted."

"It is, but this just seems more like a business arrangement." Her body did not care. Nope. Not a bit.

"This is how most matings and marriages have been arranged throughout the years," he said softly, his fingers warm against her neck. His eyes flared an unholy blue, but his hands remained gentle. "Until very recently, everybody on the planet arranged marriages. Many humans still do, and statistically, those are known to last longer than marriages entered into with feelings."

She couldn't think with his warm, hard body wrapped around her. "I understand that, but passion is good too."

"You can't have both?" His fingers trailed across her cheekbone and down to her jaw, the pads callused and rough.

She trembled and didn't try to hide it.

He leaned in and brushed his lips across her other cheekbone and then her nose. "So, do I have consent to kiss you?"

She let out an exasperated breath. "Yes."

"What about intercourse?"

He was ripping the romantic side of this to pieces. "All right." She threw her hands up. "Enough of that."

"Enough of what?" he asked mildly.

"We both signed the contract. You do not have to request consent for kissing or anything else. Since we pretty much have a relationship agreement, you can assume that consent is granted. You don't have to ask every damn time."

"Interesting." He tugged her earlobe. "You don't want me to ask for consent?"

Was he messing with her? "I did initially. Now I don't. We're in a relationship, or at least we're about to be, and you can assume that consent is given. If for some reason I'm not in the mood, I will absolutely let you know."

"All right," he said, his fingers wrapping around her nape and spearing up along her head to the crown. He pulled her head back easily and his mouth took hers.

There was nothing tentative about him, and he didn't seek consent. He took what he wanted, kissing her hard and going deep, taking her out of reality.

She shut her eyelids and kissed him back. Feeling all that hard muscle and strength surrounding her, and his kiss. Oh, could he kiss.

He overwhelmed her with just his mouth and his hand cupping her head. She murmured something, having no idea what. He gently tugged her shirt up over her head, having to break the kiss briefly. The minute the cotton disappeared, he was back on her. Shifting her to straddle him before both hands tunneled into her hair and pulled her head back as he kissed her.

She didn't know kisses could be like this. All-consuming. She moaned and shifted against him, feeling him hot and pulsing between her legs. Her yoga pants felt too tight.

He continued to kiss her, his hands moving from her head over her shoulders and down her back to cup her butt.

Fire raced through her so quickly she forgot to breathe.

He softened the kiss and stilled, leaning back.

She pressed her palms against his hard chest, marveling at the rock-cut strength there. She leaned in to kiss his chin, then caught a stillness from him. Pure alertness?

His eyes had turned a wild, chaotic blue, and yet he remained still, his chin lifting slightly.

"What is it?" she whispered.

"I'm uncertain." He lifted her off him and stood, an obvious bulge in his boxers. He reached into a drawer for a green gun and a huge, sharp blade. Much longer than any knife, it wasn't quite a sword. "Stay here." He stalked silently toward the door.

She scrambled to grab her shirt and yank it over her head.

He looked out into the hallway both ways, then walked out, disappearing from sight.

Gulping, she grabbed another gun from his nightstand and followed him, keeping her distance just in case she needed to shoot somebody. She wasn't getting in the fight. She shrieked when a bedroom door burst open and a male smashed into Vero, careening both into the far wall. Plaster rained down and turned the hallway dusty.

The attacker, dressed in all black with even his face covered, slashed a knife down Vero's arm. "I'm here for you, Prince. You die first…and then I'll take out the king."

Vero's blood spurted across the hallway, spreading across Lyrica's arm. The liquid burned her and she frantically tried to wipe it off on her yoga pants.

Silver flashed as the male in black struck again. "Vero," she yelled.

Chapter Twenty

Cold fury washed through Vero as he dropped the gun, his left arm going numb. Snarling, he forced feeling back into his hand and grabbed the attacker, flipping him over onto the hard wooden floor. "Jonathan," he yelled. He'd put the soldier into the adjoining room on purpose. The guy could fight.

A grunt of pain came from inside the bedroom.

Vero punched down and hit the attacker in the nose before yanking off the concealing balaclava. He was one of the new guys. What was his name? Shelton or something like that.

Lyrica, a weapon in her hand, kicked the guy and he snarled, reaching out to grab her ankle.

"Get back," Vero roared.

Paling, she stumbled back, her eyes wide.

Shelton punched up, hitting Vero in the nose, and he felt it crack. Damn it. He struck down several times with his bad arm while lifting the knife with his other. He tried to slam it down and Shelton, his purple eyes wide, grabbed his wrist, scissored him around the waist with his legs, and tossed him off.

Vero rolled and came up on his feet, ducking his head and charging as Shelton did the same. He lifted them up and slammed them both down the stairs, where they tumbled end over end. Pain burst in Vero's hips and shoulders. Several of his ribs cracked, but he ignored them.

When they reached the bottom, he rolled them again, his knife out, and slammed the sharp blade into Shelton's neck. The blade split into three almost instantly, and the jerk's head rolled away from his body.

Vero bounded up, blood flowing from wounds in his face and arm, and yanked his knife free. The weapon snapped back to one blade and he charged up the stairs, running into Jonathan's room.

One male was decapitated on the floor and Jonathan had another male in a headlock. Jonathan's face was a hard, furious mask, and he choked the other Kurjan out, letting him fall uselessly to the floor.

Vero ducked down, staring at the unconscious Kurjan. "His face is bloody—do you recognize him?"

Jonathan spit out blood. "He's one of the newcomers who attended the cocktail party earlier. His name is Geoff."

Vero squinted. The guy's face was mangled, but he had arrived with the newest group earlier, and he had attended the cocktail party—without a mate. "How did they get in here?"

"Window." Jonathan shook his head. "I don't know where the guards are. We better find them." His jaw hardened. "I'm hoping they're just knocked out and not dead. I can't live with our own soldiers being killed just while on guard duty."

"Okay," Vero said. "I want to take this guy down to the cells and have a little discussion before we kill him."

"Kill him?" Lyrica asked from the doorway, shaking and pale.

Vero turned. He didn't have time to argue.

"You can't just kill him."

"You're right," Vero said. "I'm going to torture him, get the answers I need, then I'm going to kill him."

She took a step back. "You have no judge? You have no jury? You have no legal system?"

"Yeah, we have a system that works," Vero retorted. "If somebody tries to kill us, we kill them." It was pretty simple, really. "I told you to stay in the room."

Color finally flooded into her face. "Apparently, I didn't listen."

"Apparently not," he said mildly. They would have more than a simple discussion about that later. He looked at Jonathan, who bled from several areas on his chest and neck. "Are you okay?"

Jonathan wiped blood off his neck. "Yeah. You came at a good time, though." The air started to shimmer around him as he no doubt sent healing cells where they needed to go.

"Do you have a gun?" Vero asked.

"I have several." Jonathan walked to the closet and reached in for jeans that he quickly drew on. He grabbed a gun out of the nearest dresser.

His guards had explaining to do. "All right, stay here," Vero said. "I'll go see where the guards are."

"Wait a sec." Jonathan tossed him a faded and ripped pair of jeans. "At least put something on. Also, I'm coming with you."

Vero caught them with one hand, his good one, and quickly put them on. "Give me a second," he said.

"All right," Jonathan murmured, gun in his hand as he reached into his closet for a shirt.

Vero walked into the hallway, grabbed Lyrica's arm, and drew her back down to their bedroom. "Shoot anybody not me, but I will have people on the lodge. Stay here."

She lifted her chin. "I should come with you. I'm an empath, and I might be able to see if he tells the truth. I'm not good with immortals yet, though."

"He'll tell me the truth," Vero said grimly. "I promise."

Her eyes widened and she looked at him. "You might want to consider a prison system and not just kill people."

"We have a system that works for us. I told you what it was. I'm not happy with you right now," he muttered.

Her head jerked. "That's just too bad."

"It really is," he agreed. "Now, stay here with the gun. I'll be back to deal with you later." With that, he yanked a shirt from the closet to pull over his head, slipping his feet into his boots. He walked down the damaged hallway to find Jonathan already waiting for him with the unconscious attacker over his shoulder.

Jonathan gingerly pulled out his front tooth to toss on the ground. "I'll have the other males who arrived with them pulled in for questioning."

"Put them all in one cell, and let's leave them there until tomorrow night. No food or water, and I have the cells under surveillance, so we can monitor what they say. The cameras are well hidden." Vero looked back at Lyrica, hovering in the doorway. "Be here when I return."

* * * *

Lyrica slept fitfully through the night, her arm still burning. She'd washed the blood off immediately before changing into panties and one of Vero's overlarge T-shirts. It fell to her knees.

While she didn't want to be all girly about it, wearing his shirt made her feel safe. Although he certainly hadn't seemed happy with her when he'd left.

At some point, soldiers came and removed the decapitated bodies. She heard them but didn't go out to watch. Instead, she lay in the bed with a gun next to her on the bedside table.

She'd never shot anybody before, and in fact had never fired one of the special green guns that fired lasers that turned into bullets upon hitting immortal flesh. She'd seen them in action, but she'd never thought she'd shoot one. She couldn't believe how cold Vero had been. Yes, he told her to stay in the room, but she thought she could help. There had to be some sort of judicial system in the Kurjan nation. They couldn't just go around killing people.

Just before dawn, the door opened and Vero walked in. She was cuddled under the covers, and she sat up, turning on the light. Blood was splattered all over the faded jeans and probably on the black shirt.

He looked at her and turned to stride into the bathroom, shutting the door. A few minutes later, the shower came on.

She shivered in the cold and ducked back down in the bed, her head feeling thick. She took several deep breaths, then began one of the breathing exercises she had learned to manage her anxiety.

All too soon, he walked out of the bathroom with a towel around his hips, his hair wet and curly around his head. Fresh bruises covered the roped muscle in his body.

Her mouth watered, but she didn't say anything.

He went to the dresser across the room and pulled out another pair of black boxers to don before tossing the towel into the bathroom.

She didn't protest, although the heavy cotton probably landed on the floor and wouldn't dry properly. "Did you kill him?"

He didn't answer her and instead walked around to the other side of the bed, lifted the covers, and settled his bulk underneath. She immediately began to roll toward him as his weight indented the mattress. "I asked you a question."

He turned on his side, facing her, his eyes a midnight blue. "I heard you."

"So answer me," she said, also turning on her side to face him, feeling uncertain and a little lost.

"I think that we should keep our relationship on a personal level."

She blinked as anger coursed through her. "Don't give me any of that 'Don't ask me about my business' Godfather bullshit," she snapped.

"Godfather bullshit?" he asked, one of his eyebrows rising.

She huffed out a breath. "You haven't seen *The Godfather*?"

"No," he murmured, "but I like the 'Don't ask me about my business,' part of it."

She shook her head. "There has to be trust between us if we're going to fulfill this contract."

"There's trust," he said easily, "but not enough of it. If I tell you to stay out of a fight, next time you do it." His voice remained level and his gaze sure. "Tell me you understand me."

She looked at him, but no words came out. "Maybe this was a bad idea," she finally said.

He shrugged. "You signed the contract. We have three months."

"And if I don't fulfill it?" she asked, fury competing with the desire running through her blood.

"You'll fulfill it," he said. "We're dating for three months. That can mean whatever you want it to mean, except we will stay in this room."

An unreasonable fury slammed through her, and she punched him in the shoulder. Her knuckles instantly protested.

He grabbed her wrist and drew her hand up to his eyes. "Did you just fracture your hand?"

"No. I may have bruised my knuckles," she muttered. "I should've hit you on your head, but I'd probably break my whole arm."

"Probably," he agreed. "I didn't think we'd have to add a no-hitting clause into the contract. I'd rather you didn't damage any of your bones."

Her ears rang. She was so angry, partly at herself. She gulped, trying to ignore his fingers around her wrist, as he absently rubbed his thumb across her palm. He was going to drive her crazy. "When you got in the fight earlier and you were cut, your blood burned my arm."

He nodded. "It is known that Kurjan blood burns other species unless you're a mate. Sometimes it doesn't burn intended mates, but sometimes it does. We don't know why." He released her. "Go to sleep, Lyrica. We only have a couple of hours until dawn, and I want to meet with Fizzlewick about the attackers. Also to see if he has anything more for me about the two female victims."

Vero's presence was warming the entire bed and her eyelids became heavy.

The image of him fighting to the death, just wearing his boxers, seared into her brain. He'd been coldly methodical and brutally powerful. She knew the immortals were stronger and faster than humans, but she'd lived with them for months and had seen fights and a deadly battle. Nobody moved as fast as he had. Tingles exploded along her skin, the purely feminine kind, and her mind tried to shut down the sensation. "Vero, I want to know if you killed that guy."

He opened his eyelids again. "I don't think it's any of your business. It has nothing to do with your job here or with our relationship."

She didn't care. "Don't make me punch you again."

"Go to sleep, Lyrica."

"No," she said, pushing his chest with both hands. "Did you kill him?"

His sigh moved them both. "No. He's still alive because he hasn't given me answers. In addition, I've had all the males who arrived at the same time as him brought in for questioning, and I'll release them after a quick discussion. Now. Go. To. Sleep."

"Stop telling me what to do," she snapped.

"Fine," he said, rolling on top of her and then rolling back over, securing her on top of him. Hard. Muscled. Male. Aroused. "You did give consent."

Chapter Twenty-One

Lyrica's body melted atop Vero's rock-hard form, unable to do anything else. Hard and soft. Male and female. Hunted and captured. No give lay in his cut muscles, and his power thrummed around them. Surprising black shards tore through the deep blue of his eyes.

She gasped, her shoulders jolting and her elbows sliding down his shoulders to the soft mattress, bringing her face closer to his. Hope had told her about the tertiary eye colors found in vampires and demons. It made sense that Kurjans had the same attribute. "What are you doing?" she whispered.

"Trying to get you to stop talking." His breath smelled minty, mixed with bourbon?

Her knees naturally fell to the sides of his hips, and they both groaned when her core met his. Only his cotton boxers and her satin panties separated them. He pulsed against her sex, and liquid heat rushed to her core. Her nipples hardened against his bare chest, the light T-shirt a laughable barrier between them. A raw craving, more intense than she'd ever felt, electrified her nerve endings.

All of them.

A soft dawn light filtered through the blinds, sliding against his chiseled features. His rough, shadowed jaw, his dark, unruly hair, and his thick, long eyelashes that framed those immortal eyes. The black had almost overcome the blue, leaving only a bright indigo rim around the fathomless darkness.

This was no man. Not even close. She could see into his depths. See him. He might be smarter and stronger than any human, but his predatory nature had fused with that intelligence, creating a cunning animal he barely managed to mask.

The thought occurred to her that he was reading her as deeply as she was reading him. Vulnerability had her levering up on her elbows to keep a modicum of control. "What do you see?" she murmured.

"You." His intense gaze poured into her, and she could almost feel him stripping away her defenses with a mere thought. A barely tamed storm hinted in his tone, and she knew on a basic, instinctive level what that sound meant.

He wanted her. Now.

A rapid pulse throbbed at the base of her throat and ticked down her body to her clit. "I see you too." And she did. In this moment, finally, she could see the wounds from betrayal he held deep. Of a life spent being harmed and of his decision to ally with his biological brother. To give loyalty to someone he didn't know but with whom he shared blood.

"You can see all of me," he said softly, his hands spreading across her upper back and sliding down to the base of her spine.

"We're temporary," she breathed, belatedly realizing her too-feminine need to heal him. To somehow provide a safe haven for him—one he didn't want.

He caressed back up to her shoulders, his hands heavy and sure. "I'm well aware that we only have three months," he murmured, his voice husky, a deep rumble that sank into her flesh and made her heart hitch. "I think you were correct."

She tried to follow his train of thought, and instead gave in and tunneled her fingers through his thick and surprisingly silky hair. "Correct about what?"

"Consent. Between us, it only needs to be given once." Without seeming to move, he captured her mouth.

There was no hesitation, no gentleness—just raw hunger and need, a collision of sensations that set her senses ablaze. He kissed her like he needed her, like she was the only thing tethering him to this world.

She closed her eyes and let herself fall into the storm.

Using his elbow as a fulcrum, he rolled them over, covering her completely. She kept a grip on his hair, holding tight, pure instinct trying to anchor them both.

The kiss deepened, and his body pressed hers into the mattress, his form hot and so alive she moaned at the force of it. Of him.

He broke the kiss to let her draw in a shaky breath, his mouth trailing down her jaw, over the sensitive skin of her neck, to her fragile collarbone. His hot, wicked tongue left a trail of fire as he explored her. The nick of a fang in the delicate skin where her neck met her shoulder had her arching up against him in reaction.

His tongue flattened over the small wound, and the masculine hum of satisfaction that resonated from his chest stole her breath. Both from warning and from need.

He'd taken her blood. The primal thought uncoiled live wires through her abdomen.

His head lifted, the look in his eyes feral. Dark and full of a possessive hunger. "Lyrica." The three syllables rolled around in a guttural sound. "While we're together, it's absolute. Complete."

What did that mean? She couldn't catch a thought. But if he was asking for exclusivity, she agreed. "I'm scared." The words shocked her. The honesty of them—she didn't mean to give him that much.

"I won't hurt you." The barest flicker of sadness cut into his eyes and quickly disappeared. "I'll protect you with my life."

She didn't think he'd hurt her. Never had. It was her heart that posed the biggest risk. For all his strength and natural, instinctive dominance, he was a soldier who never let anybody in. But he'd shown her, or perhaps she'd just been lucky enough to catch him in a rare, unguarded moment, a glimpse of the hurt he carried. The deep, ragged scars of trust and betrayal that formed him.

"I won't hurt you, either." She gave him the words he didn't seek, her chest aching as the fierce need to protect her heart warred with the equally strong need to comfort him. Before she could make sense of the whirlwind of emotions, his hand tangled in her hair and his lips descended on hers in a desperate, soul-stealing kiss.

She couldn't fight her own need. The last of her resistance crumbled, and she kissed him back, lost in the tempest of his touch, in the wild, passionate chaos that sprang from a hidden part of him.

Still kissing her, he shifted his weight to the side and off her, reaching for the hem of her shirt. She released his hair and assisted him, ducking her head for him to pull the shirt free. Even then, he was careful not to harm her.

"I won't break," she said, reaching for him.

"You're fragile. Human." He levered over her again, his heated mouth starting at her ear and wandering down to her breasts. Very heated. Did immortals have hotter mouths? Temps?

The curious thought spiraled away as his lips moved over her nipples with a mixture of demand and flaming hot desperation, his hands sliding down her arms and back up as if mapping her with each touch. His overwhelming need was palpable, a storm she couldn't escape.

Didn't want to escape.

Instead, she splayed her hands over the hard ridges of muscle flexing in his chest. Gyrating against him, she marveled at his upper arms and caressed down his flanks, finding more strength. He took her breath away.

His mouth was on her breasts, one hand twisted in her hair, the other caressing down her body, shifting again so he could touch her.

She nearly came off the bed.

His chuckle made her still. Had she ever even heard him laugh? The sound warmed her, filling her throughout. She should panic at that.

But his tongue lashed her nipple just as he slipped his fingers inside her panties, finding her no doubt wet.

His pleased rumble slid right into her heart.

Then he levered down, kissing between her breasts, his heated mouth claiming her sternum, ribs, and then hip bones.

She had a moment of vulnerability. She had more curves than many of the women in the nation. A former boyfriend had called her plush. Jerk.

Vero snapped her panties at the sides, and she forgot all about curves.

Then his mouth was on her clit. He sucked the delicate nub into his inferno of a mouth and she shot instantly into a tumultuous orgasm that had her crying out his name.

She smashed her hand against her mouth. The walls in the lodge were not that thick.

Coming down, she gasped for air.

He went at her then, his hands splaying her thighs apart and his rough tongue lashing her. "I love this," he rumbled against her, sending vibrations up to her breasts.

"Me too," she groaned, trying to chuckle. She wanted to keep this light, but the way he made her feel protected and cherished, so desperately wanted, threatened to overwhelm her. He made her feel alive. For a heartbeat, she craved a life she'd never needed.

His teeth scraped her thigh and she forgot about the world. "You're perfect," he whispered, not letting her think. He went at her with fingers, teeth, and that wicked tongue, forcing her back up again.

And then again.

After the third orgasm, she tugged on his hair. An emptiness inside her hollowed her out, even though her nerves were on freaking fire. "Vero."

He moved up her, taking his time with her breasts. She dug her nails into his flanks and then his butt, shoving the offensive boxers down his legs. There should be nothing separating them. He obliged her by kicking them the rest of the way off.

Then he continued all the way up her and kissed her mouth again, going deep. His cock pulsed at her sex and she widened her legs, wanting all of him.

He leaned up, his eyes a pure black now. "You're perfect."

She breathed in quick, taking the hit to the heart. It smacked her then, how easily he could break her. How dangerous it was to let him in. To know him. To let him know her. But she couldn't stop. Not now. Maybe not ever.

His weight settled over her, pressing her into the mattress again. She wrapped her legs around his waist and he growled, just like any dangerous predator.

The sound drove her desire even hotter. Somehow.

He pressed inside her and she arched against him, a flush heating her from her tingling ears on down to where they met. He was big. Huge. She softened and accepted him, her body moving with true instinct as if recognizing him. He went slow, carefully, his mouth taking hers again and making her head spin.

Pain rumbled through her at his invasion and she cupped his shadowed jaw, pulling her mouth free. "Are you sure we'll fit?" Maybe it wasn't possible. His blood had burned her. She wasn't his mate.

"I'm sure." He nipped her lip, and even that pain felt erotic.

More wetness spilled from her, and he moved inside her another inch.

His gaze intense, he tangled one hand in her hair and tugged her head back, sending a slight nick of pain along her skin.

More wetness and he made it another inch.

His eyes gleamed with a knowledge that made her lungs stutter. He reached down and caressed one of her nipples. Pleasure swamped her and she leaned into his touch. Then he twisted with just enough of a bite to catch her breath in her throat.

More wetness.

His nostrils flared.

That dangerous hand caressed deceptively down her side and around to her butt, lifting her an inch off the bed. His head dropped and he kissed her hard, taking over, pulling her into a wild storm as he shoved all the way inside her. She cried out into his mouth, arching against him, pleasure and pain filling her until she couldn't tell them apart.

Then he was moving. Powering inside her, overwhelming her. Giving no quarter. Accepting nothing but all of her.

What had she done?

A desperate rush of electricity arced through her as he forced her up, hammering into her so hard she could only grab his biceps and hold on. Shutting her eyes, she gave herself over to him, watching wild flashes of light behind her eyelids. His fangs sliced into her shoulder, and his entire body heated to an impossible temperature against her. His hand burned hot against her butt.

The world silenced in one perfect moment, then she exploded into an orgasm so powerful she dug her nails into his arms, tethering herself to him. The waves pummeled her and she rode them out, gasping with each wild crest and feeling his release as his body jerked against hers.

Panting, she came down, noting the rhythm of his heartbeat against hers. In perfect tune.

She relaxed her fingers and rubbed along his ribs, her body going lax. Satisfied. Exhausted. She blinked her eyes open and mumbled his name.

He kissed her nose and tightened his hold on her hair. Desire flared through her again, and she shook her head against the pillow. "There's no way."

His chuckle this time was filled with promise. "Wanna bet?"

Chapter Twenty-Two

An hour after leaving Lyrica sleeping peacefully in what he now considered their bed, Vero leaned against the wall in the medical building, banishing thoughts about her so he could do his job. He made a mental note to expand the facility as soon as possible. He had positioned himself near the door. "You still have the second victim in here?"

Dr. Fizzlewick nodded. "Yeah. I've been taking more samples of the ink in the wound to send to a colleague, but I think it's just regular ink."

Vero's eyebrows rose. "What colleague?"

Fizzlewick rubbed his square jaw. "Human one. I made friends during my time away. They don't know anything about our world, so don't worry."

Fair enough. Forcing himself to look at the dead female on the slab, covered by a white sheet, Vero pushed down anger. "Your plan with her now?"

"I'll keep her frozen as we try to identify her. We can send Tekii, the first victim, to a remote location in Alaska to be found. I can make it appear as if she was in a car crash and then froze. There's no need for her family to know of her brutal death," Fizzlewick said.

Vero exhaled slowly. "What about the circle with slashes?"

"I'll remove the skin and make it appear as damage from the crash. We'll leave Tekii's identification right next to her so her family can be notified. In her personal effects, I found a wallet she must've been carrying when the former regime kidnapped her." Dr. Fizzlewick pushed his new spectacles up his nose. As a Kurjan, he had perfect eyesight, but he'd worn the gold-rimmed glasses since he'd arrived in the territory. One of the younger soldiers had asked him why he wore the glasses, and Fizzlewick had smiled, noting he liked looking like a doctor. Since he was their doctor, Vero figured he already looked like one.

Jonathan shook his head. "I don't understand the significance of the circle and slashes."

"Neither do I." The doctor gently grasped the female's shoulder and partially turned her to show the side of her neck. A rough outline of a circle with three slashes through it had been cut into her flesh.

Fury glowed in Jonathan's eyes. The soldier had quickly become Vero's second-in-command, and they both trusted the guards left on Lyrica. "That's so wrong."

Vero couldn't agree more. A Kurjan chasing down human females to attack was like an angry grizzly bear destroying a butterfly. "We need to identify her. Now."

"Agreed." The doctor reached for a stack of photographs placed neatly on the counter. "Here are some pictures of her face as well as the symbol cut into her flesh. She wasn't mated, obviously, and she's not one of the newest rescued females, so I'm at a loss."

"As am I." Vero accepted the stack. "I'll have soldiers go cabin to cabin throughout the entire territory to find answers, even as we're investigating the bombing and most recent attack."

Jonathan scrubbed both hands down his face. "She's human, Vero."

"I know." It was unthinkable a human just wandered into camp. "Our computers should be updated by now, and I'll conduct searches for missing females in the human world." That did beg the question—how did she end up in the middle of nowhere? "I'll also go talk to Silas. I've kept him waiting and worrying long enough." Vero's stomach ached. The thought that the old soldier had brought in the human cracked something inside him. But if it wasn't Silas, then how did she arrive in the territory? The nearest town was hours away—by helicopter.

He had rotating guards around the entire property, so anybody coming in on snowmobile or UTV would've left traces.

Fizzlewick tugged on his new white lab coat. He'd ordered it the previous week, saying he wanted to appear more like the Queen of the Realm, considering the world believed her to be the best and most famous doctor. "There's something else."

"Of course there is," Vero sighed.

Fizzlewick turned and strode on new white tennis shoes—also a trademark of the queen—toward the two bodies in the rear of the building, both tossed sideways over the one remaining bed. "The attackers you killed from last night." Their legs and headless torsos hung down on either side of the bed, covered by a sheet. He pulled the sheet down to reveal their bare chests.

"Shit," Jonathan breathed.

Vero's chin went up. Awareness and irritation clocked through him. The circle with three slashes through it adorned both corpses over their hearts. Deliberate brandings. "They didn't heal those, so they must've wanted them to stay."

"What does that symbol stand for?" Jonathan snarled.

"I have enough of a reach to conduct an internet search," Vero said. He'd have to delegate that job, and he hated delegating. In fact, it had been too long since he'd worked in the lab. They needed to make the Sunshine Cure permanent so his people didn't require injections every month. As he turned and gazed at the victim, frustration heated his skin. His most important duty right now was running the entire nation, but the lab called to him.

Fizzlewick tossed the sheet back over the dead attackers, not nearly as gentle as he'd been with the female. "Burn the bodies?"

"Affirmative," Vero said. "Go forward with your plan for Tekii and the Alaska car crash. For now, keep this female on ice. In case we find her family. Humans like to bury their dead."

"So do we," Jonathan noted.

Vero nodded. "I've heard that demons and vampires burn their dead and then bury the ashes. Seems redundant to me."

"Some folks like their ashes scattered. I'd like to be scattered over a mountain in Alaska," Jonathan said thoughtfully.

Vero moved toward the door. "I want to interrogate Silas."

Jonathan followed him out into a brutal wind. "Who's been guarding him?"

"Lukas. The kid is a genius with technology and helped me to hide the cameras." Plus, keeping the kid busy kept him away from Genevieve. All Vero needed was two kids to get mated before they even knew themselves, much less each other. "We need to get everything settled before Paxton returns."

Jonathan coughed. "Are you sure the king is safe in Realm territory? I know Paxton grew up with them, but…"

Vero rolled his neck. "If anything happens to Paxton, I'll blow up the Realm. I sent that message to King Kayrs earlier today." He could be a devious son of a bitch if needed. "I also hinted that I can get to Hope in a dreamworld." Which had pissed off Dage Kayrs to no end. Even so, it was imperative they understood each other. Vero paused at seeing a pale Maeve standing off to the side, obviously waiting for them. "Hi, Maeve." He'd met the female at the cocktail party.

She gave a quick curtsy. "Prince."

Jonathon nodded at her. "Miss. Vero, I'll go give some pictures of the latest victim to Lyrica—after I fetch more coffee." He headed toward the lodge and disappeared inside.

Vero stared at the female and squared his shoulders. "What can I do for you?"

Huddled in a green wool jacket that brought out the stunning color of her eyes, Maeve clutched her mitten-covered hands together. "Ya took Ralstad last night, and he hasn't come back. That's not like him, it isn't. Beggin' yer pardon if I'm bein' too bold, but...where might he be?" Her brogue came out strong in the crisp morning air, her breath leaving a small puffy cloud.

"Let's go to the main lodge and discuss it." Vero motioned for Maeve to precede him. His skin felt stretched too tight, and his body ached. Oddly. Even his hands hurt. If he had more time, he'd discuss the matter with the doctor.

Maeve hovered hesitantly at Vero's side, the harsh wind forcing tendrils of her red hair free of her braid. "I dinna mean to bother you."

"You're not." Vero gestured her ahead of him. "Let's go talk where it's warm."

She paled and turned, her head down as she began following the path.

Vero followed her, noting the sounds of construction all around them. They had to erase any signs of weakness before the Cyst soldiers arrived. Time was working against him. Plus, he wanted enough cabins built to house at least three hundred families. All unmated males currently occupied several barracks, but he wanted to build them all their own houses. The territory needed to feel like a home so Paxton could foster loyalty and a sense of safety the Kurjan nation hadn't felt in centuries.

They reached the main lodge, and Vero paused to admire the speedy craftsmanship.

Maeve turned away from the door. "There's no need to spend yer valuable time with me, Prince. I'm worried for Ralstad and just want to know he's all right."

"He's fine, Maeve. I need to ask him a few questions, then I'll send him home to you." Vero didn't want to force the female inside if she didn't want to go. He pulled a picture of the newest human victim from his pocket. "Do you recognize this female?"

Maeve ducked her head and studied the picture carefully. "I'm sorry. I do not know her."

He slipped the picture back into his pocket and drew out the one of the circle-and-slash symbol. "What about this symbol?"

Her expression remained open and curious. "No, I've never seen that before. What is it, then?"

"I don't know." The wind whipped up, and he pivoted, placing his body between the wind and the female. "Does Ralstad have anything like this on his body?"

Her eyebrows rose, and she glanced up at him. "Of course not. He heals every injury he gets during battle. Ralstad would never allow a mark to stay on his body, he wouldn't."

Vero couldn't discern any falsehood. Maeve seemed reluctant to enter the lodge, so he remained in place. "Three of the males who arrived with you attacked me last night." Surprise altered her facial expression, and she took a step back from him. "I have Geoff in custody. The other two were named Shelton and Rogerie. How well did you know them?"

"*Did* know them?" she whispered, her nose turning red from the cold.

"Yes. Those two are dead." Vero didn't know how to soften the truth so he didn't try. "Anybody who attacks us dies." A warning for the entire camp. Plus, Lyrica could've been killed.

Maeve gulped. "Over the last two decades, we've had members come and go from our clan. There are ten couples who've been together for centuries." She pushed a wayward curl off her face. "We currently have five unmated members. Geoff, Shelton, and Rogerie arrived together about six months ago."

"Just the three of them?"

"Aye. In fact, it had been Geoff's idea for us to rejoin the Kurjan nation." Interesting. "What about the other two unmated males?"

She squinted her eyes as if trying to remember. "They arrived separately in different seasons over the last few decades."

"Would you like to come inside for sparkling water? We just replenished the kitchen." If Lyrica saw Maeve inside, maybe she wouldn't figure out he already drank three of the stockpiled crates.

"No. My worry was for my mate."

Vero tried to read her expression and saw only concern. "Ralstad is fine. I need to interview him about these men, then I'll let him know you asked about him."

"No." She held up both green mittens. "Don't tell him I'm worried."

Vero frowned and studied the female. "Why not?"

She backed away. "Ralstad is very, ah, protective? Please don't tell him I sought you out."

Perhaps Lyrica had a point about Maeve and Ralstad. "All right, but I do want you to meet with Lyrica sometime this afternoon." He'd kept her up all morning, so hopefully she was managing to catch up on sleep. "That's nonnegotiable."

"Of course, Prince." Maeve curtsied and hurried away toward a snowmobile waiting on the side of the main trail. She and Ralstad had requisitioned one since they lived on the outskirts of the property.

He watched her go. Hopefully Lyrica would know how to help her.

His chest feeling hot, he opened the lodge door, noting the coolness of the doorknob on his aching palm. What was wrong with him? He looked down at his hand and stilled. Shaking his head, he willed his eyes to clear. He had to be seeing things. There, on his right palm, was a clear marking of the letter *C* with barbed vines all around it.

The entire world tunneled in loudly, abusing his eardrums and narrowing his eyesight. He was a Kurjan. Full blooded. What was on his hand?

A fucking demon mark?

Impossible.

Another thought had him nearly swaying and then turning away from the lodge right now. If that was a mating mark, had he transferred it to Lyrica that morning?

Was he mated?

Chapter Twenty-Three

Lyrica felt...off this morning. Sure, she'd been fighting a cold all week, but today her head seemed cloudy and her body tender. The previous night with Vero would've made anybody sore. Could five orgasms count as multiple, or was there a special designation after four? Had anybody not having sex with a Kurjan ever asked that question?

Her muscles ached—some she hadn't realized she had. She shifted on her desk chair and winced as her butt cheek protested. Had he bruised her the night before? Not that the incredible sex hadn't been worth a couple of bruises, because it definitely had. The satellite phone always on her desk trilled, and she picked it up. "Hello?" She'd been ordered to answer it like any home phone, just in case. In case of what, she had no clue.

"Lyrica? Hey."

She sat back in her chair. "Hi, Hunter. How's your head?" The guy had always been nice to her, but she understood the Kurjans' irritation with him. Or downright anger, really.

"My head and neck are connected again." His voice seemed more gravelly than before, and it had been fairly deep already. "I've called Vero's sat phone three times. Is he around?"

She angled her head to see down the hallway. "Haven't seen him, but he's been busy with the attacks and two murders."

Silence ticked across the line for a heartbeat. "What two murders, and did you say attacks, as in plural?" His voice dropped impossibly low.

She faltered. Hunter no longer worked inside the Kurjan nation. She should probably keep the news private. "This is awkward."

"Because Vero has made it so," Hunter growled. "He's still my best friend. Since I've been stuck stationary for a few days, I've thought of a new concoction to try with the Sunshine injections. You know we'd both rather be in a lab than on a battlefield, right?"

She shifted her weight and winced at the quick flare of pain. "No. I didn't know that." Vero had methodically and easily subdued and killed the surprise attacker the night before. Afterward, he'd supposedly tortured a male for information and still planned to kill him. Of course, then he'd slid into bed and rocked her world, leaving her deliciously sore and uncomfortably confused. "I can't see Vero in a lab coat." Or could she? Just how much of himself had he changed to survive as a Kurjan in a lifetime of war?

Or had Jonathan been correct? Was Vero naturally a warrior?

"What's going on there, Lyrica?" Hunter asked.

She bit her lip. Surely Vero had told Paxton everything. Or had he? Was he keeping Paxton safely in the dark?

Jonathan appeared in her doorway.

"I'm so sorry. I have to go." She ended the call. "Hi, Jonathan." Lyrica lifted her cooled tea and took a sip. She'd wanted a sparkling water, but the pantry was once again empty. Who kept taking all the bottles?

"Hi." Jonathan reached into his back pocket and drew out a photographs to nudge toward her. "Vero would like for you to email these to Paxton, who can share them with the Realm experts. He's hoping the Realm computer folks can track down the identity of the second victim as well as the origin of the circle design. We're still updating our computers, and theirs are supposed to be exceptional."

Lyrica studied the pictures, her heart hurting for the unidentified victim. Sliding the picture of the victim aside, she lifted the one showing the circle symbol. Perhaps her Internet connection had been updated by now. Turning, she quickly typed in a search for the symbol, and then shook her head. The system worked perfectly. "There's nothing exactly like this, but I'll send the information to the Realm and then try a few different searches."

Jonathan nodded. "Just do what you can. I'll see you later." The hulking Kurjan disappeared from view.

Lyrica began another search for missing women, entering the victim's description. How had Lyrica managed without the internet? She'd discover the identity of the second victim, then she'd contact her friends who'd been liberated from the Kurjans to make sure their return to real life was going smoothly. She missed all of them but was so thankful they'd reached freedom.

Man, her body felt weird. Was it normal to feel like this after sex with an immortal? Shaking her head, she began another search about marketing opportunities for the Kurjan knitting online store. Even if she only stayed for three more months, she'd make a difference and help the mated females gain some independence.

A store was a good way to start.

She shifted her weight and winced as pain spread across her buttock. She didn't remember Vero spanking her, so he hadn't. Then why did her rear end hurt so much?

* * * *

Vero escorted the Kurjan males outside and set them free from the cell. Ralstad and his buddies had confirmed what Maeve had said, and he couldn't find a real connection between any of the newcomers and the attackers other than their newfound and rather short alliance.

His hand still aching, Vero stormed into the medical facility and bypassed two soldiers carrying out the headless bodies.

Dr. Fizzlewick looked up from his seat at a small desk that had been placed to the side of the room. Morning sunlight streamed through the one window behind him. "Those two will be burned and their ashes scattered across the mountains." He pulled his spectacles off to tap on a series of file folders. "You're back already?"

"Yes," Vero said grimly.

Fizzlewick nodded. "Soldiers just removed Tekii's body to fly to Alaska to arrange the fake car accident."

Dark lines dug grooves near the sides of his eyes. The male probably hadn't slept in too long.

"Thank you. I believe the internet is now up and working. So hopefully we can identify her." Vero's palm ached like a raw wound and yet felt slightly cooler, as if the brand was fading. He refused to look at it. "I know you have what few medical records we brought with us to this new location, and I'm hoping I can go through those."

"Why?" Fizzlewick asked.

Vero studied him, his gut churning. "Because I wish to."

Fizzlewick reached down for a small crate. "This is all we have. I'm expecting all of the other medical records from storage to arrive with more computer banks later today."

"Later today?" Vero rocked back on his heels.

"Yes, later today."

Vero rubbed his jaw, wondering when the last time was that he'd shaved. His whiskers scratched his still-aching palm. "I assume you read through those. Have you discovered any records of Paxton's birth or any details about the cross-breeding experiments between Kurjans and demonesses?"

Fizzlewick sat back and straightened his white lab coat. The doctor seemed inordinately proud of that smock. It was a good thing the Queen of the Realm didn't wear a bikini to work every day. "No. I was exiled from the nation when the experiments took place. You'll need to speak with the scientists involved."

"There aren't any still alive." Vero leaned against the side wall, his head reeling. How could he possibly have a demon mark on his hand? It didn't make any sense. A pit slowly dropped into his gut and spread.

"Yeah, I can see that." Fizzlewick blew on the glasses and wiped them on his lab coat. "Experiments such as those would anger many people. It can't be easy for Paxton, being the king of people he doesn't even know… added to the fact that he's half-demon. It's nearly unthinkable. It's a good thing you're his brother and back him. The nation knows you."

Did they? Did anybody really know him? Vero cleared his throat. "I was obviously alive for the tweaks and perfections of the Sunshine Cure, and we're still working to make it permanent," he said slowly. "But I had no knowledge of any experiments in crossbreeding between the Kurjans and demonesses."

"That's not a surprise."

"I know." Vero had top clearance for the nation, and he was familiar with all medical records. He had never seen a hint about the experiments, and he had little hope that more info would be coming. Frustration crawled like ants beneath his skin.

Fizzlewick nudged the crate of file folders toward him. "I've looked through everything. There are some details about the Sunshine Cure but nothing about crossbreeding with demons. To be honest, Vero, I don't know how often the earlier scientists and doctors recorded their experiments.

Secrets are rare, and usually rumors abound. I feel like we would've heard something long before you found your father's journal where he wrote about secretly fathering Paxton."

That's right. Vero had to get his hands on that journal. Hopefully, Paxton still had it. Vero studied the ancient healer. "Why were you excommunicated?"

Fizzlewick rolled his eyes. "It was about a female—as all good spats are. Several leaders ago, your, I don't know, great-great-great-great-uncle Shastin and I fell in love with the same female. She chose him, I left."

"It's that simple?"

Fizzlewick reached for a blue ballpoint pen to tap on the paper. "Yes, it was that simple. Most wars are, my young friend."

Maybe, maybe not. Vero and Paxton's biological father, Talt, had kept a journal detailing his experiments in breeding with demonesses. He succeeded with Paxton's mother, but his attempts with others had failed—or had they? "Do you know anything about other crossbreeding experiments?"

Fizzlewick dropped the pen. "No. Why would I know anything about those? I haven't dealt with the Kurjan nation in far too long. And for the record, I was quite happy living in my small village on a quite lovely island off Alaska."

"Glad to hear that," Vero said dryly. "Why did you return?"

Fizzlewick tapped the pile of paper in front of him into a semblance of order. "Maybe I became lonely for my people and more than a bit curious when word came through that the new Kurjan leader was half-demon. I had to see for myself."

Vero shook his head. "I appreciate that you've been helpful, but there has to be more to it than that."

"Not after you've lived three thousand years," Fizzlewick countered. "Sometimes curiosity is a good thing. When you go without it for too long, well, your mind starts to wander. I'm glad to be here, and I'm sad many of my colleagues are long gone."

It did appear that all the scientists who had worked on the genetics program had died afterward. Vero had no doubt they'd been killed to keep the secret. Exactly the kind of thing his father and uncles would've done.

Vero shoved his hands in his jeans pockets to keep from looking at the brand. "Do you suppose there are any other experiments walking the earth today? I mean, besides Paxton?"

Fizzlewick snorted. "Of course not. Seriously, crossbreeding a Kurjan and a demoness had probably a one in a quintillion chance of working. I would love to get my hands on those records, if there are any, which I somewhat doubt."

So did Vero. He'd learned young that if somebody wanted to keep a secret, they certainly didn't write anything down. It was shocking, frankly, that Talt had left the information about Paxton being part Kurjan in his journal. But perhaps he'd wanted the word to get out as a way to take down the demon nation and even the Realm by using Pax. Things hadn't quite worked out that way.

"Why all the questions?" Fizzlewick asked, his purple eyes narrowing with intelligence.

Vero kept his curious mask in place. "I want to know more about my brother."

Fizzlewick replaced his now clean glasses on his nose. "I understand. I've asked the king if I could draw his blood and conduct research, and he has denied me. None too politely."

Vero couldn't blame Pax. "I'd like to spend some time in the lab as soon as the equipment arrives, to study the most recent blood draws. It's time to make that Sunshine Cure permanent, like we thought it was at first."

"Of course," Fizzlewick said evenly.

Vero forced a smile. It was too bad he couldn't trust Hunter any longer. He needed his ex-friend's help to figure out why there was a fucking demon mating mark on Vero's hand. He needed to genetically test himself without anybody else knowing. This had to be a mistake. Or a manipulation of his genes just to screw with him. His heredity and connection to the Kurjan nation was the only thing keeping Paxton's head on his shoulders. If they were both half-demon, which just couldn't be possible, they'd be dead within hours.

Chapter Twenty-Four

After a quick lunch at her desk, Lyrica sat back from the computer, her mind spinning. How was it even remotely possible for the newest victim to have shown up in the middle of nowhere like that? She couldn't find a missing person report for Canada or Alaska with a description that fit the victim. The entire situation just didn't make any sense.

A shadow crossed her doorway and she looked up, her eyes focusing. "Vero." Her entire body flushed, head to toe, and heat filled her face until her cheeks ached.

"Hi," he said, his eyes a darker blue than usual. "How are you feeling?"

She blinked. "Um, good." This was awkward. She shifted uneasily on her chair and pain ticked through her hips. Even though they'd been together last night, she didn't feel close enough to him to explain the soreness she felt. Not that she was complaining, because she definitely was not. She would've bet that sex like that only happened in romance books. Dark ones. "I'd like to visit some of the newcomers later today. Maybe take them some sort of welcoming gift?"

"Sure. Just make sure you're guarded the entire time." He looked distracted...and dangerous. Sexy.

She swallowed. "That's fine by me. I'm not stupid, and somebody is killing women. And attacking Kurjan leaders." The recent attackers had been after Vero, which should terrify her. But he was so dangerous when he fought. Why did she like that about him so much? "Also, I'm creating a presentation for you and Paxton about businesses some of the Kurjan mates would like to create."

He frowned. "Why not just tell their mates?"

"They want some independence, Vero," she snapped. "Plus, apparently mates have been worried in the past about the Kurjan leadership and have kept their families out of sight."

He sighed. "That makes sense. I tried to stay out of sight as much as possible as well. I guess we need to be more obvious about our changes." He glanced at his watch. "We can do that if we all survive the Convexus."

She cocked her head. "You and Paxton have been so secretive about that. Is it just a summit?" That's the most she'd been able to get from either of them.

"Yes. The Dark Solstice for the entire Kurjan nation shall happen on Tuesday night, and it's the most holy of nights. The Cyst make all important decisions that night, and it only occurs every thousand years or so. We feel the change in the atmosphere as it nears. So, if there will be a treaty, or better yet, if they'll rejoin the nation, it has to be decided when the far shining star we call Leo Noctis goes dark." He shrugged. "The Cyst are the spiritual leaders, and that's our law."

No wonder everyone was freaking out. Hopefully the camp would look like it was in one piece by then. "Leo Noctis? Doesn't that mean Night Lion?"

"Yes. The star is in the constellation Leo, which looks like a lion, even to us. Humans call the star Regulus."

Fascinating. "Does the star really go dark?"

"Yes. Your people call it occultation, meaning a planet passes in front of it. In our case, Venus passes in front of Leo Noctis, making it go dark. Every one thousand years or so." He rolled his neck. "Our laws come from a time long before we knew that scientific fact."

Every one thousand years? So, it truly was now or never. "Do you think the Cyst have heard about the killings and attacks in Kurjan territory lately?"

His jaw firmed. "I'd like to say no, but it's possible. I'm hoping Paxton's arrival at the Realm will negate our internal problems here, but he still needs to return Tuesday morning."

Movement sounded and Dr. Fizzlewick stood next to Vero. "Have you found the identity of the newest victim?"

"No," Lyrica said, lifting both hands. "I don't understand it. How in the world could somebody have brought the victim into the territory without anybody knowing?"

Fizzlewick shook his head. "It's not possible. She had to have already been here and somehow we missed her."

Vero cut him a look, his gaze finally leaving Lyrica so she could breathe. "There's no way we missed her. We know everybody in this territory."

Frustration darkened the doctor's face. "We need to search for methods of transporting a victim here."

"There's a helicopter," Vero said flatly. "That's it. Somebody had to have flown her in here."

Grateful to return to a topic other than her tender personal parts, Lyrica relaxed. "You guys are immortal and have super strength as well as endurance. If you needed to do so, couldn't you physically run to the nearest town?"

"Sure," Vero said easily. "But it would still take a day or two through the mountains in this horrible weather. I don't see how a human could survive being brought here. If somebody snowmobiled or drove her in a UTV, we would've seen or heard it."

"Unless somebody in the territory worked with them," Lyrica said quietly.

Fizzlewick cleaned his glasses on his lab coat. "How did it go with Silas?"

"I'm going to speak with him right now," Vero said curtly, turning and striding away.

Fizzlewick watched him go. "Is it just me or is he in a mood?"

Lyrica coughed. Was it because of her? Did Vero regret the night they'd spent? She wasn't sure how she felt about it except confused. He'd been the one who'd shown up with a winter bouquet in an effort to court her. She should smack him for not being smoother about this. Worse yet, she wanted to charge after him and see what was wrong, to somehow ease him. She groaned and tapped her palm against her forehead. She really was losing her mind.

"Are you feeling all right?" Fizzlewick asked.

"I'm fine." She'd forgotten that he was even there. "I'll return to searching for the identity of the newest victim." Then she wanted to check on Maeve.

Fizzlewick nodded. "Good luck. For now, do you know where the sparkling water is being kept? I'd like to take a box to the medical facility."

"In the kitchen pantry. Bottom two shelves."

He placed his glasses back on his ancient face. "Those shelves are empty."

She sat back. "Seriously?" Who kept taking all the water? "I'll have more brought from the storage depot."

"Thank you." He turned on his spanking white tennis shoes and moved down the hallway.

She returned to the computer to broaden her search, having already checked Canada and Alaska. So it was time to try the rest of the United States. There were so many missing persons that it would take her a while to go through the data.

She worked in silence for an hour or so until a noise caught her attention from the gathering room. She paused to listen.

"I said no coffee." Ralstad's voice came out strong and irritated.

Lyrica jumped to her feet and crossed around her desk to enter the room. Many of the soldiers popped in throughout the day to freshen their cups at the coffee station. She looked at Ralstad with Maeve next to him. Today the woman wore a long purplish-green gown with a thick wool coat. Her nose and ears were red, so it must still be freezing outside.

"I know. I was getting the coffee for you," Maeve said, reaching for a bag of grounds on the lower shelf.

"I don't need coffee if you're not having coffee," Ralstad said, his eyes swirling a deep purple with red striations. He towered over the female.

Lyrica's hackles instantly rose. "I think if she wants coffee, she can have coffee."

Maeve jumped and Ralstad slowly turned, partially stepping in front of Maeve. "I don't think eavesdropping is part of your job," he said evenly.

Maeve slid to the side and into view. "Good morning, Lyrica. How is your day going?" she asked politely.

"It's going fine. How are you doing?" Lyrica asked pointedly.

"We went for a nice walk and are here to fetch more coffee. I hope it's all right. Our supplies are low," Maeve hastened to say.

Lyrica studied the tall soldier while speaking with Maeve. "Of course, it's all right. The supplies are for everyone. There's a large kitchen through that door if you need any other food, and we have just received fresh perishables."

"We're good," Ralstad said shortly.

Maeve sighed. "Actually, I would like to order a couple of items for our cabin."

"No problem," Lyrica said. "Do you want to come into the office?"

Ralstad took his mate's arm. "We don't need anything."

"We need a boot warmer," Maeve corrected him.

His face darkened. "We most certainly do not need a boot warmer." He looked sideways at Lyrica. "Thank you for your offer, though."

Irritation and temper warred inside Lyrica. She didn't want to cause a scene, but this was ridiculous. "Maeve, if you want a boot warmer, considering it's freezing outside, I am more than happy to get you one." She lifted her chin.

Maeve glanced at her mate, then over at Lyrica. "That would be lovely. Thank you."

Surprise filtered through Lyrica, then warning as Ralstad's expression darkened even more.

"We'll be going now. Have a nice day." He pivoted smartly on his humongous boots.

The woman turned to go with him.

"Are you sure you don't want to stay and hang out with me for a while?" Lyrica asked.

Maeve hustled along with her mate. "No thank you. I have bread to bake. Have a blessed day, Lyrica."

They bypassed the kitchen and went directly outside into the snowy day.

Lyrica shook her head. She had to get Maeve alone. This was an untenable position. She would help the woman if it was the last thing she did. Concern filling her, Lyrica eyed the coffee station and immediately began to replenish the automatic dispensers. A lot of the soldiers wandered in around lunchtime for more coffee.

The outside door opened again and she turned, hoping to see Maeve.

Instead, Genevieve and Lukas walked inside, holding hands, Genevieve giggling. They paused when they saw her and dropped their hands, guilt flushing across Genevieve's face.

Lukas looked at her directly.

"Sorry I'm late," Genevieve said. "We went for a walk down to the river. It's beautiful." Her eyes lit up and a pretty smile curved her lips.

Lukas nodded. "I'm off duty this morning, so we thought we'd take advantage of the pretty morning outside. Have you seen the sun?"

"No," Lyrica said, surprised. The sun finally made an appearance? She might have to actually go outside. The sky had been dark and cloudy for too long. "I appreciate that it's pretty outside, Genevieve, but please be on time for work."

The girl was an hour late.

Lyrica hadn't been worried because Genevieve rarely showed up on time. She wanted to slow down that romance.

Lukas's chest puffed out. "Vero ordered me to provide protection for you today, Lyrica. He mentioned that you wanted to visit some of the cabins, and he also ordered Jonathan to be with us. He's taking your protection very seriously."

Gee, that was great. Now if only the guy would talk to her.

Genevieve patted Lukas's hand. "I better get into work." Today the girl wore a pink sweater and jeans with what looked like new white snow boots. She shrugged off her matching white puffer jacket as she disappeared into Lyrica's office.

"What time do you want to go?" Lukas asked, his gaze on the now empty doorway.

Lyrica didn't feel hungry, so she figured she'd just skip dinner. It would soon be dark, and she was happy to have the escort. "Maybe in an hour?"

"All right, I'll be back," Lukas said. "Perhaps Genevieve can come with us."

Lyrica thought about it. She didn't want to encourage a romance between the teenagers, but perhaps Maeve would respond better to somebody younger like Genevieve. "Not tonight. It's really cold out there," she said.

Lukas's eyes lightened to a mellow violet. "That's true," he said. "But she always does make the night lighter and warmer."

Oh, for goodness' sake.

Chapter Twenty-Five

Vero strode down the stairs to the carved-out basement and walked to the first cell. He opened the heavy wooden door and moved inside to find Silas sitting on his cot, playing solitaire with a deck of cards.

Silas looked up, his light red eyes narrowing. "You know, I've been thinking."

"Really? How's that?" Vero asked, shutting the door behind himself.

"We don't have satellite hookup or our computer bank, but we have excellent prisoner cells. Does that tell you where our priorities lie?"

Vero studied the male he'd known since birth. "I think our priorities are exactly right. Unfortunately, we've never existed in an era without war."

"Ah. But whose fault is that?" Silas leaned back against the rough cement wall. "I mean, look at this place, Vero. We might as well have been trying to split a mountain in half with a hammer to make space for, what was it? Three cells?"

"Yes," Vero said smoothly. "We have three cells down here and yes, I remember the dynamite." He looked around the rough room. "Although the cells have come in handy. We have two out of the three occupied."

"Yeah, by your allies," Silas shot back, his eyes darkening to a deeper red.

Not a bad point, unfortunately. "Not any longer. I set most of the new Kurjans free. As for you, I am sorry about this," Vero pulled over a metal chair to sit. "At least we gave you cards."

Silas's chin lifted slightly. "You're being a dick."

"I am a dick," Vero agreed. "One with a problem. We have a human female victim in our territory with no record of how she got here."

"She must have been here when you arrived."

That was impossible. "No," Vero said. "I know everybody in this camp and we're in the middle of nowhere, Silas. The only person who has flown anywhere and returned this last week is you."

Silas crossed his arms. "You forget about the raiding party that brought those newest enhanced females into the territory."

Vero cocked his head. "I was part of the raiding party. I know exactly who returned with us. Tell me how you flew that female into the territory. Let me help you."

Silas shoved the cards away on the rough wool blanket. "Oh, because you want to help me?"

"I do," Vero said. "We go back a long ways."

"Kid, you're still in your first century," Silas snapped. "You don't know what you're doing."

There might be some truth to that statement because this didn't make any sense to Vero. "Did you kill her?"

Silas looked up at the rough cement ceiling and shook his head. "Why would I kill a human female?" He stared at Vero now, surprise and bewilderment on his face. "Seriously, why would anybody kill a human female? I mean, just why?"

The answer to that question kept Vero up at night. "Because they could? Because they're making a statement? Because they're trying to show that Paxton is weak as a leader?"

Silas glanced at the closed door. "That would make sense," he mused. "Having somebody killing human females who have no way of being in our territory right under Paxton's nose and yours as well?" He nodded. "Yeah, good point."

Irritation clocked through Vero, and the damn mark on his palm still burned. "Thanks."

"But still." Silas winced. "A human female. Why?"

"I'm hoping you can answer that." Vero leaned forward.

After living for three centuries, Silas was fit and trim and could fight, but he lacked Vero's broader upper body size and strength. The thought occurred to Vero that maybe he was broader than most Kurjans because— No, he wouldn't go there right now.

He focused intently on Silas. "I don't want to do this the hard way." He meant every word. "So just tell me what I need to know."

Silas chuckled, the sound lacking any true humor. "You don't want to do this the hard way? I'm ready for the hard way. You want to fight?"

"Not really," Vero said honestly. "I just want the truth."

Purple shot through the red in Silas's eyes. "The truth? The truth is I went to Anchorage to fetch all the equipment we need for interior surveillance and computer enhancement. The only people I spoke with were at the two stores I visited." His gaze flicked away and then back.

Vero straightened. "You just lied to me."

"Fine." Silas threw up his hands. "I went to the local diner and got an Oreo cookie milkshake. Sometimes a guy just wants a milkshake, Vero."

Vero sat back. He couldn't get any sense that Silas was lying. "Why would I give a fuck if you got a milkshake?"

Silas crossed his arms. "You have no right to know my personal business."

"I have a right to know everything I want to know," Vero growled. "Where'd you get the female?"

Silas shook his head, more sadness than anger in his eyes now. "You know as well as I do that I didn't bring that female back here. Trust your instincts."

Vero wanted to believe Silas. "My instincts aren't working for me right now," he snapped.

Silas attempted to hide a grin, then gave up. "Female problems of your own?"

Vero let out a low growl. Maybe he could use a good fight.

Silas lifted a hand. "All right. None of my business. Though, I have to tell you, I do like Lyrica. She's smart and spunky. Doesn't know what she wants in life."

Vero cocked his head. "What do you mean?"

"Figure it out yourself," Silas grumbled.

Vero didn't have time for this. "If you didn't bring that female back here, who did?"

"How should I know?" Silas shook his head. "You had to have missed her. There's no way that she just dropped here out of nowhere."

Vero scratched his chin. He really needed to shave. He was starting to look like one of those human movie stars who had just enough scruff to look dangerous. Well, one of the villains in a movie, anyway. He'd never come close to hero status. He reached into his back pocket and pulled out a folded piece of paper.

Silas watched him, alertness in his gaze.

"Do you recognize this symbol?" Vero unfolded the paper to show the symbol with the circle and three slashes.

Silas stared at it intently. "No. It's kind of a dumb symbol."

Exasperation clapped through Vero. "You've never seen anything like this? You've lived for three hundred years."

Silas looked from the paper to Vero. "No, it's a circle with three lines through it. It has no significance to me whatsoever and, frankly, I can't think of any kingdom through time, at least that I've studied, that had such a symbol. Why? What is it?" He sounded genuinely puzzled.

"I don't know. That's why I'm asking you."

Silas shoved the paper back at Vero. "I have no clue. Where did you see it?"

The sight seemed burned into his brain. "The killer cut the symbol into the two dead females, and it was branded onto a couple of the attackers who tried to take me out last night."

Silas looked at the paper and back up at Vero. "Then what the fuck are you talking to me about? Go talk to the guy in the next cell. He's one of the attackers, right?"

Yeah. The only one Vero had allowed to live. Hopefully he'd be conscious by now. Vero stood and replaced the paper. "That's my plan." He turned toward the door, his head starting to pound. All he needed was a blasted migraine to make this day perfect. He reached for the doorknob and paused, turning around. "You've been in the main Kurjan nation for quite a while. Do you have knowledge regarding the experiments conducted by our scientists?"

Silas's eyebrows rose. "No. I'm a computer guy and a pilot. Sometimes a soldier. I don't have anything to do with science." He shivered. "Seriously, some of the weird things they've done, like creating that virus to take out the vampires. I mean, who does that?"

It was a good question, really.

Silas shrugged. "Although I do appreciate the Sunshine Cure. You were a part of creating that, weren't you?"

"I've just tweaked it through the years. I wasn't the genius behind it, unfortunately." How Vero missed the hours he'd hid out in the labs during his childhood.

Silas nodded, his eyebrows lowering. "Yeah. Most of those scientists were killed by your uncle. I always figured it was a good thing I didn't want to go into the medical field."

"What about Paxton?" Vero asked. "Did you know anything of the experiments with crossbreeding demons and Kurjans?"

"God no," Silas breathed. "That's insane, as far as I'm concerned."

Just great. Vero had searched Paxton's room, and their father's journal wasn't there. It had described the details of Paxton's lineage but hadn't mentioned Vero's. Why did he have a demon brand on his hand? "Do you remember if any of the scientists or doctors who experimented with demon females lived?"

Silas eyed him. "Not a one. You don't want to dig further into your half-brother's genetics, Vero. Let people forget what he is and let him lead. Enough of us are concerned about his lineage, and only the fact that you're backing him is reassuring us. You're Kurjan through and through."

Yet he might not be. Fuck. Vero opened the door. "I'll be back later."

"How long are you keeping me here?" Silas asked. "You know I didn't do anything wrong."

Vero's gut feeling said the male was telling the truth. "I know. I'll talk to Paxton."

"Why? You're the enforcer. Maybe it's time you acted like it."

Fire lanced through Vero. "If I acted like it, you'd be bleeding on the floor right now."

The heavy door groaned as Vero stepped out of the cell, leaving Silas behind with his sharp tongue and unhelpful musings. The dim light of the hallway stretched out before him, casting long, flickering shadows against the rough stone walls. The cold air hung oppressive here, thick with the scent of damp earth and the faint metallic tang of blood that seemed to permeate everything underground. Vero rubbed his temples.

The symbol—the damn circle with three slashes—was an enigma, one he couldn't afford to ignore. It was etched not only into the bodies of the victims but into the fabric of their fragile peace. Silas's dismissive remarks about it being "dumb" didn't help. Vero couldn't shake the sense that it was more than just a symbol. It was a message. A declaration.

He reached the door to the adjacent cell and paused. His instincts gnawed at him, whispering that he wasn't prepared for what he might find inside. Taking a deep breath, he pushed the door open.

The male inside was slumped against the wall, his face battered and bruised, though his chest rose and fell in a steady rhythm. This was the lone survivor of last night's attack. Vero had personally ensured he wouldn't die before they got answers, though his condition suggested he might wish he had.

As Vero stepped in, the male's purple eyes fluttered open. They were bloodshot, his pupils dilated. He tried to shift his body but winced, groaning through gritted teeth. "Back for more?" he croaked, his voice ragged.

"Save your energy." Vero dragged the metal chair from the corner of the cell. The scraping sound echoed, setting Vero's nerves on edge. He dropped into the chair, leaning forward to rest his elbows on his knees. "I don't want to hurt you again—unless I have to."

The male let out a wheezy laugh. "That's what they all say."

Vero pulled out the paper again, unfolding it deliberately. He held it up for the prisoner to see. "Tell me about this."

The prisoner blinked, his gaze sharpening for a fraction of a second before he looked away. "Never seen it before."

Vero's patience wore thin. He leaned forward, his voice dropping to a growl. "Don't waste my time. This symbol was cut into the victims and branded onto you and your dead buddies. You expect me to believe you don't know what it means?"

The prisoner coughed, spitting blood onto the floor. "I don't expect you to believe anything. But if you're looking for answers, you're asking the wrong questions."

Vero frowned. "Then enlighten me."

The prisoner chuckled, a wet, gurgling sound. "It's not about the symbol. It's about what it represents. You think you're fighting rebels? Traitors? No. You're fighting ghosts."

Vero's hand shot out, grabbing the jerk by the front of his torn shirt and yanking him forward. "What the hell does that mean?"

The male grimaced, but defiance bloomed in his bloodshot eyes. "You're too young to remember, Prince, but not everything in your world was built to last. Old alliances crumble. Old sins come home to roost. You're digging into things better left buried."

Vero tightened his grip. "Who sent you?"

The prisoner smiled faintly, his teeth stained red. "You will never know."

The words sent a chill down Vero's spine. He shoved the male back against the wall and stood, pacing the small cell as he fought to piece the puzzle together. The symbol, the dead girls, the attack on Paxton and attack on Vero—it all felt connected, but how?

He turned back to the prisoner, who was watching him now with a mix of wariness and smug satisfaction. "Who do you work for?" Vero demanded. "The Realm? The humans? Someone else?"

The prisoner shook his head, his smile widening. "Kurjans always think it's about you. Always think the world revolves around petty Kurjan squabbles. It's bigger than that, you traitor. Much bigger."

"Why did you attack me?" Maybe the why would lead him to the who. Vero's headache turned into a full-blown migraine. He took a step closer, fists clenched. "Start talking. Now. Or I'll make you wish you hadn't survived the attempt on my life."

The prisoner's smile faded, replaced by a resigned expression. "You're out of your depth. By the time you figure it out, it'll be too late."

The words hit Vero harder than he expected. If he tortured this jackass any more right now, he'd kill him sooner rather than later. So he turned and exited the cell, slamming the door behind him. The sound reverberated down the hall, a fitting punctuation to his boiling frustration.

Outside, he leaned against the cold stone wall, trying to calm the storm inside him. Silas's words about trust and instincts rang in his ears. He couldn't shake the feeling that something—someone—was playing them all like chess pieces on a board. And the worst part? He didn't know their next move.

For now, he'd follow the trail, no matter how twisted it became. But he couldn't shake the nagging thought that the answers he sought might be worse than the questions haunting him. Taking a break, he looked down at his right hand.

At the perfect mating brand of a demon.

Chapter Twenty-Six

Darkness pressed in when Lyrica hurried outside, bundled up in her puffer jacket. The cold stung her cheeks as she hustled through the billowing snow and hopped inside the already warmed-up utility terrain vehicle waiting near the main lodge. She sighed, sinking into the heated leather seat of the UTV.

Lukas shut her door.

She smiled at Jonathan in the driver's seat. "This is definitely the way to go." Most of her activities took place between the lodge and nearby buildings, so she hadn't had much occasion in the last three weeks to venture out into the territory.

It struck her how Vero had made sure that everybody visited her in the nice, warm, safe lodge for their meetings. She shook her head to dislodge the thought, since it spun with too many distractions already and she needed to focus on the job at hand.

Her pleasantly sore body kept distracting her.

Jonathan snorted. "These things are a lot of fun. You should take one out and drive up the river for a while. You'd see beautiful wildlife. You wouldn't believe the size of the moose we have here."

The back door to the UTV swung open, and Lukas hopped inside, rocking the entire craft. He leaned forward between the two seats. "These aren't as much fun as snowmobiles. We only have about ten, but Vero assured me that many more are on the way since we've decided to settle here permanently. We have some UTVs coming too."

Lyrica had been too busy surviving her kidnapping, and then making a difference during the last few weeks by helping to free any of the women who wanted to return to their lives. She hadn't had the chance to explore.

Taking a deep breath, she glanced around at the jagged, white-capped mountains still visible through the storm arriving with dusk. Peering forward, she could barely make out the river flowing beneath crags of ice. A shiver ran down her spine. "Have your people always lived in cold areas like this? Because of your aversion to the sun?"

Jonathan flicked on the lights, pressed down on the gas pedal, and started them down what Lyrica considered the main drag of the territory. "Yes. We used to live underground quite a bit."

She wrinkled her nose. "Really? Like in tunnels?"

He chuckled. "No, more like cities beneath the earth. Pretty plush. We had one headquarters on the Oregon coast where all our windows looked out at the bottom of the sea. It was delightful—until the Realm bombed us, of course."

"Of course." Her gaze followed the distant mountains. "It must be strange to be allies with somebody you fought against your entire life." Jonathan had to be a couple of hundred years old.

"It really is," he admitted, chewing on his lip.

The oversized UTV provided plenty of space for Jonathan's large frame. Lyrica glanced up at the ceiling, noting how much taller it was than any other vehicle she'd seen. It made sense, considering the average height for a Kurjan male was six foot seven or eight. Jonathan matched the description perfectly.

Outside, several people worked to build additional stockpiles of food and weapons. "This is rather exciting." She wondered what spring would bring to such a remote territory. "I thought the Canadian government owned most of the land in the country. How did you all obtain ownership of this piece?"

Jonathan grinned. "Kurjans have been around much longer than most governments. We currently own twenty square acres, though we're only using ten. We purchased most of the land from defunct logging and railroad companies, but we already had a stake in it before that. I'm not sure where the original stake came from."

She sank back into the warm seat, her tender thighs protesting just enough to catch her breath in her throat. Her mind flashed back to the night with Vero and her chest tightened. Enough of that. She shifted to look at Lukas, who sat quietly in the back seat, his bulk taking up more than half of it. "So, you've grown up in Canada?"

"Yeah. I'm seventeen, and the Kurjans moved to Canada quite a while ago. Unfortunately, both of my parents perished in a skirmish with the demon nation when I was only five. Relatives raised me." He shrugged as if it didn't matter, though the slight downturn of his mouth said otherwise.

Her heart ached for him. "I'm sorry to hear that."

"It's a common story these days, but maybe now that we're at peace, that will change." He stared out at the snow, his voice quiet.

She hoped so. Some of her friends had chosen to stay with the nation, and she wanted them to have long, fulfilling lives.

Lukas leaned forward again. "I saw pictures of New York City. Is it really that jam-packed? I mean, are buildings right next to each other like that?"

"It is," she replied. "Some parts of New York are more rural, and they even have farms in different parts of the state, but the cities are like you see on TV. There's a lot of activity and excitement, and everything's open twenty-four hours."

His eyes lit up. "You can get a donut at two in the morning?"

"You can get anything you want at two in the morning. But yeah, donuts are a safe bet." She warmed to the subject. "And pizza."

He planted his hands on his knees. "Pizza. Yeah, we've had that a few times. I like it. Not as much as Glacier Ale, though."

"What's your favorite?" she asked, hoping to keep him talking. Building a good relationship with him would help both him and Genevieve make better decisions for their young lives.

"Oh, definitely pepperoni," he said. "Although the sausage was good too." He smacked Jonathan on the shoulder. "I ate several pizzas with Glacier Ale, and it was perfect. Much better than soda. We tried that too."

Lyrica had tried Glacier Ale several times, and the pale drink always tasted delicious. The Kurjans must have invented it back in the Stone Age and still infused it with rare cold-water herbs like juniper or even Arctic thyme. Each bottle she drank tasted a little different from the last.

The larger buildings began to fade in the darkness, and soon cottages came into view, scattered throughout the trees. Jonathan gestured toward a large two-story cabin set against what looked like a huge snow berm. "Many of our mated couples and their families have staked out homesteads."

Lyrica rubbed her cheek, immediately reminded of the whisker burn from Vero. "The homesteads look nice. This is a lot of territory, even though we're living in the middle of the mountains. Does the Canadian government ever come around?"

"No." Jonathan's purple eyes sparkled. "We pay our taxes, and we own the land outright. Every once in a while, we may have to make a threat or two—and believe me, we know how to do that—but it's rare."

"I'm glad it's rare." Lyrica swallowed the lump rising in her throat.

The makeshift trail narrowed even more, and Jonathan leaned forward as if concentrating on driving. Lyrica watched the trees whip by outside. "How fast are you going, anyway?" she asked, more curious than anything else.

"About one hundred fifty miles per hour," Jonathan said absently. "We tweaked these to suit our needs. Do you want me to go faster?"

Lyrica reached for the seat belt to cross over her chest and fasten. "Nope. We're good. Don't need to go faster." Sometimes she wondered if these guys remembered that not everybody lived forever. She glanced at Jonathan. "You told me that you're over a hundred years old, right?"

"I'm about a century and a half, give or take twenty years," he said, speeding up slightly. "I never paid much attention to that kind of thing."

"You don't celebrate birthdays?" She frowned at the thought.

He shook his head. "I think that's a human thing. Well, apparently a vampire and demon one too, but no, that's never been part of our culture. We do have festivals through the year, though. There'll be a fun winter one coming up in what? About five weeks?" He glanced back at Lukas.

"Oh yeah. I've already asked Genevieve to be my date," Lukas said happily. He rummaged near his seat. "I'm starving. Did you bring anything to eat?"

Jonathan sighed, reached into the side pocket of the UTV door, and tossed back three granola bars.

Lukas caught them and tore into one immediately. "I'm still growing," he said defensively, crumbs scattering.

Jonathan smirked. "I know." He glanced at Lyrica. "So, you and Vero, huh?" His attempt at small talk startled her.

The unexpected attention made Lyrica laugh despite herself. "I don't know."

"Yeah, that sounds like romance to me," Jonathan teased.

She turned the question back on him. "Are you seeing anybody?"

He shook his head. "Never had much luck with the ladies. Being kicked in the head and all."

She fought the urge to pat his arm. The Kurjans always seemed so restrained. "You know, a two hundred IQ is still beyond the extraordinary genius level. It's considered off the charts for humans."

Jonathan cut her a look.

She frowned. "Hey. Humans are smart."

Lukas mumbled through a mouthful of granola bar. "Isn't their average IQ around one hundred?"

"I think so," Lyrica said. "Above average is one-twenty. Einstein was about one-sixty."

"Poor Einstein," Jonathan muttered, shaking his head. "Was he kicked in the head too?"

She rolled her eyes, fighting the urge to smack her hand against her forehead. "No. He was a genius."

"Oh yeah, for humans." Jonathan took another sharp turn. "I believe Ralstad and Maeve claimed one of these cabins farther into the trees." He glanced around. "I think I'm going the right way."

Lukas slapped him on the arm. "It's up that way," he mumbled.

Jonathan cocked his head. "I see it." He slowed the vehicle as the trail curved into a dense grove of snow-laden trees.

Lyrica squinted through the storm, struggling to make out the faint outline of a cabin ahead. It didn't seem fair that Kurjans had superior eyesight. "Out of curiosity," she began, "if a human mates a Kurjan, do they get better eyesight?"

"I don't think so," Jonathan said, his tone thoughtful. "They get immortality and sometimes their mate's gifts. If you have a psychic Kurjan, the mate might become psychic, too. But I think that takes centuries to evolve. I don't know about eyesight, though."

"Huh." She shifted in her seat. It would be nice to have bionic vision—if that was even a thing.

Lukas slowly unwrapped another granola bar. "Mates also develop the ability to communicate telepathically."

"Really?" She turned to him. "I've never heard that." Truthfully, she hadn't been let in on many of the Kurjan secrets. The more she thought about it, the more unsettled she felt. How much about Vero did she not know? And how much did she want to know?

Lukas nodded, shoving half the bar into his mouth. "I've heard that the skill takes centuries to evolve, but there are a few who get it right away. I don't think I want anybody reading my mind all day."

Jonathan shot him a look over his shoulder. "Nobody wants in your head, kid."

Lukas snorted.

Jonathan eased up on the speed as a small structure appeared through the snow. "There it is," he said, his tone shifting. He squinted past the windshield. "Wait—what's that?"

Lukas leaned forward, frowning. "Something's on the ground over there."

Jonathan braked hard.

Lyrica yelped as her seat belt tightened against her chest. She angled her head to see beyond him into the trees, but the whipping snow, dark night, and blowing wind obscured her sight. She squinted. "Is that a foot?"

"Stay here," Jonathan ordered, tossing open his door and jumping out. Lukas followed him.

Panic shot through her as she fumbled with the belt. Ignoring his warning, she scrambled out of the UTV and stumbled into the thick snow. Kicking through the powder, she followed the others toward the disturbed surface. Her heart pounded as her gaze locked on a pale, bare foot sticking out from beneath a low-hanging branch.

That couldn't be Maeve, could it? Had Lyrica arrived too late to help the obviously frightened woman? She leaned over to see a frozen female foot with pink toenail polish. Bright pink.

Lukas aimed a flashlight on a barely there form beneath the snow.

Jonathan crouched beside the figure, his movements careful. He brushed the snow off the body, revealing long, dark hair matted with ice and blue eyes frozen wide-open. Naked and bruised, the woman lay utterly still in death.

Lyrica's stomach lurched, and she fought down bile.

"We have another one," Jonathan muttered, his voice grim.

"Do you recognize her?" Lyrica's teeth chattered as she tried to steady her breathing.

Lukas shook his head. "I don't."

"Me either." Jonathan glanced toward the cabin. "I've never seen her before. She's not from the Kurjan territory."

How was that even possible?

Chapter Twenty-Seven

Vero strode toward the main lodge, his boots crunching on the packed snow, his eyes narrowing at the conspicuous absence of guards. He stomped up the steps, shaking loose ice from his boots before stepping inside. The lodge felt eerily quiet, its emptiness prickling at his instincts. Frowning, he moved swiftly down the hallway toward Lyrica's office. The room was dark, her chair empty. He scanned the space for signs of life but found none. His mind began to churn with unease.

A glance at his watch showed it was well past ten at night, which was late but not unusual for her to still be working. Perhaps she had gone to bed early? His chest tightened as he jogged up the stairs, heading for the living quarters. His bedroom remained empty. The silence in the house grew oppressive, his unease sharpening into suspicion.

Yanking his satellite phone from his jacket pocket, he dialed Lyrica's number. The faint ring echoed from her office below. Perfect. He clenched his teeth, jogging back down the stairs. He'd handed her the sat phone for a reason, yet it proved completely useless now. Shaking his head, he punched in Jonathan's number.

"Where are you?" Vero demanded when Jonathan picked up.

"We're about two miles from headquarters, near the more remote cabins," Jonathan replied, his tone calm. "I was just about to call you."

Irritation scratched down Vero's throat. "What the hell are you doing out there?" he snapped, his voice hard as he stepped outside into the frigid night air.

"We found another body by one of the newly built family cabins," Jonathan said grimly. "A human female. She's...frozen to the ground. We're trying to extricate her now."

Vero stopped midstride, his breath visible in the cold air. "Wait a minute—" He spun toward the side of the lodge, heading for his stashed snowmobile. Jogging through the knee-deep snow, he cursed under his breath. "Why didn't you call me immediately?"

Jonathan coughed. "We've set up the lights and calmed Lyrica down. She felt deeply upset at finding yet another dead human female. I was just about to call you."

"Give me your coordinates," Vero barked, forcing his growing anger into a cold, controlled edge. The mention of Lyrica made his chest tighten. He imagined her, dark-haired and defiant, braving the brutal cold. "Lyrica is out in this weather? Tell me she's at least staying warm."

"She's fine. Want to talk to her?"

"No," Vero muttered through gritted teeth. "Before I forget to tell you, I released Silas a few minutes ago. I'm going with my gut. He didn't bring that female into the territory." He'd known Silas forever. The guy wasn't a killer.

The sound of crackling ice came over the line. "Silas was in custody when this female died. Well, maybe. I guess she could've been frozen any time," Jonathan said.

"I'll be right there." Vero ended the call and shoved the phone into his pocket. He straddled and ignited the sled, pulling away from the building and onto the main drag. His grip on the handlebars tightened as he opened up the throttle, spun around, and drove past the lodge. The freezing wind whipped him as he pushed the snowmobile harder, leaning low to avoid the worst of the biting air. He hated not having Lyrica within arm's reach, especially with an unknown enemy targeting them.

The mark on Vero's palm pulsed faintly, as if echoing his frustration. He flexed his hand, grimacing. Silas had given him no leads on the experiments with demonesses or the scientists involved in the project. If his uncles and father had eliminated everyone who knew anything, Vero had no idea where else to search for answers. The mark itself—a demon surname starting with *C*—was another mystery he couldn't solve. What demon family names began with that letter? What did it mean for him?

Ahead, lights flickered in the dark, and Vero leaned into the ride, picking up speed. He crested a ridge and spotted the scene below. His jaw clenched at the sight. Lukas and Ralstad moved between a nearby cottage and a lifeless figure lying in the snow. Strong floodlights had been affixed to nearby trees, illuminating the entire area.

Jonathan crouched over the frozen body, carefully pouring steaming water around her to melt the ice.

Vero slowed the snowmobile to a stop and jumped off, his fury rekindling as he surveyed the surroundings.

Steam rose as the water hit the ice, and Jonathan worked methodically to free her feet.

The UTV idled nearby, and Lyrica stepped out, her cheeks pink from the cold and her dark hair flecked with melting snow. The sight of her stirred something primal in Vero, the pulse in his palm intensifying with heat. She wrapped her arms around herself and trudged through the snow, teeth chattering. "Do we almost have her free?" she asked, shivering.

"Yes," Jonathan said without looking up.

Vero's gaze locked on her, his jaw tightening. "Get back in the UTV. It's too cold out here."

"I'm fine," she retorted, though the blue tinge on her lips told another story.

He stepped toward her, towering over her. "Get back in the UTV, or I'll put you there myself," he growled, his voice low and dangerous.

Her glare faltered, and after a tense moment, she spun on her heel and stalked back to the vehicle. "Fine. I want to speak with Maeve, anyway." She climbed into the driver's seat with a huff, slamming the door behind her.

Ralstad watched her go, his jaw hard. "That female's a free spirit."

"No kidding," Vero muttered as he crouched beside the body.

Ralstad ducked and began pouring water near the female's bare thighs. "You should take Lyrica in hand before she comes to harm, Vero."

Vero narrowed his gaze on the older Kurjan. "Is that a threat?"

"Of course not. It's a statement." Ralstad leaned back to study the breaking ice. "We have enemies all around us. Nobody is safe. Especially unmated human females."

An unfortunately true statement. With Paxton gone, Vero was currently running the entire Kurjan nation, and things had certainly gone to shit. The brand on his palm pulsed. He'd bitten her during sex the night before. Had he transferred the brand? He really didn't know. Lyrica might not be so unmated, after all. The UTV stopped at the cabin, and he watched her jump out, possessiveness flowing through him, dark and sure.

Jonathan poured more water, pulling Vero's focus back to the sad disaster at hand. The victim's feet were almost free, but the ice around her shoulders remained stubborn. He accepted a fresh bucket from Jonathan and began pouring water with deliberate care.

Another victim. Another mystery.

And still, no answers.

* * * *

Lyrica pulled up to the cottage, her teeth chattering despite the brief warmth of being in the UTV. Turning off the engine, she jumped out, her boots landing on a freshly shoveled path dusted with light snow. The wind cut through her layers, and she hustled as fast as her aching, frozen bones would allow. Reaching the door, she knocked firmly.

Maeve answered almost immediately, her eyes widening. "Oh, my goodness, get in here." She ushered Lyrica inside, pulling her out of the biting cold. "You're freezing. Take off your outerwear, and I'll fetch you a bit of tea."

The warm, cozy living room was a stark contrast to the icy night. Lyrica quickly removed her coat, boots, scarf, and mittens, hanging them neatly in an alcove near the door. Padding in thick socks through the inviting space, she entered the kitchen, which had been painted a cheerful yellow. Maeve was already bustling around, pouring tea into a delicate cup.

"Please, sit." Maeve motioned toward a small wooden table in the breakfast alcove. "I'll stoke the fire."

Lyrica settled into one of the chairs, wrapping her hands around the steaming mug Maeve placed in front of her. The wild berry tea was fragrant and sweet, its warmth seeping into her frozen fingers and soothing her aching lips. Maeve moved to the fireplace that bisected the living room and kitchen, adding logs with practiced ease. The crackling flames sent waves of heat into the room, instantly banishing the worst of the chill.

"Thank you," Lyrica murmured, sipping the tea. The warmth spread through her, chasing away the deep cold that had settled in her bones.

"Of course." Maeve poured herself a cup before joining Lyrica at the table. Tonight, Maeve wore a floor-length gown patterned with delicate blue flowers, its waist cinched just so. Her twin braids added a youthful softness to her face, which had pinkened from the heat of the fire. "Did they free the poor lass yet?" Concern coated her tone.

The vision of the poor victim made Lyrica's heart hurt. "Not yet. She's still frozen to the ground," Lyrica replied, her teeth still chattering slightly. The tingling in her feet became painful as warmth began to return to them.

Maeve shook her head, her brow furrowing. "Ah, what a dreadful thing. Who could've gone and done this?"

"I don't know," Lyrica admitted, gripping the mug tighter. "It doesn't make sense. No one knows how she got here."

The two sat in contemplative silence for a moment. Lyrica glanced around the sparkling clean kitchen, gathering her thoughts. "Actually, I was hoping to get a chance to speak with you anyway."

"Oh?" Maeve tilted her head. "What about?"

Lyrica hesitated, shifting uncomfortably in her chair. "I was... worried about you."

"Worried about me?" Maeve asked, her eyebrows lifting. "Why? Sure, I'm grand altogether. 'Tis a fine little cottage in a lovely, snowy place. Believe it or not, I've a great fondness for the snow. Though, truth be told, I'd take the rain any day."

Lyrica managed a faint smile. There was something starkly beautiful about these frozen mountains. Still, she pressed on, trying to find the right words. "It seems like Ralstad doesn't give you much freedom, and...I'm worried about that."

Maeve scrunched up her nose. "Ah, there's nothing to be fretting over. I'm happy as can be. Not everyone's got the itch to wander the wide world, you know."

"No, but don't you want your freedom?" Lyrica asked cautiously. She shifted in her chair again, unsure how to broach the subject without causing offense.

Maeve shrugged, taking another sip of tea. "None of us truly has freedom, you know. We're all tied to somethin'—be it kin, community, or duty."

"What about love?" Lyrica asked softly.

Maeve's gaze grew distant, and she nodded thoughtfully. "Ah, love holds us fast as well. Maybe more than anythin' else, it does."

Lyrica frowned, uncertain if Maeve truly understood her point. Did Maeve even realize she had a choice? That she didn't have to stay with Ralstad simply because of a centuries-old deal her father had made? Lyrica leaned forward, lowering her voice. "He just...he seems like the kind of male who'd hurt you if you disappointed him. I need to ask."

Maeve's eyes widened. "Ralstad doesn't harm me, so don't be puttin' that notion in your head."

"Are you sure?" Lyrica pressed gently, her concern deepening. "What about the boot warmers? You wanted them and he said no. Who would keep you from a necessity like that?"

Before Maeve could answer, the door swung open. Ralstad stepped inside, his broad shoulders filling the frame. Maeve stood quickly, setting her cup down. "Would ya like a bit of coffee, then?" she asked, moving toward him.

He shrugged off his outerwear, hanging it in the alcove, and stepped toward her. "I'd love some," he replied.

"Sure, aren't ya glad we stocked up earlier?" Maeve hurried to pour coffee from a pot warming on the stove.

Tension spiraled through Lyrica as Ralstad glanced her way. His presence dominated the room, the earlier warmth suddenly feeling stifling.

"Did they free the woman?" Lyrica asked, breaking the silence.

Ralstad accepted the mug from Maeve, his dark eyes sharp. "They're working on it. They need the UTV to transport her back to the medical facility."

Lyrica finished her tea and stood. "Did you recognize her?"

"No," Ralstad said firmly. "I've never seen her before." His gaze flicked to Maeve. "It's late. You should be sleeping."

Maeve flushed, glancing at Lyrica. "We've a guest, we do."

"I need to be going anyway," Lyrica interjected quickly, moving to the alcove to put on her boots and coat. She zipped her jacket with shaking fingers, pulling on her mittens. "Ralstad? You have Kurjan hearing and senses. Did you notice anything odd? Hear anything?" Was it possible he could've missed the woman being dumped on his property? She had a feeling he didn't miss much.

"No," Ralstad answered, taking a big drink of his coffee. "I have no idea where she came from."

Lyrica wished she could smell lies. Did Ralstad bring her in? "I noticed a snowmobile to the side of your house." Not many in the nation had their own snowmobiles yet. Vero had yet to bring a bunch in. "It's odd to have one, right?"

Ralstad shrugged, his focus solely on her across the short distance. "I requested one since we live so far out."

A likely story, but if someone was snowmobiling in victims somehow, that narrowed the suspect list significantly. Lyrica forced a smile. "Maeve, would you like to go on a walk tomorrow? I was hoping to meet some of the other new couples."

"No," Ralstad said flatly. "Maeve is otherwise occupied."

Maeve hesitated, looking from him to Lyrica. "I can't tomorrow, but maybe later in the week, aye?"

Lyrica ignored the bristling Kurjan male. "That would be great. How about Tuesday?"

"Ah, sure, I'll need to have a look at me schedule," Maeve said softly.

Ralston's lips pressed into a thin line, his eyes darkening to a deeper purple.

The air grew heavier, and Lyrica decided not to push further. "Thank you for the tea, Maeve. We'll talk soon."

Without waiting for a response, she stepped outside and pulled the door shut behind her. The biting cold stung her face, offering a sharp relief from the oppressive tension lingering inside the cottage. She climbed into the UTV, fired up the engine, and let her thoughts churn. Something felt deeply wrong, and she intended to uncover exactly what.

Chapter Twenty-Eight

Well after midnight, Lyrica sat in Vero's bed, reading a mystery novel she'd found in the kitchen. She had wavered between going back to her room or staying in his, but she really wanted to talk to him. They had to at least settle what the heck was going on between them right now. She had felt off the entire day and, frankly, it had been one of the longest days of her life. Finding that body had been both depressing and shocking. They had transported the victim to the medical facility where a grumpy Dr. Fizzlewick had waited to perform an examination.

Vero had then ordered Lukas to bring Lyrica back to the main lodge. She wanted to argue, but his tone had promised that she wouldn't win. She didn't like that. There were enough overbearing males around her right now, and she didn't like Vero thinking he could tell her what to do.

Lukas had remained quiet and somber, dropping her off and saying he'd return to cover the enforcer's back. The kid was being forced to grow up way too quickly.

The page in front of her kept blurring, and she had no clue what she'd read for the last hour. Finally, she heard Vero's heavy footsteps in the hallway outside before the door opened and he strode inside.

He'd already ditched his jacket and boots and looked tall and dangerous in a black long-sleeved T-shirt and faded jeans. He had taken quickly to wearing modern clothing, as had most of the Kurjans. The idea that they had spent most of their lives in uniforms seemed incomprehensible to her. It was nice to see them embracing some creativity.

Her mind flashed to Maeve and the old-fashioned dresses. Did the woman even want to wear dresses? Maeve might love to wear a pair of jeans.

Lyrica placed the book on the bedside table. "Hi."

"Hi," he said, just looking at her, his gaze hot.

She tried to keep her blood from racing through her veins. He was so close, his outdoorsy scent wafted toward her, tempting her. "Did they identify the newest victim, by any chance?"

"No," he said shortly.

Lyrica's shoulders slumped. "I'm sorry to hear that."

"Me too," he muttered. "The symbol of the circle with the three slashes was carved into her back."

Lyrica winced. "With a ballpoint pen?"

"Yeah, this one was black."

Lyrica shook her head. "I wish we could figure out what that symbol means."

"If it means anything," he returned, striding toward her. "It may be something this group just made up."

She gulped as he came near her. "Is this something that has happened before in the Kurjan nation? I mean, weird markings, weird symbols, and weird killings?"

"No. This is something new for us." He paused. "That is interesting though, isn't it?"

Her curiosity was piqued. "What is interesting?"

"This is new for us. A lot of things are. Somebody different brought this in," he said slowly. "We have a lot of newcomers these days."

The vampires had returned to the Realm, though. "Yet the three who attacked last night? Those were Kurjans."

"That's true." He scrubbed a broad hand down his face. "We need to talk."

"Yes," she said. Even as she burrowed under the covers, an unexpected chill crept over her. She shifted, sitting up straighter, and tucked her knees to her chest, keeping the blankets wrapped tightly around them. "Today felt weird."

He barked out a short chuckle. "Today did feel weird." He dropped his hand from his face, and his gaze met hers, the blue in his eyes undefinable. "How are you feeling today?"

"A little sore," she admitted, trying not to be embarrassed. "But in a good way," she added quickly.

Tension radiated from him. "I'm glad to hear that. Anything else?"

She tilted her head. "What do you mean?"

He shrugged. "I'm just asking if you feel different than before."

"Well," she said slowly, "like I said, I'm sore. But I'm also fighting a cold, I think."

His gaze sharpened. "Explain that."

"Why the heck do you want to know how I feel?" When his chin lowered, she gave in. This wasn't worth a fight, and exhaustion weighed down her limbs. "Fine. I feel like I'm coming down with something. Like I'm a little tired and my muscles are weak."

He swallowed. "Interesting."

"How so?"

He looked her over. She'd still been cold when she'd gone to bed, so she had donned one of his sweatshirts, thick socks, and yoga pants. "Do you notice anything else different about your body?"

"No." She frowned. "Like I said, I'm sore."

"Where?"

Okay, the embarrassment now heated her face. "Pretty much everywhere you can guess, Vero," she snapped.

He crossed muscled arms. "Give me details."

"What in the world? Do you need an ego stroke or something?"

He blinked. "No."

Good point. The guy had a huge ego. He didn't need a stroke.

"Then why are you fishing for compliments?"

He stared at her for several long, drawn-out moments. "You've lost me," he finally said.

"Oh yeah? Fine. Yes, I'm sore. Your cock was huge. I was stretched— delightfully so. Is that good enough for you?"

Amusement quickly danced in his eyes, and his lips twitched.

"If you smile, I swear to God, I'm going to punch you in the mouth." She meant every word.

He cleared his throat. "No punching in the mouth tonight, sweetheart."

Sweetheart? It was the first time he'd used an endearment with her. She should not like that as much as she did, so she glared.

"That's not exactly what I was talking about," he said.

"What are you talking about?"

He exhaled and held up his hand, palm out. "I'm talking about this."

She paused, shock grounding her. The letter *C* marked his huge palm, surrounded and crisscrossed by wicked-looking barbed vines. The design struck a balance between beauty, menace, and raw danger. "What in the world?" she breathed.

He looked at his palm. "I know. It's a demon mating mark."

She had seen Paxton's mark, which was a P for his surname, and had heard of the marks on other demons—once they met their mates. The whole thing sounded rather barbaric to her. "I didn't know Kurjans got mating marks on their hands."

He kept staring at his palm as if looking for answers. "We don't."

How did that make any sense? "You don't even have last names. What does a *C* on a Kurjan palm mean?"

"No clue."

Her mind spun off in several different directions. "Wait a minute, what do you mean 'no clue'? There is a mark on your palm. What does that mean? I thought markings only appeared when demons mated—or met their mates, or touched their mates, or kissed their mates..." She trailed off, trying to recall everything Hope had explained to her. "I can't remember all the details."

He swallowed. "Yes. That's my understanding as well."

The world went silent. "Wait a minute. Does that mean—"

He dropped his hand, his gaze stark. "I have no idea."

"Oh," she whispered softly, realization dawning. His half-brother was part demon, and Paxton had been an experiment. "Do you think that you were an experiment as well?" she asked softly.

Vero stared down at the bedspread. "I don't know." Frustration darkened the planes of his immortal face. "I believe all the scientists who worked on the projects at that time were killed afterward. I haven't been able to find any records." He looked around the room, as if not seeing any of the beautiful furnishings. "All the computers and records from headquarters arrive tomorrow, but I don't think there's going to be anything there. I can't explain this mark."

"Can you conduct a blood test?" Urgency sped up her breath.

Vero exhaled sharply, his expression turning pensive. "We'll have the lab equipment soon enough, but it won't be as simple as you think. We don't have a stash of demon blood. There must have been some at one time, but I've never seen even a trace of it in my lifetime. If I tested my blood, I wouldn't know what to look for."

"There has to be a way." Though, did this really matter? Immortal was immortal, as far as she was concerned. Perhaps it would be good for him—that he and Paxton would share that uniqueness.

He paused, tilting his head as though considering the idea further. "I could compare my blood to Paxton's, once he returns. Both of us have Kurjan markers, so I could isolate anything unfamiliar. Whatever I don't recognize might point to demon DNA."

Her heart quickened at the thought of him solving this puzzle. "You could also just ask the scientists at the Realm. Hope would help."

"No," Vero said sharply, his tone cutting through any chance of debate. "I'm not asking the Realm for anything, and I'm sure as hell not giving them my blood."

She swallowed, trying to approach the matter carefully. "I'm sure the Realm has Kurjan blood stored somewhere. From what Hope told me, the queen takes blood samples from everyone to develop cures for human diseases. If they already have Kurjan blood, they wouldn't even need—"

"Absolutely not." For a brief second, the killer they'd warned her about showed in his eyes.

She leaned closer, willing him to see reason and trying to banish her sudden fear. Of him. "They're our allies now, Vero. You need answers."

"I can't let this be public," he snapped, his frustration spilling over. "Don't you understand?"

She flinched at the heat in his voice but then shook her head. "No, I don't."

For a moment, his gaze softened, but the difference was fleeting. His expression hardened again, though his words carried a thread of quiet desperation. "Paxton is only half Kurjan. The nation accepted him because I vouched for him. Everyone believes I'm fully Kurjan. They think I'm the rightful prince—some even want me to be king. But if our enemies—or even some of our so-called allies—find out I might be part demon, too…" He shook his head, his jaw tightening with controlled fury. "We're dead."

Her stomach twisted painfully, and her world seemed to tilt. There had always been a comfort in knowing Vero had the nation's acceptance, that he could shield her from their enemies. But now, cracks formed in that safety, and fear spiraled through her chest.

"Then we need to find out if you're part demon. And we can't let anyone know." Lyrica forced herself to calm. She couldn't afford to panic—not now. "Have you told your brother?"

"No, not yet," Vero admitted. "I thought I should speak with you first."

A strange warmth bubbled up inside her at his words. She paused, trying to suppress the delight threatening to surface. Why would that make her so happy? "That's...sweet, Vero."

He stared at her, his expression unreadable. "I wasn't trying to be sweet."

She gulped, her cheeks flushing with warmth. "Then why?" Her gaze shifted to his hand, landing on the intricate mark etched into his palm. Understanding clicked into place. "Wait a minute... You bit me last night." She looked up sharply, her pulse hammering. "You don't think that you and I—"

"I have no idea," he said, cutting her off. "We were wild and... passionate." His voice softened slightly, but tension radiated off him. "But I didn't see the marking on my hand until today."

"Well," she said, trying to sound logical despite the whirlwind in her chest, "if you wanted to mate me—just as a Kurjan—did you?"

He looked at her, his eyes narrowing slightly. "Mating as a Kurjan isn't something that just happens, Lyrica. It's deliberate. It's permanent." He paused, his gaze holding hers. "And no. I didn't mate you."

Relief flooded her, and she released a breath she hadn't realized she'd been holding. Some of that might be disappointment. She'd deal with that reality later. "Oh. Okay. But..." She hesitated. "That still doesn't explain that." She motioned to his hand.

"Kurjan mates," he explained, his voice rough, "leave permanent marks during the act. We slash down to the bone of the shoulder, and the markings never heal. They don't hurt, but they stay forever. I didn't do that to you."

Yep. An additional tiny bit of disappointment hunched her shoulders until she shoved them back. She might be falling for the soldier, but first things first. "Okay. So, let's figure this out."

"Pureblooded Kurjans mate by marking to bone. But demons? Demons don't need to change the bones. The marking on the hand—transferring that marking during sex and a bite—is a permanent change."

Her breath hitched. "Oh," she whispered. Her gaze darted away, trying to process everything. "Okay. So...where were your hands when you bit me?" Heat licked at her skin, and memories of the night before surged back—wild, unrestrained, and overwhelming. Desire coiled in her belly as she tried to piece things together.

"Everywhere," he said. "But when I bit you, my hand was on—"

"My…" She trailed off, embarrassment crashing over her. "Okay. You know what? I'm sure this isn't what we think."

Vero's gaze darkened, and his jaw tightened as he stepped closer. "We need to know," he said, his voice low but firm.

Lyrica tugged at the edge of her sweatshirt before pulling it over her head and tossing it onto the bed. Left in a thin tank top, she crossed her arms over her chest. She glanced up and froze. "Did you just growl?"

He didn't move, his face implacable, but tension radiated off him.

She must've imagined the sound. Hands trembling, she reached for her yoga pants, pulling down the side just enough to expose her hip. She twisted, trying to see for herself, but there was nothing visible from her angle.

"Enough of that," Vero said gruffly. Before she could protest, he plucked her out of the bed, placing her on her feet.

"What are you doing?" she demanded.

He turned her around. "Looking for answers," he said simply.

"Hey!" She slapped back at him. "Just—just let me check."

"We have to know." His tone left no room for debate. "Trust me."

She gulped, heat rushing through her, but she nodded reluctantly. "Fine. But don't pull them all the way off." Embarrassment thickened her voice.

"Understood," he said, his voice low. His thumbs slipped under the waistband of her yoga pants, moving slowly, deliberately. He eased them down just enough to reveal the curve of her left buttock. Cool air brushed her skin, sending a shiver through her. A molten heat zipped through her body as his fingers lightly grazed her exposed skin.

He stilled. "It's here," he murmured, his voice rough and almost reverent. "There's a perfect marking that matches mine. Right here."

Her heart slammed against her ribs. "What?" she whispered, her voice trembling.

Before she could turn, his lips pressed against her skin, his touch both searing and electric. Pleasure and shock tore through her, making her knees wobble.

"Wait a minute," she gasped, yanking her pants back up and spinning to face him. Her voice rose, the words tumbling out before she could stop them. "You mean…we're mated?"

Chapter Twenty-Nine

After a night of sleeping way too peacefully next to Vero, who might be her mate, Lyrica sat at her desk and forced herself to concentrate on the computer screen in front of her. They'd decided to just get some sleep and tackle the mating issue after their brains kicked back in.

Updates to the satellite service had arrived and been installed early that morning, and she clicked several buttons, waiting patiently. She watched with anticipation as her computer linked to several Kurjan satellites at once this time. Wow.

Finally, the full power of the internet lay at her fingertips. More than she'd ever had before.

Freedom surged through her. Should she shop? Instead, she quickly devoured all the current news she could find, desperate to reconnect with the world. It had been exhausting to live unplugged for so long. Then, on a whim, she conducted a search on demon mates and Kurjan mates. One click led to another, and before she knew it, she was spiraling down a rabbit hole of monster-romance novels—anything to avoid dwelling on the fact that she'd mated Vero.

What did that even mean? He'd talked about courting her, but this was forever. Taking a deep breath, she entered an address into the updated system and tapped a few buttons. A soft ringing sounded through the computer and the screen morphed, Hope's face materializing.

"Lyrica, how are you?" Hope asked, her bright smile lighting up the screen.

"You don't seem surprised that I just video-conferenced you," Lyrica said, sinking into her chair.

Hope laughed. "Paxton and Vero already talked earlier."

"Oh." Lyrica pursed her lips. "I thought I was the first to get my computer updated."

"Sorry to disappoint you," Hope teased, her tone light. "But you're probably second."

That tracked. "I'm not sure where females rank in this nation."

Hope threw up a hand. "It's the same in the Realm. The males are all overprotective and over-the-top, but we're the ones who really run things. Trust me, you'll figure it out soon enough."

"When are you coming back?" Lyrica asked, taking a sip of her coffee.

Hope's expression sobered. "I'd like to return now, and so would Paxton, but Vero's fighting us on it. Apparently, things are more dangerous than ever."

Lyrica's fingers tightened around her mug. "Oh, really? How so?"

"Three dead female bodies, a bombing, and a rush attack," Hope said simply.

"I figured that was a normal week for the Kurjans." The breath Lyrica had been holding rushed out. "I need to talk to you," she said quickly, setting her coffee aside.

"Then talk." Hope leaned closer to the screen, her expression curious. "What's going on?"

Lyrica's stomach twisted. "Vero and I mated," she said, the words tumbling out.

Hope's jaw dropped. "Holy crap. Seriously? I figured you'd gone on a date, but mating?"

"We didn't mean to," Lyrica admitted, rubbing her temple. "It just happened."

Hope cocked her head, her gaze curious. "Huh. I didn't think Kurjans could mate accidentally. How does that even work?"

"They bite to the bone and leave permanent marks," Lyrica explained, waving a hand. "Apparently, that's their thing."

Hope's brow furrowed. "Interesting. I didn't know that. I mean, vampires do something similar, but still… Kurjans have been keeping that secret for a while, huh?"

"Seems like no secret lasts forever," Lyrica murmured. Her stomach twisted again with the weight of what she hadn't shared. Vero's lineage—his demon blood—wasn't hers to reveal. It was his truth, and she wouldn't betray that trust. Still, doubt gnawed at her. "Is there…a way out of this whole mating thing?"

Hope's eyebrows shot up. "Do you want out?"

Lyrica hesitated, her throat tightening. She wasn't sure. Infatuation wasn't love, but what she felt for Vero went deeper than anything she'd ever known. "I don't know," she admitted softly.

Hope's tone gentled. "Then give it time. You care about him, don't you? He cares about you. That's not something to run from—it's something to fight for."

Lyrica took a deep breath. She needed to know all her options so she could make an informed decision. Plus, she would let Vero know. Though, if she were being honest, he probably knew a lot more than she did.

On the screen, Hope rolled her eyes, her expression both exasperated and amused. "All right, so there's this thing called Virus 27. It was created by the Kurjans to kill vampires."

"What?" Lyrica shook her head, confused. "What are you talking about?"

Hope blew out air. "Long story. Anyway, the virus can also be used to negate a mating bond, but only in very specific situations. It's never been used on living partners. It's typically used when one mate has been dead for at least a century, sometimes two."

"Okay. I've heard about it." Lyrica's mind spun. Could she even consider such a thing? Her thoughts raced back to the night she'd spent with Vero. Hope was right—he was strong, kind, dangerous, and so sweet it made her heart ache. But forever? Immortality? That was a lot to take in. "I don't want to lose myself," she said softly.

Hope snorted, her expression turning wry. "You? Lose yourself? Please. You're one of the most grounded people I've ever met. You have valuable work there, and you can do whatever you want—mate or no mate."

Lyrica bit her lip, thinking about the work she'd done with the Kurjan nation. Helping kidnapped women find their footing again had been rewarding, even if bittersweet. That role might be fading as the Kurjans moved away from abductions, but there were other ways she could contribute. She thought of Maeve, a woman who seemed stuck in an outdated role and desperately needed someone to pull her into the modern world.

"You need to get back here," Lyrica said finally.

Hope's eyes softened. "I know. I miss you too." She glanced over her shoulder and sighed. "Oh, hey. I have to go. I talked Liam into sparring with me, and the vampire has no patience."

"All right," Lyrica said, forcing a small smile. "I'm excited to see you."

"We'll be there in time for the Convexus the day after tomorrow," Hope promised. "See you then."

As the screen went dark, Lyrica leaned back, her mind buzzing. What did she really want? She knew she wanted Vero—but forever? Centuries of being tied to one person? She'd never had a boyfriend last more than two months. Could anyone truly like her for that long?

Shaking herself free from the spiral, she reached into her desk drawer and pulled out a piece of paper. She'd kept her own records while working with the captured women and didn't need to seek out Vero for his. It was a list of email addresses for the women who had recently gained their freedom. She'd missed her new friends. Her fingers hovered over one name, Cynthia, before she typed the address and initiated a video call.

When Cynthia's face appeared, the woman frowned and leaned closer to the screen. "Can I help you?"

"Hi, Cynthia." Lyrica forced cheerfulness into her voice. "It's me, Lyrica. I just wanted to check in and see how you're settling back into your life."

Cynthia blinked a few times, her frown deepening. "I'm sorry, who are you?"

Lyrica froze. "It's me," she whispered. "Lyrica. From Canada."

The woman's eyes narrowed. "I have no idea who you are. Are you trying to scam me? How did you get this email address?"

Before Lyrica could respond, a hand came down on her mouse, cutting the connection. She looked up to find Vero standing beside her, his expression dark and dangerous.

"What was that?" she asked, her voice trembling. "I don't understand."

His mouth tightened, and his tone turned to steel. "Don't contact any of the released females."

Her lungs seized. His eyes had gone cold, and his tone sounded flat. Hard. Implacable. "What are you talking about? I just wanted to check on them."

"I said no," Vero repeated, his voice cutting through her confusion like a blade.

Fury surged through her veins, red-hot and unrelenting. "What do you mean, 'no'? I don't take orders from you."

"You do when it comes to this." Now even his blue eyes had gone flat and hard. "This is about security and safety. You will not contact those females again."

She stood abruptly, her chair scraping against the floor. "Why do I get the feeling that if I did, they wouldn't remember me?"

"Because they won't," Vero said flatly.

She couldn't breathe. "You promised. I gave you that entire presentation, and both you and Paxton said you agreed to leave their brains and memories alone."

"We didn't agree, and we didn't lie to you or promise," he said, stepping back but still radiating a deadly calm. "We wiped their memories in a very safe way. Gave them stories they could take home. Some went on vacation. Others were kidnapped and rescued without much harm. They'll move on. It's safer this way."

Her stomach turned over, and she whispered, "You messed with their minds."

"Take it however you want," he said, his tone devoid of emotion. "They're better off not knowing about the Kurjan nation."

"Did it hurt them?" she asked, her voice barely audible.

"Not in the slightest. The memory wipes were clean. This is about protecting them—and us."

Her hands itched to grab something—anything—and throw it. She glanced down at her stapler, her fingers twitching.

"Go ahead," he said, his voice dropping to a deadly whisper. "Throw it. I dare you."

Chilled by the ice in his tone, she dropped back into her chair. "I wouldn't give you the satisfaction."

"Smart girl," he said softly.

She still wanted to hit him. "Why didn't you tell me that was your decision? You both let me think that I'd convinced you."

"I didn't want to worry you."

Her chin lifted. "I don't need protection from reality."

"Fair enough." Then his tone shifted, sharper now. "Forget about Virus 27. No one is taking that. Do you understand me?"

He'd been eavesdropping? Lyrica's breath hitched as his words rolled over her, heavy and unyielding. Her pulse quickened, a strange mix of fury and desire leaving her both breathless and off balance. "Fine," she bit out. "I get it."

"Good." He glanced at his watch. "I have business. Be here when I get back. We'll discuss this mating."

"Oh, great," she said sarcastically. "I can barely wait."

When he left, the tension in the room dissipated, but her anger simmered just beneath the surface. If Vero thought he could dictate her every move, he hadn't read her accurately from the beginning. Grabbing her coat and boots, she marched toward the door.

He might have wiped memories, but he wasn't going to stop her from helping someone who needed it. Whether he liked it or not, she had her own mind—and she wasn't altering her life for anybody. Plus, she had a nice anti-immortal gun in her pocket that she'd borrowed from his bedside table.

She stepped outside, her breath fogging in the freezing air. It was a good thing she knew how to drive a UTV.

Chapter Thirty

Vero ran into Silas after he headed into the building that housed the below-ground cells. The scent of fresh pastries greeted him as Silas leaned against the wall, casually munching on one.

"What are you doing here?" Vero asked, his tone sharper than intended.

"I'm on guard duty," Silas replied through a mouthful of pastry, then gestured to the flaky treat. "That new chef who arrived last week? Really good."

Vero shook his head. If nothing else, Silas didn't hold grudges. "Hey, about your time in the cell below—sorry for that."

Silas waved a hand, brushing the apology aside. "Don't worry about it. I know you had to check every suspect, and I was the only one who'd left camp. Still, you know me. I'd never kill anyone, especially not a human female."

"I know," Vero said, meaning it.

Silas studied him, his reddish eyes narrowing before widening in surprise. "You look different. Smell different." His jaw dropped. "Wait a second. Did you mate? With Lyrica? Congrats, Prince. She's a doll." He grinned and smacked Vero hard on the arm, almost making him growl.

"Thank you. I appreciate it." Vero's voice stayed even, but his gaze probably warned Silas to tread carefully. "I'm keeping it quiet for now. She's human—she's not used to our ways." The words sounded lame even to him.

Silas nodded with a knowing smile. "Yeah, females can be tough. Takes a while to get them used to how we do things. Don't worry—I won't say a word. But, uh, you should know, she's all over you. I could smell her as soon as you walked in. It's not exactly going to stay a secret."

"Good to know," Vero muttered, eyeing the other male. Silas didn't seem bothered in the slightest, cheerfully finishing his pastry. If there had been anything unusual about the mating bond, Silas would've mentioned it. He would've asked questions. The fact that he hadn't eased some of the weight on Vero's chest.

Good. For now, no one knew about the demon blood. The mark on his hand had faded slightly, but he still wondered if there was a way to cover it completely. Maybe even remove it. He'd have to look into possibilities.

"Can I help you with anything?" Silas asked.

"No. I'm here to talk to the prisoner. Geoff."

Silas's expression darkened slightly. "Right. I took him breakfast earlier. He bitched about it the whole time, called me a traitor for following Paxton. Guy's got a real problem with the whole half-demon issue."

"Yeah, a lot of people do," Vero said grimly. "Did he say anything useful? We need to figure out what that circle with the slashes means."

"Nah. I tried to buddy up to him, ask a couple of questions, but he didn't fall for it. The guy's not stupid."

"Didn't think so." Vero clapped Silas on the shoulder. "Thanks. You can head out if you want."

Silas hesitated. "You don't want me to keep an eye on him when you leave?"

"No," Vero said flatly. "There won't be a need."

Silas's humor faded, his tone turning sober. "Got it. Well, I'll see you later. Need help with anything else? Lyrica?"

"Jonathan and Lukas are watching Lyrica anytime she leaves the lodge. I'm covered. You can get back to the helicopters or help unload the new ones we brought in today. Headquarters is setting up the new computer hub."

"Sounds good." Silas nodded, his cheer returning. He wore a green flannel shirt with dark jeans and snow boots, an unusually casual look for him.

"Where'd you get the flannel?" Vero asked as he approached the door.

Silas tugged on the shirt. "A shipment came in with the computers and some snowmobiles. I was up early and snagged this before anyone else. It's warm."

"It looks good," Vero said, a bit awkwardly.

"Thanks." Silas brushed off his shoulder, grinning. "I might even hit up the next speed dating event Lyrica organizes. I mean, it worked out for you." He whistled as he opened the door and strolled into the snowy day.

Vero shook his head. It had worked out, though not in the way he'd expected. He'd never planned on taking a mate, and when he'd allowed himself to consider it, he hadn't pictured someone as independent—or as maddening—as Lyrica.

But damn it, he liked that about her. He admired her feistiness, her drive. Hell, the mother of his children would need that fire. The idea nearly dropped him to his knees. Kids. A family. It was a dream he'd never let himself have.

Shoving the thought aside, he focused on the task at hand. He unlocked the door and descended the cold, damp stairs to the cells. The farthest door swung open with a creak as he stepped inside. Geoff sat on the cot, his face bruised from the last interrogation.

"Morning," Vero said, and without waiting, punched him square in the nose. The satisfying crack of cartilage echoed in the room.

"Asshole!" Geoff stumbled back, clutching his face as blood dripped onto his shirt.

Blood burned Vero's hand. It was common knowledge that Kurjan blood burned others, though sometimes not mates, and he wondered if this burned him because he was only half Kurjan. Something to think about once again. He could create experiments once Paxton returned, using both of their blood. "Start talking. What does the symbol stand for?"

Geoff's nose cracked back into place as his healing cells kicked in. "It's our symbol," he muttered. "It represents our group."

Vero's eyes narrowed. "What group?"

Geoff hesitated, his shoulders tense. Vero pulled a blade from his pocket, its triple edges glinting in the dim light. Geoff's eyes widened. "That's a banned blade," he stammered. "You're not supposed to have that."

"I've never cared much for rules." Vero took a step closer, his voice dropping. "If I shove this in your neck and deploy the spring, you'll lose your head. So tell me—what does the symbol mean?"

Geoff backed against the stone wall, his breathing shallow. "It's the symbol for our faction. We call ourselves the Defenders. We're independent cells working mostly autonomously."

"Doing what?" Vero let the killer inside him show.

Geoff swallowed. "Usually working against the Realm. But now? With a half-demon running the Kurjan nation..." He let the words hang in the air.

Vero's fist clenched around the blade. The threat wasn't just growing—it was already here. "How many of you are there?" His voice sounded gritty. Hoarse. Demon low.

Geoff shrugged, though sweat beaded on his forehead. "No clue. In my group, there were only the three of us. For the other cells, thousands? I truly don't know because we all branched off into our own organizations eons ago."

"Well," Vero said softly, his eyes narrowing, "I know you're lying, Geoff. Someone's killing females—human females—in my territory. The other two in your little party are dead, and you've been locked in this cell. That means someone else is out there. Who?"

Geoff shook his head, his jaw tightening. "There's no one else. Someone must be copying us. Or maybe there are more Defenders, but they're not part of my cell. I don't know who they are."

"You're lying again," Vero said, his voice turning colder. "You told me that symbol—the one carved into the bodies—was yours."

Geoff's shoulders slumped slightly. "A lot of us use it. It's been passed through centuries and different organizations, shared across groups. There could be another cell right here in the Kurjan nation, and I wouldn't even know it. Some are connected to others, and some are not. Ours is not."

"If you're lying, I'll know."

"I'm not," Geoff said, though the slight tremor in his voice betrayed him. He cocked his head, a smirk curling his lips. He sniffed the air. "You mated her. The human. She's a hot one. I don't blame you. I'd have—"

Rage surged through Vero like a tidal wave, but his expression remained calm, cold. "You have something to say about that?"

Geoff shrugged. "I just did. Gave you a compliment, didn't I? She's gorgeous. And hey, Vero—you're the rightful heir to the crown. You should be king. You're a pureblood Kurjan. Join us."

The blade felt heavy and ready in his hand. Alive. "Your pitch is pathetic."

"I'm serious," Geoff said, his tone sharpening. "Your brother won't live through the next month, no matter what you do. Even if you kill me and wipe out my cell, we're not alone. There are more of us than you think—and some of us are already inside your precious headquarters. Join us, Vero. We'll make sure you get the throne you deserve."

"Well, gee, Geoff," Vero said dryly, lifting his right hand to reveal the demon mark. "Can't really do that."

Geoff's smirk faltered. "You're part demon? You're kidding me."

"Now, tell me the truth. You were a scientist, weren't you? A lab rat."

Geoff's jaw slackened for a moment, but then hatred filled his eyes. "You're a half-demon, aren't you? You're one of them."

Vero's voice turned mocking. "Apparently. It was a shock to me too. But you—you were in the labs, weren't you? Back when they were experimenting on demons. Or maybe you don't remember all the lovely little projects involving Kurjans and demons?"

"I don't know anything about that," Geoff spat. "Finding out about Paxton was bad enough, but this?" He threw back his head and laughed, the sound harsh and bitter. "You're dead. Just like your brother. And that bitch you mated? She's as good as dead too."

Vero's rage darkened, but his voice stayed calm and cold. "Careful."

Geoff leaned forward, his grin vicious. "She's human. Mortal. Not even an immortal female, like Hope Kayrs-Kyllwood, who could handle mating a Kurjan-demon hybrid such as your brother, Paxton. Lyrica needs to be studied—cut apart, put back together, studied some more."

Vero struck, slamming the knife into Geoff's throat and pinning him against the wall. Blood spattered his hand, the familiar burn scorching his skin, but he didn't flinch. Geoff's eyes widened, his hands clawing at the blade.

"Wait," Vero said, his tone conversational. "Tell me now—who else is in your cell? How many cells are there?"

Geoff choked, blood dribbling from his mouth as his gaze darted wildly. "I don't know! Hundreds, maybe. We're separate for a reason—so we can't betray each other. We all have different goals. Mine is to put the nation back together. To make it strong again."

"Who else is with you?" Vero pressed. His thumb hovered over the button on the hilt of the knife.

Geoff's eyes flashed with defiance, though panic flickered beneath. "Fuck you, demon."

Vero hit the button. The blade split into three, slicing through Geoff's neck with brutal precision. His head hit the floor with a sickening thud, his body crumpling seconds later.

Vero stepped back, his chest heaving as he fought to steady himself. Geoff's words echoed in his mind, twisted and vile. Of enemies who'd want to study Lyrica—by harming her. The thought of anyone touching Lyrica like that, treating her like a thing instead of the incredible female she was, made his blood boil.

He clenched his fists, forcing himself to breathe. He needed to run— hard and fast—to work off the searing rage threatening to consume him. But first, he had to see her.

She was in more danger than he'd ever imagined, and she had to know. Whatever it took, he'd protect her. No one would touch her. No one would take her from him.

Vero turned and strode out of the cell, leaving Geoff's lifeless body behind as he headed toward the only person who could ease this rage in him.

His mate.

Chapter Thirty-One

Lyrica wasn't entirely sure she'd ever been this angry. How dare they mess with those poor women's memories? Those women had already endured enough. And how dare Vero lie to her? He did. An omission hurt just like a lie.

A tiny voice in the back of her mind reminded her that now the women were safe. They didn't know about Kurjans or immortality, so nobody would target them for what they'd seen or experienced. Plus, they no longer had to relive the terrifying ordeal of being kidnapped by immortals.

Still, it didn't matter. She was furious.

She jumped into a UTV, starting it up with a harsh growl. The vehicle's low hum cut through the snowy quiet as she pulled away, no one paying her any attention. Vero had insisted she call for help if needed, but she didn't plan to follow any of his damn orders. She patted the pocket of her heavy coat, reassured by the feel of the sleek green gun inside. If anyone crossed her, she would shoot first and explain later.

Right now, she needed to talk to Maeve. Ralstad should be at work, and Maeve would be baking or doing something equally domestic. This was Lyrica's chance. A small, rebellious satisfaction filled her chest. Vero needed to understand right now that she wasn't the obedient type.

She drove through the main part of the Kurjan settlement before turning toward the outskirts. The vehicle's pace was slower than when Jonathan had driven her, but she didn't mind. The time allowed her to gather her thoughts, though she pointedly avoided glancing at the area where the body had been found. That poor woman. They needed to figure out who was behind the killings—and fast.

For the first time, she fully understood Vero's obsession with keeping guards close. It was smart, necessary even. But that didn't mean she wanted to be shadowed every second of the day. Maeve wouldn't talk with anyone else around. This conversation required privacy.

When Lyrica finally reached Maeve and Ralstad's home, she parked and stepped out, her boots sinking an inch into freshly shoveled snow. At least Ralstad kept his walkway clear.

Big, fat flakes drifted lazily from the sky, dotting her nose. She glanced up, marveling at the white powder swirling in the muted light. The storm had abated, though it seemed likely to snow every day. For now, the wind had granted a welcome reprieve from its blustery power.

She approached the door quietly, her breath frosting in the air, but stilled when raised voices reached her.

"I said no," Maeve yelled, her voice sharp with defiance.

"Too fucking bad," Ralstad bellowed in return.

A scuffle followed, punctuated by a loud clatter. Panic jolted through Lyrica. Her hand darted to her pocket, pulling out the green gun as she burst through the door.

"Stop right now, or I'll shoot," she shouted, her voice shaking with adrenaline. She winced immediately. Had she really just yelled a line straight out of a police procedural?

Ralstad and Maeve froze mid-action, both turning to stare at her. Maeve sat on the kitchen floor. Ralstad had his hands on what looked like a pair of fur-lined tights wrapped around Maeve's thighs, while Maeve had one hand on his head, as if swatting him away.

"What the hell is going on here?" Lyrica demanded, fury making her hand tremble as she kept the gun raised.

Ralstad straightened, still holding the offending tights. "Get out of my house. You don't just barge in waving a gun around."

"Let her go," Lyrica snapped. Her anger was a living thing now, feeding off every second of this ridiculous scene.

Ralstad's eyes flicked to the gun in her shaking hands before he sighed and released Maeve. "It's time for you to leave."

"Ah, damn it, Ralstad," Maeve said, yanking the tights off and flinging them at him. They landed square on his broad shoulder, one leg smacking him straight on the nose. "I'm not wearin' these, so I'm not. They're too big, and they make me look like a bloody elephant. Besides, I'm roastin'. Not in a million years will I put those atrocities on me."

"Yes, you will wear these," he growled, stepping between her and the gun. "If you're going outside, you're wearing more layers, for Pete's sake."

Maeve stood to her feet, fire sparking in her green eyes. "I'm with child, not chilled, and I'll not be told otherwise, mark ye that."

Ralstad extended the tights toward Maeve. "Yes, you're pregnant, and you're not going out without enough layers on. You'll freeze."

"I'm immortal, you daft fool," Maeve shot back, grabbing the nearest object—a cast-iron pan.

Lyrica gasped as Maeve swung the heavy pan without hesitation, the sharp clang of metal meeting flesh echoing in the small space.

Ralstad howled, clutching his ear as he staggered back. "Damn it, woman," he shouted. "Your arm gets stronger every year. We might as well send you off for spring training with the damn Yankees."

"Maybe if you heeded me for once, I wouldn't be gettin' so much practice," Maeve countered, her tone thunderous as she brandished the cast-iron pan like a weapon. "And you know bloody well I'm a Dodgers fan, you daft clod. Now, we're goin' to set some things to rights. Do you understand me?"

Ralstad blinked, keeping one hand pressed against his injured ear. He looked at Lyrica, his voice lowering. "Put down the gun. I don't want you to hurt her."

Lyrica gaped at him. "I wasn't going to shoot her. I was going to shoot you."

Ralstad paused, his gaze narrowing. "Not helping."

Maeve crossed her arms, the pan still clutched in one hand. "Lyrica, put the gun away, will you? He's naught but bark and no bite, so he is."

Lyrica hesitated, then slowly tucked the gun back into her pocket. "What is going on here?"

Ralstad sighed and rubbed his ear, his shoulders broadening and his scowl darkening. "I just want her to dress warmly if she's going outside. There's someone out there killing people."

"I've walked this earth immortal for years," Maeve snapped.

"I don't care," Ralstad thundered. "You're wearing those bloomin' tights, or you're not leaving this house."

Maeve shook the pan again, and Lyrica stepped back instinctively. "I am not wearin' them," she declared, her tone brimming with disdain. "They look utterly ridiculous, and I'm no mere mortal woman in need of fleece. *Fleece*, Ralstad—have you lost your senses?"

Ralstad glared at her, his patience clearly fraying. "Then I'm not leaving this house either. We can argue all day if you want."

Lyrica couldn't help it—a laugh burst out of her before she could stop it. Both Ralstad and Maeve turned to glare at her. "You two are impossible," she said, shaking her head. "But I guess I should be glad to see someone fighting about something other than murder for once."

Ralstad grunted, still rubbing his ear, while Maeve's lips twitched with reluctant amusement. The tension in the room eased, though Lyrica suspected this wasn't the last round in their ongoing battle.

At least Maeve seemed safe—for now. Lyrica wasn't entirely sure about Ralstad. His other ear might be a good target.

"Well," Ralstad said, his tone softening despite the exasperation in his eyes, "listen, Maeve. We've been trying to have a baby for a century. You're finally pregnant, and you're going to be careful. I can't have you slipping out there."

Maeve set the cast-iron pan down gently on the counter and crossed her arms. "Whether I wear those absurd tights or not, this babe will be just fine. You can't go frettin' over every little thing, Ralstad."

"Of course I worry," he said, letting go of his ear, now swollen and bright red. "You're every breath I take."

Maeve's expression softened, her fiery demeanor shifting to tenderness. "You've been awfully cranky of late," she said, a teasing smile curling her lips. "You're lucky that's the first time I've taken the pan to you, so you are."

His lips quirked upward despite himself. "This month," he muttered, rubbing his ear.

Maeve laughed, the sound soft and warm, as she stepped closer and reached for his hand. "It's been some time, hasn't it?"

Ralstad grumbled but allowed her to take his hand. "It doesn't feel like a while," he muttered, leaning down so she could kiss his cheek.

Maeve kissed his injured ear instead.

"You're an evil one," he said, a smile softening his gruff tone. "I knew it the moment I laid eyes on you in that field all those years ago."

"You knew exactly what you were gettin' yourself into," Maeve replied, a mischievous gleam in her eyes as she kissed him again. "Now stop yer fussin'. I love you, and I'll be just fine."

Ralstad puffed out his chest, trying to look stern but failing under her warmth. "I know you'll be safe. I'll make sure of it." He leaned in, pressing a kiss to her nose before stepping back, his cheeks tinged red when he glanced at Lyrica. The big, grumpy soldier looked almost sheepish. Lyrica bit back a grin. The male was a giant teddy bear wrapped in a storm cloud.

Maeve noticed her expression and laughed, the sound soft and warm. "Lyrica, why don't we sit and have a bit of tea while Ralstad goes to clear the walkway again?"

Ralstad snapped to attention, clearly relieved by the excuse to leave. "That's a good idea," he said, kissing Maeve one last time before walking to the door. He opened it, paused, and scanned the area outside. "There's no guard on duty out here."

Then he turned back, his gaze locking on Lyrica. His nostrils flared slightly as he sniffed the air. "You drove here without guards? The prince let you?"

Lyrica wavered, crossing her arms. "That's none of Vero's business."

One of Ralstad's eyebrows shot up. "Huh. That's not true." He shrugged and stepped out into the cold, shutting the door behind him.

Maeve walked to the stove, placing a pretty pink kettle on the burner. "Can't believe ya nearly shot me mate," she said over her shoulder.

Lyrica shook her head and moved to take the same chair she'd sat in during her last visit. The warm and comfy kitchen provided a welcome peace. "I thought he was abusing you, not the other way around."

Maeve waved a hand dismissively. "Oh, please. Every one of 'em needs a smack to the head now and then. You should know that by now."

Lyrica stared at her, trying to process everything. "I had this all wrong."

"Why? Because I like to wear dresses and braid my hair?" Maeve arched a brow.

"Well...yeah. Plus, you don't want to go anywhere."

Maeve shrugged, pulling two mugs from the cupboard and dropping tea bags into them. "We might've kept under the radar thanks to the old leadership, but that's why we've come back now. I like it here. I love me mate. We've been tryin' for a baby for ages, and now we finally are." She glanced back, her smile softening. "I'm right where I want to be."

"But Ralstad seems so…cranky. Kind of mean and bossy."

"Oh, he is," Maeve said with a laugh. "Cranky, mean, bossy. That's just Ralstad. And that's why I love him."

Lyrica blinked, unable to wrap her mind around Maeve's perspective. "What about the boot warmer? He said no."

Maeve rolled her eyes. "I want the boot warmer for him. The poor lad gets fierce cold feet, but he reckons it's a weakness to slip into warm boots each day. Daft eejit."

Boy, had Lyrica read this situation wrong. "I don't think I belong here. Not in this nation."

Maeve placed the mugs on the table and sat down, her green eyes warm and wise. "Ah, sure you do. You belong wherever you choose to belong. And you can be whoever you've a mind to be."

The kettle began to whistle, and Maeve rose to pour the hot water into their mugs. She returned to the table, handing Lyrica a steaming cup. "If you've a mind to be like me—a bit of an old-fashioned Irish witch who loves her dresses and keeps a traditional home—then go ahead and do that. But if it's a modern life you're after, wanderin' the world and such, then follow that path instead. Whatever sits right with your soul is what you should chase."

Lyrica's throat tightened. She'd come here to save Maeve. Instead, Maeve might end up saving her. "I don't know what I want," she admitted quietly, wrapping her hands around the mug for warmth.

Maeve's smile turned knowing. "Ah, sure, I've been there meself. Do ya love him?"

Lyrica didn't bother pretending they weren't talking about Vero. "I don't know. I was drawn to him from the first time I met him. Every time I see him, the pull is stronger." After one night with him, she couldn't imagine being with anybody else. "It's part of why I wanted to stay and work here. It wasn't just about helping the kidnapped women or modernizing the nation."

"Maybe," Maeve said, her voice thoughtful, "ya stayed to get to know him. Sure, there's nothin' wrong with that."

Lyrica hesitated. "I've never trusted anyone fully. It's hard." Though she felt right at home in the snowy wilderness, just like she had as a kid when lucky enough to stay with her grandfather. Vero made her feel that safe as well.

Maeve leaned forward, her tone firm. "It's never too late to make a fresh start, so it isn't."

The distant hum of a snowmobile cut through their conversation. Lyrica froze, her pulse spiking.

Maeve winced. "I had a feeling Ralstad might ring Vero."

Panic tightened Lyrica's chest as she stood, looking wildly around the room.

"Ah, there's nowhere to go," Maeve pointed out, holding up her cast-iron pan. "Do ya want to borrow this?"

The door burst open, and Vero filled the space like a thunderstorm. His fury radiated from every inch of his broad frame, his face a hard mask of rage. "You came here without guards?" he said, his voice a gritty whisper that was more terrifying than a shout.

Lyrica's knees threatened to give way, but she snapped her head up defiantly. "Yes. I have a gun, and I can drive a UTV just fine."

He stared at her for so long she thought she might combust under the intensity of his gaze.

Maeve wisely kept silent.

"Get your coat," Vero ordered. "We'll take this discussion elsewhere."

Lyrica wanted to run. She wanted to fight. Every emotion from the past week crashed into her, igniting her temper. She turned to Maeve, lifting her chin. "I need to borrow that pan."

Chapter Thirty-Two

Vero killed the snowmobile's engine, the sharp silence of the snowy expanse slamming into him like a physical force. Lyrica sat stiffly behind him, her arms wrapped around his waist, her body vibrating with defiance. She hadn't spoken a word since he'd dragged her out of Maeve's place, but her anger simmered in every breath she took.

Good. He was pissed too.

Without a word, he swung off the snowmobile, gripping her waist and lifting her down before she could protest. She wobbled slightly on the icy ground, her lips pressing into a tight line as she cinched her coat tighter. Her fierce glare was adorable, but he'd appreciate that later. For now, if she thought her anger could match his, she was wrong.

"Inside," he said, his voice low and commanding as he took her arm. They had mated, which meant there was no going back. Their courting and their sex had been consensual, and neither of them had thought mating a possibility. He'd had no fucking clue he was a demon. But now, it was done.

It wasn't until he'd discovered she was out alone, with a serial killer stalking victims in his territory, that the reality of that truth nearly took him to his knees.

She was his.

"Let go of me, Vero," she snapped, her tone sharp enough to cut glass.

"Not happening," he growled, tugging her toward the lodge. Snow crunched beneath their boots as he led her into the warmth of the main building, his grip firm despite her attempts to wrench free. He didn't stop until they reached her office, slamming the door shut behind them and flipping the lock.

Her glare intensified as she ripped her arm free. "What is your problem?"

"My problem?" He stalked toward her, his broad frame dwarfing hers as he backed her against the desk. "You are my problem, Lyrica. You don't listen. You put yourself in danger—alone—then act like I'm a human asshole for caring about your safety."

"I can take care of myself," she shot back, her voice shaking with fury.

"Really?" he asked, his tone cutting. "Because from what I've seen, you couldn't care less if you're hurt. Or worse."

Her eyes widened, her breath hitching as his words struck home. But just as quickly, her chin jutted out in defiance. "I'm not one of your soldiers. You don't get to order me around."

"No," he said, his voice dropping to a dangerous whisper. "You're my mate. And that means I'll damn well order you around if it keeps you alive." Taking the virus to break the mating bond while both mates still lived was too dangerous, even if they both wanted that. Which he did not.

The word "mate" hung in the air between them.

"You're not understanding me," she said, vulnerability in her eyes now.

He pressed forward, his hands bracing the desk on either side of her hips, caging her in. "Oh, I understand you. Scared little girl who's afraid to take a chance. Terrified of counting on somebody. Of being let down."

She sucked in a breath. "Shut up."

"Mature," he countered. "But you're not seeing me." His tone turned raw, his chest heaving as he reined in the storm inside him. "I have spent my entire life keeping people safe, Lyrica. My people. My cousin until he betrayed me. My newly found brother. And now you. Do you think I can just turn that off because you want to play like some rebel from a television show?"

She blinked up at him, her breath coming faster now. He could feel the heat of her body, the way she responded to his nearness even as her instinct for self-preservation, the one that forced her to shield her heart, tried to kick in.

"I'm not playing anything." The war battling inside her emerged with a new octave in her voice. "This is who I am, Vero. You don't get to decide that."

"You don't get to decide my role in this," he shot back. "I do."

She froze at his words, her lips parting as if to speak, but no sound came for several tense seconds. Finally, she swallowed. "We didn't mate on purpose."

"I know." He gentled his tone. Somewhat. "But this is where we are. It's too dangerous to take that virus, so we're not doing that."

She faltered. "You can't want to stay mated."

Ah, there she was. The female who thought she was alone in the world. "I do—with everything I am."

She blinked. Desire darkened her stunning eyes along with a healthy note of disbelief.

He'd have to show her. His hand slid into her hair just enough to tilt her head back and expose the column of her throat.

"Take all the time you need to learn this," he said, his voice rough, his thumb brushing her jaw. "You're mine, Lyrica. I won't let anybody harm you—whether you like that fact or not." Whether she worked with him or not.

Her pupils dilated, her lips trembling as his words washed over her. "You can't control me," she whispered, though the defiance in her voice was fading.

"Control has a lot of connotations," he said, his other hand sliding to her hip, possessiveness gripping him. "I want to protect you. To shelter you. You're a fighter, and I like that, but this fight you can't win. So don't waste your time." He couldn't be anybody other than who he'd become, so he let her see all of him.

Her breath hitched, and he didn't give her a chance to argue. His mouth crashed down on hers, claiming her with all the emotion he didn't know how to express. She gasped against his lips, her hands fisting in his shirt as she gave in to the pull between them.

Fire and fury, the kiss turned into a battle of wills that spiraled heat through his body as if he'd been shocked. He swept his tongue into her mouth, tasting sass and berry tea, demanding everything she had to give. She met him with equal passion, her nails biting into his shoulders as if trying to anchor herself.

His hands moved to her waist, lifting her onto the desk with effortless strength. She made a sound—a mix of protest and surrender—but he silenced it with another kiss, his lips trailing down her neck to the twin indents he'd already marked her with. But they weren't deep enough. Not even close.

"You drive me insane," he murmured against her skin, his voice hoarse with need. "Do you have any idea how hard it is to know there's someone out there who would kill you just to get to me?"

Her hands slid into his hair, tugging hard enough to make him growl. "I was relatively safe."

"Relatively is unacceptable." His lips trailed lower, his teeth grazing her collarbone. "I'm telling you that I'll tear apart anyone who tries to hurt you. Keep that in mind next time you venture out against orders."

Her breath shuddered out, and she arched against him as his hands slid under her sweater. Her skin was warm beneath his palms, her heartbeat hammering against his touch.

"Vero," she said, her voice breaking on his name.

He pulled back just enough to meet her gaze, his hands framing her face. "You have never had anyone put you first, have you?"

She blinked at him, her lips trembling, but she didn't answer. She didn't have to. He already knew.

"I will, Lyrica," he said, his voice fierce. "Every single day, I will put you first."

Her lips parted, and for a moment, he thought she might push him away. But then she pulled him closer, her body melting into his as if she'd finally stopped fighting.

For the first time since he'd heard she was out there alone, the furious storm inside him shifted from anger to something else.

Hunger.

* * * *

Lyrica's breath came in short, shallow bursts as Vero's lips moved against hers, demanding and consuming. The weight of his body caged her in, pressed her against the desk, and shock slammed through her at how much she wanted to let him take over.

How much she wanted to trust him.

She plastered both hands against the hard muscles of his chest, and that defined masculinity made her knees weak. "Vero. What do you want?"

"You. All of you."

Panic jerked her shoulders toward him. "It's too much."

Slowly, he shook his head, his callused fingers brushing her bare abdomen. "No. There is no 'too much.'"

She gulped, her lungs on fire. Her entire body felt like she'd been dipped into a volcano, and every time she breathed in, she breathed him. Male, wilderness, even the snow. "This isn't sane. We barely know each other. Mating was an accident."

His hands stilled on the sweater, his fingers merely touching her skin and shooting sparks of electricity to her clit. "My people? They believe in fate." His gaze darkened to the blue of twilight just before the darkness smothers the day.

Her heart hitched and her brain rebelled. "Fate? That's just a cop-out. An easy way out of taking a risk. Of taking responsibility."

He whipped the sweater over her head, tossing it across the desk. "I'm taking responsibility. And I'm sure as hell taking a risk, woman. The question remaining is whether you have the guts to do the same."

"That's a dare," she whispered, her eyes widening. "Give me a break. I know what I'm doing." But did she? Really?

"Do you?" he asked, his tone cutting. "Because I'm not seeing it. What I see is someone who thinks she can take on the world alone, who refuses to acknowledge her own vulnerabilities."

Her lips parted to argue, but no words came. His gaze pinned her, sharp and unyielding, and she hated how much truth there was in his words.

"I'm not alone," she said finally, her voice trembling despite her best effort to sound strong. "I'm here. With you."

"Yet you're still fighting us," he said, his voice softening. "Still trying to prove you don't need me."

Her stomach twisted, the weight of his words hitting harder than she wanted to admit. She'd spent so long fighting for every scrap of independence, every shred of control over her own life, that letting someone else step in—even someone like Vero—felt like giving up.

"I don't know how to let someone in," she admitted, the words spilling out before she could stop them. Her voice cracked, and she hated herself for the vulnerability that crept in, but it was the truth.

Vero's expression softened, though his eyes remained intense. "Baby, you didn't stay in this territory because you wanted a job."

Her mouth dropped open and she quickly shut it. Had she been that transparent? If she truly looked at herself, if she finally went for honest reflection, she'd been falling for the deadly warrior since the first day they'd met. That timeline she'd put on her job here had been to protect herself.

"I felt it too." He cupped her face with one hand, his thumb brushing her cheek. "Dreamed at night about you. Wanted you. But I figured that I'd be dead soon, so I didn't let myself dream in the daylight. Now, I can."

His vulnerability, true honesty, halted any retort she might've made. "But your so-called fate took away those thoughts."

"Fate just spurred me along," he countered, one finger releasing her bra. "There was no turning back for either of us, but we just didn't know it. I'm never turning back."

The promise held weight. "What are you saying?"

"I mated you as a demon. There's no going back from that." He kissed her again, scraping his fangs along her neck. "I want to mate you as a Kurjan. I am going to do so." He flicked her ear, his chuckle low when she shuddered. "But not until you ask nicely."

She couldn't think with his mouth on her skin. "I, ah, I wouldn't, um, hold your breath."

"Kurjans can hold their breath for hours." Slowly, his fangs sank into her neck, right as his hand shot into her pants, cupping her.

Her knees went weak.

He licked the wound. "You taste like berries. Sweet with just a hint of sass." He slipped inside her panties, brushing easily through wetness. "For now, I want a promise that you won't go into danger again."

Her breath stopped. If he just moved his hand slightly upward, she might orgasm. "I'm not, I mean, I don't answer to you."

He paused.

Awareness ran through her.

His free hand jerked her pants and panties right down to her ankles. "We can do this one of two ways. You're gonna want to answer to me right about now. Promise me." He plunged two fingers inside her.

She cried out from the delicious invasion. Streaks moved across her vision. "No," she gasped, so close to orgasm she held her breath.

"Hmm. Unfortunate." His fingers twisted and he pressed his thumb against her clit, shooting her instantly into an orgasm that had her eyelids shutting and her body gyrating against him.

She whimpered as she came down, shocked. He'd taken her right over the edge with just his hand. Quickly. She blinked. So, defying him led to spectacular orgasms. Good to know.

"Wrong conclusion," he drawled.

She stilled. Had she said that out loud?

Still keeping his hand in place, he flipped her around. His other hand, strong and wide, flattened against her upper back and pushed her down.

She went easily, turning her head on the cool oak surface, desire ripping through her. He kicked her legs farther apart with one booted foot and she tried to lift up and protest.

He kept her in place.

Live wires uncoiled inside her, sending more wetness to coat his fingers.

He chuckled, brushing her clit again. "I've asked very nicely, Lyrica. Give me what I want."

She shut her eyes as more waves of pleasure rippled along her every nerve ending. "No."

The hand on her back slid up to clasp her neck, while he removed his fingers.

She bit her lip to refrain from moaning. Or begging.

The air whistled, a slap echoed loudly, then pain careened through her bottom.

She jerked, trying to lift herself, but the hand on her nape kept her pinned. "What in the world?" she snapped.

"The hard way," he said congenially, spanking her again.

Hard.

Her body jolted, and fire spread from her butt to her sex and up her entire torso to her breasts. She couldn't breathe. Nobody in her entire life had dared to spank her.

He nudged her legs even farther apart and slipped his hand between them, brushing her clit.

She gasped.

"You might like this. We'll see." He spanked her again, setting up a hard and oddly rhythmic motion that forced her up on her tiptoes in a worthless attempt to avoid the blows.

The pain spread with electric tingles through her skin, her body taking both pleasure and pain, confusing her.

At her nape, his hold relented. "Stay here."

"Or what?" she gasped, butt aching, her body empty and needing him. She flattened both hands on the desk to push up. To defy him.

"Or I use my belt."

She stopped moving.

"Good girl." Clothing rustled, his head brushed her thigh, then he turned, between her sex and the desk.

"What—" She gasped as his heated tongue scraped across her clit. She relaxed against the desk, no longer wanting to move away.

His hands grasped her butt, strong fingers digging into bruised skin, but before she could protest, his mouth and tongue went at her. Another orgasm rushed through her, and she gasped, her body vibrating. Then another.

She mumbled something against the desk.

Then he moved again, sliding back behind her. She was too spent to argue. The release of a zipper echoed around them, his hands grabbed her hips, and he powered inside her to the hilt.

She stiffened, breathing out as pain and pleasure mixed so there were only feelings. All of them. Then he started to pound, holding her with rough hands, taking this time. Gasping, stiffening, she climbed toward that pinnacle, still unable to move. She felt him everywhere.

The desire to ask for his fangs, to ask nicely, as he put it, had her biting her lip again. She couldn't think. Only feel. When she crested this time, she cried out his name, her body going lax as he shuddered against her.

Silence fell.

She couldn't move. She might never move again.

He must've fixed his clothing before pulling up her pants and yanking his shirt over her head. Tugging her around, he ducked and tossed her over a shoulder.

"Wait. What are you doing?" she asked groggily. Spent.

"Taking you to bed. You're not ready to ask nicely to be mated by a Kurjan. However, you are going to promise to behave yourself and stay safe." He punctuated the last with a firm slap to her abused butt. "I promise, before the night is over, you will give me those words."

It turned out the Kurjan warrior was right.

Chapter Thirty-Three

Vero walked down the stairs, rolling his shoulders as a morning chill filled the lodge. The atmosphere thickened, proving the Convexus would take place the following night. For now, he'd left Lyrica sleeping peacefully in their room, her dark hair spilling across the pillow. The brand on his hand had calmed, the pulsing heat from the night before fading, leaving his mind clearer than it had been in weeks.

In the main lodge, Jonathan and Lukas had already set up a checkerboard near the fireplace, the faint sound of their banter carrying through the space. Silas leaned against the wall near the coffee station, drinking from a big cup.

Vero stopped, crossing his arms as his gaze pinned them. "She doesn't leave without you on her six, and I want advance notice if she so much as steps outside. If anything happens to her," he added, his voice low, "I'll kill you both."

Jonathan snorted while Lukas's eyes widened.

"Got it," Lukas coughed.

"Here. We found the belongings stashed by the idiots who attacked us the other night." Jonathan nodded toward a couple of knapsacks at his feet. "From what I can tell, the cell with the stupid symbol had six members here in our territory. We killed three, leaving three still within our encampment. I can't tell if there are more of their cell members in contact on the outside."

"Damn it," Vero muttered. He should have pushed Geoff harder. "I killed him too quickly."

"Maybe, maybe not," Jonathan said, folding his arms behind his head. "Some people don't break, and he knew you were going to kill him anyway." Vero didn't reply. The truth was, his temper had gotten the better of him. The bastard had talked about Lyrica—about hurting her—and Vero hadn't been able to think past his rage. "I'll do better next time."

Jonathan shrugged. "We'll get them. I analyzed their communications. There are definitely six participants, and they call themselves the Defenders. From what I can tell, there are many different cells and they don't communicate much with each other. Seems smart. Nobody can betray the others." He took a deep breath. "I consider you both my boss and my friend."

Vero stilled. "Ditto." He'd known Jonathan his entire life, and the soldier had always been kind, even when training Vero years ago. But friendship? This was new. "Why do you mention it now?"

"I scent your mate on you. That puts her in danger, and I wanted to let you know." Jonathan kept his gaze. "Without pissing you off."

Something settled in Vero's chest. Mated. He had a mate. "I appreciate it." Nobody had picked up on his being part demon as of yet. That was good. The brand on Vero's hand had lightened, but it was still there. "She's still vulnerable even without this new danger." Nobody really knew how long it took for a human to become immortal. It seemed to vary with each human.

Lukas glanced at him from beneath his brows. "Um, I'm dating a girl, you know. They like weddings. Just an FYI. Are you going to marry Lyrica?"

Vero hesitated. "Kurjans don't marry much anymore. Centuries ago, sure."

"She's human," Lukas reminded him. "They like that kind of thing."

Vero hadn't considered that fact. "I'll think about it." He had also only mated her as a demon and not a Kurjan, not that it probably mattered biologically or genetically. He'd promised Lyrica time to adjust, but there was a part of him that wanted—needed—to finish the bond. He shoved the thought aside. "I want to see the doc, then I'll interview anybody I can find who knew the attackers." He'd barely known them.

"Nobody seemed to know them well," Jonathan said. "From what I can tell, they joined that small band a while back."

"They were from the Donbas region, right?" Vero asked, sifting through his memory.

"That's what it looks like," Jonathan agreed. "Either they met three more Defenders here, or they joined the movement once they were already in the nation."

That possibility seemed the most logical.

"That's my guess. Otherwise, what's the point? It's not like they knew that Paxton would become our king," Silas said, finally taking his face out of his huge coffee mug.

Lukas nodded. "That's good news in a way. It means they haven't had time to plan."

"I'll start asking around," Vero said.

Silas reached into his pocket to toss a cell phone at Vero. "We now have cell service and the internet. I had a teenager program all our numbers into each one."

Vero snatched the phone out of the air. "Finally. Do you have one for—" He caught the next phone. These were way beyond what the humans currently used. "Thanks." He pressed a couple of buttons to note that his number was the first one programmed into Lyrica's, with Hope and Paxton next. Good. That's what he would've done.

Vero tossed Lyrica's phone at Lukas, impressed when the young soldier caught it easily. "Give that to Lyrica when she comes down. Do you two have phones?"

"Yep," Lukas said, placing Lyrica's phone on the table. "I put Genevieve as my number one."

"Good thought." Vero headed toward the door. "Text me if Lyrica wants to leave the lodge." As he stepped into the frigid morning air, he noted the guards stationed at their posts and gave them a short nod. The crisp cold helped sharpen his focus as he walked toward the medical facility and opened the heavy door.

Inside, the oppressive heat hit him immediately. "What the hell, Fizzlewick?" he muttered. "It's like a sauna in here."

Dr. Fizzlewick looked up from his desk, his black hair wild with the red tips curling, his purple eyes bloodshot. "Sorry. I was up all night and the temp dropped precipitously."

"Why haven't you slept?"

Fizzlewick rubbed his temples. "I looked over the bodies of the two remaining human females again. Poor young victims. We had to put them in a snowbank until we figure out who they are. I also searched the internet for any missing person reports, but so far, nothing."

Vero frowned. "Lyrica was looking into that yesterday. We may need to widen the search."

"I'm already running it through the new computers," Fizzlewick said, nodding toward the new, recently set-up, glowing monitors. "The newest upgrades are impressive."

"Good," Vero said. But his thoughts were already spinning ahead, back to Lyrica—and the dangers she didn't yet understand. "Have you found anything else?" He leaned against the desk, his arms crossed as he studied the ancient doctor.

Dr. Fizzlewick rubbed his temples. "Yes. I found gasoline traces on the last victim, but that could've come from anything. Even just riding in a UTV. Also, the attacker had to have immense or immortal strength to carve those symbols into the victims' flesh to that depth, but those females were just human—fragile, breakable, killable." He sat back in his chair, looking every bit his three thousand–plus years. "I just don't understand, Vero. None of this makes sense to me."

"Me either," Vero said, exhaling heavily. "We'll give them a proper burial if necessary, but first, we'll find out who they were. It's the least we can do. They were killed in our territory on purpose, to make Paxton look weak—and because someone out there is a sick bastard." His jaw tightened. "I can't wait to get my hands on the killer." The Convexus was the next night, and he wasn't ready. Couldn't even make sure the territory was safe enough for Paxton to return.

Fizzlewick lifted his empty mug and scowled. "Out of coffee again." He placed it down with a loud clink. "Any leads on who might've done this?"

Vero shook his head. "Not yet. Jonathan found and went through the belongings of the three attackers we killed—those wearing the mark. He's confirmed there are six of them in total here in our territory. That leaves three still here and who knows how many on the outside."

"Do you know anything about the dead three?" Fizzlewick asked, leaning forward.

"Not yet, and there's nobody to really ask." Vero frowned.

Fizzlewick nodded, his expression grim. "I'll ask around. Sometimes people will talk to a doctor when they won't talk to anyone else. But it's clear this group was secretive. Whoever the remaining three are, they've probably gone underground."

"Except they keep killing human females," Vero said, frustration heating his throat. "We can't even figure out where the females came from."

Fizzlewick steepled his fingers. "That trace of gasoline on the last victim could be from riding a snowmobile for days, but nobody's been absent that long from our ranks—not that we've found, anyway."

"Unless," Vero mused, "they have an accomplice bringing the females here."

Fizzlewick removed his glasses to rub his eyes. "Which means the killer might not even be part of the Kurjan nation."

"No. Strangers here? We'd sense them. Smell them. Patrols would see and sense signs of vehicles bringing them in, which means somebody on the inside is working with them to mask their arrival. How are we supposed to track someone like that?" Vero muttered, anger flaring hot inside him.

Fizzlewick raised a hand. "Take a breath, Vero. You're one of the best hunters we have. I've heard of your successes and exploits. You'll find these males."

"Thanks," Vero said tightly, though the weight on his chest didn't lessen.

"Have you looked through the new medical records that arrived yesterday?" Fizzlewick asked, motioning to a pile of manila folders.

"Not yet," Vero admitted.

Fizzlewick grabbed the top folder and flipped it open. "I was up all night going through the medical files. There's nothing in here about impregnating demons with Kurjan DNA or anything close to it."

Vero's chin dipped as frustration bubbled beneath his calm exterior. "I wish that surprised me, but it doesn't. If my uncles wanted to keep something secret, they'd have done it right. There'd be no paper trail."

The door to the medical facility swung open abruptly, and two soldiers stumbled inside. Romer and Dalax, both young and strong, looked as though they'd been through hell. Their faces were more pale than usual, bruises marring their skin, and they hunched over as if they'd taken bullets to the gut.

"What is wrong with you two?" Vero stepped toward them.

Dalax, who was tall even by Kurjan standards, dropped to one knee before collapsing entirely. "Something's wrong," he slurred, his words thick. "I feel...off."

"What do you mean?" Vero crouched beside him, gripping his shoulder. "What happened?"

"I don't know," Dalax muttered, his head lolling to the side. "It hit me out of nowhere."

Romer swayed before crumpling to the floor.

Vero lunged, catching him before his face hit the concrete. "Fizzlewick, help me out here."

Fizzlewick was already moving, his sharp gaze assessing the situation. "Lay him flat," he ordered. "Dalax, have you ingested anything unusual? Anything new or rotten or that could've been drugged?"

"No...nothing..." Dalax mumbled, his head rolling again.

Before Fizzlewick could respond, another knock came at the door. Silas stumbled in, looking as pale and sickly as the other two. "Damn it, Vero. I'm sick."

Vero grabbed Silas by the arm and helped him to a chair. "What's going on?"

Silas shook his head, sweat beading on his brow. "I feel dizzy. My head hurts. My stomach's churning like crazy, and I think—hell, I think my brain's swelling."

Fizzlewick threw up his hands. "I don't know what's causing this."

"Figure it out," Vero snapped. "Run tests. Ask questions. Do something. I need answers."

As if on cue, Vero's phone buzzed in his pocket. He pulled it out, his irritation mounting when he saw a text from Lukas: LYRICA WANTS TO VISIT A FRIEND. MAEVE CALLED IN EARLIER SAYING THAT HER MATE HAS FALLEN ILL.

Vero's jaw tightened as he slipped the phone back into his pocket. Was Lyrica feeling okay? Was there a new illness now threatening his fragile, still possibly human, sweet mate? He had to see for himself. "I have to go," he told Fizzlewick, turning toward the door. "Figure out what's going on. I'll be back in thirty minutes."

Before Fizzlewick could respond, the door swung open again, and three more soldiers stumbled inside, their faces pale and their movements sluggish.

Vero stopped, staring in disbelief. "Did you all eat the same thing? Have you been in the same area?"

One of the soldiers, Lance, turned to the side and vomited green bile into the snow just outside the doorway.

"Gross," Buclaw muttered, stepping around him as he staggered inside.

"We've got three more," Vero called to Fizzlewick. "Find out what they ate, where they've been, and lock this down. Now."

Fizzlewick nodded, already moving to assist the new arrivals.

Vero's hands clenched into fists as he stepped back outside. The cold air hit his face, doing little to cool the fire raging within him. His thoughts turned immediately to Lyrica. What if she'd eaten whatever was rotten? Or even worse, poisoned?

The fear that shot through him was unlike anything he'd felt before. For most of his life, he'd only been responsible for himself—or for Paxton, once Vero had made his choice about loyalty. But this was different. This was absolute.

She was his mate, his everything, and he would burn the world down to keep her safe.

Chapter Thirty-Four

Lyrica tried to hide her discomfort as she poured herself a travel mug of coffee and carefully balanced a plate of donuts she'd snagged from the kitchen. The new chef had created incredible pastries, and she wanted a chance to talk with him more, but he'd left the kitchen without leaving a note.

Her entire body felt sore and well-used. There wasn't an inch that Vero hadn't kissed, bitten, or claimed the night before. Not to mention spanked. She wanted to be angry, but her body felt too deliciously satisfied. Yet it hurt to move even a little.

She had finally given him the words he wanted by agreeing to take safety precautions at all times, and now she felt more vulnerable than ever. Her heart was definitely involved, but he was overbearing and bossy, and she didn't want to like that. She didn't want to find security in that. And yet...she had never felt safer.

Did she want to be mated as a Kurjan? Did it even matter? Probably not physically, but to Vero, it mattered. Could she take that risk with her heart? Or was it already too late?

The door swung open, and there Vero stood, his towering frame filling the doorway. "Where are you going?"

She glanced at Lukas, who looked down at the checkerboard between Jonathan and him. A sheen of sweat covered his brow. "Tattletale," she muttered under her breath.

Lukas's ears turned red, but he didn't respond.

"I'm going to visit Maeve and take her donuts," Lyrica said, lifting her chin. "She called in and said that Ralstad is sick. She's worried, and I want to check on them both."

Amusement flickered in Vero's blue eyes. "I'll take you because I want to check on Ralstad. But ditch the donuts, and nobody eat anything until we figure out why some of the soldiers are getting sick. My guess is that we have a food poisoning situation."

She hastily slipped the donut tray onto the bar shelf. "Can Kurjans get food poisoning?"

"Not often," Vero said, glancing at Lukas. "How are you guys feeling?"

Lukas shrugged, planting a hand on his stomach. "Not great."

Jonathan grimaced. "Not sure."

"Go see the doctor and tell him everything you've eaten recently. There has to be a common food." Vero's gaze narrowed on Lyrica. "How are you feeling?"

"Fine." She patted her hair into place. "But I haven't eaten anything yet today." She'd been counting on having a donut at Maeve's and reluctantly put her mug next to the donuts, which still looked delicious. She shuffled toward him, grabbing her coat off the sofa and shrugging into it. Checking out Lukas's pale face, she frowned and followed Vero outside into the biting cold. The freshly shoveled walkway crunched under her boots as she carefully made her way to the UTV.

Pleasure swept through her as she settled against the heated seat, letting the warmth surround her.

Vero climbed in next to her, the UTV rocking under his weight. Once inside, he turned to her, his intense gaze locking on hers. "How are you?"

How was she? That was a loaded question. She hesitated, unsure how to answer. "I'm fine," she said finally.

His lips thinned. "I may not have been mated long, but I know 'I'm fine' isn't a good sign. How sore are you?"

Her head jerked up, and she could almost feel fire flash from her eyes. "Well, my butt is very sore, thank you very much. You bruised me."

"I spanked you," he corrected, his voice firm but tinged with amusement. "It's not supposed to feel good. Well…not too good, anyway." A wicked grin lifted his lips.

Heat surged to her face, the blush actually painful. The things she had let him do to her the night before, she could barely believe. Yet it had been worth every second. She crossed her arms, glaring.

"Still." His gaze softened. "Having you bruised isn't ideal."

His fangs dropped, glinting in the morning light.

She cringed back against the door. "What are you doing?"

He held out his wrist and slashed his fangs into it. Blood welled immediately. "Here. Take blood. We're *mated*. It won't hurt you—it'll help you."

"I'm not drinking your blood," she snapped.

He sighed, clearly losing patience. Before she could react, he reached out, cradled the back of her head, and pressed his wrist against her lips.

She tried to fight him, but the liquid slid over her tongue, sparking like wildfire. Her eyes watered, but to her surprise, the taste wasn't bad. In fact, it was...delicious. Spicy and dark, with a hint of sweetness she couldn't quite place. Against her will, she swallowed several mouthfuls, warmth spreading from her belly to the rest of her body.

He finally pulled his wrist away. "We're mated, so my blood should help you—won't burn you any longer."

She licked her lips, shaking her head slightly. "It's like I just tasted something very spicy. But I like spicy food."

The warmth continued to spread through her limbs, and she suddenly felt lighter. Stronger. Healed. She rolled her shoulders, shifting her weight on the seat experimentally. "That's...amazing," she breathed.

The soreness had vanished entirely. When was the last time she hadn't experienced any pain? She looked at him, wide-eyed. "You feel like this all the time?"

He chuckled. "I'm usually getting punched in the face, but yeah, we feel like that when we're not in battle."

"Wow." She leaned back, still marveling at the sensation. "Hey, as I become more immortal...how does that work? Once my chromosomal pairs combine, I mean...will I feel like this?"

He shrugged. "I have no idea. Probably."

"Wow," she said again. This might be worth the occasional spanking. She pulled a wrapped candy out of her pocket. "I've been eating these all week, and they're wrapped. No poison." She unwrapped it and popped the chocolate morsel into her mouth. The instant the treat touched her tongue, her eyes widened. "Even this tastes better. Does food taste better to you?"

He put the UTV in drive, frowning slightly. "I don't know. I don't have anything to compare it to. But food tastes good, usually."

"You don't understand," she said, savoring the deliciousness. "It's like I can taste every molecule of this chocolate. The cocoa beans that created it. The sun that nourished the plants. The water that hydrated the soil."

He cast her a quick glance, his brow furrowing as two soldiers stumbled past outside. "I just usually taste chocolate."

"This is amazing." She swallowed the candy and even her stomach warmed. No wonder Maeve seemed so content. The world tasted incredible. She paused mid-thought, watching the soldiers. "Are those soldiers drunk?"

"No. Looks like they're sick. We need to figure out what everyone has eaten. I haven't had anything yet today, either." He turned his attention back to her, speeding up and driving out of the main hub of the territory. Trees surrounded them. "Are you sure you feel healthy?"

"I just told you. Incredible. Nothing hurts."

His gaze raked her, head to toe. "Good. Tell me if that changes."

Bossy.

A flash of green light seared the air, and Lyrica turned just as a laser tore through the UTV's front window, striking Vero in the face. His head snapped back, blood spurted across the broken glass, and the vehicle screeched to a halt, the sudden stop throwing her against the dash. She gasped, pain ricocheting through her ribs as her door was wrenched open. Rough hands grabbed her, dragging her into the cold.

Her breath hitched as she twisted, trying to break free. "Vero!" she screamed, the word raw and desperate. He wasn't moving. Fear coiled around her throat, threatening to choke her.

Coron, a soldier she recognized from camp, gripped her arm hard enough that tears sprang to her eyes. His face, once familiar, twisted into something cruel and foreign.

"What are you doing?" She attempted to wrench her arm free, but his grip tightened painfully.

Another Kurjan soldier emerged from the tree line, his boots crunching through the snow. What was his name? Saren. That's right. "Silence her," he snapped, his tone sharp and irritated. "She's drawing attention."

"She's not going anywhere," Coron grunted, pulling her closer. His grip bit into her skin, sending pain lancing up her arm.

"Vero!" she screamed again, desperation breaking through her fear.

His eyes opened suddenly. A guttural sound tore from his chest, deep and feral. He jolted upright in the UTV, a primal roar ripping from his throat. Her blood froze. The sound was inhuman, otherworldly—raw fury made audible.

He vaulted out of the vehicle, charging straight toward Saren. The impact was brutal. The male's body slammed against a tree, bark cracking beneath the force. The sickening thud of skull against wood made her stomach churn, the sound reminding her of a watermelon smashing onto the ground.

Before the male could react, Vero's fangs sank into his neck with swift precision. In one brutal motion, he jerked his head, tearing out half of the Kurjan's throat. Blood sprayed in vivid arcs against the snow as Vero punched through Saren's throat to the bloody tree. Saren's head rolled off his shoulders before his body fell.

Lyrica froze, the air rushing from her lungs. She'd never seen violence so unrestrained, so absolute. Vero turned, blood dripping from the fresh bullet wound in his cheek. His eyes, darker than she'd ever seen, glinted with a ring of pale blue.

"Let her go," he demanded, his voice low and cold, a predator's growl.

Coron yanked her closer. "Not a chance, trait—"

She acted on instinct, letting her knees buckle and her body go slack into dead weight. Her sudden drop startled him enough to loosen his grip, and she hit the icy ground with a jarring thud. In the same instant, Vero was on him.

They collided in a flurry of movement, fists flying, grunts of effort punctuating the chaos. The fight was vicious, raw. Snow scattered as they rolled, each seeking the upper hand. Coron managed to land a punch directly to Vero's injured cheek. Blood sprayed, staining the ground.

The sight jolted Lyrica into action. Scrambling on hands and knees, she searched for a weapon. Her eyes landed on the glint of a gun half buried in the snow near the first soldier's body. She reached for it, but her boots skidded out from under her. She fell, her palms scraping against ice.

A roar cut through the air, and she looked up in time to see Vero drive a knife into Coron's throat. The soldier's eyes went wide with shock and his hands clawed at the blade, but Vero didn't stop. He twisted the knife, his expression unrelenting. Then he clapped both hands against Coron's temples, and the Kurjan's eyes rolled back in his head before he dropped, unconscious.

The fight ended abruptly. Silence fell, broken only by the ragged sound of her breathing. Lyrica stared as Vero stood, his chest heaving. He yanked Coron's body up by the jacket.

"Get in the UTV," Vero ordered, turning so his gaze locked on hers.

Her body obeyed before her mind could catch up. She scrambled into the passenger seat, gripping the edge of the console to ground herself to reality. Moments later, Vero tossed Coron's limp body into the back. "Stay here."

She gulped and stared back at the unconscious Kurjan with the blade still embedded in his throat. Her stomach lurched, but she turned to see Vero tearing the jacket and shirt off the headless body outside. His shoulders straightened, and he turned, walking around to take the driver's seat.

"His torso?" she whispered.

He nodded. "Yeah. The brand of the circle with the three slashes was over his heart." He started the engine. "I'll send soldiers out to check on Maeve and Ralstad."

"Are you all right?" she managed, her voice trembling. She turned to him, her gaze falling on the wound marring his cheek.

He kept his gaze on the snowy trail ahead. "I'm fine," he said curtly.

"You're bleeding," she pressed, her words unsteady. "Badly."

"I'll manage." His tone softened, just enough to make her chest ache.

She hesitated, then held out her wrist. "Would my blood help?"

His eyes flicked to hers, something unreadable passing through his expression. Slowly, he nodded. "Thank you," he said, the words quiet.

Her pulse quickened as he took her wrist in one hand, his grip firm but careful. His lips brushed against her skin, and then his fangs pierced her. The sting was brief, a sharpness that gave way to warmth. She gasped as he drew from her, the pull of her blood intimate. Her heart thudded in her chest, each beat echoing in her ears.

When he pulled back, he licked the wound closed, his eyes meeting hers. "Thank you," he said again, his voice steady.

"Why did they want me?" she whispered, her voice barely audible.

"To make a point," he replied, his jaw tightening. "I knew you were in danger. I shouldn't have let you leave the lodge."

The weight of his words pressed against her, heavy and unyielding. She looked down at her hands, her fingers trembling. "To make a point?" Why would anybody take her to make a point?

"They know you're mine," he said, his voice firm. "If they kill you, they kill me."

The raw honesty in his tone left her breathless. She leaned back in her seat, her mind racing. Despite all his strength, his power, he wasn't invincible. If he had a weakness, it was *her.*

Chapter Thirty-Five

Lyrica huddled at her desk, a space heater from the new shipment blasting at her feet. No matter what she did, she couldn't seem to get warm. Outside her office door, two guards stood at attention, while Vero busily tortured Coron for information in some underground cell. Vero thought there were six members of the cell who wore the weird symbol, and with four dead, that left two—Coron and someone unknown. For now.

Which one of them was attacking human females?

She had discovered an unopened box of tea and deemed it safe to drink. More of the Kurjans had fallen ill, and Fizzlewick still hadn't identified the source of the poisoned food. Even the chef had succumbed. At this point, they couldn't be sure if the poisoning was accidental—or something far more sinister.

Taking another sip, her mind scattered and refused to focus. She set the mug down and stared at her computer console, deciding to take a chance. Dialing up Hope, she waited, and soon her friend's face appeared on the screen.

"Hey." Hope's voice sounded bright, though her sharp blue eyes immediately searched Lyrica's expression. "Vero called Paxton earlier about the illness and about your near kidnapping. Are you okay?"

"I'm not physically ill, but my mind is spinning," Lyrica admitted, her words tumbling out before she could think. "Honestly, I've never seen anything like it. Vero is such a good guy. He gave up the crown for Paxton, supports him every way he can. He's selfless. Loyal. But—" She paused, taking a deep breath. "I thought I could save him. God, I feel so stupid."

"Who says you can't?" Hope replied, her cheerfulness intact, though her gaze turned serious.

Lyrica's chest tightened as the memories clawed at her. "You didn't see him kill. It was...terrifying." She hesitated before lowering her voice. "I think it was because of me."

"Oh, it was absolutely because of you," Hope said matter-of-factly.

Lyrica blinked. "Hey, you're supposed to make me feel better, not worse."

"Nope." Hope grinned, shaking her head. "I'm here to give you the truth, not coddle you. You're in danger because you're his mate. That's how it works."

"Remind me not to put myself in danger again," Lyrica muttered.

Hope snorted. "Yeah, believe me, I've been there."

Lyrica studied her friend through the screen, noting the worn expression softened only by her easy smile. "You really do get it, don't you? Paxton would tear the world apart for you, wouldn't he?" Like actually and not figuratively do it.

Hope's smile faded into something quieter, a little heavier. "Yes, he would."

Before today, such devotion had sounded romantic, almost poetic. Now, Lyrica understood the brutal reality behind those words.

"Vero would never hurt you, though," Hope added gently. "You know that, right?"

Lyrica exhaled shakily. "Yes. I do know that. But I don't know if..."

"If what?"

"How can I love someone who kills like that?" Lyrica stared down at her tea.

Hope leaned back, her own expression shifting. "Ah. That." She rubbed at her temple. "Yeah, I get it. You grew up human, not among immortals who are always at war, so it's a lot to take in. But...what would you do to protect him?"

The question hit harder than Lyrica expected. She reached for her tea blindly, taking a sip while her mind spun. "I guess...I'd defend him."

Hope nodded. "There's your answer. That's what you do for the people you love."

"We haven't talked about love," Lyrica admitted, her voice soft. "I don't know how he feels about—well, any of this."

Hope held up her hand, her palm bruised. "I doubt he knows how to talk about feelings. You might have to lead him on that one."

Lyrica's gaze sharpened. "Wait, why is your hand bruised?"

"I was sparring with Collin," Hope said with a shrug. "I just haven't bothered to send any healing cells to it yet."

Lyrica's lips quirked. "I have to ask—does everything taste amazing to you? Like, is food just beyond excellent?"

Hope snickered. "I don't know. But I don't like broccoli."

"Huh. Now I want to try some to see if I like it," Lyrica mused, half to herself.

Her thoughts drifted to earlier, to the way she'd offered her wrist without hesitation. Vero could have drained her dry, and she'd have let him, just to make sure he healed from that bullet wound. "He got shot in the face," she murmured. "He killed one immortal for me, knocked another out like it was nothing."

Hope, unbothered, peeled open a candy bar and took a bite. "Yep. That's how they are. Makes you feel all the responsibility, doesn't it?"

"Yes." Lyrica's voice rose. "Exactly. I didn't think I'd feel like this. I mean, I'm glad he can protect me—I've never felt safer—but now I feel like it's my job to make sure he doesn't have to."

"Exactly," Hope said with a knowing nod. "It's a partnership. You make his life easier; he does the same for you."

Lyrica sat back, her tea forgotten. "I don't want to get anyone killed."

Hope tilted her head, her smile sly. "You love him."

"Shut up," Lyrica muttered, her cheeks heating. "When are you coming home?"

The screen fell silent as both women paused. Lyrica hadn't missed the way Hope's brows arched at her choice of words. Coming home. To the Kurjan nation. The realization tightened something in her chest.

Hope, gracious as always, didn't call her on it. "Tomorrow morning in time for the Convexus. Can't wait to see you."

But half the Kurjan nation had fallen ill. So far. How could they hide that from the Cyst soldiers? Lyrica's head began to ache.

Hope leaned closer to the camera. "Forget about the violence for a minute."

"Gladly," Lyrica replied, her shoulders sagging.

"How's the sex?" Hope asked, her grin impish.

* * * *

Vero was on the third hour of torturing the prisoner for information. The bastard wasn't giving anything up easily. He knew he was going to die today, but Vero intended to make him beg for it first. Blood dripped from the edge of his blade, pooling on the cold floor, and Vero decided to take a break. Sometimes mental torture worked better than physical.

Vero exited the room and glanced down at his blood-soaked clothes. He paused on the steps, still feeling the dull ache in his cheekbone. He'd heal, but the residual pain annoyed him. Jogging outside, he stopped abruptly, noticing the eerie stillness that had settled over the camp.

He stomped inside the main lodge, only to pause when a few females shrieked. He glanced down at his gore-covered shirt and jeans and tried for casual. "I skinned a deer."

Lyrica's sharp gaze locked on him. "Are you all right?"

"Yes." He scanned the room, his eyes landing on the assembled human females, who stared at him as though he'd just stepped out of a horror movie. "Does everyone here feel okay?"

"Not really," a blonde offered, her voice shaky. He vaguely remembered her name—Sandy? Mandy? "You look like death," she added.

He felt like death.

Lyrica gulped. "We're all feeling fine, but the doctor wants to see you."

"I'll be right back." He strode toward the stairs and took them three at a time

Upstairs, he scrubbed the blood from his skin in a hot shower, his movements brisk and efficient. Once clean, he threw on fresh clothes and headed back down, his gaze immediately catching Lukas leaning heavily against the far wall next to a sitting down and pale Silas.

"Lukas," Vero called sharply.

The younger male blinked slowly. "I promised I wouldn't leave. I haven't left." His knees buckled.

"Lukas," Lyrica yelled as the kid's eyes rolled back in his head.

Vero surged forward, catching Lukas before he hit the ground. Throwing the unconscious soldier over his shoulder, he looked down at Silas. "How bad are you?"

"Not great." Silas pushed to his feet, swaying, his face grave. "Most of the soldiers are down, but I'm armed and can shoot. I'll protect the females. Just get me backup when you can."

"I'll be back," Vero said. His gaze lingered on Lyrica until she nodded, and then he strode outside into the frigid air. Soldiers lined the area, most of them slumped on the ground or huddled over the snow, their faces pale and sickly. A few were violently retching onto the ice, the sound grating on Vero's already frayed nerves.

He shoved open the door to the medical facility, his jaw tight as he placed Lukas on one of the beds. "Do we know anything?"

The doctor crouched to check the pulse of an unconscious soldier. His lab coat flapped as he stood, his lined face creased with worry. "No." Fizzlewick threw up his hands, exasperation sharp in his voice. "Everyone's sick. The barracks are a disaster zone—vomit, diarrhea, you name it. People are stuck in their cabins."

"You're taking note of what everyone has eaten?"

"Yes, and so far, no common denominator. We have so many schedules, and some are too sick to speak." Fizzlewick's movements were quick as he checked Lukas's pulse and examined his pupils. "I talked to the chef. He's sicker than anyone."

"So it's the food?" Vero pressed.

Fizzlewick looked around at the line of groaning soldiers. "How? You're fine. I'm fine. The females are fine. That's the key. Why are the females just fine? They've eaten the same food. At least a couple of them should be ill."

"So, if this just affects all of the males, it's deliberate. But why are you and I healthy?" Vero asked, his tone sharper than intended.

Fizzlewick sagged against the wall. "I started thinking. The only common denominator that males have and females do not is the Sunshine Cure. Could somebody have contaminated it?" Fizzlewick straightened, his glasses slipping down his nose. "Except *you* aren't ill."

Vero's fists clenched at his sides. "Neither are you."

The doctor hesitated before adjusting his glasses. "Full disclosure—I don't take the inoculations."

"What?" Vero frowned, a new thread of unease tightening in his chest.

Fizzlewick pushed up his glasses, his movements frenetic. "I don't like it," the doctor muttered. "Never have liked the sun. Don't go into it. Don't need to be inoculated against it."

Interesting. "Go on."

Fizzlewick hesitated, his brow furrowing. "If it's the inoculations, it makes sense that I'm not ill. But you..." He pointed at Vero, his finger shaking slightly. "You've had the Sunshine Cure, and yet you're fine."

The revelation hit Vero hard. "Just Kurjans require inoculations. How easy would it be to get to the concoction?"

"Very. Why would we guard it?" Fizzlewick admitted. "But that can't be it. I personally inoculated you last week. Some of these guys haven't had a shot for two weeks, yet suddenly they're all sick."

Vero scanned the room, his gaze lingering on the two soldiers curled in the corner, groaning in agony. "Is there a pattern?"

Fizzlewick nodded and moved toward a counter cluttered with hastily scribbled notes. "Yes. The older the Kurjan, the longer it took for the illness to hit them. Remember, we started the inoculations by age? I injected the younger soldiers yesterday and the day before, and they're already sick. But the older soldiers, who got their injections last week, are just now falling ill." He crossed the room to a large fridge and yanked it open. "I need to run some tests."

"Agreed," Vero said tightly, "but we need to find out fast. Everyone's weak. There's no one left to defend the territory."

Fizzlewick slammed the fridge shut and turned, his face pale but determined. "We have to figure out why you're fine. Maybe the cure is all right and they were all infected some other way. I have new lab equipment I haven't unpacked yet."

"Where?" Vero demanded, his tone sharp.

"The building next door," Fizzlewick replied, pointing out the window. "I want to use it as a dedicated lab and keep this for medical purposes. I figured, now that we're settled, some of the mates might start having babies again. We could use the space for prenatal care."

"One thing at a time." Vero cut him off, his voice steely. "We need to figure out what's happening here. Has anyone died?"

"Not yet," Fizzlewick said grimly, "but several have slipped into comas. Kurjans don't go into comas, Vero. I've never seen anything like this."

"Come on, Doc. Show me the lab," Vero said, motioning toward the door.

Fizzlewick cast one last glance at the unconscious soldiers before leading the way outside.

The biting wind stung Vero's cheeks as they navigated the icy path, stepping over more sick soldiers who had collapsed onto the ground. The air smelled faintly of vomit and misery, and Vero's temper simmered. Inside the new lab, he stopped short. "You've already started setting this up."

Fizzlewick hustled toward a stack of boxes. "I figured we'd need it eventually." He pointed to a sleek counter. "I requisitioned that. Pretty nice, huh?"

Vero ignored the comment, his focus on the array of equipment Fizzlewick began unpacking—microscopes, centrifuges, and instruments Vero would love to use again. "We need answers. Fast."

Fizzlewick straightened, his expression suddenly intense. "Talk to me, Vero. Please."

That was a fair request. He no longer had a choice. So much for keeping his secret. Vero lifted his palm, the mark faint but still visible.

"Holy shit," Fizzlewick whispered, his jaw slackening.

"Exactly," Vero muttered.

The doctor's mind seemed to race as he paced the room. "You're part demon. That's why you were asking about the crossbreeding experiments and any remaining medical records."

"Yes. This mark came as a hell of a surprise." Vero didn't like exposing his secret, but he didn't have a choice.

"So, it's the demon blood that has protected you," Fizzlewick concluded. "That's the only explanation. Whatever's in the inoculations can harm Kurjans, but not you. That also means someone deliberately tampered with it."

Vero's jaw tightened. "The medical facility wasn't exactly under lock and key. Everyone had access."

Fizzlewick nodded. "You need to find out who. This is a targeted attack. Making the entire territory ill at once is no accident."

"I'll continue questioning the Defender in my cell," Vero said. "I'll get answers. Soon."

"Good." Fizzlewick turned back to his equipment. "I need your blood. I'll analyze it and see if there's anything in it we can use to create a defense. We need to figure out whether this is fatal or if it'll burn out like a virus."

"Do it," Vero ordered, his mind already shifting to the larger implications as he held out his arm for the doctor to draw blood. "Let's keep this between us for now, all right?"

Fizzlewick pulled blood and then retracted the syringe, turning toward his equipment. "Of course. Also, I need somebody who's still upright to start checking on Kurjans out in the cabins. I'm concerned about them."

"I'm the only one who should be driving right now." Vero rolled down his sleeve and walked out of the lab, letting the frigid air cool his temper as he pulled out his phone. His thumb hesitated over the screen for a split second before dialing a number he never thought he'd use. The line connected on the first ring.

"Vero," Hunter's voice came through, immediately alert. "What's wrong?"

Vero blew out a breath, Hunter's real face flashing on the screen. He looked like his father, the king. Broad face, sharp angles, metallic blue eyes. "You were better looking as a Kurjan."

Hunter chuckled. "You would say that. What's going on? You wouldn't call unless it was serious."

Vero's jaw clenched. "I might need the Realm's help."

Hunter sobered instantly, his predatory eyes narrowing. "What kind of help?"

"A virus issue. If I remember right, you and the queen know a thing or two about those."

Hunter's expression hardened. "Tell me what you need."

Vero exhaled slowly. "We've been attacked from the inside, and that's all I know. Paxton has to return to the territory tomorrow morning, no matter what, so I have to get this figured out. We have a contagion on our hands that has infected every Kurjan, and we're just getting our lab up and running." If Paxton asked the Realm for protection of the Kurjan territory, would the Kurjan nation reject him for good?

Hunter's voice remained calm. "I'll call in my mother. For now, you don't look ill. Are you sure all the Kurjans are infected?"

"Yeah. About that..."

Chapter Thirty-Six

Lyrica finished pouring water into the large coffeepot, glancing over her shoulder at the worried females behind her. They'd been drinking coffee all morning, so at least the coffee was safe. The women scattered around the room, chatting quietly, playing board games, or gathering near the pool table in small, tense groups. Though they moved as if calm, an undeniable tension thickened the air.

All of the unmated women and more than twenty Kurjan mates filled the lodge now. More arrived sporadically as the few functioning soldiers continued escorting females to safety. Those soldiers, however, looked worse with each passing hour.

Lyrica nodded at Genevieve, who handed out bottled water, before heading toward the office where Vero leaned against the doorframe, a grim expression on his face. His shoulders carried the weight of too much responsibility.

"What do you think?" she asked, her voice low.

Knives and guns strapped to his body made him look every inch a war-hardened soldier. "We're in trouble," he said, his tone even but heavy. "Guards are posted at every entrance, and soldiers are patrolling the territory, but they're moving at half speed. Too many have collapsed." He paused, glancing back toward the main room. "I've requested backup from the Realm."

Her stomach churned. "Is that a good idea?"

"It's all I've got." His sharp blue eyes met hers. "I've ordered Realm forces to stick to the outer perimeter and stay out of the main territory. My gut says whoever did this doesn't have the numbers to stage a full attack. This isn't a rival nation moving against us."

"Unless it's the Realm itself," she murmured, the words slipping out before she could stop them.

"I spoke to Paxton and believe the Realm hasn't moved against us," Vero said, his tone firm and leaving no room for doubt. "Hope is the heir to everything in the Realm—they wouldn't attack their own."

Lyrica's brow furrowed as unease swirled in her chest. "But if it's an organized group trying to hurt us?"

Vero's jaw tightened. "Displaced Kurjans who don't like Paxton taking the throne is the most likely answer. There are scattered factions of them across the world. If they've managed to organize, they'll attack."

"And if they have?" She forced herself to breathe evenly.

"I hope the Realm arrives quickly."

The room around her seemed to blur as the weight of his words pressed against her chest. Losing the Kurjan nation felt unthinkable. "This...virus or whatever it is—" Her voice broke slightly, but she steadied it. "You're immortal. You can't die from something like this, can you?"

Power radiated from him. "Normally, no. But there has been a virus or two through the millennia that have harmed immortals. It's possible somebody created another one."

Lyrica's mind struggled to process the implications. "This doesn't feel real."

Vero's lips pressed into a tight line. "It's hard to grasp. Fizzlewick is testing the Sunshine Cure right now. I think somebody contaminated it, and I'm fine since I have demon blood in me." His voice lowered to a growl. "Fizzlewick doesn't take the cure. So at least our doctor is upright."

Her chest tightened. "So you're sure that someone did this deliberately."

"Fairly." His expression hardened, his voice like steel. "Either this virus is designed to kill us, or it's meant to weaken us for an attack—the night before our summit."

Her breath caught as his grim words settled like stones in her stomach. She glanced toward the women in the main room, their pale faces showing resolve despite the tension. "What do we do?"

"We stay ready," he said, his voice sharp with command. "I've got guards posted at every door. If someone gets too sick, they're replaced. It's not perfect, but it's the best we can do right now."

She nodded, her heart pounding. "All right. We've only been eating unopened packaged food. I guess we can eat the perishables."

"No. Just in case, don't eat anything that has been opened," Vero said, his tone softening. "Stay inside. The guards may not be perfect, but they're stationed everywhere." He rubbed his knuckles across her cheekbone, making her skin tingle. "I need to check on the outlying families and will return soon." His phone buzzed and he looked down at the face before lifting it to his ear, turning, and walking toward the door. "Hi, Paxton. Tell me the Realm is in place."

Lyrica watched him step outside and then shook herself. Her outward composure remained steady, though her mind raced. She moved through the room, spending time trying to reassure many of the women. Reaching the kitchen, she looked back at Silas across the room, who appeared ready to fall to his butt again. "I'll get more water."

He nodded, his eyes glassy.

She opened the door to the warm space and headed toward the pantry, her thoughts circling back to Vero's words. If this virus truly targeted Kurjans, it meant someone had declared war—on the entire nation.

The aroma of the pecan pastries created earlier by the chef before he'd taken ill lingered in the air, their sweet scent clinging despite the tension surrounding the lodge. Lyrica's stomach growled. She'd already thrown out the treats just in case.

The sudden creak of the side door startled her. She turned as Jonathan stumbled in, his movements shaky and erratic.

"Jonathan, you look terrible." She grabbed one of the chairs by the tall counter and pushed it toward him. "Sit down."

"No." His voice rasped as he grabbed her arm, his grip stronger than expected. "We have to go. Now."

She pulled against his hold, noting the pale cast of his skin and the unnatural glow of blue veins beneath the surface. "You're feverish. Have you been to see the doctor?"

"Come on," he insisted, his body trembling as he tried to pull her toward the door. "We're leaving now."

"No," she said firmly, planting her feet. "You're not thinking clearly. Stop."

He groaned and wiped a hand down his face, looking at her with desperation in his fevered eyes. "You don't understand," he muttered.

Reaching up, she touched his forehead, the heat radiating from him burning her palm. She yanked her hand back. "Holy crap, you're burning up."

Jonathan's chest heaved as he grabbed her with more force. "I'm not going to argue with you," he said, his voice rough and breaking. He lifted her, groaning as he carried her toward the door.

She screamed. A crash sounded from the other room. Had Silas just fallen?

Panic spiked through her, making her struggle harder. Jonathan's hands only touched her shirt, so he wasn't risking the allergy. "Jonathan, what are you doing? Put me down."

The icy wind slapped her face as he pushed through the door and into the frigid air. Snow had stopped falling, but the bitter wind burned with every gust. A UTV rumbled nearby, and she scanned the area frantically, her eyes widening at the sight of two guards lying unconscious in the snow. Dark streaks of blood painted the ground beneath them.

She sucked in air to scream, and he jerked her head back with enough force that she felt dizzy. His steps faltered, and his head shook. "Stop fighting me," he sputtered, dragging her across the icy ground.

Her stomach twisted as realization hit. "Did you knock out those guards? Are you one of the Defenders?" she asked, her voice trembling with equal parts fury and fear.

He turned to her, his expression crumbling. This close she could see blood pooling above his ear. He'd fought the guards? "Just get in the UTV."

Yanking open the door, he shoved her inside. She fought to push herself back out, but he reached across her, securing the seat belt tightly over her arms and chest. With a swift motion, he jammed a knife into the lever, preventing her from unbuckling it.

"Hold still," he growled before slamming the door shut and stumbling around the vehicle to enter the driver's side.

Her heart raced as she tugged against the seat belt, fury and terror battling for dominance. "Jonathan, I can't believe this is you. You're supposed to be a nice guy."

He grunted as he started the engine, his knuckles white on the wheel. "I did get kicked in the head," he muttered, leaning heavily against the seat. He pressed the gas pedal, and soon they zipped through the main hub and into the forest. "Just hold still."

"Let me loose." She fought against the restraints, terror filling her.

A flash of movement caught her eye just before a snowmobile zipped out from the forest, cutting directly in front of them. Jonathan cursed and yanked the wheel hard. The UTV spun out, the back end crashing into a tree. Her head whipped back, the impact jarring her spine as stars exploded behind her eyelids.

Darkness threatened to pull her under, but the sound of a door being ripped open brought her back. Bitter cold flooded the cabin, and she blinked several times, trying to clear her dazed mind. Lukas stood there, his expression grim.

"I told you, Jonathan. You can't take her," Lukas said, his voice low but fierce.

Jonathan groaned as Lukas yanked him out of the driver's seat and slammed a fist into his jaw. The force sent Jonathan stumbling, but he swung back, landing a weak punch against Lukas's shoulder. Lukas growled and struck again, this time knocking Jonathan to the ground.

"Lukas," Lyrica shouted, struggling against the seat belt. "Help me!"

"Just a second," he said through gritted teeth, crouching to deliver another blow to Jonathan's already bloodied face.

Jonathan slumped into the snow, unmoving.

Lukas wiped his knuckles on his pants before climbing into the UTV and reaching for the controls. "Are you okay?" he asked, his gaze briefly meeting hers.

"No," she snapped. "I can't believe this was Jonathan."

Lukas's face tightened as he reversed the vehicle, maneuvering it back onto the icy trail. "I know," he said grimly. "But we have to move."

Her pulse raced as she studied him. Something felt off. "Lukas, you need to turn the vehicle around," she said, her voice rising.

He didn't respond, his eyes fixed on the path ahead.

"Lukas," she repeated, sharper this time.

When he glanced her way, the chill in his expression made her stomach drop. "Wait a minute," she murmured, her gaze narrowing. "You're not sick. You knocked Jonathan out without any trouble. You look...healthy."

"Of course I'm healthy," he said, a mocking edge in his tone. "Do you honestly think I'd let them inject me with the contaminated virus?"

Silence crashed between them. She stared, disbelief warring with horror. "Lukas," she whispered. "No. It can't be you."

His lips twisted into a smirk. "Why not? Because I'm seventeen? Because I have a thing for Genevieve? Please."

Her chest heaved as she tried to process his words. "This has to be some kind of sick joke."

"Genevieve's a stupid girl," he said, the disdain in his voice cutting like a blade. "But she made for a good cover."

Her mind reeled. "Oh my God. You're one of the Defenders."

He chuckled, the sound dark and twisted. "Stupid fucking name, isn't it? I don't know who came up with that, but yeah. I proudly wear the symbol on my chest. The circle symbolizes the organized powers in our world, and the three slashes are us...tearing it all down with blades."

Her breath came in shallow gasps. "Lukas, this isn't you. It can't be."

He glanced at her, his grin widening to reveal his fangs. "Oh, it's me," he said, the glint in his eyes pure malice. "I faked being sick."

It was too much to take in. "So Jonathan was trying to save me," Lyrica said, her voice trembling.

"Yeah," Lukas replied, his tone indifferent. "He figured out who I was. We fought. He got to you before I could." Shaking his head, he added, "The guy has a fever of about 125, though. Wasn't thinking clearly. Obviously. Should've gone to find Vero."

Lyrica's breaths came quick and shallow as she struggled against the restraints. Her gaze darted to the knife stuck in the seat belt connection.

Lukas noticed and glanced down at it, his mouth curving into a cold smirk. "Huh. He did a good job with that."

"You have to let me go," she demanded, trying to keep the fear from her voice. "You can't do this."

"Of course I can," he said, his tone mockingly cheerful. "In fact, I'll rather enjoy doing this." His eyes gleamed with something dark and twisted.

She shrank away from him, leaning as far as the seat belt allowed. "Wait a minute. You're the one who's been attacking human females." Her voice faltered as the horrifying realization took shape.

"Oh yeah. I took that task on myself." He shifted his grip on the wheel. "We were just supposed to kill a couple to make Paxton look weak, like he couldn't protect his territory, while we waited for the virus to take effect."

Her stomach churned. "The sexual assaults?" she whispered, bile rising in her throat.

"That was for fun," he said casually, as if discussing the weather.

She turned her face away, the nausea overwhelming her. She clenched her eyes shut. "Oh God," she gasped, swallowing hard to keep from throwing up. "How many of you are there in your little group? Five of you are dead. Are there only six?" she forced out, desperation lacing her words.

"Four are dead," Lukas corrected smugly. "Coron is still alive in the cells underground. I'll spring him once everyone dies."

Her chest tightened, her lungs struggling to draw in air. "You think the virus will kill everyone?"

"We hope." He turned the UTV toward the river. "Don't know, really."

Her pulse hammered in her ears. "What's in the virus?"

"I have no idea. Not my purview. I just cause chaos, and now we just need to wait to see if everyone dies. It looks good so far." He grinned, a predator toying with his prey. "For now, you and I are going to have some fun."

The UTV rumbled to a halt in front of a sweet-looking, newly constructed A-frame cabin nestled near the river. Snow clung to its sloped roof, and icicles dangled from the eaves, glittering in the cold light. Lyrica's heart plummeted as Lukas turned to face her, his grin widening.

Chapter Thirty-Seven

Vero halted his UTV in front of the lodge headquarters and quickly assisted the six mates out that he'd crammed inside. One by one, they climbed out, worry etched into every line of their faces. Normally, their chatter filled any space they occupied, but today, they moved in silence, weighed down by fear for their ill mates. He ushered them toward the lodge entrance, his promise to the soldiers echoing in his mind—he would return for them once the females were safe.

As the UTV door clicked shut, Silas limped out of the lodge, his steps heavy. His expression was grim, his words clipped, his hands shaking. "Lyrica's gone," he said without preamble.

Jonathan stumbled out behind him, pale and shuddering wildly. Blood trickled from a deep gash above his ear, his normally steady hands trembling as if they wouldn't obey his commands. "I'm so sorry," he rasped, his voice hoarse. "I tried to stop him, but I couldn't."

Vero froze, words catching in his throat before he forced himself to speak. "Who?" His tone was ice, dangerous in its calm.

"Lukas." Jonathan doubled over and dry-heaved into a snowbank. No vomit came, just raw, wrenching gasps. He clutched his stomach, his voice breaking as he continued. "I figured out he's one of the Defenders. Something he said, it just clicked. God, I tried to stop him, but he got to Lyrica before I could get her away."

"You're telling me that kid is one of the Defenders?" Vero's fists clenched at his sides, his voice low and vibrating with restrained fury.

Jonathan nodded weakly. "Yeah. I think he's the one killing the human females. And now he's taken Lyrica."

Rage shot through Vero like wildfire, hot and all-consuming. His boots crunched against the snow as he surged toward Jonathan, fists ready to make him pay for his failure.

Silas stepped in, placing a shaking hand on Vero's chest. "Stop. Jonathan tried to save her. He fought hard. Look at him—he crawled back here, bleeding and puking, just to tell us what happened. He did everything he could."

Vero stopped, forcing himself to breathe. His vision blurred with fury, but he stepped back, giving Jonathan a moment of reprieve. "Fine," he growled. "Tell me everything."

Jonathan wiped a pale hand across his mouth. "They headed east in the UTV," he said weakly. "I tried to follow on his snowmobile, but I crashed into a tree. It wouldn't start again. I passed out and... I don't even remember crawling back here. I just knew I had to tell you." He looked up, guilt etched deeply into his fevered face.

Vero's chest constricted, fear clawing at him like a living thing. It was foreign, unwelcome, but impossible to ignore. He turned to Silas, his expression tight.

Silas's phone buzzed sharply, breaking the tense silence. He answered immediately. "Hi, King Paxton. What've you got? You do? Okay, can you trace it back?" He paused, his free hand tightening into a fist. "You're sure? Yeah, I'll hold." Seconds stretched into eternity before he nodded sharply. "Got it." He ended the call and turned back to Vero. "As soon as Jonathan showed up, I called Paxton, and he had the Realm hack into the nearest satellites since I didn't want to leave the main lodge and find a computer. Plus, the Realm is fast. Hope traced the UTV's last location." He rattled off the coordinates.

Jonathan groaned, his legs giving out as he collapsed onto the snow.

Vero went cold. "Stay inside and guard the females. I'll be back."

"Of course," Silas muttered, crouching to lift the unconscious soldier. He hefted Jonathan's limp body over his shoulder. "I'll drag him into the kitchen," he said, meeting Vero's gaze. "King Paxton is headed this way, just so you know."

Vero didn't think he could keep his brother away. "Call him and tell him to remain with the Realm soldiers on the perimeter when they finally arrive." Hopefully in time to protect the territory from any oncoming threat. "I don't want to see him until tomorrow night, in time for the Convexus. Remind him to fucking stay safe."

"Yes, sir," Silas said, sweating profusely and staggering under Jonathan's weight.

Vero nodded, his lips pressed into a thin line. "I'll be back with my mate...and answers." He ran to the UTV. The frigid air bit at his face, but he barely felt it. His mate needed him, and nothing—not snow, not Defenders, not death itself—would stop him.

* * * *

Lyrica fought with every ounce of strength she could muster as Lukas dragged her from the UTV, his grip unrelenting as he hauled her toward the cabin. She shrieked, her legs kicking wildly, and managed to drive her elbow into his groin. He let out a strangled curse and dropped her. Scrambling to get away, she had barely moved when he recovered, grabbing her hair and twisting hard enough to make her scalp burn.

"Stop fighting," he growled, dragging her across the icy, rocky ground. Each sharp edge and jagged patch of ice tore into her thighs and legs, shredding her jeans. Lyrica clawed at his hands, her nails biting into his gloves, but he only chuckled.

"Feisty. I like that," he said, yanking her roughly up the two wooden porch stairs. The door creaked as he shoved it open, and she tumbled into a sofa table. Pain radiated through her temple as she slammed into the edge.

Lukas kicked the door shut and turned to face her, his grin stretching wide. "I made it nice and toasty for you." He gestured to the roaring fire crackling in the stone hearth.

Lyrica staggered to her feet, one hand braced on the sofa table for balance. She forced herself to look at him despite the pounding in her skull. "You're seventeen," she spat. "You can't seriously be a psychopathic rapist and killer already."

"Oh, but I can," he replied cheerfully, spreading his arms wide. "I'm just getting started. Think how good I'll be in fifty years. Or two hundred."

The thought churned her stomach. She glanced around frantically, searching for a weapon. The coffee table held nothing more than a few magazines, and the quiet kitchen gleamed with its pristine, untouched countertops.

Lukas followed her gaze and smirked. "Yeah, this place is brand new.
No one's moved in yet. I figured you and I could make good use of it. Well,
until I strangle you and freeze you."

His words hit her like a punch. "You're insane."

"Not even close. Do you have a favorite snowbank in mind? I'll let
you choose your resting place. But first, we have some fun." He started
toward her, and she took a step back.

"What about the virus?" she asked quickly, desperate to buy time.
"Will it kill everyone?"

He paused as if willing to play with her a bit. "Maybe. Like I already
said, that's not my department."

"Whose is it?"

"You don't know him. A guy named Laker, who is some genius
virologist." Lukas tilted his head, as if considering her. "He's not here,
though. Stays outside the territory."

Her mind raced, trying to place the name. She came up blank. "He
brought in the victims, didn't he? The ones we couldn't identify."

"Oh yeah. I'd meet him while on patrol and then report in all was well
since our satellites weren't live yet. We're supposed to patrol in pairs, but
as a kid, I can take off on my own and nobody really cares. So, if I went
hill climbing and met my buddy, no one was the wiser." He snorted. "The
human females didn't like the several days of riding to get here, but by the
time they reached me, they still had some fight left. That made it more fun."

Lyrica gagged, pivoting slightly, readying herself to strike. "Who were
those poor women?"

"My playthings," he said. "Laker found them in different cities, both
homeless and probably sex workers."

She had to get out of there and track down their relatives. Somehow.
"You're sick," she snapped, her voice shaking.

"You don't have any training, do you?" Lukas's expression turned almost
pitying, though his amusement remained. "That's what I thought." He sighed,
his face dropping into something colder. "Too bad. I do love a good fight."

"What about Genevieve?" she asked, grasping for any leverage she
could. Had she been mated long enough for the mating allergy to have
kicked in? Hopefully? "Genevieve loves you."

"She's a stupid female," he said with a scoff. "But she was a good
cover. I'll kill her next."

Lyrica's stomach twisted violently. "Lukas, this isn't who you want to be."

"It's exactly who I want to be," he said. "Now, take off your clothes." His hand lifted. "Or I'll do it myself."

"I'm going to throw up on you."

"Wouldn't be the first time," he said, taking a step closer.

Her legs trembled, her heart hammering. She tried to steel herself, but his size and strength loomed over her like a shadow. At six foot seven, the trained soldier could crush her. She needed a plan, and she needed it fast. "You know Vero's going to kill you, right?" she asked, her voice rising as panic seeped in.

He snorted. "Vero should be puking his guts out by now. But even if he isn't, he has no clue it's me. I could take him from behind so fast—"

"No, you can't," she interrupted, hoping her mating allergy had kicked in already. "He'll destroy you."

Lukas's jaw tightened. "Then we'll make sure he doesn't get the chance."

He lunged for her. Before his hands could reach her, the front door exploded inward, splintering in all directions. Lyrica stumbled back, her breath caught in her chest. Lukas spun, but Vero was already on him. He grabbed the traitor by the neck and flung him face-first into the fire. Lukas screamed, his voice high and piercing as flames licked at his skin.

"Are you okay?" Vero asked over the sound of burning flesh. His black eyes, rimmed with the faintest touch of blue, locked on hers.

She nodded, trembling. "Yeah. Bruised, but I'm fine. Is Jonathan—"

"Not great," Vero interrupted, pressing Lukas harder into the flames. The smell of scorched flesh filled the room, acrid and suffocating.

The smell nearly dropped her to her knees. "Vero," she shouted. "You can't—"

"Oh, he's going to die," Vero said coldly. "But not yet. He's going to answer a lot of questions first." With one sharp yank, he pulled the unconscious soldier out of the fire and dropped him to the ground. "Don't look."

Lyrica swallowed hard and forced her gaze away.

"Go wait in my UTV," Vero ordered. His tone left no room for argument.

Her legs shook. "Vero, don't—"

"Now."

The raw command in his voice propelled her outside. The freezing wind bit into her cheeks as she reached the UTV, the hum of its engine a

small comfort in the oppressive quiet. She climbed inside and gripped the
heated seat, her entire body shaking.

It was half an hour before Vero emerged. His hands were burned
red and raw, his expression grim. He climbed into the driver's seat,
silent and seething.

"What did you do?" she whispered.

"Exactly what needed to be done," he said, peeling away from the cabin.

Chapter Thirty-Eight

Vero finished giving instructions to Maeve as she stood guard at the front door, flanked by two other heavily armed mates. Her expression remained calm, but her posture appeared battle-ready. "You good?" he asked.

"Not a problem," Maeve replied, her Irish lilt softening the steel in her tone as she adjusted the grip on her green gun. "We'll be rotating every two hours, so we will. Everyone'll get a bit of sleep. Don't you be worryin', Vero. We've got this, and soon Ralstad and the rest will be okay. They're too strong and stubborn to be otherwise."

Vero nodded, grateful for her confidence. He glanced around the main room of the lodge, now stripped of its usual furniture. Rows of sleeping bags blanketed the floor, providing a makeshift barracks for the females who had sought refuge. Half would rest while the other half kept watch, paired strategically with trained mates interspersed among the untrained humans.

It was a solid plan. Many of the Kurjan mates had chosen to stay in their fortified homes, and since most of them were well trained and well armed, he had agreed. There wasn't enough room in the lodge for everyone anyway.

Silas hovered at the back door, scanning the snowy expanse with a soldier's vigilance. Vero made his way over, noting the tension in the ill male's shoulders. "You need sleep," Vero said. "You haven't slept in twenty-four hours."

"I'm afraid I have. I fell asleep a few times, and the females took point. Some of these mates would make excellent soldiers," Silas shot back, his tone grim.

That was something to consider, if any of them wanted the job. "Thank you. I know you're ill."

Silas nodded. "Have you spoken with Paxton?"

A mild relief filtered through Vero. For now. "Yes. The Realm has circled the perimeter. No one's getting in. Their satellites—and ours, now that they're fully operational—don't show any forces heading our way. So if there's danger, it's from the virus or infection."

Silas's shoulders relaxed slightly. "Good."

Vero took a deep breath. "Also, the Realm picked up Laker, the other traitor, right outside our perimeter."

"Excellent."

Vero needed coffee. A lot of it. "He put up a fight, though."

"How bad of a fight?"

"He doesn't have his head anymore." Vero couldn't feel bad about that.

Silas scrubbed both hands down his face, a weary sigh escaping his lips. "Well, all right then. Is the summit going to happen tomorrow night?"

"Yes. Of course. Waiting another thousand years isn't feasible." Vero straightened and glanced at the patrol rotation chart pinned to the wall. "Lukas said there were only six cell members inside our territory with Laker on the outside bringing in the victims. Apparently he created the poison that infected us. We might never know if he worked with anybody else. The Realm's intel matches ours, so it's good to know we're not missing any immediate threats. At least there's no army coming for us today."

Silas eyed the quiet room. "When will we have medical updates?"

Hopefully soon, damn it. "We drew everyone's blood, and I instigated a genetic stripping and analysis that should be concluded in a few hours. I can't do anything else absent those results."

Silas shook his head. "I won't ask for more details right now. We need you alert, Vero. Please get just a couple hours of sleep. You're in charge and we need you at least slightly rested."

Vero didn't require the luxury of sleep, but he did want some time with his mate. They needed to get on the same page and now. "I won't be long." His thoughts drifted to Lyrica. She hadn't said much on the way back from the cabin, and he could only imagine how much she was processing—her ordeal with Lukas, the violence she'd witnessed, and the grim reality of what Vero had done to end the threat.

There had been no other choice. Lukas had loved hurting females too much. He'd been a monster, and there was no redeeming him.

Vero's gaze strayed to the corner of the room, where Genevieve sat huddled with a few human females. She was crying quietly, her delicate face etched with heartbreak and terror. Though she'd been duped by Lukas, she had survived—and one day, Vero hoped she'd realize how lucky she was. For now, he turned away and strode toward the stairs.

Each step felt heavier than the last, the exhaustion of the past days settling in his bones. When he reached their bedroom, he pushed the door open to find Lyrica sitting on the bed, facing the screen on her phone. Her dark hair cascaded in soft waves down her back, her face pale but still strikingly beautiful.

"Vero's here," she said. "I have to go. Okay, I'll talk to you soon."

Hope's voice carried through the receiver, clear and cheerful. "Good. Rest, Lyrica, and I'll see you soon."

Lyrica ended the call and set the phone aside, her eyes tired. "Any news?"

He closed the door behind him. "I'm running tests in the lab, and there's nothing more I can do until those conclude." He pulled off his sweatshirt. "It's going to take a few hours to get results." He glanced at her. "Did I hear Hope say she'd see you soon?"

Lyrica winced. "Yes. She and Paxton arrived with the Realm soldiers and are now guarding our perimeter."

"Good." Vero concentrated on his pretty mate. "How are you?" he asked, stepping closer.

She jumped into his arms, shocking him, burying her face in his neck. "I'm fine. A little sore, but more freaked out than anything. How did Lukas trick all of us like that?"

"I don't know." Vero brushed her hair back from her face and studied her eyes, losing himself in the deep chocolate of her gaze. "It nearly killed me when I found out you'd been taken," he admitted. "I've never felt like that before in my life."

She gingerly touched the healed spot on his face. "I felt the same when you were shot and didn't move. It's terrifying." Her fingers trembled against his skin.

"I love you," he said, the words rough with emotion. "I didn't really know what those words meant or what that felt like. But I think I get it now. I think this is what it is."

Her smile was soft, sweet, and filled with something that hit him straight in the chest. "Yes, Vero. This is what it is."

She leaned up to kiss him, her lips warm and soft against his. He let her take the lead for a moment, savoring her tenderness, then took over, deepening the kiss and tugging her T-shirt over her head.

She laughed as she leaned back. "Vero, seriously, the nation could be dying. We don't have time for this."

"I need to sleep," he said, his hands hooking into the waistband of her yoga pants and tugging them down, along with her panties. "This will help me get there faster."

"Oh, get there faster, huh?" she teased.

He didn't bother answering. Still kissing her, he unbuttoned his jeans, pushed them down, and kicked off his boots. She squeaked in mock protest as he tackled her to the bed, laughing even as she winced.

"Hey," she said, breathless. "I'm a little bruised."

"I can fix that." His voice dropped as he hovered over her. "I'll give you blood in a minute."

"Oh, promises, promises."

He kissed her again, loving the way her body fit against his. She was all soft, female curves, and they were skin to skin. He paused to brush his lips over her jawline, letting his tongue tease the delicate curve of her ear before nipping it lightly.

"There's nothing more we can do for anyone else right now," he murmured, his lips trailing down her throat. "The tests are running under Fizzlewick's watchful eye, the perimeter is secure, and all the females are safe. Soldiers are ill, but the Realm has us covered from attack. So, I thought we'd take this time to get our mating situation sorted out."

He leaned back just enough to meet her gaze, enjoying the heat simmering between them. "This is where you ask nicely."

* * * *

Lyrica paused, her breath catching as emotions swirled inside her. He was violent—there was no denying that. He was a warrior in every sense, an enforcer in the Kurjan nation. And yet, somehow, he made her feel safer than she'd ever felt in her life. Was it because she'd never known shelter before? Or was it something deeper? She needed to reconcile his duality—the protector and the predator—because this was who he was. She had to accept him. All of him.

Her heart spun, but she whispered the truth anyway. "I love you, too."

"Yeah, I know," he said, his grin wicked as his hand trailed possessively over her hip.

"You do not know," she challenged, a spark of defiance lighting in her chest. Her nails scraped down the impossibly hard planes of his torso, tracing the indents and ripples of his abs, marveling at the strength in him.

"Maybe not before," he admitted, his voice dropping, "but I do now. You taught me."

His words were raw, and the honesty behind them struck a chord deep within her. She was his weakness, and as terrifying as that knowledge was, it also filled her with a fierce sense of belonging.

"Ask me," he said, his tone soft but insistent.

Oh, for goodness' sake. She blinked up at him. "Fine. Can you mate me Kurjan style without biting me all the way to the bone?"

He was on top of her now, their skin pressed together, his warmth enveloping her. "No. Your very bone will wear my mark."

Her pulse quickened at his words. There was no hesitation in his voice, just raw possession. "You sure?"

His grin returned, dark and alluring. "You'll like it. I promise."

She didn't doubt that. She'd liked everything he'd done to her so far—more than liked. Everything about Vero was intense, consuming, and exhilarating. He didn't just touch her body; he reached her soul.

"Okay," she whispered.

His eyes flared with colors so deep and rich they made her breath hitch. Blues, darker than midnight and lighter than the ocean, swirling together in a way that was uniquely him. "Good," he said, his tone carrying a promise she felt down to her bones.

But she had to warn him. "I'm not the obedient, meek type."

He smirked, leaning down to press his lips to the pulse point in her neck. "I'm well aware of that," he murmured against her skin. His voice was gravelly and full of heat. "But you'll obey when I want you to."

Her body jerked at the promise in his tone. She tunneled her fingers into his hair, tugging sharply. "I have absolutely no intention of obeying."

His laugh rumbled through him, low and dark. "We'll see about that."

Then his mouth claimed hers, going deep, dominant, and possessive. She moaned, surrendering to the fire between them. His kiss was more than just a physical connection—it was a promise of a life together. Yes, they'd butt heads; yes, they'd clash. But it would keep things exciting, and deep down, she knew they'd make it work.

His hand slid down her side before gliding lower to find her wet and ready. His lips wandered to her jawline, teasing her skin before nipping at her ear. She shuddered, arching into him as he moved lower, his tongue flicking over one nipple, then the other.

Her thoughts scattered as pleasure consumed her. The warrior above her—the violent, unapologetic protector—was her world. Though he terrified others, he made her feel invincible.

Vero continued his journey down her body, his mouth finding her most sensitive spot. She gasped, her hands fisting in the sheets as he drove her higher. Her orgasm slammed into her so fast she couldn't hold back the cry that escaped her lips.

He chuckled, the sound full of male satisfaction. Then, slowly, he did it again, this time more leisurely. The second climax was just as devastating, leaving her trembling as she came down with a soft whimper.

"There you go," he said, his voice rough and full of affection.

Before she could catch her breath, he slid a hand beneath her and flipped her over onto her stomach.

"Hey," she laughed, pushing her hair out of her face as she glanced back at him.

"Hey, yourself," he said, his grin mischievous as he pulled her onto her hands and knees.

"Oh," she murmured, heat flooding her face.

He laughed and smacked her rear, just enough to make her squeal.

"You still haven't given me blood yet," she pointed out, though her voice sounded more breathless than accusatory.

"That's okay," he replied, leaning down to kiss a small bruise beneath her hipbone. "I only see one little bruise."

Her breath caught as a familiar hunger flared through her, heating her entire torso.

"Vero," she whispered.

"I know," he said, his voice softening as he grasped her hips.

He entered her slowly, deliberately, taking his time as if he wanted her to remember every second. And she would—she'd never forget this moment. Finally, he pushed all the way in, holding her tight as he stilled.

"I do love you," he said quietly, his voice raw.

Her heart all but exploded. "I love you too," she whispered, the words barely audible.

"I know," he said, his tone filled with emotion.

Then he started to move, each thrust powerful and unrelenting. Her body climbed higher and higher, every nerve ending sparking with electricity. Just as she teetered on the edge, he struck, sinking his fangs deep into her shoulder.

She cried out, the pain burning bright before morphing into pure pleasure. Something clicked into place, a connection so profound she couldn't describe it. Her shoulder went numb, and her body shattered, the orgasm tearing through her with a force that left her breathless. She screamed his name as she flew into oblivion, riding the waves of ecstasy until they brought her back to him.

His body shuddered above her as he found his own release, his fingers flexing against her skin before he withdrew.

Gently, he turned her onto her back and lay atop her, his eyes still swirling with those impossible blue hues. He kissed her softly, reverently.

"I love you," he said again, brushing her hair away from her face.

She smiled, smoothing a hand through his messy locks. "I love you too. By the way," she grumbled, "my shoulder still feels like it's on fire."

His grin turned wicked, full of male pride. "I can live with that."

Chapter Thirty-Nine

Vero dressed quietly, making sure the bedclothes were tucked securely around his mate. Lyrica slept peacefully, curled into a tight ball with faint traces of healing cells shimmering in the air around her. The sight surprised him. She'd gained the ability to manifest healing cells much faster than he'd anticipated. Then again, Lyrica was no ordinary female—she was his mate. Spirited, brilliant, and a touch dangerous. He couldn't have asked for more.

A grin tugged at his lips as he walked to the window, checking the triple lock. Not that anyone in the territory was likely strong or desperate enough to scale the two stories to their bedroom, but he wouldn't leave anything to chance. A green gun rested on her bedside table, cocked and ready for her use if needed. Quietly, he grabbed his boots and carried them out of the bedroom to avoid disturbing her.

The atmosphere felt heavy with anticipation. The day of the Convexus had arrived. Ready or not, Venus would darken the Leo Noctis tonight. He and Paxton had to bring those Cyst back into the nation.

In the silence of the hallway, a rare moment of peace filled him. Lyrica loved him. He'd mated her as both a demon and a Kurjan, bonding them forever. That knowledge settled into his bones, a deep sense of contentment tempering his usual sharp-edged focus. But only for a moment.

He couldn't afford to bask in his happiness for too long—his people were sick, and they needed answers. His trial run and research on the blood samples should be complete by now. It was time to head back to the lab.

Descending the stairs, he noticed a fully armed Silas standing near the main entrance, his presence as steady as ever. The sleeping arrangements in the lodge had shifted; new females now rested on makeshift bedding, and the guards had rotated. He recognized several of the armed females as seasoned Kurjan mates. Their readiness reassured him.

Walking over, he addressed his soldier. "Anything?"

"No," Silas replied, his voice low to avoid disturbing the others. His lips were blue, matching the veins that stood out starkly against his pale skin. "I did sleep while Jonathan watched over this crew, and I'm good for a while. Unfortunately, Jonathan passed out, and I had a couple of the younger soldiers carry his ass to the doctor. I've been waiting for Fizzlewick to call, but no news yet."

Vero checked his watch. "I should have results in about fifteen minutes," he said. "I ran a series of tests on the blood samples—antigen analysis, chromosomal stability checks, and clotting factor evaluations."

Silas frowned. "Clotting factors?"

Vero nodded, slipping into the mindset of the scientist he rarely admitted to being. "Viruses often alter blood's viscosity and clotting response. If this is an engineered pathogen, I'm looking for irregularities. I also compared immune response markers to baseline samples from before we were inoculated. If there's a shared anomaly, it'll point to contamination in the Sunshine Cure."

Silas exhaled slowly, his jaw tightening. "Good. Let's hope you cure this thing."

"I'm cautiously optimistic," Vero said. "But don't get your hopes too high—I need to verify the results."

Silas leaned back, crossing his trembling arms. "I have things covered here, and Jonathan will be back soon. He feels terrible about everything, although it wasn't his fault."

"I'll be in touch." Vero moved quietly through the lodge, impressed with how the older male had stepped up to protect and defend. The calm felt fragile, the tension heavy, but he let himself enjoy the sound of quiet breathing and the occasional murmur from the sleeping females.

He stepped outside, noting the cold bite of the predawn air. The horizon remained cloaked in shadows, with no sign of the sun breaking through. It matched the mood of the territory—waiting for answers, waiting for relief. He headed toward the lab, his mind already sifting through possibilities for what the blood tests might reveal. If he was right, and the Sunshine Cure had been compromised, they'd need to devise a countermeasure immediately. And if he was wrong?

Well, failure wasn't an option.

He strode down the walkway toward the medical facility, noting the absence of soldiers in the snow. That was a good sign. He'd ordered everyone to find shelter and stick with groups of at least two or three in case anyone deteriorated suddenly. So far, no deaths had been reported, but the fear lingered.

He opened the door to the lab and stopped short. Dr. Fizzlewick sat hunched over a computer in the far corner, his focus glued to a data screen, and Jonathan lay on a stretcher attached to an IV of saline. But it was the broad-shouldered male who turned to face him that made Vero freeze.

"Vero," Hunter said with a slight grin.

Vero glanced at Fizzlewick and back. "How did you get into the territory?"

Hunter rolled his naturally blue eyes. He looked odd without the purple hue. "Seriously? We're the ones guarding the perimeter."

Vero studied him, struck once again by how much Hunter resembled his father, whose picture had been seen far and wide in the Kurjan nation. Jet-black hair, sharp cheekbones, and those piercing eyes. Hunter was a fighting machine, but his mind was just as sharp—one of the most brilliant strategists and researchers Vero had ever known.

"You looked better as a Kurjan," Vero muttered.

Hunter chuckled. "So you've said. And I've explained that I lied because I was undercover. But you're still my best friend, so let's focus on not letting your people die."

Fizzlewick glanced up briefly, then returned to his screen. The doctor had ditched his glasses, his wrinkled lab coat draped awkwardly over his lanky frame. "If we're going to solve this, less chatting and more working," he muttered.

Vero's breath heated. "Is my brother also inside the territory?" He'd wanted Paxton to stay under Realm protection until the ceremony commenced.

"Yep," Hunter said cheerfully. "The cousins have him covered, and he's just fine—probably at the main lodge by now. He's a big boy, Vero."

Yeah, but he was the king of the entire Kurjan nation. Vero glanced at his watch. He had exactly ten hours until the Cyst contingent descended upon his territory, and right now, most of his soldiers could be taken down by a mild rainstorm.

"I can help," Hunter said, his tone more serious now. "I noticed from your antigen-binding analyses that something is off in the protein markers. It reminded me of something my mother taught me about viral mutations and cellular uptake inhibitors."

Vero's interest was piqued. He moved toward a microscope. "What did you add to the analysis?"

Hunter gestured to a separate tray of slides. "I layered your samples with a viral binding agent and ran them through an active enzyme disruption model. It's crude, but it replicates how certain pathogens latch onto blood cells."

Intrigued, Vero peered into the microscope. The slide revealed the binding activity of a mutated antigen inhibiting cellular repair. The virus seemed to interfere with cell regeneration pathways, which explained why healing cells weren't functioning in the infected soldiers.

"I see what you mean," Vero said. "But the problem is that these inhibitors are overriding the usual healing cell responses. If the virus has been engineered to disrupt cell communication, it's targeting something unique to Kurjans."

Hunter nodded. "Exactly. And that's why the Sunshine Cure is implicated. It's enhancing cellular permeability to the virus, essentially creating a back door for it to replicate."

Fizzlewick joined them, his lanky frame hovering over Vero's shoulder. "What if you counteracted the permeability with a stabilizer? Something to reinforce the cellular membrane?"

Vero straightened, thinking fast. "That could work, but we'd need to introduce a protein that can outcompete the virus for binding sites. Something that's compatible with Kurjan cells but also resistant to the antigen."

Hunter snapped his fingers, his face lighting up. "You're onto something with the demon blood tests, Vero, but you're overlooking one thing."

Fizzlewick squinted at him. "What's that?"

Hunter leaned forward, his voice gaining urgency. "The binding mechanism. If the virus can't latch onto your cells, it's not just because of the blood's demonic origin—it's the interaction at the chromosomal level. You're testing proteins, right?"

Vero nodded. "Yes. I've been isolating the blood's unique proteins, but so far, I haven't identified which one is creating resistance."

"Exactly." Hunter gestured toward the centrifuge. "It's not just the proteins—it's the *way* the demon chromosomal pairs interact with the cellular membrane. The structural difference in demon hybrids might create a barrier that disrupts the virus's ability to bind."

Fizzlewick straightened. "So, you're saying the resistance isn't just biochemical. It's structural."

"Exactly," Hunter said. "If we target that mechanism directly—essentially replicate it—we can synthesize a compound that mimics the demon-specific cellular structure. That would block the virus from binding to infected cells."

Vero frowned, the idea sparking possibilities. "I've been focusing on isolating the proteins, but if we model the membrane's structure and reinforce it in infected cells…"

"…we create a shield," Fizzlewick finished, already moving to his equipment. "We'll need to use the blood you've already been working on. I can refine it through structural modeling and combine it with what's left of the serum trials."

Hunter nodded. "Let's add enzyme inhibitors to disrupt the virus's life cycle while we're at it. If we attack from both angles—blocking binding and preventing replication—we might just have something."

Vero's mind raced. The pieces were coming together. "I'll run simulations on how the membrane interacts with the virus. Fizzlewick, you prep the serum."

"I'm on it," the doctor said, reaching for his pipettes.

Hunter grabbed a notebook. "I'll handle the computational modeling. Let's see if this idea holds up."

For the next few hours, the three males worked in tandem, falling into an easy rhythm. Hunter isolated the key proteins from Vero's and Paxton's blood samples, while Vero ran compatibility tests with the infected soldiers' blood. Fizzlewick fine-tuned the serum, adjusting ratios and running simulations.

Finally, Vero held up a syringe filled with a pale blue solution. "We need a guinea pig."

From the corner of the room, Jonathan groaned. "Use me."

Vero turned, frowning. "You've been through enough."

"I don't care," Jonathan rasped, forcing himself to stand. He shuffled toward them like an old human, his shoulders hunched and his movements slow. "It can't make me feel any worse."

Vero hesitated, searching Jonathan's feverish gaze. "We don't have an antidote if this goes wrong."

Jonathan swayed but stood firm. "I don't care. Just do it."

Hunter and Fizzlewick exchanged wary glances. Finally, Vero nodded and tapped on the syringe. He pressed it against Jonathan's arm and injected the serum.

Jonathan gasped, stumbling back against the counter. His breath hitched, and his eyes fluttered shut. Hunter reached for him, but Jonathan held up a hand. "No—just give me a second."

The air around him shimmered. Tiny pops of light danced like fireflies, sparking and dissipating as the energy in the room shifted. Vero stepped back, his instincts on high alert. "What's happening?"

Fizzlewick hurried closer, squinting. "Oh my God. Those are healing cells—on steroids."

"On steroids?" Hunter echoed, raising an eyebrow.

Fizzlewick shrugged. "What? We have the internet now. I've been watching modern movies in my spare time."

Jonathan groaned, his face flushing red before the color evened out. He stood straighter, his movements less sluggish. "I feel...incredible. Like, I need to go punch something. Or—" He paused, grinning. "I need a female."

"Hold on," Vero snapped, grabbing Jonathan's arm. "How do you feel? Any nausea? Pain?"

"Nope." Jonathan stretched his arms, his energy palpable. "I feel like my healing cells are in overdrive. They're fixing everything."

Hunter clapped Vero on the shoulder, his expression triumphant. "I think we've got it."

Vero examined Jonathan closely, noting the male's steady breathing and clear eyes. Relief flooded through him, loosening the knots in his shoulders. "Looks like we do."

Fizzlewick, already at his equipment, called out, "Let's mass-produce this serum. Fast."

Vero nodded, feeling hope. Finally. "For the record, Hunter—you're still my best friend too."

Chapter Forty

Vero stepped out of the medical facility and into a blistering wind. Snowflakes pelted him like bullets under the harsh glare of the lights. He squinted through the storm, his gaze drifting toward the area where he'd planned to build a proper reception space for the Convexus tonight. Of course, he hadn't gotten the chance. Quickly recalculating, he considered his options, only finding one. They'd have to hold the ceremony outside by the river.

If the forty Cyst didn't rejoin the Kurjan nation, he didn't really have a plan B. They could try to survive on their own. There's a chance they'd succeed—especially if they aligned with the Realm. The idea didn't sit well with him. Aligning with only half his people felt like a failure. There had to be a better way.

Nodding at several soldiers limping toward the medical facility, he noted their grim but relieved expressions. Word must already be spreading that they had a cure. At least that was one thing off his plate. It was too bad Laker had died. Vero would like to know if he'd had help creating the poison. He stomped through the snow, irritation and worry churning together in his chest. Where was his brother? Paxton should've been under guard but was no doubt front and center in the chaos somewhere. Vero had no idea how he was going to train the male to be king. He understood Paxton's reluctance, though.

Soldiering seemed to live in their blood.

He reached the main lodge and ducked inside, shaking off the snow. The warmth was almost a shock after the relentless cold outside. He looked around, noting that all the females had already cleared out. Word had definitely spread fast. Grunting, he caught faint noises coming from the lone conference room.

Detouring to the treat-laden counter on the side wall, he poured himself a cup of coffee, the scent grounding him slightly. With his steaming mug in hand, he maneuvered through the space, stepping carefully over several sleeping bags strewn toward the back. Reaching the conference room, he paused, expecting to find his brother. Instead, he stopped short, his coffee halfway to his mouth.

"What the fuck?" he muttered.

Paxton sat at the table with General Waxton, the leader of the forty Cysts, of all people. Vero's first instinct was to reach for the weapon holstered at the back of his waist.

"Relax," came a voice from behind him. He whirled, finding Collin and Liam strolling toward him from the kitchen, both munching on pastries. Relief filtered through him, but his instincts remained sharp. Turning back to the room, he stepped inside, already calculating the best way to position himself between Paxton and the general.

Waxton, towering at over seven feet tall with broad shoulders and muscled arms, was impossible to miss. He stood, the white strip of hair thick on his head and trailing down to a long braid. His amethyst eyes were calm, his voice booming as he greeted, "Vero, good to see you."

Vero crossed the room and shook the general's hand, his expression neutral. "You as well." His tone remained automatic as his attention cut to his brother.

Paxton grinned, entirely too relaxed. "Turns out kings use diplomacy. Who knew?"

"Diplomacy?" Vero echoed, lowering himself into a chair while keeping his body angled slightly, ready to move if necessary. "Do you mind explaining that to me, King?"

Paxton gestured to the file folder in front of him. "Take a load off. Looks like you've been through a war."

"I'm fine," Vero replied curtly, flipping open the folder. Inside was a neatly typed contract, the precision catching his attention. He glanced up, his brows lifting. "You tried diplomacy?"

Paxton leaned back, looking entirely too pleased with himself. "Figured what the hell. Couldn't be out there fighting, so I took a page from the

King of the Realm. We met off-site and the king acted as mediator. It was quite civilized. Then we started drinking bourbon, the good stuff, and we came up with some interesting ideas."

The general nodded. "We're prepared to return to the fold as spiritual leaders and soldiers. In exchange, we'd like to be fully integrated into the Kurjan nation. No more separation between Cyst members and Kurjan members."

"I'd like that," Vero said instantly. "The more integrated we are, the stronger we are."

"Exactly," Waxton said, his voice firm as he planted a massive hand on the table. "I'd also like to determine if the Sunshine Cure works for us."

Vero studied the leader. "Most of the Cyst have refused to try the cure, believing it to be unnatural."

The general shrugged. "Which is why I'm now the leader—at least of these forty. We want to join the modern times and venture into the sun. We want to work with you, Vero. As equals." He smiled, revealing dangerous canines. "I even agreed to perform marriages. The human kind."

Vero arched a brow and looked at his brother.

Paxton cleared his throat. "Hope was involved in some of the negotiations. Apparently, females like weddings, so we figured, why not?"

The general chuckled, a surprising sound coming from someone so stoic. "Believe it or not, I'm quite the romantic."

Vero had never known that about Waxton, but he couldn't deny the male would serve as a good choice to lead. "Do you believe you can draw more Cyst into the nation?"

Waxton nodded. "Yes. If we show a year of prosperity, the others will likely return. We could become quite prosperous when at peace." His gaze burned with conviction.

Peace. It was all Vero had ever wanted. He glanced at Paxton. "So… diplomacy, huh?"

Paxton grinned, reaching for another donut. "Yeah. Apparently, we still need to perform the Convexus ritual at midnight. Just the four of us: you, me, Waxton, and his second, Erford. We each say our parts, do a quick handshake vow in blood, sign the contract again, and it's done."

Vero blinked. "Erford?" The name stirred something deep within him. Erford had trained him as a young soldier, a male known for his kindness and rowdy sense of humor. He'd been considerate yet mischievous, with a strong penchant for practical jokes that left lasting memories.

"Yes," Waxton confirmed. "He's scouting the area now to assess where we might build new facilities once we move here."

These Cyst weren't just negotiating—they were preparing for the long haul. Vero sat back, sipping his coffee as his mind reeled. He'd spent days worrying about this ritual, but Paxton had handled it with ease. Diplomatically.

He grinned, finally allowing himself a breath of relief. "Welcome back, brother."

* * * *

Lyrica sat on the bed, wrapped in one of Vero's oversized T-shirts, the scent of her mate surrounding her like a warm cocoon. She had the bedside lamp on, her phone in hand, scrolling through news articles about recent studies in fission power. While she and Hope had chatted for an hour and enjoyed a very good champagne, Hope had headed to bed a while ago. Lyrica tried to focus, but the thought of the Convexus occurring outside near the river wouldn't leave her mind.

They had to be about finished by now. Unless the entire situation had been a setup. Then there would be fighting, beheading, and dead bodies.

Heavy footsteps echoed outside the door and she looked up as it opened. Vero stepped inside, kicking off his boots with practiced ease.

"Hi," she said, smiling despite the tightness in her chest. Her heart leaped at the sight of him. "You're all right."

He moved toward her. "I thought you were sleeping."

"I was," she said as he sat down, plucked her from the bed, and cradled her in his lap. "But I woke up and missed you." She rested her forehead against his broad shoulder, inhaling deeply. "Please tell me you have good news."

He kissed her lightly on the nose, his lips warm and tender. "I do," he said simply. "We performed the quick ritual, Paxton and the general signed the agreement again, and we sent out the video to the entire immortal world. It was surprisingly easy to find peace."

She pulled back, her eyes widening. "Really?"

"Yes," he replied, his grin easing some of the tension coiling in her chest. "We need to order a lot more building supplies as soon as possible."

He moved so his back rested against the headboard with his legs extended, her safely ensconced in his arms. "Also a lot more of the sparkling water. Apparently the Cyst soldiers love it."

Sure they did. "No problem," she said, snuggling against him. "We didn't have time to talk earlier with all your preparations. You just told me that Hunter showed up and you two came up with a cure for the illness knocking out all your soldiers. I've heard laughing and whistling all night from those patrolling outside, so I figured it worked."

"Oh, it's definitely working," he admitted, though his expression turned wry. "But, uh, it has a side effect."

Her brows knitted. "What kind of side effect?"

"It seems to kick the soldiers' healing cells into overdrive," he said with a slight grimace, "which also makes them hornier than hell."

She blinked, her lips parting. "Horny?"

He nodded, his mouth twitching. "I've already had to put guards on the single human females for their safety—not that anyone would hurt them, but they might get...courted very enthusiastically."

She laughed, her tension finally breaking. "Courted enthusiastically? That doesn't sound so bad."

He shook his head, clearly not amused. "Let's just say I won't forget the sight of Jonathan climbing a fur-laden, icy tree to pick perfect pine cones for a bouquet. He nearly broke his neck."

Lyrica snorted, unable to hold back her amusement. "Pine cones?"

"Pine cones," he confirmed, shaking his head. "The effects seem to be wearing off, so I think everything will be back to normal in a couple of days. But for now, romance is running rampant in the Kurjan nation."

Her laughter softened into a gentle smile as she rubbed her palm along his whiskered jawline. "I could live with romance being strong in the Kurjan nation. It sounds...nice."

"That would be a first," he admitted, leaning down to kiss her, his lips firm and sure. The kiss spread heat through her body, a sense of home and belonging warming her from the inside out. He paused and leaned over to glance at the laptop she'd left open on the bed. "Another PowerPoint?"

Excitement thrilled through her. "Yeah. It's a proposal for a new store owned by the knitting groups here in the territory. With their skills, I project they'll make a profit within the first few months. It'd be nice to give the mates some financial security."

He flicked through screens. "You're impressive, sweetheart. A bit bossy, but in a way that takes care of people."

She placed her hand over his heart. Nobody had ever seen her this clearly. Of course, he ruffled her structured composure any time he wanted. Even though her entire personality had rebelled against relying on him, he'd worked his way right into her heart. She trusted him and realized that gave her strength. And a new freedom to explore. "Also, I'd like to look at the finances, if that's okay. I'm wondering if paying people more will gain loyalty."

"Sure. You probably need a raise as well."

She hadn't thought about that. "I figured my million dollars was pay enough once I left."

"You're not leaving," he said evenly. "But you can still have the money."

She perked up, having no intention of leaving, ever. "I don't want to take that much."

He shrugged. "I have a few billion of my own, so spend all you like."

A few billion? Dollars? "Wow." She'd have to think about that one.

"Like I said, you're staying, but I hope you don't mind the cold and snow."

She could feel his heartbeat beneath her palm. So steady and strong. "I love the cold and snow. It reminds me of the happy and safe times of my childhood. So," she said, her voice teasing, "we're mated, huh?"

"In every way possible." He held her close. His body heat alone could have chased away any lingering chill. His lips twitched. "Paxton just went to find Hope. The walls are thin. We might want to turn on some music." His grin turned mischievous as he shifted her to straddle his lap. "We have the rest of the night before I need to return to work."

"I love your smile. It's rare, and I can change that. I'd like to see it all the time." Her legs tightened around his waist as her hands landed on his thick shoulders.

His gaze softened. "You have ways to do that?"

She leaned in closer, her nose brushing his. "I can think of a couple," she murmured, her voice dropping. "I love you."

"I know," he said, his grin softening into something deeper. His lips brushed hers in a slow, reverent kiss. "I love you too."

Epilogue

Three weeks later

Vero finished checking the rotation of the guards, his sharp eyes scanning the room as Paxton paced beside him in the main lodge with his newly arrived dog stretched out by the fireplace, watching him while yawning once in a while. Snow fell heavily outside, blanketing the ground in a pristine white, but the tension inside made the atmosphere anything but serene.

"Would you relax?" Vero asked, glancing sideways at his brother.

"Are you kidding?" Paxton shot back, his tone incredulous. "My father-in-law is landing in a moment. Zane Kyllwood is a force of nature."

Vero shrugged. "His daughter loves you. Though this makes me somewhat appreciative that I don't have a father-in-law."

Paxton cut him a look, his mouth twitching. "Yeah, I envy you. But not really—because Zane's the best. As a part-demon, you're his relative as well."

"Now that's a thought," Vero replied, adjusting his sleeve to expose the demon brand on his hand. Though faded, it would always remain. It marked him as more than just a Kurjan, and the nation had accepted both him and Paxton despite their demon blood. After all, that blood had saved everyone. Without it, the virus might still have them puking their guts out—or worse, dead.

He glanced at the C on his palm. Unsurprisingly, there hadn't been anything in Talt's journal about Vero's true ancestry. Should he try to find his demon relatives, if any had lived through the last wars? It was something to think about...later.

Vero glanced around the lodge. The soldiers had finally recovered, the forty Cyst members had moved in and had already recruited ten more members, and the loyalty coalescing around Paxton as their king was absolute. The Kurjan nation was strong again.

The thrum of a helicopter outside drew his attention, and he followed his brother into the cold, whipping wind. Paxton's steps faltered slightly, betraying his nerves.

Vero smirked. "Are you nervous?"

"No," Paxton said, though the sharpness in his tone betrayed him.

From across the snowy expanse, Hope and Lyrica emerged from the medical facility, their heads close as they spoke. The sight of his mate warmed Vero in a way that had nothing to do with the heavy coat he wore. She moved toward him, her face lighting up despite the storm.

"Stay here," he murmured, stepping into her path. He held her back gently, shielding her from the pelting snow as the helicopter descended.

The whirling blades slowed, the back door opened, and Collin and Liam jumped out first, scanning the area with sharp precision, their weapons visible.

Paxton raised his hand in greeting. "You can relax. We're safe. There's not even a guard patrol around the lodge right now."

Liam didn't smile, but he did nod and step aside.

A bundle of energy barreled out in the form of a lovely female with tawny eyes and blondish-brown hair. "Hope," she yelled, running toward her.

Vero stiffened.

Paxton grasped his arm. "That's Libby."

Libby hugged Hope, lifting her off the ground before dropping her and running full bore to be snatched in a hug by Paxton.

He placed her on her feet, obviously careful not to touch her skin. "Vero, this is Libby, our best friend. Libs, this is my brother."

Libby held out a hand, her smile contagious. "It's so weird to keep from shooting any of you."

Vero chuckled. "You're a shifter." He'd have to keep Jonathan at bay. "Yep. Feline."

Vero introduced Lyrica, pride filling him as he claimed her as his mate.

They shook hands. Curiosity filled Lyrica's eyes. "Can I see you actually shift into an animal?"

"Sure," Libby said easily. "It's fun, but you have to stand back so the energy release doesn't flatten you."

Lyrica snuggled into Vero's side. "That's awesome."

Vero turned his attention back to the craft.

Zane Kyllwood, the legendary leader of the demon nation, disembarked next, his movements lean and efficient. Without hesitation, he reached back into the helicopter and helped a petite, brunette female out onto the snow.

"That's the queen of the demons," Lyrica whispered beside Vero, her tone filled with awe. "Janie Kayrs. Hope told me all about her mother, and they look like twins. Apparently we're all true allies now."

Vero liked that she said the word "we." Lyrica already considered herself part of his world, and the realization settled warmly in his chest.

Paxton moved forward, greeting Zane and his queen with hugs. As introductions were exchanged, another figure emerged from the helicopter. Vero's eyes narrowed as a massive, metallic-eyed male stepped out with the grace of a predator. Recognition hit him like a blow.

"That's Benjamin Reese," he muttered. The bastard had kidnapped Karma long ago.

Benny carefully lifted a heavily pregnant female out of the aircraft.

Her face broke into a smile the moment she spotted him. "Vero!" she cried, starting toward him.

The giant male at her side growled low. "Wait."

She slapped his hand away without breaking stride. "Stop it, Benny. We're safe, and you're going to be nice."

Benjamin hesitated, his expression unreadable.

Vero moved to meet her halfway, pulling Lyrica with him just in case.

Karma threw her arms around Vero in a quick but warm hug, careful not to touch the exposed skin on his neck. "It's so good to see you," she said, leaning back to study him. "You look wonderful."

"You too," Vero said, his voice softening. He glanced at her belly. "And you're...busy."

She laughed, introducing herself to Lyrica with an easy charm. "Aren't you stunning?" She pulled Lyrica into an embrace.

Vero felt the weight of Benny's gaze like a physical force. He straightened, meeting the massive male's sharp eyes.

Karma stepped between them, planting her hands on her hips. "Oh, you two knock it off," she said, her tone exasperated. She rubbed her belly and gave them both a look. "Behave."

They both nodded, breaking eye contact.

Lyrica laughed, her voice light and bright, cutting through the tension.

Karma's smile softened as she linked her arm through Benny's. "We're happy," she said, her voice directed toward Vero. "He keeps me safe, and the girls are thriving and have come up with some intriguing twin speak that somehow insults their brothers. This is our fourth boy," she added, patting her belly. "We wanted to visit with just the two of us this time, but next trip, we'll bring the kids. The girls would love to see you."

"I'd like that," Vero said, his voice steady. For the first time in years, everything felt right. His world clicked into place. Karma was happy, the Kurjan nation was healing, and his place in it—by Paxton's side—was solid. He looked down at Lyrica.

"Are you happy?" Karma asked softly.

Vero didn't look away from his mate, his gaze locked on hers. "I am," he said, surprising even himself.

Lyrica's smile was soft, her eyes full of warmth. She reached up and kissed his chin. "Me too. Always."

* * *

Kensington Publishing Corp.
Joyce Kaplan
900 Third Avenue, 26th Floor
US-NY, 10022
US
jkaplan@kensingtonbooks.com
212-407-1515

The authorized representative in the EU for product safety and compliance is

eucomply OÜ
Marko Novkovic
Pärnu mnt 139b-14
ECZ, 11317
EE
https://www.eucompliancepartner.com
hello@eucompliancepartner.com
+372 536 865 02

ISBN: 9781516111831
Release ID: 151442730

Printed in the United States
by Baker & Taylor Publisher Services